ALL THE LOVE IN THE LAND, ALICE

An Historical Biographical Novel

Joan R. Lisi

D1737015

© 2016 Joan Lisi

The persons and places portrayed in this book are real. Some names have been changed to protect privacy. Some events have been altered for optimal flow.

Book Trailer by Shannon Bae on Vimeo & YouTube
Cover by Elizabeth Mackey
www.elizabethmackey.com

Lost

I am here.
No light upon this place.
I am here.
No sign to show the way.
I am here.
No music to give me form.
I am here.
Bound. Hidden. Timeless. Suspended.
I am here.
Come and find me.

Joan Rothbury Lisi

Experience teaches us that we do not always receive the blessings we ask for in prayer.
—Mary Baker Eddy

Prologue

A Conversation with Gran'mere

No one ever mentioned that you chose to end your life, Gran'mere, by taking poison in a hotel room in Phoenix, three days before your son's wedding day. No one inscribed your name on the plaque in that vaulted niche in the Hollywood cemetery; it held not just your ashes, but those of both your beloved husband Jerry and his sister Sue and husband Griff. Their remains were contained in lovely boxes; yours, however, were packaged in the crematorium's mailing carton.

Debt and anguish were your legacies. While your debts were easily settled, the anguish solidified in your grown children until it was a wall over which we glimpsed you rarely during all those years of our childhood.

Forty years later, after both your children were also dead, what remained of your life made its first appearance. For that day my brother delivered prodigious boxes of files and an extraordinary Louis Vuitton traveling secretary trunk, wrestled from the attic of a house where they sat hidden for a generation. I still wonder why they were never discarded, which set me up to believe that you had a hand in writing this story. But you and I will get to that.

For months, that trunk and lifetime of files remained on my office floor as I chronologically sorted your life—paper-clipped notes, lists on backs of stray envelopes, invitations, scrapbooks, address books, menus, letters, deeds, contracts, photographs, invoices, and inventories.

Your traveling secretary trunk was as you left it in 1938, the canvas body stamped with the company's distinguished initials "LV": an extravagant piece of luggage by today's standards. It was gouged a little in places, no doubt by a careless stevedore. The brass hinges and clasp still functioned. I found the contents orderly—carbon and typing paper and those thin yellow sheets used for carbon copies in my own younger days. Sadly, no portable typewriter. That would have been a nice surprise. The trunk unfolded magically into a miniature desk with a file cabinet, set of leather-bound drawers, and storage cubby.

Then you came to me one night— an inner voice and image conjured from my thoughts of you, but able to speak of things I didn't know. We were sitting together at my dining table watching the full moon through the trees, softening as it crossed time and distance, drawing you into my present. Moonlight, I knew from reading your letters, opened your heart. Would you reveal some answers to the secrets of your life? For though your papers overflowed with details, there were pieces missing. Sometimes, in my frustration, I felt you deliberately left those pieces out to taunt me, as if it were all planned, this hide and seek.

"What should I call you?" I asked. The answer seemed important, now that we had a relationship of sorts. But not at all one of the burning questions on my list.

"Gran'mere," you replied

"I thought you disliked French. You said German was easier on the tongue."

Gran'mere arched a beautifully shaped dark eyebrow. "Ah, but French, though quite difficult for me, was… well, perhaps *lyrical* might be the best word. Call me Gran'mere."

I said, "I am frustrated, Gran'mere. Your papers hold onto more secrets than they tell."

Gran'mere smiled, though I could see sadness in her eyes. "I suppose, then, you will be forced to guess. At those times, my dear, I will visit and we can talk."

"Beware of my good intentions, Gran'mere. Your story, of necessity, will be told in many voices. Whose will speak the loudest?"

Gran'mere gave the slightest of shrugs and turned her gray eyes toward me. Then she began to fade as the moon slipped under a cloud.

"Wait!" I said. "Tell me, was it worth it?"

"Oh yes," she replied in the barest of whispers. The moon went dark, and she was gone.

***

She left with promises to return. Now, I get on with it, starting with her entrance to college. As good a place as any to begin, she was reinventing herself for a glorious new life, in a century of extravagant promise.

.

Part One: The Reshaping of Alice

July 21, 1938

It was 29 years ago next month, in 1909, that Jerry Muma requested some of my fraternity brothers in the Alpha Delta Phi do what they could to see that his young lady friend Alice Hicks, who was just arriving at the University as a freshman, should have the proper advice and assistance. And through the usual channel, I as a sophomore was instructed to call at the ladies dormitory to offer my and the fraternity's assistance. Alice was very attractive, with extraordinary culture, poise and charm, and she and I became quite friendly. She joined the Kappa Alpha Thetas and I escorted her to numerous functions, but she adhered strongly to her former intentions to wed Jerry Muma, doubtless quite fortunate for her. Jerry Muma was magnetic, dynamic and a powerful man both in college and in business. ...

Sincerely,
John Rankin

Chapter 1

First Day at the University of California-1909

Alice Ena Cuthbertson Hicks, five feet nine inches, in her summer white shirtwaist, gored skirt, cotton lace gloves and beribboned straw boater, stepped down from the train onto the platform of the 16th Street station. She smiled against the terrible pounding of her heart. This great adventure at the University of California was beginning today, August 13, this morning, in the bright sun.

Alice shaded her eyes, scanning the crowd for Jerry's cousin, L.B. In just seconds she spotted him in the throng. L.B. looked slim and dapper in his pale seersucker suit—also ramrod straight and anxious. He was a lawyer-turned-schoolteacher whom she had met only a few times before, when he had visited Jerry in Los Angeles from San Luis Obispo. She raised her arm. He saw her signal and crossed the platform, trailing a baggage handler.

"Alice, how good to see you again," said L.B, a slight smile showing under his mustache. "How was the overnight ride? Not too taxing, I hope."

"Not at all. My compartment was luxurious. The *Overland* is quite the train." She did not mention the overwhelming loneliness after sharing departing hugs and kisses with her family and Jerry. Nor did she talk about the butterflies of anticipation that kept her away from the elegant dining car, nor the growing excitement she felt as she gazed at the moonlit landscape north of Los Angeles.

"My trunks are just here along with several small cases," said Alice, returning his smile.

L.B. directed the baggage handler to her pile of luggage on the platform.

They chatted throughout the fifteen-minute drive to College Hall on Hearst Avenue. Alice, deep in thought, barely heard his words. After he delivered her to her dormitory's reception hall, she would be alone. A joyful beginning, college—but she had secrets to keep. Only her family and L.B. knew of her engagement. Maybe she would reveal it in time, depending. The dark secret behind it, however, would remain forever untold. Hiding close behind was the identity of her benefactor for this year of college. Who would understand it? The fourth secret was silly, really, but she was several years older than the other freshmen, and it would not do for anyone to know. Four secrets; they should pose no problems. She would enjoy herself for a year and then wed her Jerry.

***

This day had been in the making since February 28. "Will you marry me?" he had asked, swiveling in his saddle as their horses walked abreast. They had ridden up Laurel Canyon Trail near the construction site of the new Bungalow Land to view its progress, but this was an excuse, really, to be alone.

"Yes," she said. Just like that. Alice had sensed his proposal coming for weeks, and church that morning had been an agony of waiting.

Jerry reined in his mount. Alice's docile mare followed suit. They met over their horses for a soft kiss. A whoop of pure delight flew unrepressed from Alice, and before another second had passed, the jubilant couple turned their horses and cantered back to the stables.

***

Now, Alice's cab stopped in front of the four-story, redbrick College Hall. L.B. directed her luggage to the waiting porters. He said his good-byes and good luck, handing her over to the waiting House Mother. Alice stepped over the threshold to begin her new life.

College Hall was humming with chatter. Dominating the middle of the room was a huge refectory table covered with embroidered linen, matching tea napkins, two fine silver tea and coffee services, and silver serving trays of sandwiches, cakes and cookies. Perhaps as many as fifty young women were gathered around, talking in groups of three or four. The House Mother asked her name and promptly steered her toward the piano. "Let me introduce you to your roommate, Miss Hicks."

"Mildred, this is Alice Hicks. Alice, this is Mildred Ahlf."

Alice smiled in delight at the willowy figure before her, thinking how unusual it was to meet a woman taller than herself. "A pleasure to meet you, Mildred. I hope we will be great friends." It would turn out to be a lifelong bond.

"Secondly," said the House Mother, "the Treble Clef Society is of interest to you both. I encourage you to discuss their tryouts. Please be ready to join the others shortly for a tour of your new dormitory."

The small gathering of women sipped their tea and munched cookies while they all discussed the university's prestigious women's choral group and the upcoming tryouts for the fall production of the comic opera, *Erminie*.

Twenty minutes later a woman identified by Mildred as the Assistant Dean of Women spoke to the room. "As some of you already experienced, we are only two blocks from the Euclid line, which will take you to the ferry crossing, and the university is a few minutes' walk. This is the first women's dormitory, and we expect you all to uphold the standards of behavior and to govern yourselves. Six committees will be formed, under the guidance of floor

3

mothers." She went on speaking as she led the crowd to the back of the dining hall, to the kitchen door, and then turned left onto the first floor of bedrooms. "Each floor is identical on both wings. Three floors of rooms, each floor with a sitting area and two porches, four baths and eight toilets. There are forty women per floor, two to a bedroom. Your rooms have two each of beds, bureaus, rockers, study chairs and scatter rugs, and one large desk and a sink. Follow me upstairs, please."

Everyone was breathless by the time they reached the fourth-floor roof garden. The views into the arboretum-like campus grounds were magnificent. Potted flowers fluttered in the sunny breeze. Under a partial roof, scattered lounge chairs invited peace and quiet.

***

Alice and Mildred eventually made their way to their shared room. Working through their piles of luggage, they found linens and made beds, hung their dresses in the wardrobe, and stuffed underwear in the bureaus. It was suppertime before they knew it, and they flew down the stairs to the dining room for roast chicken and dumplings.

Back in their room at the end of the day, Alice finally sat, unbuttoned her shoes and pulled them off with relief. She scooted to the head of her bed, shoving a pillow behind her back against the head rails.

"Mildred, I better prepare for tomorrow, and read through my mail, if I don't fall fast asleep first. I can't think when I have been this tired!"

Mildred nodded. "We'll go together to register for classes, if that's all right?" She sat in the rocker and piled her lap with registration papers.

"Will you come with me, too, to the Treble Clef tryouts?"

"I wouldn't miss it," replied Mildred.

Still keyed up from the strangeness of it all, she decided to read her Mother's letter before trying to sleep.

My wish for dear Alice,

"I desire for my dear child, neither great beauty, wealth nor fame, nor anything to mar her happiness. But give her a contented spirit, ministering hands and willing feet that her presence may radiate joy wherever she may be." A quote from Lillian Bell.

May your experience this fall be wonderful and fulfilling. We all wish you happiness. Please write.

Love, Mother

Wasn't it just like her dear mother? She was so good at finding the correct quote for the moment. Tears filmed Alice's eyes at the memory of leave-taking. Her mother had held Alice's face between her arthritic hands and kissed her on the forehead. "You have our blessings, dear, though it is hard to

4

see my last fledged baby fly away. Jerry has given you a great gift of this education. I know you will not squander it."

All Alice could do was hug her, taking in the lily-of-the-valley eau de toilette scent that was so much a part of her mother. Thank goodness Brother George and his wife, Annie, were there to take care of her. Father, still in Canada, was so far away.

George came to her for a final hug and held her for a long time.

"Take care of yourself, kid." He stepped back and smiled.

"Kid, indeed, George. I'm all grown up," retorted Alice, smiling, trying not to cry.

"You were dubbed 'the kid' and so shall you be forever, to me and to Jo and Kate and Bill and the rest of our tribe."

She pulled her unfinished letter to Jerry from her pocket. Feeling loneliness creeping in, she put pen to paper, determined to be gay and cheerful.

Chapter 2

Erminie

Sept 8–9
College Hall
Wednesday eve
Jerry Dear:

What do you think, but I made Erminie, the principal part in the opera. Oh, how I wish I could see you tonight. I went to Treble Clef this afternoon and then heard it quite officially. I am just too delighted for anything and all the girls in the hall think it is so fine. It is to be given in a theater in Oakland about October 20th. This all seems much more than I dared hope, that I just prayed that I would be able to carry it out successfully, for success like this is apt to make me forgetful. What a part it is, for I must be funny as well as sing love songs to the male lead, a British young man by the name of George Manship. But you must not be jealous. I heard him sing so beautifully at the Freshman Rally that I fully realize what I am into. It means work, but I am so pleased I will set to work at once to practice with a will.

There is much to be made of this part, for while it is a large cast, there are only three women in it, with mine being the largest role. The plot involves farcical twists and turns, kidnapping, drunkenness, thieving and swordplay. In the end I get to marry the man I want. How do you like that!

And now to mention a practical thing: I must have voice lessons. My roommate, Mildred, takes them in Oakland, and has kindly asked if I would like to come and meet the teacher. I cannot imagine that I would not like her, as Mildred is so very sweet, with a voice like an angel. Should it work out, I will need a draft to cover lessons through the October performance.

Good night, Jerry dear. All the love in the world for you. I am so happy.
Alice

* * *

The next evening Alice danced home to College Hall, even tired as she was after a full day of classes and rehearsal. In the large sitting room, fifteen women ambushed her as she came through the door. With congratulatory words and laughter, they swept her to the piano for a song. Alice chose to sing "Dream Song," the one she had practiced for tryouts. Many of her friends joined in, as they had been drawn in time and again during practice, having memorized the lyrics along with her.

At midnight on my pillow lying
By my daily toil oppress'd
To me weary care denying
Deep profound that giveth rest;
When a tiny bird alighted
On my latticed windowsill,
Welcome guest though uninvited,
Cheering by his joyous trill.
Song of promise, soft and clear.
Sounds that fill the tranquil grove,
Glad, joyous trill of hope and love.

"And now, goodnight, goodnight to one and all. I absolutely must go to bed," said Alice, looking pale but happy. After she had given and received fifteen hugs, she climbed the stairs.

The anticipation of performing—really, it was beyond imagining.

The paper due at the end of the week, and homework yet undone for an early morning class, did not even get a nod.

College Hall
Saturday
October 2nd
My Dear Jerry:
Your special delivery was pinned to my pillow so that I would surely find it, and when I came in from the Pajamerino Rally in my silk pajamas, there it was. I devoured every word and how I had been thinking of you all through the rally. It was just great. Those glorious yells, and the speakers were enough to infuse enthusiasm and spirit into anyone.

What do you think but I got an invitation to the Alpha Delt Dance, and I never hoped to get one. It will be quite an affair at the country club. I am just picking out the ones (fraternity dances) I want to go to most.

Today is simply a glorious one. The sun is out and you can see the new green grass shooting up all over. Just the kind of a day you feel glad to be alive.

Black ink on paper is always a splendid substitute, but I am just longing for the real joy of seeing you again.

My best love,
Alice

Wednesday morning
October 13, 1909
My dear Jerry:

Just two months today since I arrived and how innumerable are the events: some grand times—some lonely times—and "experience" withal. This is a lovely cool morning and I wish I was out, instead of in the infirmary. I feel such a quitter! The pain in my side has been coming on gradually. At first I thought I must have pulled a muscle playing tennis but the doctors say no. I am quite concerned about the opera and feel certain they will pull me from the part.

I had a visit from two Gamma Phi girls just as I was going to get up. They are so ladylike—in fact, all the girls of the sorority are. After they went away, my pain came back and Doctor says I must not be discouraged, for it won't leave me at once. Then I had to leave my room where I was alone and could practice my part, and move down the hall to let in a sick boy. But, my roommate turned out to be an Alpha Chi Omega I had met before, who now has an infected thumb. So, we help each other. I can't do much, though, for I can't get around very fast. After lunch I am going to rest for a few minutes and then try and get up and out onto the porch.

Did you see in yesterday's "Cal" where they still have me down for *Erminie*? Tomorrow, though, is absolutely the last day they will wait. ... I am saving all my strength for it and you are so interested in it—that helps me on.

I am using the lessons in the little Christian Science book you gave me last year. Hopefully it will help me win back my health. I am remembering the words the speaker quoted from Mary Baker Eddy's book, "Science and Health," the first time you took me to a C. S. meeting: "The physical healing of Christian Science results now, as in Jesus' time, from the operation of divine Principle, before which sin and disease lose their reality in Human conscience and disappear naturally."

My love to you,
Alice

October 21, 1909, 6 a.m.
My Dear Jerry,
I am sitting on my little bed and writing with the handsome pen you gave me. Was it only last Xmas? Seems ages and a lifetime ago.

John Rankin escorted me, with Mildred and her beau, to the Delta dance last night. It was held at the prestigious country club. We had just heaps of fun and wore our lily-of-the-valley corsages, which smelled heavenly. John saw that my dance card was full and so I had a chance to meet the best. Gracious and attentive, and up on all the newest dance steps. I wore my blue silk dress with the silver buckle belt you gave me. I felt like a princess all evening.

Jerry, the most amazing thing was one of the boys has a motor of his very own. His father paid extra dues to the fraternity to garage it in a renovated horse stall! He has offered to take us all for a ride, and I am certainly looking forward to that!

Goodbye for now, Jerry. I will write you my usual Sunday night letter tonight. I am hoping to see a letter from you as I drop this off at the post office.

Your loving Alice

College Hall
Sunday eve
October 24, 1909
My Dear Jerry:

By next Sabbath you will be here and what a happy girl I will be. I got in from the theater last night with Alpha Chi Omega girls to see *Time, Place and the Girl*. How well I remembered going with you to hear it. We had two boxes and it was altogether a very nice little party. I had to let the Delta Gamma date pass as they were going on a picnic and that would have been too much. ... But did go with Allan for a while to the game, and the varsity beat them 19–0. I left before it was over to go in to Oakland to see my voice teacher. I was having trouble with some of my high notes. He gave me from five o'clock to 6:30 and we went through the entire opera and everything went so much better today as a result. We have dress rehearsal Thursday morning and I expect will finish about four or five, and will see him again. Allan has asked me to have dinner in Oakland but I want to hear from you as to what time you will arrive. You will be my escort home. How I have looked forward to all this and it's too good to be true that it has come.

October 24 '09
Los Angeles
My Dearest Alice,

Letters come with remarkable regularity at about 10:30 a.m. I pop out of my quarters and on the end of the counter lies a letter sealed up from you that makes my heart swell with pride for the most deserving and lovable girl in all this land. If I don't get your letter I am out of tune with everything. I never imagined that I would ever know anyone who could so completely become a part of my life. Alice, you are the only-only, and while I used to think your influence was wonderful, it is growing greater every day.

Now, about the trip north. I don't know what your plans are. I think I had better not put in an appearance until after the night of the opera. Think it over and tell me what you want. There are at least a bunch of plans in embryo.

Don't miss the Glee performance. The only consideration in the matter is your health. And you, my dear, must of necessity all too soon put aside the playthings and tinsel. ... Through all the years to come, what we are to be together, your life at UC is to be the setting of our first dream of home. Somewhere we two will show the world that the old ideals are not lost; that a man and a woman may still live together in supreme and lasting content.

9

One year at college at the pace you are setting will make you a great girl. Too bad you can't stay the regular four.

Best love to the best girl.

Yours, Jerry

Oct 28 '09
Los Angeles
My Dearest Alice,

Yesterday I was compelled to disappoint you by sending that wire. The auditor came here out of season. Two changes have been made in office help and I could not leave. I hope my not coming will not upset your plans. It is now 8 p.m. You are in the midst of the big event and I know the big success you are making. The "Calif" today said that the male lead was supposed to "make violent love" to you. Don't you cheat any, you little rascal. I have sent a wire to you addressed to the theatre and I am hoping and praying for best success to you, my dear.

By Sunday you will be rested and we can have a ramble somewhere. I have one business appointment in Piedmont and then the rest is free. I ought to leave on the "owl" returning Sunday night.

Goodnight with the same loving heart that prompted me on the epoch making 28th day of Feb just eight months ago,

Your Jerry.

On October 28, a nervous and excited Alice performed *Erminie* in the Oakland Theater. Her costume was a replica of the one used in the first British performance in the late 1890s. Her dress of pink muslin was gathered with lace and frills in the style of Marie Antoinette. Her hair was done in tight ringlets that peeked out from under an outrageously pleated bonnet. Alice played to the comedy well, beautifully delivering her songs between swordfights and drunken brawling.

Seats were sold out, the audience went wild with pleasure during all three acts. And Jerry was not there to see it. Alice stuffed her great disappointment deep inside. *I could not have acknowledged him, anyway*, she admitted, though it was only the anticipation of the performance that had overcome her wretched despair at his refusal to witness her most astonishing accomplishment.

The next morning the paper arrived with breakfast in the College Hall dining room. Alice confiscated it to clip out the article. Even though she would see him on Sunday, she would send it to him in her next letter.

San Francisco Chronicle
October 29

Erminie, presented at the University of California's newest venue, the Greek Theatre, was a resounding success. Performed first in 1895 in England,

10

and then the next year at the Casino on Broadway in New York City, this tuneful and pleasing work is one of the most performed light operas. The performance by Alice C. Hicks is of particular note. She is just a freshman and it is her extraordinary singing voice and sparkling eye which gave her access to a part usually reserved for upper class women. Miss Hicks is to be commended for her poise and her lyrical and comedic delivery.

Nov. 1 '09
The Owl Limited
Southern Pacific
San Francisco and Los AngelesMy Dearest Alice,
A lonesome sad trip back to LA, but the pleasure of being with you and knowing you are happy and contented will make the sunshine brighter tomorrow. I have the love and confidence of the most deserving girl.
Good night at 50 miles per hour,
Jerry.

November 2, 1909
Tuesday evening
College Hall
Dearest Jerry:
Another minute and you were gone and I realized I was alone once more. It was so good to be with you and have a chat. Your dear wee note was waiting for me when I got back from class and I sat by my window after rereading it, dreaming away until Mildred brought me back to Earth. She said it was her duty as my roommate to read all letters that affected me. Of course I didn't show it to her.
All the love in the land, Jerry.
Your Alice

Chapter 3

Jerry's November Surprise

The aroma of burning leaves rose up to the third story and drifted through the dorm's open window. Silence reigned like a commandment. Alice slipped out of the covers to grab her pen and stationery before sneaking back to bed, grateful that Mildred had not stirred.

Nov. 8th '09
College Hall
Dearest Jerry:
I sat alone in the lamplight last evening, having just come in from the Chi Psi dance. I like the quiet—everything is so still. It was an informal affair and I wore my plain white dress. Their house is very pretty and we had a fine time. Earle Grant knows how to take a girl to a dance—filled my program and found all my partners. I think I have been exceptionally lucky in having such nice boys take me to the dances. There is nothing like going with the boys who "are on top" and Earle Grant seemed to have the whole affair in charge. Dear little Irene, who was Cerise in *Erminie,* sang her song and I sang the lullaby and "When Love Is Young." It was so nice to do it and they all stood around the grate fire while we sang. The dance is over—the boys can come and go, but I am glad there is one who doesn't forget me.

Bidding day is Friday. The excitement grows and all the boys can't wait to find out what we are going to do. Poor Mildred is so nervous over the outcome that I know she will be glad when it is over. I think there is no doubt she will get a bid from the Alpha O. As for myself the girls are still camping in our room, though not just now of course, and I don't know what the result will be.

I am looking for a letter from you this afternoon, telling me how it goes with your "conditional acceptance" of Chicago. I can hardly bear to hear. How perplexing it is to have it come up again, for I know how it must worry you.

Mildred spoke suddenly from under her bedclothes. "Alice, my dear. The dance at Chi Phi was pretty fine. You and Earle Grant looked wonderful together. Is there anything going on between the two of you? And, who is this—*person,* you write to and get so much mail from?"

Alice squashed an impulse to blurt out the truth. "Jerry is just a boy I know from work at home. And, definitely no, there is nothing going on with Earle."

Mildred smiled. "Say, didn't we have a glorious time singing songs from *Erminie*? How grand to have some of the cast at the dance."

"So many turned out to be good friends," said Alice. Her gaze drifted toward the other end of the room, where two deflated gowns lay draped over the chairs. "I hope we keep our friends forever." She threw the bedcovers back, obscuring the letter. "I'm going down to shower my laziness away. You should as well. Then let's have a pig's breakfast!"

And off Alice went in her robe, bare feet slapping down the oak corridor, sponge bag dangling from her arm, her thick brunette braid swinging across her back.

They bounded down two flights of stairs to Saturday's buffet breakfast. Alice tilted her head up and sniffed. It was the rich, deep aroma of coffee in giant silver urns that greeted them first. Alice had loved that smell since moving with her mother to Los Angeles from the tiny Canadian town of Mitchell a couple of years ago. Thoroughly American, that scent.

Today, as on all weekends, breakfast was laid out on a long sideboard. The Chinese cook worked half days and the washing-up girl kept an eye on things, but the residents served themselves. Green and red apples, leaves still attached, were piled in a basket. A yellow bowl of brown-shelled hardboiled eggs came next. Soft white rolls lay in platters surrounded by delicately textured butter pats, and blueberry jam in silver-lidded jars lay within easy reach.

Coffee in hand, and choices made, they carried their plates to the refectory table. Patty Chickering and Pauline Pierson popped in a split second later and poured coffee for themselves. Alice waved for their attention.

"Come sit with us," said Alice, "and let's natter on about the end of Rush and Bidding Day, and what kind of mischief you got yourselves into last night." The conversation jumped back and forth about dates and dances. Patty and Pauline had double-dated at another fraternity dance, not yet thinking seriously about any one boy, but days were early! Alice was teased about Earle Grant's intentions, and just who was this John Rankin that kept coming by the hall to escort her to this and that? Weren't the Thetas the absolute tops and didn't they all wish mightily that all four of them would be chosen on Bidding Day and would live together at the sorority in the spring?

Breakfast over, Patty, Pauline, and Mildred went out to accomplish their various errands. Alice, intent on finding a letter from Jerry at the post office, was just about to leave the hall when the receptionist said she had a telegram marked "urgent." Alice ripped open the envelope and read:

ARRIVING OAKLAND 1PM STOP ON WAY TO SACRAMENTO STOP JERRY

She thought her heart would burst with happiness.

***

13

There he was. Six feet two inches of charcoal gray pinstripe, homburg and white shirt. Thick, straight black hair was swept back with pomade. His large clean-shaven jaw boasted a broad smile. He hadn't changed one whit since that day she met him in the Los Angeles insurance office, he a salesman just down from San Francisco, and she the new typist just out of high school. She ached to run into his arms, be enfolded in his embrace. Propriety forbade it, and so with joy radiating from her eyes, Alice took his arm and they walked to the trolley to catch the ferry to San Francisco.

"What a delightful cad you are to arrive so abruptly, expecting me to be at the ready!" But, of course she would be and they both knew it. She grinned in acknowledgement. "It is so very wonderful to see you, though you were just here, what? A week ago? How long do we have, and where shall we spend our time?"

"Alice, my heart, one question at a time! I'll be here for a couple of hours. Let's hop in a cab and go to the Fairmont Hotel, where we can have tea and hide in a corner."

"But, why are you here?"

"I am on my way to Sacramento for a managers' meeting. I have already made a stop at the Buckeye Ranch to see Mother and Anne and Sue. They seem to be holding up the ranch pretty well."

"They must still miss your father's guiding hand, Jerry."

"It has been two years since his passing. Mother can't get beyond the fact that life is not the same without him," replied Jerry with feeling.

"Of course," said Alice, "How could it *ever* be the same?" Not that she had ever met the family, not yet. Perhaps when their engagement was not so secret Jerry would take her to the ranch. She was thinking rather of her dear mother's sadness that had lingered over the death of Alice's older sister, Jo.

Returning to thoughts of Jerry, she asked, "The foreman must be competent?"

"He is. Anne and Sue deal with him well enough, but there is a restlessness about him. I suspect it is because our family is being pressured by Phoebe Hearst to sell. He could be dismissed quite suddenly if the ranch is sold. My Aunt Mary and Uncle Tom and the rest of the ranchers are also being pestered by Hearst, too. I guess her son wants to look out his bedroom window and see Hearst to the horizon. But, enough of family matters." Jerry sighed and turned loving eyes on Alice.

The cab ride was a most sensual experience, pressed shoulder and thigh together. Alice's hand was clasped in his, and it seemed that every inch of her body was humming with electricity. Too soon they arrived at the top of Nob Hill where the enormous Fairmont Hotel perched like a palace.

Jerry paid the driver, and the doorman extended his hand to Alice as she stepped out. The hotel doors opened, and they were swept into the exquisite lobby. Alice was stunned. Alabaster walls stretched upward to gilded ceilings

14

that reached yet another three stories high. A marble Corinthian colonnade framed the long curved reception desk. Jerry gently slipped his hand under her elbow and steered her to the left of reception and then back toward a grove of potted palms to the tearoom.

A nod to the maître d' and they were seated far back in a private alcove. Tail-coated waiters materialized, unfolded linen napkins onto laps and handed out menus. Another nod brought the waiter and Jerry placed the order. Alice was mesmerized. She finally focused as Jerry scooted his chair closer to her so he could hold her hand under the table.

"Jerry, in all the times I have been to the city I have never dared to come here. This is absolutely overwhelming—something right out of Europe. You must have come here before. The maître d' seems to know you."

"I have, but not often. Last time was with my old fraternity brother Arthur—you remember him from our insurance office here? We had to make plans to open the LA Rotary Club."

Alice knew all about the results of that first organizational meeting in June. He had insisted that members boost one another's business, an approach frowned upon by other clubs. The headquarters was in the Travelers Insurance offices where he and she had worked before Alice left for college. The Rotary election was soon, and Jerry would be its first president.

"I have so much to say to you, but words are having a hard time forming in my mind," said Alice. "Just feasting my eyes on you seems to fill me up."

"Dear Alice." He squeezed her hand and leaned over to kiss her softly. "Mmm," he said, withdrawing from her eager lips. "We have the palm trees to thank for that little departure from etiquette."

Alice caught her breath, and thinking it best to change the subject before her heart gave way, said, "Jerry, can we spend Thanksgiving together with your cousin L.B.?"

"Not this year, dearest. I will be playing golf with some important characters from the Chicago office."

"Well, then, I will make plans with Mildred. Maybe we'll see each other for Christmas. Perhaps you can come down to George's ranch over the holidays." Alice struggled to keep it light, disguising her disappointment with a smile. It had not been an altogether diversionary question. She wanted to be with him and find out when the wedding plans would come to fruition.

"That's my Alice. I know all this separation is hard to bear. I am so proud of all your accomplishments. It has at least been fun, I think. Am I right?"

"You know there have been heaps of events. It's just… I miss you."

Jerry squeezed her hand as if to acknowledge her loneliness. And then his lips turned into an impish grin. "Are you looking forward to the Axe Rally?"

"I cannot wait to see it in action," she replied, animated once again at the anticipation, remembering the story he had related months ago.

15

The Axe Rally was the symbol of intense rivalry with Stanford University. It began with the April 1899 three game baseball series; Stanford had already lost game one. Needing a symbol with which to whip up the crowds, the Stanford Yell leaders bought a lumberman's axe and painted the handle red. At a rally before the second game, the axe was raised high to the students, then brought down sharply on the neck of a straw University of California effigy.

The Stanford Yell Team brought the axe with them to the second game, stirring up the crowd with the newly composed Axe Yell, brandishing the axe and cleaving blue and gold ribbons at every run. For all the encouragement, Stanford lost to UC. Victorious UC students, Jerry Muma and Clint Miller among them, stole the axe. During the chase through the city Stanford team members recovered the axe by pretending to be UC students. Jerry followed the pretenders onto a cable car and snatched the offending axe away. It cost one Stanford pretender bruises and a broken finger. Clint Miller then cut the handle off the axe, hid both pieces under his jacket and boarded the ferry to Oakland.

In November, Clint Miller took the axe from its hiding place in his mother's upright piano to the UC Yell Team for the pregame rally.

***

Alice and Jerry sat until the afternoon light began to dim. She forgot to be impressed by the panoramic views as they climbed back into a cab for the descent to the ferry. The four-faced clock tower rang out six o'clock as Jerry escorted Alice over the bay to the Berkeley station. They made small talk while Alice tried to be brave at the thought she would not see him for Thanksgiving. She could not even imagine Christmas without him, but the doubt was creeping in faster than she could sweep it away. He boarded the train to sit by a window, and tipped his hat. She waved, resisting the impulse to blow him a kiss. The knot below her heart refused to unwind.

Nov. 9
College Hall
Dearest Jerry:
I had dinner with a lot of Kappas tonight. We went to a meeting of all girls here for Thanksgiving to arrange some jinks, then out for chorus in Hearst Hall. Guess what? I am excused from all missed classes when the professors found out I was in *Erminie.*

Allan was in the courtyard last night with the Mandolin Club. They sang and all the girls encouraged them by clapping. He was on the Euclid car just after I left you and walked up with me. I really wanted to be alone—tears were not far off. Cruel train, I thought, as you tipped your hat from the platform. Except for the train that brings you back.

Your loving Alice

Chapter 4

The Axe Rally and the Big Stanford–UC Game

So it was this year, as the previous ten, that the Axe was removed from the secret vault, placed in an armored car and paraded to the rally from the Greek Theatre. An excited Alice and her friends from Gamma Phi Sorority watched the parade in the pouring rain, and then massed in Harmon Gym for the rally.

College Hall
Nov 10, 1909
Oh, Jerry, when John Hartigan started to read the telegram I knew it was from you. And then he told the boys you were one who helped get it. Then came three cheers. Jerry Muma, hurrah, hurrah, hurrah, Jerry Muma. Harmon Gym seemed transformed into some kind of a—I don't know what, and I felt I could have cheered with them had I not feared the astonishment of the girls with me.

The axe surely is a funny-looking article. It had a blue-and-gold ribbon twisted around the handle. I am awfully glad to have seen a rally and it was great of you to remember it with the telegram.

I wanted to tell every being around me who you were. To have to keep quiet and file out was more than a punishment.

I was asked today to sing at the Freshman Jinks in Hearst Hall on the 19th. I am glad to do it, for I am afraid I have lost out with my class lately for I haven't been to any of the functions. One of the Gamma Phi girls is going to play my accompaniment. An Alpha O girl and I are going to sing a duet after Thanksgiving, so I surely will have to start to practice.

All my love,
Your Alice

***

Saturday, John Rankin drove Alice, Mildred and her date Les to the Stanford campus in Palo Alto. The women were dropped off at the Alpha Phi Sorority for an early luncheon (rivalry not withstanding) and then picked up again in time for the game. Crowds shouldered their way through the gates; the anticipation was palpable for this last game of the football season. Thickening gray clouds did nothing to dampen the spirit.

17

Yell teams whipped the fans in the bleachers into a frenzy of screaming chants and waving banners as the rhythmic foot stomping sent seismic waves through the boards. Alice, John, Mildred and Les were hoarse from cheering. The Delta Fraternity brothers sitting around them soothed their throats with potent medicine from hip flasks, and so by the end of the game, there were more than a few glassy eyed young men. No matter, for as drunk as they were, it did not keep them from pouring onto the Stanford field to celebrate UC's victory. The score was 19–13 in favor of the UC "Oskies." A live bear cub mascot wearing the blue-and-gold collar headed the serpentine parade around the Stanford field.

It began to rain.

November 14
Sunday night
My Dearest Alice,
Oskies won. Now that was sweet music to a little bunch of fellows crowded around a table at Longs last night. I am so glad that you could participate in so glorious a victory. You will remember it all your days. I remember events that took place in the games of 1897–'98 and '99 just as if they only happened yesterday.

I found three of your letters waiting for me at the office, and by Jove, they were appreciated. No one was at the office when I arrived so I just sat me down before my desk and numbered them one, two, three and read them, knowing of the victory and that you were there to enjoy it. I do want so much to have you enter into the spirit of all the college activities and your success and good luck have been way beyond my fondest hopes. Soon it will be bidding day and I know you will be pleased with the opportunity. Whichever one you choose, you will get the pearl ring. It is all made and is a little beaut!

The Home Office still wants me in Chicago, and as much as I do not want to go, they are so insistent that there may be a time when I will say goodbye to dear old California for a while, but I would need your agreement before it comes to that. All my best love to you, Alice.

Jerry

Her shoulders slumped as she gazed out of the window at the rain streaking down outside. Her joy at sharing the game with him evaporated with the fear of their separation. Would the wedding be postponed? She could see herself, pale reflection looking back through the rivulets. *How will I bear it? What will I do?* Perhaps he would not go. And she put the thought of separation away.

Chapter 5

Dash and Disappointment at Year's End

Nov. 24 '09
Wednesday morning
My Dear Jerry:
Ever so many thanks for letting me hear from you at once. I have decided definitely that sorority Bidding Day is over for me. I am so relieved but still feel more than sorry that everything got so mixed up and I have only myself to blame for mistakenly turning down the sororities. All the girls are too nice for anything and it doesn't look as if they had any ill feeling toward me. I must put it behind me and study hard for the two exams next week. Tomorrow I will write from Hoytie's house where I am spending Thanksgiving—and how I wish we could be together.
Much love,
Alice

What a Thanksgiving she had with Hoytie's family. She had been placed to the right of Professor Hoyt and had just finished chatting with his sister-in-law sitting on her left when the professor tapped Alice on the shoulder.

"Alice, my dear, I had mentioned to my brother that you were born near Toronto. He has come up with some interesting gossip from the paper. You have seen *Pippa Passes,* I think. I recall that you and Hoytie went together to the nickelodeon a while ago."

"We did, yes," replied Alice. She turned to include the professor and his brother, who was sitting in the next seat. "Though we agreed the movie had almost no connection with Robert Browning's poem, we enjoyed it."

"I understand that little Mary Pickford, who had a small role in this D. W. Griffith fellow's first movie, has caught the public eye," said the professor. "She is only sixteen. My goodness, two years younger than you and Hoytie! Imagine."

"She's Canadian, you know," replied Alice, choosing to ignore any reference to age, lest she betray that she was Hoytie's elder. "From Toronto."

"Are you talking about me, Father?" Hoytie broke in from across the table, having just heard her name.

19

"No, my dear, just mentioning that movie, *Pippa Passes.* I was just getting to the part about your uncle mentioning that Mary Pickford was born in Toronto. And, Alice stole my line!"

By this time the whole end of the table was listening. Alice turned toward the professor. "'God's in his Heaven / All's right with the world.' That's the only line from Browning's poem in the script. UC's literature professors would shudder at the cavalier use of such fine poetry."

"Well, that aside, my dear girl," said Professor Hoyt, "the moving picture is about the healing power of song, and *that's* right up your alley."

And so the conversation went, roaming through the events of the growing Los Angeles movie industry—and did Alice and her family live next to the studios? And what was it like to have film crews running through the neighborhoods?

November 29, 1909
Sunday evening
College Hall
My Dear Jerry,

It seems more than two days since I have written you—so much has happened, and oh, such a good time. I was at Hoytie's when I closed my last letter. Well, I just got back to the hall in time to dress and be ready for the Junior Farce. Les called for Mildred—and John, just out of the infirmary after a bout of influenza, picked us all up in his machine.

We had such a splendid time at the farce that I am sending you my program so you may see just how jolly it was. And I am putting my dance card from the prom, marked full of dances, in my memory book. Someday, we will go over it together.

I went for a walk to Berkeley town and found your letter waiting for me when I returned and sat down near a window in East Hall to read it. I was all alone, and when I finished reading it, I just sat there loving you with all my heart, and to think it had rained and you had no cheery Thanksgiving dinner. I just pictured next Thanksgiving Day in our own home, with everything so different—no more lonely times. I am loving you better all the time. Never fear with all these other boys. You have something they don't begin to have in their inexperience. You will laugh at that expression I know, but I mean more than perhaps the words imply.

Your loving Alice

Dec. 5 '09
Los Angeles
My Dearest Alice,

You have wondered why I did not write you Wednesday as I promised. The settlement of the Chicago matter did not take place until yesterday and you have problems enough of your own. Exams are important enough to take all one's thought and time.

I believe I should have said yes this time and gone on to Chicago Jan. 1st if I had been feeling just right. I have been fighting off the grippe or some other, just-as-disagreeable malady for past ten days and my poor "koko" was aching simply awful. If I had been in better humour and you had consented, I would have said good-bye to dear old California and associations that are so dear to me. ...

I had dinner with your brother George, but was poor company on account of not feeling well.

The *Erminie* photo occupies the center position on my dresser. What a fine collection of pictures I am getting. Four on the dresser and three on the wall. My fraternity brother Jim Osborn says he just believes there is something going on.

It doesn't look like a trip north for me until perhaps Xmas Eve. You know we are in the midst of the closing (sales) campaign. In arranging your Xmas holiday, leave me out of consideration. I mean by that, you determine what you want to do and where you want to visit and let me know. I will adjust my coming to suit your plans. If I get to spend the New Year with you, I will be lucky. ...

Good night my dear and good luck with the exams.

Lovingly, Jerry

***

Alice and Mildred left for a stroll through the campus to Berkeley town. Exams had just finished. Alice was exhausted. Her face reflected her sleepless nights during the weeks after Thanksgiving. Mildred had to coax her to luncheon at The Bear, which was eerily quiet without the sounds of student chatter.

"I am just so thankful it is finished," said Alice as she picked at her salad. "The days and weeks of studying have pretty much finished me." How could she tell Mildred what was also on her mind—that Jerry was leaving for Chicago? Did he mean that it would it be in January? She could not think anymore, could not find a cheerful way around it. Bidding Day was a disaster, Jerry might leave her for Chicago, and exams had been brutal.

"Do you think you passed your exams?" asked Mildred.

Alice shook her head. "I know I didn't make first section for most of them."

"Well, it is over now. Try not to worry. It is me who must worry for you— not to go home to Los Angeles for the holidays."

"Well, Hoytie wants me. I am so tired that the trip would do me in entirely. I'll stay with her family. You know me. I will bounce back after I can rest. I have been thinking of staying in the infirmary for a few days beforehand."

21

"That sounds like a smart idea. Please, Alice, have some soup. You will need your strength to walk back up the hill," Mildred said with a grin, trying to find a little humor.

Alice slid her soup bowl in front of her and dipped her spoon into the beef and vegetables. She thought she did not have a better friend in the world right now than Mildred.

They walked slowly back, passing the Avenue Theatre Nickelodeon on Telegraph Hill. It was closed until the university opened again in January, their best customers having left for Christmas.

***

There were several other students in the infirmary when Alice checked in. There were no books to study and no parties or teas to distract. And so she slept and dreamed of last year's Christmas with Jerry, only to awake in sadness. She resolved to take her joy in the warmth of Hoytie's family.

December 24, 1909
407 Fairmont Ave., the Hoyts
Dear, Dear Jerry,
Almost Christmas Eve and when I think of being away from you tomorrow I can hardly stand it. I do hope you have some nice invitation for Christmas dinner. Boxes are arriving all the time and Mrs. Hoyt carries them away to her room. We are to hang up stockings, too, for the children's benefit, and get up at 5 o'clock to see the result.

I have made twelve place cards decorated with berries for the dinner table. We are to dine at two tomorrow afternoon. Carolers are expected tonight and we all have sealed boxes of candy to throw down to them at the finish.

I am so thankful for your pearl ring and look forward to wearing it to dinner. I know it was to celebrate my sorority bid, but never mind. It is beautiful nonetheless.

You will see by my "personal" on this envelope that I am trusting you to get the mail at the post office. The fact is I have used all the small business envelopes and cannot let on to anyone why I need more. But there won't be much more of this, will there, Jerry? The year 1910 is nearly here, I am waiting to hear the result of your trip to the ranch. I hope you will make it north to see me. And now, Jerry dear, I hope Christmas will be bright and happy for you and let us look forward to a "righte merrie" one next year.

Your loving Alice

December 25 '09
407 Fairmount Ave
My Darling Jerry:
Christmas Day is nearly over and what a day! I can't begin to tell you how good everyone has been, and the messages and packages from Jerry dear. ...

22

The doorbell kept ringing and it was something from you. The lovely little clock is striking now and every time I hear its sweet chime, I think of you. And the belt buckle, the fan, the New Year cards, and the telegram—I believe you planned that they would come in, one at a time, the way they did. ...

We were up early and diving into our stockings, all sitting around the grate fire in Mrs. Hoyt's sitting room. I gave one of Hoytie's sisters a photo, and an embroidered apron for another. Cousin L.B. sent me a pretty motto card. ...

And now, Jerry dear, I must say good night. I cannot tell you how many times I have thought of you and loved you with all my heart. I have been wondering what all the dear people at the Muma Ranch are doing and hope to hear soon. This has been as happy a Xmas as any girl could ever hope to spend away from those she loves most dearly. My mind is full of thoughts and plans for the New Year—wonderful year of "1910."

Chapter 6

Changing Horizons, 1910

A Conversation with Gran'mere

"The year began well for you, didn't it, Gran'mere? You didn't expect the invitation from the Thetas in January for your initiation." Was that a grin I saw bloom on her beautiful young face?

"Wasn't it fine?" she replied, and emphasized the comment with a flourish by sticking the last hairpin into her lustrous pompadour. "Jerry wrote me later, on the twenty-fourth, the day of the induction: *You are up to ride the goat at this hour, and good luck to you.* I laughed out loud at the rude phrase, which referred, of course, to the initiation shenanigans in a fraternity. Nothing so crude for the women, all of whom seemed perfect ladies. Oh, but it was heaps of fun, that day. Mildred was there and lots of other girls I knew. After the ceremony we sang and had a little informal dance."

"Somehow, it all worked out, then," I said. "You were chosen for the very sorority you felt was tops. But they never explained their silence on Bidding Day?"

Gran'mere looked away. "No, and as I must have had a part in their delayed decision, I would never ask."

It was a small thing not to know, and there were other things I wished to press.

"That same letter was fraught with other issues, if I remember correctly," I said.

I could visualize her pacing the dorm room. Her red kimono, a Christmas gift from Hoytie, flowed out behind her. "Jerry was involved in the creation of the Rotary in San Diego and had a team from Travelers working with him. I was so proud of him for creating a national organization."

"What about this move to Chicago?" I said, being blunt. I was tired of being deflected by all the news of Jerry's pioneering efforts with Rotary, his success on the golf course, etc.

Gran'mere stopped looping a path around the room and sat down abruptly in her rocker. She forced her hands into her lap. I could see them beginning to tremble. "I was very upset by a line at the end of his letter, suggesting that he was going East after all, away from me. He said he wouldn't go without my blessing. He said he would not decide without me. And then, then... That seeming offhand remark, *too bad you cannot stay the four years*, truly scared

24

me. Did he *want* me to stay for that long? We had planned to be married in the fall. One year, he said."

"But, he did decide. And, why was that, do you think? You never said."

"I sent him a telegram within the hour, GODS PLAN REQUIRES MORE STRENGTH THAN I POSSESS STOP RING SOONEST STOP ALICE. And then he called."

"Gran'mere, it was more than Travelers sending him on a promotion to Chicago, wasn't it? That was just a lucky convenience. It was about the reason behind your engagement."

Gran'mere did her best to disappear, but I held her firmly in my mind.

She finally began to speak of the secret she'd hidden from all of us. "My Jerry became engaged to me last year. But before that, he was engaged to a younger girl from Oakland. As you know, an engagement is a binding contract—which was why our engagement had to remain a secret until he could extricate himself. Her mother would not consent to break the contract. And, of course, they are all right next door, so to speak. She was a girl of some standing in the community, always in the society pages with her mother. If our engagement were made public, she would sue. The publicity would ruin Jerry, he would have lost his credibility. ... Who would trust a man who would break a contract? By association, my reputation would be in tatters, and my dear mother and Brother George would have suffered."

"What else, Gran'mere? If you want me to tell your story, you must speak of what was so dark that it could not be committed to paper."

She took a shaky breath, and began to rock. "She was pregnant, and seventeen. Jerry paid for an abortion in Los Angeles and had his fraternity brother Jim Osborn drive her there, and then back to Oakland after an overnight stay in a hotel. Of course the mother and daughter got even more insistent that Jerry marry her.

"And I was so worried that this would never end, and Jerry really wanted me to stay in school forever, and that he would hide out in Chicago because serving papers on him would be difficult." It all came out in a rush of anguish.

"In the end, you agreed to his going," I said, "if for nothing else than that there was no other choice. And Jerry said he would be gone a year and make so much money for Chicago Travelers that he could write his own ticket back to California after a year."

"And I would stay the semester and see what might be resolved."

She left me, then. I sighed. The emotional tug of war between Gran'mere and me to get to the truth had left me drained. Not able to face another minute with her papers, I, too, left the room.

March 9th
Thursday afternoon
Dearest Jerry:

25

We are nearly swimming away here, for we have had so much rain. I am sorry it is raining tonight, for I am going over to the city to a musicale. It is to be a very smart affair. Last night I sang a solo down at the little church, as it was the beginning of a series of good old-fashioned revival services. They are to last ten days. I will go again next week.

I had a lesson yesterday. My teacher believes me to have "unlimited possibilities." Getting better, isn't it?

Chapter 7

Chicago Bound

April 4, 1910
San Francisco *Overland* Limited
Chicago–San Francisco
Union Pacific and Southern Pacific
My Dearest Alice,
Arthur left me at Sacramento, and since that time I have been in the observation car taking a last look at dear old California. The most beautiful time of the year. It all would not be half bad if I only had you along. You and California are the dearest on earth to me.

I don't know whether I gave you my address in Chicago. American Trust Bldg., 7th floor.

Yours for brighter skies,
Jerry.

Monday evening
My Dear Jerry:
Two letters from you today. Why Jerry, I can hardly believe it! I don't know of anything better.

I have just come in from a sorority meeting and it has been an exceptional one. We have visitors who played for us while we danced after the meeting, and then we met to arrange for the Senior Freshman Banquet. ... How glad I am to be a Theta. 'Tis well to be satisfied, isn't it?

Today everyone has been saying, "Four years today since the earthquake," and so it is. What a tremendous amount has been accomplished in the city. Helen told me something on the ferry yesterday, as we stood out in front holding our hats, about the seagulls and how they went away after the fire. They are only now coming back in such great numbers. I didn't know it before.

We are all so lucky. The Floral Fete on the Faculty Club lawn comes off on Wednesday and I think it will be very pretty, all the girls in white with garlands of roses to wave in our dance. The Treble Clef concert is only a week off and on Monday night I am going to sing a Spanish song at the Spanish Club meeting.

At noon today I walked home via Strawberry Creek and the end of Piedmont Ave. past the little bench where we sat, when I wanted to say so many things to you and just couldn't. It was all so short, and you were away before I knew it. How I have enjoyed your letters! Do write two every day.

Chapter 8

A Visit from Harry

Several days later, between a hurried breakfast and a rush to class, the desk clerk announced, "Alice, dear, you have a visitor. He says he is your brother, Harry."

Oh, drat. What terrible timing, Alice thought, and resigned herself to be put out for her wonderful, vagabond elder brother. George had discovered on one of Harry's visits that he carried liquor in his suitcase. In Alice's mind, that did not make him a drunk. George was not so sure. Harry had, at a much younger age, joined the Canadian military, went to fight the Boer War in South Africa, and lived. Perhaps that would account for his drinking, for none of the rest of the family imbibed.

"Harry, you're a sight for my eyes!" Alice leaped into his arms for an enveloping hug and a kiss. She was pleased to see him in spite of the inconvenience, arriving as he did during this last crazy week before exams, with two concerts to perform, daily rehearsals, and the freshman–senior banquet. Well, she would just manage.

"You are perfectly horrible not to let me know. How long can you stay?"

"The kid looks so grown up. University agrees with you. Until Thursday." Harry smiled down at her.

"I will drag you to a few classes and rehearsals and you in turn will take me to dinner at the pub on Center Street and a show at the nickelodeon."

Harry nodded assent. "Did you see Jerry on his way to Chicago?"

"Yes, he stopped by between trains on his way. He writes that he is settled finally at the Athletic Club, lived through a late-April blizzard, is working way too hard, and longs for California. More of that later. I need to grab my books and dash to English class. You must attend this fiasco and see firsthand how my English professor has it in for me."

Alice, her arm hooked snuggly into Harry's elbow, made haste through the campus to her English Literature class. "Now, Harry, don't laugh, but this professor—this spiteful, arrogant nit—has assigned me the part of Sir Toby Belch in *Twelfth Night*. Perhaps at the end of class you will figure out what his problem is?"

Harry sat through the class, inconspicuous at the back of the auditorium, as Alice growled her way through Sir Toby. When they had joined up again, Harry said, "Kiddo, he's in love with your beauty and is punishing you for it!"

Alice blushed, smacked him with her playbook and marched him to anthropometry.

"What in the world is anthropometry?"

"Ah-ha!" said Alice. "You will learn a few things about yourself this next hour. It's all about measuring the human body and brain's anatomy for comparing the races, things like that. You'll see. In any case, it's geared to non-science students and not as hard as it might be."

After classes, Harry escorted Alice to the promised pub, ordering a beer for himself and steak and kidney pie for two.

"How is Mother, Harry? I do worry about her, though dear George and Annie take great care."

"She is getting older, a little frail, but otherwise well. She misses Father just as awfully as ever. I hear from Bill that he and Father are thinking of packing it in for good and coming down. Bill, I think, is finally reconciled to the death of Lucy, his fiancée, and willing to part with Canada."

"How good it would be for us to be together," said Alice, "but poor Bill." In truth Bill was more uncle than brother, being so much her elder. "I must make the trip to the ranch for Christmas. Haven't been home in so long, and it makes me homesick to see you. Will you stay long in Los Angeles?"

"No," replied Harry. "Must be off. Too bad to miss Jerry. Now that he is in Chicago, there is no one around to cheer up the folks and talk about you."

"Harry, I miss him. Silly, because I did not see him much—only brief visits on his way to someplace else." Alice paused, breathing out the tension beginning in her throat. "It just feels awful, his being so far away."

"I know, kid, but it won't be long now before you are married. What's he up to these days?"

"He is living temporarily at the Chicago Athletic Club, and working hard to make it permanent. Just the place to entertain business friends, like it was in LA. He tells me that by May first, his increased business will begin to pay off, and if it goes well, he will be out of there soon. Calls me his California Sunbeam, isn't that silly? But he misses his old state dreadfully."

"Likely, Alice my dear, he misses you more."

"Oh, pooh." But it felt good to hear him say it. "Jerry's still mightily connected with the state. His fraternity brother Clint Miller is starting up a California oil investment business of some kind."

Harry replied, "Wouldn't be surprised if ol' Jerry didn't have a piece of that one."

Alice smiled knowingly. "I'm confident you are right on that score." She paused and chewed the last of her savory pie. "Can you tell me where you are traveling next? Please, please, Harry—you are always so secretive."

"Ah, now you know I can't, kid. But I can tell you it is a government job and I am going to a hot climate."

"Still a telegrapher, then," said Alice. It was not really a question.
Harry nodded.

Over dessert, they chatted about Brother George and his growing babies, and reminisced about Mitchell and the cousins, "Mur" and Jean, who wrote occasionally to Alice and to their mother. Alice did not share the sordid details of the reason behind Jerry's flight to Chicago. Her family thought Jerry was a fine fellow. He *was*. It would not do to cast aspersions.

Harry left from the 16th Street station to travel south to George's Riverside Ranch for a brief visit. Alice waved good-bye and turned back toward Theta House. Sunlight slanted through evening clouds, and the promised rain held off for the time it took for her to make it through the front door.

Chapter 9

May Exams and Graduation

Sunday, "May Day," 1910
My Dear Jerry:

A "May Day surprise," surely, to have your lettergram arrive while I was at breakfast this morning.

I have had a lovely Sabbath day, although rather a selfish one. After dinner I read some interesting anatomy books, and perchance fell asleep, for the couch on the sleeping porch was so comfortable. This morning I went to the First Congregational Church in Oakland with Alice Earl. The whole family of six leaves in less than two weeks for Europe, to see the Passion play and to stay until next December. ...

At the Freshman–Senior Banquet, when the "engagement course" arrived, everyone looked expectant at who might announce their impending marriage. Two girls at least were suspected, but we were disappointed. If I had gotten up I think they would have fallen over. But when I am at the Theta House, and the postman delivers the same handwriting, they will find it out.

The grand concert was Friday night. Much to our sorrow, we had a very cold night, so there were only a handful of people there. Everyone said the Japanese chorus was very pretty. They turned all the lights off and I ran out first in a beautiful borrowed kimono, with a lantern, and when all the lantern girls got in, they flashed on the lights.

And now for a week of work. I will be studying with a friend all day tomorrow. Thanks for your good wishes for the "exes." I need them.

Good night and heaps of love to you,
Alice

May 5, 1910
Thursday evening
My Dear Jerry:

Two very bad days are over and I wish I had a better report to make, but yesterday the exam was very hard and I won't be surprised if I flunked it. By way of dissipation after such strenuousness, I went over to the Theta House for luncheon, and Peggy and I took pictures of as many freshmen as we could get together. Then we went to the library, even into a recess of the periodicals room, but I fear neither of us is a wonderful student with a natural love for study, for in about an hour we couldn't stand it any longer and went out and walked down to Center Street and purchased a box of graham wafers and those

31

new Lorna Doones and had a tea party away up on the third floor—
"Freshman's Paradise" of Theta House—with Pauline and some others. It was
Pauline's last afternoon here, as she leaves for home in Oregon and sails from
New York on the 29th for Liverpool, England, where her fiancé meets her.

I worked hard in the library today and finished my paper and handed it in.
Tomorrow, May and I go up in the hills to practice our speeches for our English
ex on Saturday morning, but not before an early game of tennis. ...How very
often I feel, just as you said in your last letter, about "handling matters on
paper." Parchment does seem cold and unsympathetic sometimes, doesn't it?
Many of the sweet things I'd love to say, I can't somehow, but I will someday.

Good night, Jerry dear,

Alice.

P.S. I went with the Earls to the exquisite little Swedenborgian Church near
the Presidio, with its brightly lit fireplace and beautiful paintings, and thought
it would be perfect for our wedding.

P.P.S. John Rankin invited me to the Greek Theatre to hear the New York
Symphony Orchestra program of Wagner. I fairly drank it in. I do hope you
have been hearing some good music. What a joy it is.

May 17, 1910
MY DEAR ONE STOP JUST SENT A WIRE TO THE MEN OF 1900
AND ASKED THEM TO SING PALMS OF VICTORY AS WE USED TO
SING IT TEN LONG YEARS AGO STOP WE CELEBRATED TONIGHT
AND I DRANK EVERY TOAST TO YOU AND CALIFORNIA STOP
LOVE AND BLESSINGS JERRY

May 17th
Theta House, Graduation Celebrations
My Dear Jerry,

What a happy, happy time we are having, going to first one thing and then
the other.

This morning all the alumni gathered in the Greek Theatre and the President
of Harvard gave the address. The Treble Clef and Glee Club sang with the
university orchestra, and I stood right in front of Mrs. Hearst while I sang. So
many alumni were there clutching different banners—from the class of '87,
the year of my birth, to your year of graduation, 1900. After the ceremony, all
rushed down the hill to the Faculty Club lawn for luncheon.

Afterward I went over to the Theta House and sang with the girls. We are
going to have tea in the hills tonight and watch the sunset.

Yesterday was the class pilgrimage and speeches, and I tell you, Jerry, I
enjoyed it. In the afternoon there were receptions at two "frat" houses. Peggy,
Helen and I hitched a ride in a machine to the Beta House. That was the nicest
place, for they served out on the lawn under huge Japanese umbrellas. Then

we went to the Chi Phi house for an informal dance, and then to the Greek Theatre for the extravaganza which was so good we clapped for ten minutes at the end.

Then there was the Grand Jubilee Parade which was a great success— classes of '09, etc. marched with colored Japanese lanterns, Chinese students had a dragon, and the Hindoos, a most unusual display. We serpentined over California field, down onto Shattuck, through the campus to College Ave., down Bancroft, and through an opening in the fence to the south side of the field.

There were cheers and class yells, and your class of 1900 was there with the wagon with the little black coffin. Oh, how I thought of the good times you must have had. The electrical engineers had Halley's Comet fixed up splendidly and an auto carried a huge electric "C." Then the "BIG C" on Charter Hill was lighted and shone so beautifully through the fog.

Last night, there were most of us left at the house, and we chatted about staying for the full four years in college. I always feel so guilty when they start on that topic. They have an idea I am not coming back, but the easiest way is not to tell them now, I think. What do you think?

I am a sophomore now!

Good night, I hope this week will be a successful one with you.

Your Alice

Chapter 10

Chicago Heat

My Dearest Alice, I enjoyed your dandy letter received just before I left the office. It came when things had me all stirred up and I just sat down and read your message twice and started all over again. ...

Your lover Jerry

* * *

Black and white bathroom tiles felt cool on his bare feet. Jerry stood in the bathroom, still damp from the shower, lathering his brush in the shaving mug. The mug's faded gold bands framed the angular Masonic crest. Jerry remembered his father explaining the meaning of the symbols as they stood beside each other in the ranch bathroom when he was a little boy—in a bathroom not like this, in a time and place as remote from here as the moon. This mug had come to him three years ago when his eighty-two-year-old father had succumbed to influenza.

Jerry was bleary-eyed. Six days a week he was up early for a routine of showering, shaving, eating breakfast, and working. Sundays were for golfing with business connections; evenings were for dining and conniving over the best Chicago steak, port and cigars. Next week's trip to the home office in Hartford with new hire Stumes was all work, too, but at least it would get him out of this damnable heat. Perhaps he would take a weekend trip on the lake just to break the pace.

Alice popped to mind as the razor rounded his jaw on the left side. Last week he wrote her that he was "as good as elected to membership in the club." It had happened. Against the odds, *this* out-of-towner had moved into the heart of the business community—the Chicago Athletic Club. Jerry could smell the success.

Alice had written back praise and congratulations, and she informed him that she had moved into a little house with some of the summer school Thetas. Summer school—a godsend to keep her occupied, and worth the expense. The girls were teasingly calling her "mother" because she was watering the lawn and supervising the cleaning lady, Mrs. Fakuda. Her spirits had swung back to her ebullient self once she had accepted the whole Norah mess, and his reasons for fleeing to Chicago. It was not over, but it would be. It might take months, but it would finally end. And Alice was tough. No scholar for sure, but that was not the point. He could talk her into another semester. She was excited to be learning German to help with her singing, and she had added folksongs to

34

her repertoire. She wanted to learn Spanish and participate in Rush. Yes, she would do it, would go back for the fall semester. He would wait a little while to tell her, though.

Jerry jerked his razor away but not in time to avoid the nick.

"Damnation!"

The soap turned pink with blood. He splashed his face to rinse off the last of the lather and stabbed the cut with his styptic pencil. Satisfied that the blood would not drip down his chin, he walked into the bedroom. Flinging down the towel from around his waist with the surety of a man with maid service, he dressed for the day.

***

Jerry's starched, stiff collar was already wilting as he draped his jacket on the back of his chair. It had been a sweltering walk to work. His office in the upper floors of the American Trust Building had that new air cooled system, but this high up it served mostly to spread the odor of sweat from office to office.

Miss Mathews, his secretary, had already put the day's files on the corner of the desk. He rifled through the stack, looking for a letter from Alice. Most days there was at least one to savor. But, no, there was no letter from her and he felt a twinge of disappointment, an edge of worry. For throughout his busy days, he missed her more than he liked to admit. Those letters back and forth were their lifeline. If there was none by tonight, he would send her a lettergram and ask if anything was wrong. Lord knows there were times he received a frantic telegram from her when she had not heard from him for a couple of days! No, for now he would start on the work his secretary had laid out. Half-year stats on the Chicago/Cook County sales stared at him from the top of the pile.

He knew without looking that sales were ahead for the year. He had seen to that. Nonetheless it was rewarding to see it in print, knowing the whole office was aware. Now for the next move—to draw the best of the new breed of insurance salesmen to his Travelers office. To do that he would institute a new commission plan that would leave upper management incredulous. But in the end they would go for it—just a few more icebergs to melt, as he had put it to Alice.

The day's *Chicago Tribune* lay folded by his ashtray. Jerry lit a cigar. Comfortable with the glow, he opened the paper to the financial section.

Scanning down the columns he found a summary of his recent investments, the Coalinga oil fields in California.

Air compressors experiences promise to be an entire success in drawing water off flooded oil sands in Coalinga parcels.

T. L. Hannah well drilled into oil at 156 ft. Cosmo Oil Company still going at 1,300 ft.

35

Southern Pacific lays heavy rails along the road from Kings River to Huron. Railroad bed heavily ballasted and in first-class shape.

"Trust the railroad to keep smellin' the money," Jerry murmured, then said into the intercom, "Miss Mathews, please get C. O. Miller on the line. The West Coast wakes up any minute now. His number is Broadway 3062 in LA."

While waiting, Jerry turned the pages to the automobile advertisements. There it was:

1911 Winton Six, a real beauty, self-cranking, four speeds, all-wood interior with leather seats for five, a convertible top folded back to show the rich interior, multiple disc clutch, reliable brakes. It combined the sweetness of electricity and the flexibility of steam with the highest-possible efficiency of the gasoline motor. It was available September first for $3,150.

Jerry's fantasy drive around town was interrupted by his secretary.

"Mr. Muma," Miss Mathew's voice droned from the intercom, "I have Mr. Miller on the line."

"Thank you, Miss Mathews. Hello, Clint. Get you first thing in the a.m., did I?"

"Hell, yes, Jerry. Got to start early out here to keep up with you Easterners."

"Received your telegram about the bad report on the Coalinga fields. Tell me the particulars."

"It's no good on those outlying parcels," replied Clint. "We hired Hazeltine of the Nevada Petroleum Company, you know—those gold field capitalists. He says oil's too deep to drill at 4,000 feet."

"You trust his judgment?"

"Yeah, but he can get a little radical, in my opinion. I'm going up there to check it out. Might spend two months, including looking over your interest in the Devils' Den District. For now, don't put any money in it."

"What's happening on my Diablo Lost Hills claims?" asked Jerry. "Are all the partners happy with the progress?"

"Wells around it are doing okay," replied Clint. "Associated Oil Company came in at 257 feet with 300 barrels a day. Four rigs going and a branch pipeline passing through any day now. Jerry, how are you situated with capital outside your own?"

"There's interest here in making some side money on California oil."

"Good. If you can persuade anyone to purchase land or oil company stock, you get a share of the profits. I'm thinking that I can get land at forty dollars net, and if you can sell it for me, there's five dollars an acre in it for you."

"Great, Clint. Thanks for the chat."

"Oh, hey, Jerry, I just moved in with Jim Osborne to your old rooms at the Athletic Club."

"Now you are making me homesick for my old fraternity chums. Damn you!" Jerry laughed as he put down the phone.

36

"Mr. Muma," droned the intercom again. "You have an interview in ten minutes with a Mr. Stumes, then a sales force meeting, and lunch with the Fresno manager at one. Oh, and you have a personal letter. The mailroom just brought it up. Shall I just put it on your desk during lunch?"

"Thank you, Miss Mathews. That will be fine." Jerry breathed a sigh of relief and regret. Alice's letter was prompt, after all, but he could not take any pleasure in her words until the end of the day.

***

At five p.m. Jerry was back at his desk plowing through the afternoon paperwork, determined to clear it all before dinner. It was after seven when he pulled on his jacket and walked out of the darkened office.

Back at the club, Jerry went straight to the locker room, peeled off his sweat-soaked clothes, showered off the perspiration, and dove in. Chlorine stung his eyes; the rest was bliss.

He could feel his brain disengage and muscles come alive in the cool water. Grateful for the dinnertime solitude, Jerry paced his laps for a good thirty minutes.

Back up in his rooms after a quick bite, he tore open his letter from Alice.

Dearest Jerry,

We have just come in from visiting friends at an old-fashioned rambling house on Piedmont Ave. They have a tower room and we gazed over the whole country in the moonlight. Then we talked downstairs in the library in the light from candles and the grate fire, and I couldn't help picturing just such a little room where you and I can read and enjoy each other next winter. My thoughts are never far away from that. They had a library table, round with a pedestal and four big claws. It reminded me of the one we had back home in Canada, which I have many times pictured in our home (draped) with a partial cover of brown Chinese tapestry. Long ago, Mother promised it to the first one of us girls who had a house to put it in—so I guess I win! We will see about that later on.

Your good letter arrived this morning with all the enthusiastic news of your progress with the office. Please keep sending me those clippings of Rotary doings; I so enjoyed reading about the ladies' night dinner and the honors bestowed upon you that evening. I am looking forward to our attending such a gala together soon.

All the love in the land, Jerry dear,
Alice

***

The sleeper left Chicago on July 19, bringing Jerry and Mr. Stumes to New York the next day. They took a taxi from Penn Station to Grand Central, boarded a train and were in the Hartford home office for a late lunch. After introductions among fellow managers from other Travelers offices, and after

37

sitting through an interminable meeting in a room only marginally cooler than Jerry's Chicago office, the visitors were chauffeured to the Hartford Club for their stay.

Next day, he breakfasted with his new hire. Stumes was young, recently married, and congenial, and he was also a remarkably productive salesman with an enviable golf handicap. He made it clear to Jerry that he was cognizant of the honor of being here: after all, he was a star candidate for the new, aggressive insurance sales force that Jerry had in mind.

Jerry closeted himself the rest of the morning with President Dunham, defending his plan to offer an astonishing thirty percent commission on all life insurance plans written in Cook County. Dunham sputtered and squawked and finally agreed to take it up with the board.

After two days of golfing, lunches, and touring the cool Berkshires, Jerry and Stumes were back aboard the train, heading into the Chicago heat.

August 10, 1910
Chicago Athletic Club
My Dear Girl,

We are just having regular old Eastern thunderstorms. I recognize them from my sojourn to Hartford. It sounds as if they were coming down right on top of the club.

What do you think! I met a fellow by the name of Hamilton from whom we finally stole the Stamford axe in '99. I remember pushing him off a Castro Street car when he had the axe under his arm. He fell and hurt himself and we ran off with the axe. Today, just as I was turning the corner to come to the club tonight, I ran into him. Ten years since I have seen him. We both stopped short. We made up and he has invited me out to his home.

Your letter from Marysville came along today. It was a dandy and made me brim full of gladness. What great fun you and Peggy are having touring the countryside. I do hope the visit will be restful for you. It will be no good to be tired before you even start the new semester. How delightful that you and the Powells are so fond of one another. Now, you must see that all those who meet you, love you.

Some important matters are up for settlement, and while I am trying always to find a good-enough excuse to justify a trip west, still that opportunity has not presented itself. My sisters are to visit me here at the end of the month. The Eastern Convention comes off about September 15. The fall campaign for business is on in earnest through October and November. But above all is the news that my mother is not in good health and it is possible I may be obliged to go out to her on that account.

Clint Miller and I made a lucky investment in oil land. He wired me today that oil had been discovered about one half mile from our property. I bought

20 acres outright in Feb. this year and 10 acres more since. I hope the information is well-founded.

This letter may not reach you in Marysville before you leave for school on the 18th. I am sorry to be so slow in writing, but the Rotary Club National Convention kept me going until very late. It has been a busy three-day session and very important things are to be done. I enclose a copy of the program.

Here's my dearest and sincerest love,

Jerry

Chapter 11

Summer's Secret Revelations

A Conversation with Gran'mere

It was August 3rd. Gran'mere sat on the bench at the 16th Street station, waiting for Peggy. I could see exhaustion slump her normally upright posture. The dismal final exams followed immediately by packing out of the little summer cottage were no doubt the immediate cause.

I slipped in beside her and touched her shoulder. "Why, Gran'mere, are you not headed back south to Los Angeles and your family? Two weeks, surely, would be enough to regain your health."

Gran'mere wouldn't look at me, but her expression fell into one of great sadness. "Jerry has just asked me to continue for another year. How would I explain this to my dear mother? We were to be married this fall. The dilemma for me is, will I get back into school at all, with failing grades? I just can't face the muddle right now without Jerry here by my side."

"So Peggy's family has offered you a holiday from your decisions?" I suggested.

A train whistle screeched, covering up the need to answer. She stood, expectant as the startled pigeons scattered. The *Overland* from Los Angeles snorted steam from its giant boilers and ground to a halt.

Peggy dashed onto the platform, followed by a porter with her luggage. She apologized for being so late.

"All aboard!" shouted the conductor, and the three of us climbed into the train car. The struggle of the locomotive to gain momentum was to me what Gran'mere must have felt herself, as if still tethered to her worries. Would she confide to Peggy that the *Overland* was the same train that carried Jerry away to Chicago?

No. Quite soon they began chatting about their upcoming visit: the parching heat, heavenly peaches ripening in the orchards, and the delights of being on the river at dusk.

"Perhaps, Gran'mere, the train's easy rocking motion had dissolved those tethers of depression that had held you fast to your seat on the platform. Perhaps there was nothing like a new adventure to keep you from looking back."

"Perhaps you are right, "she whispered.

***

I watched you, Gran'mere, through your letters during the two weeks of your stay, soaking up the attention of the lively, loving family and returning it with true affection. I see you playing tennis, cavorting on a riverbank, and picnicking with friends in the light of a bonfire that dispelled the moonless dark.

Jerry had mentioned that the town had staked its own claim to commerce long ago by providing supplies to the gold miners working the Yuba and Feather Rivers. He said his father had one such claim on the Yuba over fifty years ago. He had never struck it rich, instead teamed up with his future brother-in-law to make a considerable sum running a supply wagon for the miners. The Mumas settled near San Luis Obispo. Jerry had to go to high school in Oakland, then had worked his way through UC Berkeley and then met you, Gran'mere. How much of a circle was life, even back in those times?

Oh, Gran'mere, I thought, three friends would announce their engagements in the fall semester. There would be no ringing of spoons on glasses to announce your own betrothal, nor gossip around the fire of wedding plans.

Still, I believe I heard you whisper, "I am one of you." Isn't that what you wanted?

Chapter 12

The Rush of a Sophomore

August 19th, 1910
Friday evening
2723 Durant St., Theta House
My Dearest Jerry:
Oh, if you could only know what fun I have had today. "Rushing" is going on in full force, and we served a buffet luncheon at noon and had a number of freshman. Tonight for dinner we had two very choice ones. This is the first night we have had dinner in the house, and the jollification would have done your heart good. We sang and danced and only now (after 10) have I been able to sit down and write to you.

My charge, to help freshman register, was Harriett Passmore of San Francisco. Perhaps you have heard of the Passmore Trio. They are a very clever and musical family, and if we "get" her, we will be very lucky.

You asked me if I was "in college" yet. I have to appear before two men to gain their sanction, but I will know by Tuesday.

Brother George has just written me with news of the arrival of a wee baby daughter, and he seems just as enthused as he did over the first daughter. He wants me to come down and visit them.

Peggy and her beau have been walking in the moonlight. They look so happy.

Heaps of love, Jerry dear,
Alice

Friday evening
2723 Durant
My Dearest Jerry:
The doorbell has just rung, which announces the arrival of a "suitor." How I wish it was you, for me! But you will just be leaving the city now, and you know how I will be thinking of you. Oh, you just seemed to be snatched away from me this afternoon, but now my hopes are high for seeing you next week on your way back. We will chat by the grate fire downstairs and I will tell you all about our new pledges. Send me a telegram about the success of the Los Angeles Rotary Convention!

Goodnight, my own Jerry,
Alice

August 22
ALICE HICKS, THETA HOUSE, BERKELEY, CALIFORNIA 9 AM
MOTHER DIED STOP SAN SIMEON TOMORROW STOP WILL
CALL STOP JERRY

Dearest Jerry:
If thinking of you and loving you more than ever will help you these next
few days, then Jerry dear, I can be helping you even if I can't be with you.
All the love in the land,
Alice

September 3rd
Palace Hotel
San Francisco
My Dearest Jerry,
I am spending the day in the city with Peggy, and just before I left this
morning your lettergram arrived. I am as happy as a lark to think that tomorrow
I will see you, and would that I could give vent to my joy in a manner befitting
my smile.
I would like nothing better than to wander over the Berkeley hills with you
in the morning and tell you of a plan I have for the afternoon.
Do hurry over—I can't wait to see you.
Your loving Alice

Wednesday, Sept. 28, 1910
2723 Durant Ave.
Berkeley, California
My Dearest Jerry:
I have just come in from an "ex" in German and if ever a letter was
welcome, your most surely was this afternoon. I have had my share of exams,
I think. One yesterday in chemistry, one this morning in Spanish and the
German one a few minutes ago. A history section comes tomorrow, so I can't
breathe normally yet.
There was a general commotion in the house over the masquerade held last
night in Harmon Gym, and I had a far better time than last year. Don't be
shocked when I tell you I went in a typical rooter costume, as I was in a
basketball stunt. The girls were astounded to see me in corduroys, a white shirt,
and a blue and gold rooter hat. The basketball team played a spectacular rugby
game and there were two rooting sections. I was on the California side, and of
course we won and serpentined around.
To tell you the truth, I haven't been feeling well for several weeks, but
haven't missed many days and am better now. You don't know what a comfort

my little C. S. Science and Health book has been. You gave it to me the first of August 1908, and, oh, I was so pleased, although I don't believe you ever knew just how much, for I always kept my feelings so bottled up, for some unknown reason. I have never used this book as much as I have this summer, and now more than ever.

I didn't make the part in the opera, *Mikado*, this year. I am just a chorus girl, but I will have some fun all the same. I will, as well, play a lady in waiting in Shaw's comedy Caesar and Cleopatra. George Manship (the Englishman who played in *Erminie* last year, if you remember) is Caesar. We will all be sorry to see him go, as he has been offered some Shakespearean roles in London at Christmas.

Good-bye, Jerry dear. I'll write again soon.

Much love,

Alice

October 18th, 1910
Los Angeles
Dear Alice,
With fond love and good wishes for a happy birthday, from your loving mother.
"Christ's Own"
Christ's Own, His polished jewel,
Preserved by his own hand;
His own to sparkle for him,
When round His throne you stand.

Tuesday, November 29th
Berkeley
My Dearest Jerry:
After the wild excitement over the Stanford football game, everyone is thoroughly conscious that the awfulness of "exes" is upon us, and already a strange depression can be felt. ...

Peggy announced her engagement and flashed a diamond in a platinum setting. She was mobbed by the girls, but at midnight, Peggy and I betook ourselves to the large alumni room on the third floor and chatted. As I have told you a dozen times, I don't know what I would do if I couldn't talk to Peggy about you. You know, girls can't stand it like men can. I am sure of that.

The musical organizations including Treble Clef are scheduled to sing at the Greek Theatre next Sunday if it does not rain, and, guess what, at the meeting of Treble Clef yesterday, I was reelected as a member of the executive committee, which makes the third term. I believe I will not run again.

Goodnight, Jerry dear, must away to dreamland, where I surely did meet you the other night.

Alice

Chapter 13

Christmas at the Ranch

Dear Diary:

December 23, 1910—We all came to Rosebine for Christmas. George has bought this ranch in the San Gabriel foothills. I arrived this afternoon ahead of Mother and dear Father, who himself has just traveled from Canada. Not a bad train ride up from home, only an hour north. George met me with the buggy. Good thing, with all the packages and luggage.

December 24—Expected Mother, Father and Brother Will this evening but they didn't come. Annie is in a tizzy with all the cooking, and the big fat turkey sits ready for the oven very early Xmas morn'.

Gifts and mail arrived at the station, so down we went to get it, the handyman and I. It has been so long since I rode that George provided me a gentle mare, but could do nothing for the saddle sores on my behind afterwards! Jerry's exquisite present of a fur muff, so silky and soft and warm, is just the right size; the exaggerated ones will surely be out of style next year.

His letter was full of holiday cheer, including splendid news of his Chicago office competition in the sales campaign. He will win, of that I am sure, and, well, that should stand for some time off for our honeymoon! His sweet telegram of Xmas greetings, phoned in this evening, was almost the same as hearing his voice.

11 p.m.—I finally had the time to read the letter from Pauline, which included a photo of her and her new husband. I put it with all the other mementos into my "strongbox" to share with Jerry. Thank goodness for the telegraph and the phone, for the post office is just too far away to run to with letters every time I think of it. But for all that, it is pretty fine up here.

December 25—What a wonderful day this has been! Father, Mother and Brother Will arrived early. The handyman picked them up as ol' Brother George had to lift and carry in the kitchen for Annie while I watched the children and saw to their breakfast.

The six long years have changed my daddy very much. He is a little bent but has kept his fine hair, now white. He looks at me, bewildered, and remarks every so often on how much I have grown. I think he expected to find me with my hair down my back and in short dresses! To see dear Father officiate at the turkey was a joy. His thin face was radiant with all the family around him after so long. Aileen is very shy of him and hides behind Annie, but baby Helen is so little she reaches out for him and tries to pull his mustache.

We are all trying not to think of poor Jo's passing so soon after Xmas almost four years ago. And Mother and Father miss Kate, but Will, George and I are just as happy her sharp tongue does not intrude on our happy reunion.

Christmas is almost over for another year. The tree is beside me. Aileen plays with her new doll and Helen lies in her cot cooing at the sparkles in the tree. We are alone by the grate fire; the rest of the family talking away in another room. I am sad this splendid day is over and am missing Jerry with my whole heart.

December 26—A deer roamed by this morning. There is snow up in the canyon, which may have driven it down to feed, or perhaps he knows there is hay in the barn and grain for the horses. George is thinking of turning this place into a camp for the summer months and so has been adding a few horses as he finds them. He and I will go riding up to the snow line, weather permitting.

***

December 31st

The Ranch

My Dearest Jerry:

Before the old year is entirely gone, I must send a good-night note to you. I have just looked at my little diary for last year and it describes the watching of the incoming 1910 from Sausalito, where, if you remember, I spent a few days on a house party (boat). What a happy time we had, Patty Chickering, Pauline and I—watching the fireworks toward Oakland and hearing the whistles and gongs from the bay boats.

Here I am at the old ranch and I am wondering where you and I will be next year. How I have been thinking of it and wishing I could see you tonight.

Today was the close of the contest and I have pictured you with flying colors. I know I am not wrong. What a relief it will be for you, and I would like nothing better than to hear that you were going to take a vacation. You most surely deserve it, for what an eventful year it has been.

Goodnight, my own dear Jerry, and here is every good wish for the new year of 1911.

Your love,

Alice

Chapter 14

Jerry's Madness in Chicago

Jerry slogged through the snow at the end of his day, his thoughts as dreary as the miserable weather. No cabs. God, this frozen pile. How could a man make a living in the winter? He was sick to death of deals over dinner in the club room and would have given the world to get on the golf course, where at least a man could breathe some fresh air! Well, no dinner deals tonight; he was grateful for the respite from cigar smoke and too much brandy. Jerry stopped at the desk to scoop up his mail. When he finally had made himself comfortable in his favorite overstuffed chair, he realized with a shock that he was holding letters from Norah. His hunger for a rare steak evaporated, replaced by stomach-churning dread.

Tuesday, January 26, 1910
Oakland, California
Raining hard
Dear Jerry,
Thanks for sending me "Noon Madness." I like it, but, you know, mon cher, that's no book for me. I don't need any encouragement along those lines.

I think I have always been the nut of the bunch. My friends have nothing but a continued round of pleasure, and my good friend Hazel calls me to give me the dope. Mother says she does it to make me mad. What do I care—one of these days I will go so darned high in the air that none of you will find me.

By the way, my boudoir is going to be lavender and I am going to have plenty of perfumed cigarettes. Does it suit you? I made the mistake of altering that black skirt, and if I should sneeze in it, we will all go to jail. ...

Jerry's hands were shaking. Norah's lavender colored letters unnerved him with their dark gaiety, their unpredictable changes of direction.

...When I get so lonesome for my far away pal—and it seems as tho' I can't stand it any longer—can you guess what I do? Get out the cherry kimono, put it on and parade around just as I would if you were here. It's sort of fun and relieves the monotony. Let's play you were here and what I would do. First I would find out if you were tired, and if you were, I would put you on the couch and let you listen to the fine old piano player—any tunes you like. Then we would have a really cheery tea party—maybe a game of pinochle—and after that, I would smother you with kisses. Pretty flashy for an old maid who is thinking of turning up her toes and traveling the journey of the great traverse.

But hope springs eternal in the human breast, consequentially hope may win out. ...

My God, but he had given her that kimono. And, the "turning up of the toes" reference to death was alarming. Jim, his fraternity brother from UC who had stayed close all these years, was supposed to be visiting Norah to keep her from doing something stupid. Jerry had actually begged, and Jim had been willing. Jerry owed Jim a very large favor.

My only complaint with Jimsie is that he stays away too long and here too short. He's peculiar, rather. You know, being your fraternity brother and bosom buddy down in Los Angeles. Listen, dear, I have the real cherry satin petticoat—the best ever. Can anyone tell me why I admire red and cherry so much? I'm just crazy for Jim to admire it. I know he will—you see, he is the only pal I know intimately enough to show it to. He always likes all my things and clothes I show him.

Did I tell you I have a new ring? Not a solitaire. Got it for Christmas so nothing to be suspicious about—for my little finger.

Here goes a lot of love to you, my nicest dear.

Norah

Jerry dropped the letter, refusing to think about Norah's "intimate" relationship with Jim, and picked up the next letter. His anxiety grew with every sentence.

My Dear Jerry,

I just finished reading your rather pathetic letter, and while I am heaps worse off than you, still my heart can't help but sympathize with you even tho' it is your fault that you think life doesn't hold much for a Tom Cat. You will realize it someday. I hope before things go too far, but believe me, truly it is bound to come. Look at all the "old coots" around you and ask them if they had it to do over. Really, you are a dear and you will never find a person who admires you in so many ways and loves to sing your praises more than this Girl of the Golden West—but you have, if I may say, unreasonable ideas—very, very unnatural ideas that have about almost swamped me; and if insisted upon, many more years will be the means of making you a very miserable old man!

I ask myself often if I am really such a terror. All you have to do is feed me on plenty of bird seed, and I'll guarantee a song every hour.

Your affectionate Norah

His letters to her were written to make himself out to be a corruptible bachelor and a cad—were they working? That was part of the deal he had made with Jim, to convince her. Jerry wiped his brow and steadied his hands by lighting his cigar.

49

Jerry vowed to call Jim in Los Angeles and ask how things were really going with Norah. She seemed on the edge of doing something drastic, and he counted on Jim to continue visiting Norah to get her through this. Suddenly, his anxiety overflowed; his gut gripped him with pain, and the nausea threatened to rise up and out. Jerry was barely able to get his cigar in the ashtray before he made a dash to the bathroom.

***

Several days later, when Alice was safely ensconced in the bosom of Peggy's family in Marysville for the winter break from UC, Jerry received a letter from Norah's mother.

February 26, 1911
Ferrand Piano Company
Oakland, California
My Dear Mr. Muma,

I have been expecting to hear from you since January 7th, 1911 in regard to the settlement of the affair I went east to see you about last summer. It is no more than fair to both yourself and Norah that some definite arrangement be made, and I should be able to formally announce your engagement. If I do not hear from you I will take it that this is agreeable to you. The large acquaintances you have around the bay should make you a successful Piano Man. I trust I have not taken your breath away with this offer. ...

Jerry exploded. "Indeed, madam, I would suffocate!" The impudence of the woman. Her letter, charmingly worded, was a pretense. She could not possibly like him. She was a viper ready to strike.

Her summer visit to Chicago still scared him with its audacity. Jerry had shared this visit with Alice because it meant that she and he had to be extra vigilant with their secret engagement. Alice had sensibly agreed to postpone their wedding, though it upset her.

Thank the Lord he had Alice's letters as a balm against anxiety. Was even Alice showing signs of distress? She filled pages with mundane goings on, miring him in the minutiae of her life—delightfully. To him, it was a way to hear her joyful voice, feel her presence. And, always, he loved her endings. *Good night, Jerry dear. If only you were here, too.*

***

This was a dangerous waiting game, this Norah debacle. Still, he had not yet been sued for breach of promise. Jerry guessed that Norah had run interference several times to keep her mother in check on that score. However, if Norah killed herself, the guilt of her death would lie heavy on him and sit like a stone in Alice's heart. Their marriage and his career would be ruined.

Jerry stuffed a cigar into his jacket pocket and left for the club room. It was just too damn cold to go for a walk to clear his head. He dreaded his next letter to Alice, suggesting they put off yet again plans for their marriage. He would need to come up with an alternative to save her sanity, which he feared might slip away.

Chapter 15

March Breakdown

A Conversation with Gran'mere

Your letter to Jerry lay incomplete. The golden light from the little brass lamp Jerry had given you laid bare the words you had just penned.

March, 1911
My Dear Jerry, I hope I didn't put things too strongly in that letter. You know I am not incapacitated, but am going the usual round of two or three things at once. Only you know, too, that when your nerves are tired it isn't a breakdown that comes in a minute, but is a gradual thing. This last injury has made everything more acute. Before it, I felt I could go along all right until the end of the term. Doctors can usually persuade a person that there is more the matter with them than there really is. But I know how I feel and how the C. S. treatments have helped me. Honestly, I do hate to give up, but I suppose there is no use in going on and on. It is better to stop awhile then resume with renewed vigor. Isn't that it? I am going to get over this and be just as spry as ever.

I sang my solo lustily on Sunday, or so Ruth said. I am to sing another one tomorrow evening. Yesterday I went over to the city with Peggy. ...

I knew that you were back at Theta House. You were recovering from what the doctors at the infirmary deemed exhaustion. Was that term a euphemism for "nerves?" Had you suffered bouts of this "thing" during your childhood? You never said.

***

Gran'mere was sitting alone in her room, and I felt it was time to settle in beside her.

"What was it, Gran'mere, that so exhausted you? A leave of absence is a drastic thing."

"I fear it was seeing the bottom of Peggy's bridal chest," Gran'mere said. "You know that I went to her in Marysville after finals in February. I had been so brave, pleased to be helping her prepare—happy for her all these months... Then it was over." Her throat moved as if to swallow her anguish. "I wanted a hope chest of my very own," she whispered.

"I think," I replied, "it might it have been those letters from Norah. Jerry must have told you about them." I wondered how he managed that. Surely a phone conversation would have been out of the question with operators' prying ears on the lines. "But, I am just guessing."

She would not answer, and her gaze dropped from the window to her hands, which were clenched together in her lap.

"It was just—everything," Gran'mere continued. "I am no scholar, but I loved the languages. German and Spanish courses seemed easier to take than chemistry and history. Of course I could relate even then to arias and folksongs in foreign languages. I had given up Treble Clef but continued my voice lessons with Mildred's tutor. I sang all the time. Even at Peggy's house in Marysville. It was lovely. Some of the *Erminie* cast were up."

I sensed that she was doing to me what she had done with Jerry, deflecting pain that she could not afford to acknowledge. In her mind Jerry had more than enough challenges in that purgatory called Chicago, what with Norah and her mother.

"What was that pain in your side that brought you to the infirmary this time?"

"The same one that bothered me my freshman year, I guess," Gran'mere responded. "Some weakness the doctors tested for subnormal blood pressure, which makes no sense to me. Jerry was relieved to know that I did not have what killed my sister Jo—cerebral apoplexy."

"You said that you fell, remember?"

"Perhaps I did. Maybe I fainted from the pain, or I was having trouble breathing. I just don't know."

I watched her for a while. The beautiful profile, the long straight nose and strong chin. Her dark brown hair was braided down her back. She was full-busted, and she emphasized it with a tightly belted robe. She stood and paced across the small space. Even exhausted as she was, her movements were full of grace.

A slip of paper in her mother's old-fashioned hand fell to the floor. It must have come from her bedside table, near the little black C. S. reader peeking from the opened drawer. "Do your mother's numerous sayings soothe you at all?"

"Oh, yes. She is so good at sending me these little notes when I complain of this or that."

I retrieved the paper from the floor.

Serene, I fold my hands, wait,
Nor care for wind or tide or sea;
I rave no more 'gainst time or fate,
For, lo, my own shall come to me.
—John Burroughs

"And the other," Gran'mere said. "*Remember sorrow and love go side by side.* I have memorized and repeated it when the nights are so dark."

I tried another angle. "Had Jerry just told you of Mrs. Ferrand's demanding letter?"

Before Gran'mere could answer, the gibbous moon slipped past the window. I could no longer hold her fast as I might have with a full one. Wait! I wanted to shout. I haven't had time to ask you about your decision to set off for your own European tour.

No matter. I felt her near and stayed the night, dreaming of her predicament as she slept. I knew there were other issues that increased her anguish, not the least of which seemed the incredulity many of her Theta friends expressed for Christian Science. Not wishing to be scorned, Gran'mere hid her little C. S. book out of sight. Only a girl named Helen had, surprisingly, walked with her to Wednesday night prayers one week ago. Helen would grow to be a friend in the decades to come, become a C.S. Practitioner herself—and she would help hold Gran'mere up as she fought her demons, and mourn her at the end.

***

In the morning, I knew Gran'mere would rise early for quartet practice before classes began. As the early light played colors of palest gold and rose on scudding clouds, the trees still dark silhouettes, I thought I could hear her humming. I hoped, as she got close to Hearst Hall, that her heart was at peace for a little while, anticipating the joy of song.

Chapter 16

The Decision to Travel Abroad

Monday, April 4th, 1911
Theta House
My Dear Jerry:
Congratulations on being appointed manager of the Travelers branch office. You certainly deserve it after winning all those awards at the end of the year.

Your draft came today, which I turned over to the steamship company and, oh, it seems so wonderful that I can book for Naples. When I first mentioned about Miss Freuler, I told you her plans to sail directly there. Then she wants to go to Florence and stay a month, learning about the Italian Method, and from there to Berlin to stay the greater part of the time.

I can't think much past April 25th, which will be the day I arrive in Chicago. Miss F. explained to me the intricacies of a letter of credit, which I will need upon my arrival in Berlin, but I know you will let me know all about that. After I get my ticket to New York, I will be all fixed and will only have to think of packing. Only two girls know so far, and one is planning an informal tea so I can share the news. I can just imagine their enthusiasm.

My only thought is what fun it would be to plan this together.

I am looking up Pauline's address in Harrogate and all the other Thetas living abroad. Oh, Jerry, what more wonderful conclusion could there be to my two years here?

And now I must away to bed to dream of you and Naples. Two weeks today and I will be on my way.

My best love,
Alice

***

"You are a wretched girl to leave me in need of a maid of honor," said Peggy as they sat down. "Show me those tickets."

Alice opened her purse, pulling out the precious tickets and waved them in front of Peggy.

"Ah-ha!" exclaimed Peggy. "Cunard Line, the Carpathia, April 27. That's it, then."

They sat in Ghirardelli's for their last ritual hot chocolate. The brilliant spring sunshine splashed through the front windows. Alice's face glowed with it. Excited butterflies danced in her belly. What a change from the anxiety that had been clutching at her heart.

Peggy pulled a long face. "Oh, Alice, I wish you just the best voyage, but I am bereft."

Alice placed her hand over Peggy's. "I will be sorry to miss your most important day. But, you must be happy for me. Only you know my secret engagement to be married at the end of the tour. I will not be at your wedding, nor you to mine."

"Right, then," said Peggy. "Tell me about your traveling companion."

"Miss Freuler, she's a concert singer from Oakland. She's petite, plump and quite jolly. She was looking for a roommate, and the steamship company put me on to her. Goes to Europe to study voice and just knows heaps."

"How old is she?"

"Oh, thirtyish I would say. Speaks German, Italian and a little French."

"Perfect."

"And," continued Alice, "she will be in Chicago for a concert the week before I am due to leave here. She will meet with Jerry to handle the foreign bank draft required for Naples."

"Are you going to see Jerry on your way to New York?"

"For five hours only." Alice's face lit up at the mention, but then she had to shake her head to force the tears back. "And then off on a new adventure."

***

On, Sunday, April 16, they were all there—her dear friends gathered in the parlor to wish her bon voyage. Alice thought her heart would burst looking at each smiling face. There was Mildred, her singing companion, Ruth and Enid from summer school, Miriam Clapp who would be leaving for the Continent soon, Alice Earl and Patty Chickering back from Europe months ago and looking svelte and fashionable. And Peggy.

Miriam had compiled a collaboration in her fine hand as the parting gift. It was presented in a Blue Book used for exams, with the title *Alice Hicks: A Final Examination in "One Trip Abroad." Course 2b.*

Within its pages were ten exam questions about the voyage, answered in imaginative rhyme and illustrated with cutouts from the paper. The opening verse set the tone.

There was a young maiden named Allie
Who went to a college named Cal-ie
When they bade her goodbye
All her friends had to cry
But they wished her good luck
On her Sally.

***

San Francisco Chronicle, April 21

56

"Sorority Singer Will Be Heard at Church"
Miss Alice Hicks Leaves for Europe Saturday

Miss Alice Hicks, a popular sorority girl of Berkeley, who is to leave on Saturday to study music in Europe, is to be one of the singers at the first annual concert by the choir of the First Baptist Church on Friday evening, the 21st.... She plans to continue her work in Paris and Berlin, and will remain abroad some years.

Chapter 17

Jerry's Five-Hour Visit in Chicago

Jerry scanned the letter from the home office announcing the extra bonus that would accompany his larger paycheck. A smile played around his mouth as he read to the bottom. He had done it. Alice would be pleased. He folded the letter inside his jacket pocket, and ignoring his overcoat and hat, left the office and hailed a cab for Union Station.

The gusts were fierce. A flag atop the gabled turret snapped loudly. But he gave no thought to the chill on his neck as he exited the cab nor to the wind grabbing at his pomaded hair and suit coat. Alice was almost here.

Once inside, he looked up at the schedule board in the main hall. There it was, the *Overland* from California, due at 3:45. He had ten minutes to walk to that familiar platform, the place where he had taken this very train back and forth from home. Just a few minutes before he could gaze into Alice's face and feel the measure of her.

Jerry heard the blast of a whistle and watched as the train pulled in, staring hard through the streams of passengers, catching Alice's tall form. He raised his arm and shouted to her, and she made a straight line through the crowd. Then there she was standing before him, coat unbuttoned to reveal a white shirtwaist with a narrow black ribbon at her neck. At long last she was hugging him. He took in the feel of her against his chest, her lips against his neck. Her lustrous brown hair smelled of lavender and cigar smoke. He wanted to free all those carefully placed pins and let it spill down over his hands. Instead, as she was fairly crushing him, he returned the bear hug, slipping his arms beneath her coat.

They stood together until most of the passengers had disappeared into the terminal. Then he released her at arm's length.

"Tired?" He smiled with his whole face, hiding his concern at the drawn look of hers. He reached up to touch her cheek.

"I'm all right now I have you in front of me…" Alice paused, and shook her head. Suddenly she blurted, "What are we going to do? I have hardly more than a glimpse of you," and she leaned into Jerry's shoulder.

He put his arm around her again, feeling her ribs beneath her shirtwaist. "There's a restaurant in the waiting area. I have a table in the back reserved for as long as we need it." He picked up her overnight case, and escorted her to their table.

The waiter brought menus. "Thank you, Fred, but we won't be needing those. Would you bring me a beer, and for the lady a glass of your best red wine. We'll have steaks medium rare when I give the signal. We would like to sit awhile before eating."

When Alice had been relieved of her coat, she sat close to Jerry and grabbed his hand.

"Strange predicament, this talking instead of writing," Jerry said, trying to tease Alice out of her malaise. "Ah, here comes your wine. Now, a big sip to get you warm and relaxed. I know, I know, you don't drink. Think of this as a tonic. Good for your blood, get your appetite going." Alice tried to smile and took a sip, following it with a piece of roll from the basket. "Now, dearest, tell me of your sendoff."

Alice frowned as if trying to drag up the memory of some long-ago event. "Quite a good one, as you might imagine. Waves and shouts from my Thetas and a professor or two. Peggy came down especially, and at the last minute stuffed an envelope full of addresses of Thetas living in Florence and Paris into my bag. Goodness, what a pile of luggage the porters dealt with. I had a bag for the compartment, and the rest marked for Chicago and then New York. Some were also marked for the ship cabin and the remainder for the hold. What a help Alice Earl was, having done just this last year."

The wine had its effect. Alice told how the Treble Clef quartette had sung her aboard the train, though she was too emotional to sing a note. She mentioned how sad it was to pass by Marysville and know she would not be at Peggy's wedding. Color came back into her cheeks, and the worry line between her brows lessened.

"How did your meeting with Miss Freuler go?"

"Well, at the risk of another major worry, I never did manage to find her, Alice. I have my doubts about her reliability. I went to the address she gave— that friend of hers she was staying with—only to be told they had recently moved."

"Oh, dear. What does that mean? Well, I am sure I will meet her in New York." But her face revealed none of the optimism in her words. "I will send you a lettergram to let you know."

Jerry leaned in to kiss her cheek. "You must not worry, my pet. It will go well. Now, it's the time to feed you up on a good Chicago steak."

Jerry signaled the waiter. Dinner arrived quickly. He watched Alice tuck into her meal and breathed a sigh of relief. For the moment, she seemed her old self.

"Jerry, you will never believe it, but I met a princess in the dining car."

"What, royalty on the train? Never spotted a celebrity on my trips."

"Well, you were likely scheming and planning and paying no attention whatsoever to fellow passengers."

"Right on that score," admitted Jerry.

"She was a princess from Hawaii, she said, on her way to marry none other than Mr. Jay Gould, Jr. So, you must watch for the announcement and tell me if it is true."

Jerry laughed. "I promise! Now, tell me, what did you see of the glorious Western scenery?"

Alice shrugged her shoulders. "I did really enjoy it when awake. I was in a fog much of the time and dropped off for naps at odd moments. I suppose it was the rocking of the train. Gracious, but that was a long ride! Almost sixty hours is forever, Jerry. I don't know how you managed it all those times back and forth." And changing subjects abruptly, said, "Here, let me show you. My dear mother sent me this." She handed over a tiny envelope. Inside was a folded note, and in a corner was written, *For Alice to read on the train.*

Jerry opened the note. It was Matthew 28:20, *Lo, I am with you always*, and a poem about consolation and faith dated Christmas, 1902. Jerry looked up, a question on his face.

"Mother's way of blessing this trip for me—for us," said Alice. "She was hardest hit by my not coming home at the end of this semester. Brother George and Annie had nothing but praise and encouragement for this adventure, but Mother was heartbroken. She misses me terribly. She must have written this long ago for herself and tucked it away. It is a little odd, Christmas being so much behind us. But I know it was her way of telling me she accepts my being away."

Jerry and Alice continued to speak in quiet tones, leaning toward each other, their joined hands resting on the damask cloth amidst the silver and crockery. When the waiter arrived to collect the course, Jerry requested tea for Alice and coffee for himself. As the drinks arrived, he let go of Alice's hand and reached into his jacket pocket and handed her the letter he had placed there as he left the office.

"In here is the contract agreement from Travelers home office to authorize 30 percent commission to certain brokers. Agreement is given with 'hesitation and apprehension' as they said, and my head is on the block if the plan should fail. Let me read just this sentence to you." Jerry took back the letter and opened it. *Just how you are going to avoid the pitfalls remains to be seen. The outcome of the experiment will be watched. Needless to say we hope it will be as you expect.*

"Jerry, they seem to look forward to your failure."

"That is almost true, my dear. There are those who resent my being made manager, and many also of the old school who have no idea of this industry's exploding potential. The home office has seen what I have already done for the revenues in Chicago. My failure will cost them nothing—my success will bring them millions."

"What a sendoff this is for me, to know you are finally being recognized. You will be so busy you won't have time to miss me."

"Alice, dearest, I will miss you every day. I will count the months till I am on that boat for Liverpool. But if I can do this, I will be able to free myself for a long-deserved leave to be with you and enjoy the Europe you will discover." Jerry looked at his watch. "Alice, it's time, my love. We must get you to New York."

Alice slumped in her chair. Her face showed her panic as she grabbed his hand. "What if Miss Freuler is not in New York as she promised? After all, she never did see you here. What if something has happened?"

"Dearest Alice, it will be fine." Then, seeing her desperation, he added, "Shall I ride part way with you? Would that help?"

"Oh, Jerry, please… please."

"Come on, then, let's get my ticket and be on our way." Jerry took her elbow as she stood, helped her on with her coat, and then grabbed her overnight bag. On his way, he dropped cash for dinner into the hands of the waiter.

"One round trip to Toledo, please," Jerry said to the ticket master.

They boarded the train at nine thirty and found their first-class seats. During the trek east, Jerry held fast to Alice's hand. As the train slowed for his stop, he wiped the tears from her face with his handkerchief, and then tucked it into her pocket. From the platform he saw her desolate face in the window, and she pressed her hand against the pane as if to keep the connection.

After her train pulled out, he caught the return within a half hour. During the lonely ride back, he composed a little note to cheer her, thinking to send it special delivery to the Carpathia. Jerry's train pulled in to Chicago at seven a.m.; his eyes were grainy and spirits low. And, he regretted having left his damn overcoat in the office.

Chapter 18

Sailing to Italy

April 27, 1911
New York City, S. S. Carpathia
My Jerry Dear:
Here we are aboard (and my pen is giving out). Everything has gone well this morning. Miss F. is now reserving our seats in the dining room and also deck chairs. She knows it all.

As I came over the gangplank I thought of the merriment when we do it together. Our cabin is a beauty. I don't see that it could be better.

What do you think—a Mrs. Lovejoy, an old friend of Mother's, has been in to see me. Mother wrote her and she came over from Brooklyn to the steamer. Wasn't that nice to have someone knock and have a nice book tucked under her arm for me to read!

I am going up on deck with her to watch the proceedings. Oh, it is great, Jerry dear. This is the best yet. My baggage is all here—my little steamer trunk is tucked away under my berth, and I am all fixed.

If I could just give you one more big hug and kiss I would be all right. Miss Freuler is so jolly she will keep me going, and may you find someone to help the time pass quickly till we are together again. Words are simply of no use here, but you know my love, and may that help you in the months to come, my own dear Jerry.

Your Alice

Jerry's red roses sat glowing on her stateroom table. Stacked around the vase was the bon voyage telegram from the Thetas, Jerry's special delivery letter, and his small packet of artwork drawn in his own hand: seven humorous cartoons about life abroad, done in colored inks. Alice had already laughed at the first six, her favorite being a cartoon of a scruffy Italian gentleman in fedora, smoking a cigar and eating spaghetti. But when she came to the largest drawing, she gasped. It was dapper Jerry, in black suit and bowler hat standing at the pier, a little dog sitting at his feet, waving goodbye with a handkerchief at the *Carpathia* as she steamed away. He had thought of everything.

***

Alice found a comfortable routine. Breakfast at eight thirty, a constitutional around the decks, then reading and napping in her assigned deck chair, wrapped in a blanket and her brown wool coat with wide plaid lapels. At eleven the stewards brought around a cup of hot bouillon. A lively bugle horn sounded for luncheon at one, tea at five, and dinner at seven.

A Miss Singer, in a broad-brimmed hat and trimmed silk dress, introduced herself at tea one day. The Turner sisters met Alice at shuffleboard. They were thin to a fault, long faces under piles of pale brown hair. The evening promenade often found these four by the ship's rail outside the saloon, singing popular melodies to entertain and delight the other passengers. Instead of cards, they sat around the table studying Italian phrasebooks. It was Miss Singer who suggested one evening that Alice write to one Regina de Sales, a voice teacher in Paris who had an exceptional reputation in her field for training opera singers. Alice was excited at the possibility and quickly wrote an inquiry to be included with her growing packet of letters to be mailed from the steamship office in Genoa.

On Sunday, May seventh, Gibraltar poked over the watery horizon. Passengers pressed at the rail anxious to see terra firma, thrilled at the prospect of the promised excursion, impatient to hear the anchor rattle to the bottom of the bay and hold them fast. Alice and Miss F. piled into the tender with the others and headed off.

My Dearest Jerry:

The high Atlas Mountains of Africa were on our right and Spain on our left. We could see several Spanish villages. ... The white houses with the tiled roofs are the ones after which the California houses are built. So I was seeing the original. The good old rock hardly looks natural without "Prudential" written across it!

We took a "Cooks Carriage" with the Turners, and I sat up with the driver, who was a dandy in giving information. It tickled him when I knew a few Spanish words.

We saw Moors dressed in their garb with their children in tow, the Governors Palace, the old gates and a dress parade of families out for a stroll along the streets and parks.

I am speechless with the wonder of the blue water and sunset tints on the great old rock. While looking over the rail, up shot a whale spout—the first we've seen. The crew promised a great many more, plus sightings of the black beasts themselves, before landing in Genoa Bay.

I will write some more to record it all before we land. It's hard to think that when you read this, I will already be in Florence.

***

Alice woke at five a.m. to peer through her upper berth porthole at Italy. She sat for almost two hours watching Genoa Bay materialize in the hazy morning light. When Miss F. emerged from her lower berth, they raced to dress. Without a thought for breakfast, they tendered ashore.

For six lire, a carriage and guide named Professore Migliano would show them the sights. Using their Baedeker's and his promptings, they rolled through the narrow streets past churches and palaces, eyes wide with appreciation at the rich marble architecture.

It wasn't until they departed south for Naples that hunger overtook them. They had not eaten since the night before.

A day later Alice lined up with Miss F. and the other passengers to gaze at the smoking Mount Vesuvius while the *Carpathia* made its way into the Bay of Naples. As they docked, steam whistles blew and shouts went up from the sailors securing the behemoth rope lines. Huge ship's doors rumbled open. Gangplanks screeched, stretching across the gap to shore. Sousa marches blared from a band on the nearby *Hamburg*. Street urchins on the dock heckled passengers to pitch pennies, as was custom. *"Trovo'lo!"*—"Get it!" *"Bravo!"* yelled the passengers, as the children dove into the water to catch the treasure.

Customs was a trial. Alice's luggage sat waiting, marked with the required yellow crosses indicating customs clearance. Miss F.'s trunk, however, had failed to make an appearance. And once her trunk had been located, there was a long delay in organizing delivery to the hotel. Finally they boarded the carriage for the Hotel Hassler, where they would spend their first night on land in two weeks. The delay cost Alice precious time in retrieving Jerry's longed-for letters; Cook and Sons had closed for the day.

Alice's impatience to get her mail had her out of bed early and through breakfast in a flash. She and Miss F. rushed to Galleria Vittoria and were first through the doorway. Alice marched to the counter, collected her mail, and ran out into the courtyard to be alone while she opened one of the treasured blue envelopes. All other letters, including mail from Alice Earl, she tucked into her purse.

May 1st, 1911
Sunday evening
Naples, Italy
Dearest Alice,

How did you relish your Sunday dinner on the Atlantic? I thought of you the whole time tonight as I sat alone at my dinner. Yesterday brought two letters from you. They just filled the old boy with joy. I never thought I was going to get one for weeks yet.

I went to church today with three of my agents. C. S. Church is on the North Side. We may go there later because the North Side is where we will live.

What do you think? Just two long years and two months ago we were together in Hollywood. Since that night we seem to be putting the miles between us instead of getting together. However, we have been doing things and that makes for compensation.

I am glad you had a beautiful day in which to sail out of New York. Today it has rained all day long. Good weather for business. I have been at it, hammer and tongs. I want to finish my allotment by Sept. 1st and not worry when I am in Scotland later on in the year. I am longing for a rest and trip myself.

Bye-bye, Alice.

Your devoted lover,

Jerry

Alice walked to the telegraph window. "I'd like to send a telegram to Chicago, please, to the Athletic Club." The man behind the counter took the piece of paper she offered him, which contained one-word message and the address of the club. She knew Jerry would know she had arrived. *Safely*, it read.

Miss F. went to a separate window to collect their tickets for Florence with a stopover in Rome. There was a sudden "Yoo-hoo!" from across the room, and through the crowd plowed *Carpathia* passengers Mrs. Cahill and Miss Singer. They were waving tickets.

"What a pleasure to see you," said Alice. "Are you off on an excursion?"

"Yes. Number nine, a three-day tour of Pompeii, Amalfi, Sorrento, and Capri. Please come with us!" said Mrs. Cahill.

Alice looked at Miss F. "Wouldn't it be heaps of fun? We are not due in Florence for a week."

Miss F. caught the enthusiasm and returned to the window to purchase tickets for the jaunt. Back at the hotel arrangements were made to store some luggage for their return, and then the four women headed down to the harbor to catch the tour boat to Pompeii.

The four of them explored the ruined city. It was laid out perfectly in long lines of intersecting streets. Alice marveled at the exquisitely preserved mosaic floors and worn partial frescoes, which had glowed with color before the volcanic eruption. Awful fascination gripped her at the sight of those ashy casts—poor creatures, both humans and dogs, caught in the agony of death. Alice felt growing respect for the still-smoking Vesuvius.

Early luncheon restored their cheerfulness. Their guide led them to a little restaurant built just beyond an old lava flow. The tour was escorted to wicker chairs and tables laid out under a large trellis. A little three-piece orchestra tuned up and began to play. Alice, Miss F., Miss Singer and Mrs. Cahill sat at one table, comparing their experiences. When the pasta course arrived, a simple dish of spaghetti pomodoro with fresh basil, the waiter dusted each portion with a grating of parmesan. The women tucked large white napkins under their chins. Alice glanced around for guidance, picked up her large spoon and luncheon fork, and began to wind the pasta slowly onto the tines. As she became engrossed in the difficult task of eating spaghetti with grace, the women's giggles crested over. Each successful bite was celebrated with sips of Apollonius water, for the hour was entirely too early (in their American minds) for a glass of wine.

Their trip continued to Amalfi through green hills covered in grapevines and wildflowers. Climbing roses massed in village gardens, scenting the heat. Winding upward on the cliff road to their hotel, Alice memorized the vision of the passing traffic; the two-wheeled carts loaded with hay and vegetables, the fat friar astride a donkey, a road crew of women carrying heavy loads of rocks on their heads. There were no men here, the guide said—they were all in the army. Alice's gaze was drawn upward to the hanging gardens, trellised lemon trees, and pots of flowers all glowing with rich color in the sun. She had a sudden stab of homesickness, for it reminded her of Santa Barbara.

Their destination was the Hotel Capuccini, a converted twelfth-century monastery that was perched at the very top of town. Alice and Miss F. made plans with Miss Singer and Mrs. Cahill to meet at dinner, then found their beautifully furnished room. It tempted them with a bath and a nap. Following a candlelight dinner, the four companions strolled the piazza to catch sight of the moon gleaming on the sea. And sleep came easily.

Sorrento was accomplished the next day, preparing them for a visit to the magnificent blue grotto of Capri. Once deposited at the Hotel Tramontano, Alice and Miss F. took their leisure through the winding cobbled streets in a successful quest for souvenir prints. Instead of luncheon, they relaxed over late-afternoon coffee and sweet cheese pastry. After the requisite nap and bath, they met up with Miss Singer and Mrs. Cahill for dinner.

"I think we should all go swimming before breakfast," said Alice as she sliced into the fried zucchini, which was sprinkled with vinegar and fresh mint.

"My dear," said Miss F., "what will we do for bathing costumes?"

"I imagine the front desk will supply us," said Mrs. Cahill. "Who here has their Italian down well enough to negotiate?"

"What a lark," chimed in Miss Singer. "A splendid way to start the day. Miss F., will you speak with the concierge?"

The sweet smell of strawberries for dessert interrupted their conversation. Then they rose and marched en masse to the front desk. Ancient bathing costumes were produced and sorted out with much hilarity. Brown and black baggy bloomers and full skirts made of wool. Over-blouses voluminous enough to sink them when filled with water were passed around, and accepted with merry spirit.

The next morning at six they took the elevator down to the beach level and plunged in. A porter assigned to the task escorted them through the water, carefully rowing his small boat alongside the frolicking females.

Back in time for a bath and breakfast with the tour, they went afterwards to shop. Just before luncheon Alice and the others boarded small boats to meet the larger tour of the Blue Grotto. The sea was calm, and the small craft slipped easily under the low cave wall—arriving into a magical world of transparent blue water. The slanting light changed the boats and oars into silver, and the roof of the cave into a rainbow of color. Alice could not wait to record it all for Jerry.

Completely done in by three days of glorious sightseeing, Alice and Miss F., along with most of the tour group, nodded off on the long carriage ride back to the Hotel Hassler in Naples.

***

Tuesday, May 16th
Eden Hotel, Rome
Dearest Jerry,

Here we are in Rome and it is altogether too modern to suit me. But I haven't seen much yet for we only arrived this afternoon.

I have certainly been collecting small souvenirs of this splendid adventure. Just seven pairs of gloves in Naples (Miss Little bought a dozen!), and several pictures of Pompeii and Amalfi with which to adorn the walls of our California sitting room, for if I never get you to return here with me, I can at least regale you with my memories.

To keep clean is no small matter in Italy. We actually have to pay 2 lire (40 cents) for every bath—hot or cold. This has happened in every hotel since my arrival, and must therefore be a national custom.

Another funny thing is the system of tipping. You are supposed to give every little "facchino" who opens a door for you or touches your suitcase a penny or more. They hardly pay the porters anything, so that is what they depend on.

We arrived here after five hours on the train, and what a scramble we had getting our suitcases in the funny little compartments of the Italian trains. We arrived around six to this highly recommended hotel, and it is nice in every way.

After dinner, which is the grand meal over here—and I never ate so much in my life—we went to a concert.

Tonight at table, Miss F. said something that I know you will be glad to hear: that I was looking a hundred times better than when I started. I feel it, too. Altho' we have not had much rest, everything has been delightful. And I am doing as you told me to, to put all worried thoughts out of my mind. I am having the time of my life.

Just now someone in a window opposite was whistling one of the good old songs I learned in Los Angeles. Little did I think I would hear it in Rome.

I must stop now or I will never get up in the morning. Goodnight, my Jerry.
Heaps of love,
Alice

67

Chapter 19

Florence and Venice, then a little Munich

Lelli's Pension Nouvelle
3 Rue Palestro
Tout Près de l'Arno
Wednesday, May 31st, 1911
My Darling Jerry:
Yesterday I wondered how you were spending Decoration Day, for I went out to Pisa with Miss Singer and saw the world-renowned leaning tower. It is made of white marble, and when the sun shone on it, you couldn't gaze upon it. We climbed to the very tip-top, and you are always rewarded for any effort of this kind by seeing the country for miles around.

The inhabitants were so quaint, but we are looked upon as curiosities here! To be sure, we don't dress like the European women, and I am deeply thankful for that, such sights as some of them are. ...

We saw peasants at the fountains with their bronze pitchers which they carry on their shoulders or heads. They wore little shawls, short skirts of all colors, and shoes something like Chinese ones, only with heels. They chatted along, and the whole scene was like something you would write about. ...

Tomorrow I go for another Italian lesson, and if I work at it, well, I ought to know quite a bit at the end of a month. I am looking forward to Germany to have a chance to air my Deutsch. As for French in Paris, I am decidedly shaky. Everyone on shipboard was studying out of Cook's little books of convenient phrases. I learned a few, but you feel so idiotic when you find you cannot make a person understand.

The chief thing is to know the numerals so you can count and reckon. One phrase I have used continually is, "Quanto costa questa," which asks, how much? And then you say, "Troppo," which means too much. Miss F. is a great bargainer, and I am surely learning a lot.

I dropped into the hall where the Christian Science meetings are held. They have the meetings on Wednesday afternoon.

June 6, 1911
Dearest Jerry:
Miss F., three ladies from the pension, and I strolled after supper—oh, it was heavenly in the moonlight. Our destination was Piazza Michelangelo, overlooking the city. We crossed over one of the old bridges and could look

for miles in each direction, and the streetlights on the bank twinkled in the water. I don't see how Venice can be more beautiful. We went through a residential part where the villas were huge palaces, and the gardens were of palms and cypress and lovely trailing honeysuckle. I am sitting and writing, seized with a most exalted mood. What I have seen in the softness of the moonlight is fairly stamped on my memory and will be something to feast upon. Oh, Jerry, the blessed privilege of traveling about! My heart is just full of love and joy in being alive. God bless you, dear, and give you great success each and every day.

Good night,
Alice

June 11th
Sunday evening
Darling Jerry:
Great news has reached me tonight by receiving the sweet note from Madam de Sales telling me to come to Paris. To have her say she has a place for me sounds inviting, doesn't it? And to think what a great teacher she is, I am indeed privileged. ...

In three letters now you have spoken as if September would be the fine time when you can sail out of New York Harbour. How I wish I could talk it over about which route for you to come. I can think of a dozen arguments in favor of almost every plan, but I am simply crazy for you to see Italy. It is the acme of sublimity for a honeymoon, and really, I have lived every inch of what I have seen with you in mind. ...

The little rose that you find is one I have carried in my Baedeker's since we visited Sorrento. I am sending it to you for safekeeping.

Friday, June 16th
My Darling Jerry,
By the time you get this letter I will be in enchanting Venice, riding through the Canal Grande in a gondola. I know I will think of our little Venice near Ocean Park and compare the two. Wouldn't a Venetian be flattered to hear me say that?

This morning, after I wrote postals to Canada, Miss F. and I went again to the Pitti Gallery, and I feel I know something about the pictures. Every single one is so choice. The grounds and palace are all in exquisite taste. We sat at the top of a terrace above a fountain, and there was something about the lay of the land that reminded me again of Santa Barbara, the view we got away up on the hills.

I walked across the Ponte Vecchio in the morning sunshine and along Via di Bardi to a little shop where I drew a pattern for a sweet dress to be made. It was really one of the joys of my life to do it. I have thought a long time and I have made myself believe you would want me to do it, and so I did. If it turns out as I plan, no girl ever had a much sweeter gown—indescribable Belgian cloth with Italian embroidery.

What a strange mood has seized me tonight. I am capable of many, as my letters do testify.

Withall, I am loath to leave Italy. But I know there are great and glorious sights ahead of me. Miss F. is sitting opposite me, and of course she guesses to whom I am writing. She says she realized what she missed in Chicago by not meeting you, and says good morning to your picture every day.

A heart full of love to you,

Alice

P.S. In your last letter you referred to me as a Scottish lassie. I surely like to be called that. I am proud of all the Scotch that is in me.

***

June 29
Pension Gregory
Grand Canal, Venice
My Darling Jerry:

In the letterhead is a drawing of our pension. I have x'ed where we are staying up on the fourth floor, where I am sitting now writing you. Oh, the air is so fresh and good, right off the Adriatic. I can see the boats flying back and forth and the bells from "the salute" are chiming seven o'clock. I can see everything complete with you and me in a gondola, with a sturdy gondolier singing lustily—as we hear them doing at night. The one and only city built with canals for streets!

We came from the station in a gondola, winding through the narrow canals and under arched bridges, and it didn't seem as if it could be real life to be acting this way.

The scenery between here and Florence is exquisite. Switzerland must be like it, only better. We crossed the Apennine Mountains, and in doing so, went through upwards of fifty tunnels. It was the hottest day I have ever experienced and we couldn't stand the windows closed, so when we went through the tunnels you ought to have seen the old gentlemen and the doctor draw the curtains vainly trying to keep the smoke out. They had kept the window seats so jealously—at first we were disappointed—but when we found how they had to work we were very glad. We were as black as Negroes when we arrived. But it was the jolliest trip we have had in all Italy.

After dinner last night we walked along the canals, over the bridges to St. Mark's Square and listened to a band. It being the evening of a festa day, we are going to take a gondola and view the celebration from the Grand Canal. Doesn't that sound fine! Oh, my Jerry, I am having such a good time. We walked miles this morning, for you can walk in Venice in spite of the canals,

70

but the streets are just like alleys. You can touch both sides. The shops are alluring here as elsewhere, and we are pursued in the usual manner by the shopkeepers. The old marble buildings which were originally white are almost black, caused by the sea breezes. It gives the city a very old and dilapidated appearance. All the trees and shrubs are beautifully green, and the gardens go right to the water's edge. The first floors of the houses are given over to the servants—the higher up you are, the better. The rooms we have are very nice. I will write more soon after our tour and get it all in a letter to you before we leave.

June 30th

Yesterday afternoon we took one of the steamboats which go up and down the Grand Canal and went its entire length, under the Rialto Bridge, saw lots of fine palaces, and stayed the night on the boat while it went over to the Lido—the fashionable summer resort, and have only now come back. It was a fine swim.

On the way a military airship passed just above us, so you see, there are different modes of travel in Venice besides the gondola and the gondoliers in their colorful garb. A heart full of love, Jerry dear.

Alice

***

Two days later, Alice and Miss F. departed Venice. The train made a stop in Austria for luncheon in a town surrounded by green valleys and snowy mountain vistas. They crossed into Germany, rolling by prosperous looking farms. Three hours later they were settled into the pension in Munich. After a quick wash at the basin in their room, they left to walk to Cooks to find their mail and book a carriage to tour the Englischer Garten.

In the early evening, they dressed for supper and went down to meet the other guests. Their hostess made introductions all around to the teachers from Vassar and some German professors. All twelve sat to supper, and afterwards, retired to the library for a smoke. A silver cigarette case was passed along with the lighter, and guests were asked to help themselves. Alice declined, taken aback and trying to be polite.

"I have seen it all through Italy, but was never actually asked before," she whispered to Miss F.

"You are in Germany, now, my dear. It is quite the thing."

The hostess announced to the guests, "We have two Americans on their way to Berlin and Paris to study voice. Miss Freuler, Miss Hicks, would you honor us with a few songs?"

Miss Freuler, having prepared Alice for such an occasion, launched them both into arias and German tunes, all wildly applauded.

Next morning they left with some of the guests for Schwaben, where they swam in the lake's cold waters, and were back for dinner at noon.

71

"Shall we go for coffee?" suggested one of the guests in German.

"A marvelous idea," said Miss F.

They gathered their purses and went around the corner to the café.

Alice looked bewildered at the costumed crowd. "Are they students?" asked Alice to Miss F.

"Different altogether from the Berkeley kind, aren't they?"

Alice tried to understand what she was seeing. The students ebbed and flowed through the doors. Each man—for there were no women today—had his own stein in his hand and a colorful hat or black skullcap on his head. The color matched a wide band going across the front of his coat. Here and there a face showed a scar.

Alice, feeling woefully inadequate in German, asked Miss F. to ask what she was seeing. Miss F. eventually translated the extraordinary sight.

"Because this is a university town, there are a great number of students about. Their colorful hats and bands each represent a different fraternity, each one more snobbish than the next. Those scars you see are healed dueling wounds proudly worn, and under the skull caps one would find additional wounds of battle. It's what comes of drinking so much during the day, and the pride of the fraternities."

***

After another day of sightseeing and listening to the bands that played during tea, the companions moved on to Nuremberg (yet another city on the must-see list from Alice Earl) and then Berlin, arriving at a pension between Cooks and Miss F.'s lessons. It was full to the brim with Europeans. She wrote to Jerry as soon as she could.

I am getting brain fag. They converse in German and French at table. There are seven different nationalities represented: two Spanish ladies and they talk Spanish, French, English, German, and Italian with equal ease. It was these ladies who warned us the first night, as they sat smoking after dinner that one must be careful to avoid disputing the word of a guide or official of any sort. Such men have proven to be most unreasonable, and they enforce the law and show their authority to the limit. It turned out to be true. The other day when Miss F. and I went to the National Museum, we were asked quite abruptly to either wear our coats or give them up. It seemed such a funny request, and Miss F. protested. But from the gleam in the eyes of the guard and his tone of voice, we quickly and meekly submitted. We found out later that there was a theft at the museum. Some relic had been slipped into a coat that was carried. And, as to hatpins, long ones are a great grievance here. One may be stopped in the street and asked for inspection. You will be glad to know our pins are considered of a medium length!

In spite of Germany's officious officials, I find it to be an orderly and beautiful country. Why, even the weather has cooled for us. I am delighted to be here.

But, I digress. There is a little girl from Rumania who speaks, apart from the Rumanian dialect, German, French, and English. There is a Russian lady who speaks German and French, a Frenchman who is studying German, and a Herr Professor who understands English but speaks very little. And then there is American Miss F. and Canadian me.

I am humbled and appalled by my own ignorance, but it does me good, for it makes me resolve to dig in and learn something.

On her way to mail her letter, Alice stopped into the camera shop to buy some film. Who should be standing at the counter with his camera open, loading film, but a member of the UC Glee Club.

"Why, isn't it Arthur Sake?" shouted Alice.

He turned abruptly, dropping the new film. "What on Earth? Alice Hicks." Both stared dumbfounded, but it was Alice who found her voice first.

"Are you on vacation with your family, Arthur?"

"No, goodness, we have quite a stunt. In two days we will be giving a concert here in Berlin. You must come. We are doing songs from *Erminie* and such."

"You could not keep me away! I have been so homesick. Hearing your good American has already cheered me up. I am booking an overnight in Dresden but promise to be back in time."

Alice's overnight to Dresden, the "Florence of Germany," was all it was promised to be. The fun part was struggling in her rudimentary German to answer the questions from her companions on the train. After an hour of furtive glances, one of the ladies asked her how long she would be in Germany. Alice replied, *zwei woche* (two weeks) and received a compliment on her accent. She immediately decided that Germany was romantic enough for a honeymoon, and decided to write Jerry to that effect.

Alice rushed back the next afternoon to be in time for the Glee Club performance. She wept as they sang "All Hail" and yelled an Oski cheer, and after the concert, danced with Arthur, the boy she first met through *Erminie* during her first semester in 1909.

Two days after the concert, Alice hugged Miss F. good-bye. She left for Paris via Cologne, on the good advice of Alice Earl.

Chapter 20

August in Paris

July 24, 1911
Hotel Louis La Grand
Paris
My Dearest Jerry:

Just a good-night note to let you know I am all fixed up in a nice little room at this hotel, safe and sound. The day has been a scorcher, and the trip seemed longer on that account. There was a party of twelve Americans in the car today and consequently everything was lively, and it did sound good to hear English spoken. They came from Texas, Colorado and Maine—quite a mixture. I overheard a man ask for a stamp, and as I had one, offered it to him, and that broke the ice. He was a Baptist minister who was conducting his party through Europe. In my compartment was the dearest little Norwegian girl, and she spoke French and English a little, and she said she could understand what I said, so we had a nice time together. We had the compartment to ourselves all afternoon, but for a while in the morning we had three of the worst specimens of German women I ever encountered. One old dame insisted upon having the windows closed and the shades up, and the sun just blazed in. We soon were driven to the passageway and abandoned our seats, so you may be sure we hurrahed when they all departed.

It was a relief to find it raining as we neared Paris. The little Norwegian girl was so concerned to think I should see Paris first in the rain. … She came out with me until I found a carriage and was safely in it. Now here I am, and I am going to rest. Tomorrow, I will let Madame de Sales hear from me.

Just before dinner I went to Cooks, which is just two blocks away, and was disappointed to find that all my mail had all been transferred to Berlin. I asked the girl how many were sent and she said, "Well, there were several of those blue envelopes, you know, with a C in the corner." How is that for observation! They can't come back too quickly, for I want them. Heaps of love, Jerry.

P.S. I waited until the next day to check for your mail, and lo, three letters from you, which I read before leaving the Cooks and Sons reading room. One was written at the Hartford Club and another on the train coming back to

Chicago, and you seemed so near, for your last letter was mailed the 17th and reached me the 25th, which is only eight days—the best traverse time yet!

I went with two ladies to a typical Parisian dressmaking establishment when they were having gowns made. The madame was very solicitous, but I evaded her, for I want to look around well before I have any gowns made. My poor little blue suit, which I so carefully selected with an eye to having it "hold its own" for style when I reached Paris, looks almost as if Mrs. Noah had worn it in the ark. I think I will have it remodeled.

Your loving Alice

Two days later Alice walked to the de Sales studio on Rue Villejust, off the Bois du Boulogne. The afternoon heat bore down on her taut nerves like the devil, but she would not allow her spirit to be defeated. *So far to come. I could not have imagined me, walking alone on the streets of Paris.* She knocked on the door promptly at three o'clock, hand trembling inside the lace glove.

"I am here for my appointment with Madame de Sales," said Alice, handing her card to the maid who answered the door.

The maid nodded and gestured for Alice to wait in the reception room. Alice breathed deeply, rooted to the spot while the maid ascended, presumably to locate Madame on an upper floor. Quiet footsteps descended immediately. Alice found herself facing a woman dressed in a dark, scooped-neck dress and almost no jewelry. She was of average height and full-fleshed, as most women in their middle years were. Her eyes reflected a calm intelligence and some humor. Alice could feel herself relaxing.

Madame extended her hand and smiled directly at Alice. "Miss Hicks, finally we meet in person."

"It is a pleasure to be here," said Alice, and thought she detected a hint of Scottish brogue in Madame de Sales speech.

"Please, won't you sit? The heat is terrible but there is a breeze just here by the windows."

They both sat. As they chatted about Alice's adventures of the summer and of the musical events unfolding in Paris, Alice felt herself not only relaxing, but enjoying herself.

To bring the conversation gently back to the present, Madame asked, "Have you visited Villa Copernic?"

"Yes, you were most kind to provide me the list of pensions It seems quite nice."

"If it would help you decide, I stayed there myself years ago, when Madame Chalamel first purchased the pension. You will like the other residents. Many are my students, so you will have company back and forth for your lessons.

"The stairway is wide and will accommodate the hire of a practice piano, which you will definitely need, Miss Hicks." Madame paused then laughed. "That is a great deal to recommend it all by itself."

"Then, Madame de Sales, I shall definitely stay there."

"Excellent decision, my dear. I *am* pleased. I will call Madame Chalamel and let her know. I will also recommend that she sit you on her right at table. She has the most impeccable French and will be a boon to your instruction."

"Shall I have French lessons at the pension, then?" said Alice.

"No, Miss Hicks, with my staff here at the studio. It is part of my course of instruction."

They stood and walked about the studio as Madame gestured to pictures on the walls. "Many of these men and women are artists in Munich and London, close enough to be summoned for a visit—they come occasionally to give a small performance for my students. I even get American artists back for additional training, and they often perform at my weekly teas.

"Let me tell you a little about my vocal training technique. I myself am a soprano. What you are will be determined by hard work and devotion to the best principles of the French vocal school and of the German, as well as the Bel Canto school in Italy. In addition, Miss Hicks, I set great store by being sympathetic to my students' personal life. I can promise you that I will not interfere, offering only support when you might be confused or unhappy. Please don't hesitate to come to me with anything that confounds you."

Alice realized that without much fuss, Madame de Sales had guided them gracefully to the piano. After a little discussion of the sheet music, Alice sang, accompanied for the one and only time by Madame herself.

"Miss Hicks, your voice is good. Lots of back in it." Madame looked straight at Alice, then tilted her head, waiting for a response.

Alice smiled, relief plain on her face. "Thank you for your confidence in me."

"And what do you want to do with your voice, my dear?"

"I want... to make the most I can out of it."

"How long do I have you?"

"Well," said Alice, "I cannot say definitely how long I will be here." *I should not be so vague. She will think I am not serious. But how to explain about Jerry's coming?*

"Indeed. None of us can tell," replied Madame. "What does it matter right now? So, my dear Miss Hicks, shall we begin?"

"Oh, yes, Madame. I am ready to start this afternoon." Alice could see Madame's smile playing around the corners of her mouth, and realized with embarrassment that she had been too enthusiastic.

"No, tomorrow will be soon enough, say ten thirty in the morning for your first lesson. I want to see you every day until you can learn to practice yourself. Please hire a piano as soon as you can. I will help you with the arrangements."

They both stood, and Alice extended her hand to Madame de Sales. "Thank you so much. You are very gracious."

Madame shook Alice's hand firmly and then gave her some forms. "Please take these back with you. You will see how to pay for the lessons and the excursions to the opera. The season begins soon. Payments for the lessons are due monthly and require you to fill out the enclosed cards for each month. I am sure you will find it a comfortable arrangement."

"I have just received a cable with funds from Cooks. I shall bring a draft with me tomorrow to cover the first month. Thank you, Madame." Alice felt her throat close with emotion, swallowing anything else she might have said.

Madame noticed, and placed her hand gently over Alice's throat. "We will learn how to open your voice so that will not happen again."

Alice walked back to the hotel, so elated that she forgot the blazing sun. On the way she stopped at Villa Copernic to arrange for a room large enough for a piano, and then to the American Express Company to pay for her trunks to be delivered to the pension. They had been in storage since she had left Florence—it seemed a lifetime ago

.

Chapter 21

Summer View from Chicago

Jerry stood at the window of his new air cooled room, enjoying his view from the seventh floor of the Athletic Club. Moving day had been last week. What a view he had, looking out over the avenue into the park. He had stripped down to his underwear after playing golf in the oppressive heat; his tanned forearms, neck and face were dark against his torso and shorts.

Record heat and humidity stretched east to Connecticut, jumped the Atlantic, and covered much of Europe, including France. Alice had written that the one-hundred-degree temperatures were immobilizing the entire population of Paris. It had followed just weeks after the cholera outbreak in Italy, which Alice had brushed off *as nothing to do with me so never mind what you may read.* She was his very own fresh air; hell and damnation, he had never needed it more.

A loud whine caught Jerry's attention. There they went: Grant Park was having an aviation meet. Two birdmen had been lost yesterday—he still couldn't get the crumpled, beautiful yellow wings of their aeroplanes out of his head. Today the meet ran smoothly, as if the tragedy had never happened. They were taking off, one after the other, led by the astonishing red tri wing around the field, toward home. Jerry propped his feet up on a stool and lit his last cigar of the day. He allowed his mind to wander through his own struggles of the last months.

It had been a close thing to keep his wits. He faced his biggest challenge with Travelers yet—to argue a more lucrative contract. Just in time, as it turned out, to accommodate Alice's monthly expenses of $150, of which he begrudged her not one cent. And then there was the possibly awful financial burden of Norah, should that not turn out well.

Just weeks ago, he stamped "refused" on his paltry contract raise and sent it back. The home office in Hartford registered it with a shock of earthquake proportions.

"Get your ass to Hartford," they said. "We'll talk."

Jerry knew then that he had them; he had brought more business to the Chicago area than any in the company's history, and successfully challenged the whole sales percentage approach for top-performing salesmen. A short, very hot trip back to the home office had produced a new contract worth $9,500. He had doubled his own income in a year.

Mr. Nolan, his boss from the beginning of his incarceration in the Midwest, had turned from foe to friend. New respect for Jerry's sales record warmed their relationship, and Nolan's recent marriage secured it. After Nolan's engagement, Jerry had shared his own plans to be married, discussing pros and cons of a continental wedding and how to time his leave from the office. Nolan was eager to arrange his own honeymoon, so with Alice off on her toot and sending almost daily tour reports, Jerry was able to give Nolan advice on destinations. Nolan reciprocated with recommendations for steamship bookings and contacts for legal advice on the contrary nature of Americans marrying on foreign soil.

***

Goddamn, it was a shock to see Norah turn up in the reception room of the Athletic Club, tall and fair, with her dark hair imprisoned under a large hat. Somehow she had absconded from her Oakland nest to plead her case. Jerry had managed to send her back safely to her mother's roof, with promises from her to get interested in something and be a good girl. He would call her twice a week, he said. Of course he hadn't and was greeted a week later with one of her scariest letters.

August 3, 1911
I think, Jerry, your letter about making progress came too soon. While my letters have been full of the "big talk," my heart has been far from feeling as hilarious as my letters sounded.

I am famished for want of a little sympathy, a few words of affection. I have raved and ranted and cried until my pillow got so wet I couldn't sleep on it. Still, what good does it do? I have learned not to look to you for much sympathy, and Mother is just as bad. I am restless and unhappy, and your attitude doesn't help me ease things a bit.

I haven't bothered you since I have been home and that waiting and waiting has been the hardest battle. Just give me a few days' notice when you are ready to keep your side of the bargain. Unfair you have been with me, but the good instinct in me has prevailed so far. But maybe it won't always.

A medium told me I was not going to live long—a few months more, that something was going to happen unless I was very careful. So, what's the use? In heaven all the angels sing. Really, I'm not afraid to die. I didn't tell Mother but I can use my trousseau to be buried in. I have to get some use out of that $45 petticoat!

Jerry had scrubbed his face hard with his hands in a marginally successful attempt to bring sanity to his fear. After agonizing over the missive, he sat down to inform Alice of his decision to postpone their marriage. For now he would not mention the alarming letters from Norah.

August 15, 1911
My Dearest Alice,

I don't know who is the happier over your success with Madame, you or I. The good news in your last two letters made me the happiest man in Chicago. The reason for the trip abroad is now apparent and justified. It seems to me that I have told you that I knew there was nothing in your ambitions which you could not accomplish if given the opportunity. I am just as happy tonight as I was the night you told me you loved me. Now I know you will be happy and contented, thanks to your accounts of meeting so many people who could help make your life in Paris more pleasant—and I was beginning to wonder if you were not a little homesick!

My first impulse is to take passage on the next boat for France, but that won't do right now. How dreadfully my presence would upset your progress in her hands. No, my dear, it must be sometime in October. By that time you will be transformed into a little French damsel. The instruction in French is of course the right thing, but please don't you work too hard at it. You are over there to play most of the time, you know.

How long does it take to go over to London from Paris? Does London seem close by?

I went to Cooks and cabled you 1,000 francs. On August 1st I mailed you in care of Cooks 500 francs which you no doubt have received. Another 1,000 francs will be mailed Sep. 1st.

I am busy with a Mr. Kenny of Seattle, who has seen your picture and has heard me brag of your wonderful stay in Paris. His wife, also taking vocal lessons, will be anxious to meet you. Perhaps we will visit the Kenny's in Seattle after our return.

Your old love,
Jerry

Alice, she was a trump. Each place she visited became a possible location for a honeymoon. Her letters rolled out lists of steamship companies, their pros and cons, travel timing, luggage restrictions, things to eat, places to stay and see, *and please, bring my string of pearls and kunzite necklace for me to wear with my trousseau. Register them before leaving or customs will be a nightmare on our return.* How it would hurt her to put off his trip! He had written to make it positive for her while he waited for the Norah issue to resolve itself. And, what would he do if he waited until the end of the year and simply could not leave the office? The national Travelers end-of-year sales contest took place then. Well, he had done what he could in the letter to ease her fears. It rankled him no end to be so helpless.

Then a week later Jerry received a letter from a very different Norah. She had written to say she was in Tahoe with her great friend Hazel.

August 14
Tahoe

My Dear Jerry,

I am at the Hortons' camp. Pine scented air, warm days, chilly nights and the attention of Joe—you know, the Joe we both know. Yesterday he and I drove through miles of virgin pine forest. I never had enjoyed myself so much. Little chipmunks flitted across the road, birds calling—it really made a picture. Joe sang for me and I closed my eyes and almost imagined Caruso beside me. I recited "My Mountain, My Sierras" from Girl of the Golden West....

Could he hope that Norah's suicide threats were a thing of the past?

Chapter 22

Coming of Age in Paris

August 4th, 1911
Villa Copernic
My Darling Jerry:
I was thinking this afternoon that the very day that I spent in Cologne riding my lonely self up and down the Rhine, you were in Hartford. Just the width of the Atlantic and a little more between us. But not for long. Please, don't forget to put the extra five-cent stamp on your letters, for if you don't, I must wait ten days to hear from you instead of seven. I can't wait for every slow boat!

Madame Chapin, the dear old French teacher, sometimes turns up her eyes to heaven in a hopeless sort of way at my pronunciation of certain words. French is so much harder than German and I never have any patience with anything I can't get all in a minute, and that is a bad way to be. She is teaching me the words to *Mignon* so Madame de Sales will be successful with my lessons from Handel's *Oratorios*.

I had a fine afternoon with Madame de Sales and was proud as punch when she introduced me as one of her "chickens" at her tea after the lessons. All sorts of her students are gathered here from America. I wore my blue-over-red dress, the one I got in San Francisco, and I am glad to find it is in good style over here. My new chapeau is a dream. I got it at a milliner who supplies hats for the famous Mary Gardner, whom you have heard sing in Chicago. So you see I am patronizing great people! And, Miss Gardner is here to appear in Monsieur Massenet's opera, *Thais*, which we will be seeing during the upcoming season.

Madame has pronounced me a mezzo-soprano, but has cautioned me to keep practicing my high notes, for she is thinking of giving me an aria from *Madame Butterfly*. I am amazed to think I should be ready for such a part with my voice in the lower tones. It is such a joy to soar up the way I have been going the last few days, and I can do it so easily. It seems like a "bird out of prison," and Madame has taught me how to let it go.

Dear Miss F. arrives tomorrow to start lessons with Madame. How wonderful to have her here with me again, and for two whole months.

Write "tout suite."
Your loving Alice

Aug 8th, 1911
40 Rue Copernic,

My Darling Jerry,

I had almost forgotten what blue envelopes looked like, but the sight of my breakfast tray this morning revived my drooping spirit, for there were two letters from you.

Yesterday afternoon I had tea with Madame de Sales, just we two, and she came with me to get a piano. It is coming tomorrow. When we were walking to her home she said, "Come tell me some more about this nice person in America," and asked if we were going to be married here. It seems it is quite as difficult to be married in Germany as it is in France. All require a residence of about three weeks. Madame says she has a lawyer friend with whom she will inquire, concerning what is necessary.

My lesson this morning went off with great gusto. Madame has given me such pretty new songs and I am struggling away with the French. I had two visitors at my lesson and I must say it is a unique experience, this being exhibited as a prize pupil. I overheard Madame tell a friend that she could do more with my voice in three months than with some in a year, so I ought to be able to sing for you when you get over here.

Since luncheon I have been speaking German with the Russian lady. I must say I like "Deutsch" better than French, so I will keep it up. I must say "au revoir" and hie myself down to Cooks. I hope there is another letter on tomorrow's breakfast tray.

Heaps of love to you,
Alice

August 16th,
Villa Copernic
My Darling Jerry,

Cool weather at last and I understand the weather is better with you, too.

I met a friend of Madame's in a house outside Fontainebleau and we spent the afternoon in song. My contribution was a little Scotch ballad. I felt thrills while performing it.

My dress from Italy is arriving. I have never paid for it, but send other people to her so hope it will make amends. Still, I need new clothes and will wait and have a new suit to go home—with you! Every letter is waited for so eagerly in hopes of hearing news of your coming. If you cannot come, I will go back with Miss F. in November. But I hope no business complication or anything else hinders me from hearing that you leave on such-and-such a date and arrive nine days hence. Be it Berlin or here, I am ready, and, oh, my Jerry, come soon.

Alice

August 27th
Sunday evening

My Dearest Jerry:

Great was the excitement this afternoon when an aeroplane passed right over Rue Copernic and was so near it seemed like a huge monarch of the air ready to swoop down upon us. As I watched it disappearing, I thought of the great sight you have been witnessing in seeing so many in the air at once. I have been enjoying the accounts in the papers.

My last letter was full of impatience, and here today brings your definite word that October is the time. Three cheers for October. I don't know how I will last until then. I have been all excitement today and don't see how I am going to sleep tonight, so I will just keep on writing to you. You must be here before October 18th, of course. No more birthday celebrations without you.

My throat is better after my C. S. treatment yesterday. I have not sung in a week or so. Madame blames it on the weather. Madame—you will remember I told you she is a Christian Scientist, quelle surprise—had recommended a Mrs. Breckson, who lives in the Latin Quarter with all the students and artists. She is very nice, and we had a long talk. I haven't had a chance to talk Science with anyone for a long time, and you surely slip back when you aren't in touch with it all the time. And, well, though I am not feeling very spry, I did sally forth to the C. S. church off the "Champs." There are so many Americans there, some of whom I have met on my travels. But, no more singing lessons for a week.

I am working hard on my French ballads, struggling mightily with the words until Madame permits me to use my voice to sing. It is most elusive, but no language can compare with it for light and dark shades of vowels, and that is what makes it hard. In German you are ALLOWED to pronounce all the letters of a word.

I found out from Madame's lawyer M. Carpoit that Americans can be married here in Paris by an American clergyman as American citizens without conforming to the residence laws of the country. He says you must fill out the enclosed papers and take them to the consul in Chicago.

I am planning the wedding to be as simple and quiet as possible. For all that, M. Carpoit suggested it would be easier to be married in England. I know you have very little time so close to the end of the year. Perhaps it would be best to come here so that you may meet Madame as well as little Miss F. who is eagerly awaiting your arrival. All of Paris will be at our feet, dear Jerry. We shall visit Fontainebleau and walk in the vineyards and see all the things I have been saving for your coming.

Your loving Alice

Aug 30, 1911
Chicago
My Darling Alice,

...The truth is I am laid up again. I was at the office Monday and Tuesday but today I could not quite make it. My Science practitioner came about noon, so now I am feeling so much better and will be back on the job tomorrow. Just after the C. S. man left, a bellboy brought your letter written Sunday August 20th. This letter just beat the C. S. treatment all to smash. I could not have received one from you when it would have been more welcome.

I am glad you continue to go to the C. S. Church and that you meet familiar American faces.

Yes, of course we'll get back here in time for the Chicago Opera season. It runs through the holidays. ...

I love you just lots and lots,

Jerry

Chapter 23

September Blows Hot and Cold

September 5th, Sat. evening
Villa Copernic
My Darling Jerry,
Today has been hot again. All the trees on the once lovely Champs Elysees
are all brown and withered from the sun. But it can't last much longer and I
hear great tales of Parisian rains.

Today when I went over to Madame's, Miss F. was still at her lesson, and
instead of the accompanist the Baroness Dubonsky, there sat M. Priod, the
great Chef du Chant of Paris. He is a great coach and hobnobs with Massenet,
the French composer, so Madame says. She made me perform while he
accompanied me and I sang an Italian Spring song. It is very bright and gay
and has a dandy fine finale. After the finish I got a look of approval.

Do not trouble to bring the Blue and Gold yearbook to me; just keep it for
our collection. I am so glad to hear you have decided to bring over only
suitcases instead of bothering with trunks. Mine will be nuisance enough.

Forgive me for not writing for so long. My room seems to have become
rather a rendezvous for long chats lately, and I have not been able to steal away
and write. But now I am alone in my little eyrie, unmolested.

Goodbye for now, more tomorrow.
Heaps of love,
Alice

Sunday, September 10th, 1911
My Darling Jerry,
This morning the sight of blue envelopes cheered my drooping spirits so
much that I forgot to eat breakfast until it was quite cold. How sorry I am to
hear you have been laid up again. We were both having troubles about the
same time, for my throat was bothering me. But I hope you are as all right as
I am. The fact that you are looking to Science for help allays my fears, or else
I would be so worried. How good it is that your trip comes soon, for that will
do you so much good. As soon as I hear from you the exact date you will
expect to leave, then won't I count the days! I really can't write you many
more letters, can I? For this won't reach you until around the 20th. Oh, Jerry,
Jerry, I am so glad you are coming. I don't know what to do or what to say! I
suppose before this reaches you, you will have decided on the steamer and
where to land. Cherbourg is the best coming direct to France.

Last night Miss F. and I were chaperoned by a Mrs. Perkins and an Armenian madame from Constantinople for a trip to the Latin Quarter. That is a part of Paris on the other side of the Seine where all the students live, and they carry on all manner of capers there and are quite immune from the regular laws governing Paris. The whole of the opera, *La Boheme,* is laid just around part where we were on the Boulevard San Michel. There were dozens of artists with long hair, little velvet caps and coats, just as you see them depicted in the opera. The cafes were gay and just packed and revelry ran high.

September 11th, 1911
Monday evening
My Darling Jerry,
Yesterday I had such a lovely surprise in having Mildred Ahlf, one of the first girls I met at College Hall, call and see me with Ruth Fuller. She arrived on Friday and had been so recently in Berkeley that we had a fine talkfest. Mildred came over to be with Ruth, but now Ruth and her mother say it is better for Ruth that she study art in Germany. Mildred wants to stay here for a while and see Paris and take singing lessons. ... She wants to study French, then travel with her uncle after a year or so. Mildred is a very clever girl, having passed college with flying colors. How nice it would be if I could get her all settled with Madame de Sales before I leave.

I received a sad letter from Peggy. The engagement appears to be off and she is suffering so. Also, I heard from Pauline in the north of England of the arrival of a baby girl. She is so happy, which is wonderful, as her parents were quite opposed to her marriage, wanting her to stay in the U. S.

This morning I had an unusually fine lesson. I knew the words of my song right off and that pleased Madame. Madame Chapin gave me encouragement with my French tonight, which cheers me mightily. I was beginning to think I was hopelessly stupid. She says I am getting "une bonne accent," so by the time you get here I may be able to make myself understood.

I must say goodnight now and write a letter to Pauline.
A heart full of love for you,
Alice

September 18th
Chicago Athletic Club
My Dearest Alice,
Two letters from you today—Monday usually brings them. I had one for breakfast and one at the office. I must say that your coach and teacher Madame de Sales is a wonder. She has gathered about her the famous and talented men and women of Paris, and how easy she makes it for you to meet them. When you sing at her reception you will meet more of the famous artists. You are not half as happy over these reports and evidences of progress as I am. You don't

know how much it helps a fellow who plods on over the bumpy insurance road. It's not the smooth, straight path here that I had in Los Angeles. You are all that I seem to have left of my list of ideals.

Lovingly,
Jerry

September 24th
40 Rue Copernic, Paris,
My Dearest Jerry,
I have not heard from you in four days. So I just couldn't stand it and sent you a cable. I have looked and looked each morning and in vain until I was so disappointed my patience was at the breaking point...

Don't forget that letters are part of my subsistence over here.
Your Alice

ALICE HICKS PARIS 24SEP1911
ARRIVAL AFTER NOV 1 STOP FAVOR ROTHBURY STOP LETTER FOLLOWS STOP JERRY

Chapter 24

Jerry's Explanation

September 24th

My Darling Alice,

Your cable came yesterday when I was out to Evanston making up a foursome at the club. Well now, my honey bug, I am all well and trying to be happy without you. I have just come back from the cable office where I sent you a message telling you that I could not arrive before Nov. 1st and that I favored Rothbury in Northumberland rather than Paris for the wedding. I know you will be angry with me in delaying and postponing my coming but I am not yet my own boss and my friends at Hartford don't say or even intimate that they are willing for me to go away at this particular season of the year.

Let us give up considering France. There is a possibility that you could come to New York and we could be married at Thanksgiving. Or, if you went to Rothbury late in October and I landed there about Nov. 1st, we could start back sooner because I would give up my plan to visit Paris at this time. It would be a quick trip over and back for me that would include the big event and just a peep at England. Now, dear, this is only one plan that may not be feasible at all. It would never do unless your cousin at Rothbury is favorably inclined. She seems to be a dear old lady and I can't conceive of her doing anything else but invite you up to her home to be married. I just know that by Oct. 1st you will send me word that she has guessed what our trouble is and has come to our rescue.

Miss F. does not leave Paris until Nov. 1st and in consequence, you will have her company until I can get there. Alice, my pet, I feel a bit derelict in not coming on the next boat when I read your good letters. I guess I am too fussy and particular altogether. When I see you and tell you what has been going on this summer I know you will forgive me. In fact, I think you would agree to live in Paris or London until the later part of December or first of January, if I had thought it best to have written you all that is going on for me at work and at home. The storm is all over now and we have other things to occupy ourselves. You will never understand if I try to write you all the details, so please let's not upset any of our ideas except possibly to consider a delay in carrying them out. That delay, however, is to be only a short one. I could do as I see fit but I want the H. O. to approve this particular move. ...

...Now about that flat or hotel question when we come back to Chicago. I think it is just about right that you do not know all about "domestic science."

We will get along okay in a hotel until we can find a good flat and a good neighborhood. Of course a maid will do what you are unnecessarily worrying about. Leave that to me, dear. I will arrange the hotel before I leave. We will get a furnished apartment until we find out what we want.

Now, dearie, I am going to move heaven and earth to come as soon as I can and believe me I want to stay over there as long as I can. Now don't be surprised if you get a cable announcing a change to an earlier date.

Enclosed are two letters for your eyes only that will go some way to resolving "the issues."

Your ever-loving Jerry

Sept. 6
Redding, California
Hotel Lorenz
My Dear Old Pal, Jerry:

Well, Jerry, things did look pretty serious for a while. I did all I could to make the girl to take a sensible view but it took a long time before she would give up. I've not seen her since June but just received a letter from her, a page of which I enclose. Please destroy it and never let it be known I wrote you or sent this. Perhaps she has written you. Anyway, Jerry, if you are out of this scrape now, don't start any more unless you mean to carry it through.

Sincerely,
Jim

Oakland, California

Here, Jim, is where I'm serious. I guess you are wondering what I have done in regards to Jerry. Well, my dear, I thought this all over good and thank the Lord I didn't do anything crazy but took your advice, and am going to let him go to the devil or any other place he likes better. Honest, for my good mother's sake, I couldn't drag her into a suit of any kind. Do you know, Jim, your words came to me so often when I was making the decision: "I'm thinking of you and you have got too much to lose." That's the truth, and so I thought, What's the use?

Norah

Thursday, October 5th
My Darling Jerry:

As I sit here and think of how much I want to say to you, I find I am pages ahead of my pen. Your good long letter of September 24th came at noon today and since then I have read it more than once—into a rag.

Today's letter contained so much of what I have been longing to hear. Explanations don't hurt, Jerry dear, and I have known all along that there was something you had in hand which had to be wound up before you could get away. But I have been wanting to hear about it and felt it was slow in coming. I try with all my might to be reasonable, and consider how hard it is to go into details on paper, and I have trusted you that it was the same good reason that kept you. I have wondered how you would be able to leave as the year draws nearer and nearer the end, and we must not let our personal plans out-stride our being practical. I am so anxious to wait, if by the waiting you can stay longer when you come. ... I am wondering how you can hope to leave any later and have the approbation of the H. O. for an absence at that time of year.

If you can't come over here, I can go back to you. I am ready to stay over here alone over the New Year, if you could surely come then, but if you are doubtful about being able to get away then, I want you to let me come home to you. ... My "thought paramount" is to do what is best in the long run. I don't want my homesick letters to influence you to come.

In speaking of the happenings of the summer, you were rather indefinite, for you did not give me the slightest intimation as to how you had been attacked. I find my imagination taking "aeroplanic" leaps, but I must curb myself, and trust you to bring, whatever it is, 'round all right. And you trust me to be fair and reasonable, won't you, Jerry? But I cannot make myself see that it is right for us to be at the opposite sides of the globe much longer. I have felt all summer that I have shared so little with you in your real difficulties, and when it is so hard to discuss matters of importance by letter, that is all the more reason why we should not be apart longer—for that is not living. ...

As yet, I have not received any word from Mrs. Fogo, but am thinking about it so much. I don't see how she can fail to recognize our dilemma and help us. What a predicament, to be at the mercy of a person's intuitive sight, although I put everything so plainly as far as courtesy would allow. ...

I must say goodnight now, and if I could throw my arms around you, I would say "bon courage" to you, but as I can't I very reverently ask God to give you strength and protect you and bring us to each other somewhere sometime soon.

Your loving Alice

Chapter 25

Apple Pie and a Recital

Alice, her lesson just over in the studio, waited in the music room for Miss F. and Mildred to arrive. The three students had been invited to a rare luncheon with Madame. The two suddenly burst through the door, not late but excited, with three huge hatboxes on carrying strings. The orders they had placed a week ago with the milliner were inside.

"We simply could *not* pass by without collecting our new treasurers," exclaimed Mildred.

Lids were lifted and gentle hands removed the new purchases, each a dark confection uniquely suited to its wearer, variations of tulle, silk flowers, feathers, and ribbons. They exclaimed and modeled in hushed tones, not wanting Madame de Sales to hear the commotion, but the maid, charged with keeping an eye on the three, peeked in the door to ogle the finery.

"A good hat is just the thing," said Mildred. "Too bad you two didn't have them for the Student's Hostel performance last week."

"Nevertheless," replied Miss F., gentling her hat back in the nest of tissue in her box, "the performances went well. I'm not one to deny our audience the best, but the hostel guests and invited public were not the upper crust. Quite a good turnout for our first public appearance, though."

"Quite a good rehearsal, as well, for my own recital here tomorrow," said Alice. "I am all aflutter. Madame told me she expected me to 'carry the laurels.'"

"You will," said Miss F., leaning over to pat Alice on the shoulder. "Didn't you tell me that the baron thought you were a professional when he was accompanying you during your lesson?"

"That was before I practiced my Italian song. He picked up several mispronounced words."

"Never mind," said Mildred. She leaned over in a conspiratorial manner and quipped, "With your new hat, the audience will be mesmerized."

Miss F. said, "The Baron von Mariansburg he may be, a direct descendent of the Austrian throne, an accomplished pianist, consul in Italy, and dear friend of Madame de Sales. But he does not play piano as well as Monsieur Priad, the 'Chef de Chant' of Paris. It is he who will be accompanying you and guiding you through the whole performance."

"Of course, you are right," said Alice as she took off her new hat and smoothed her hair. "He is marvelous." She thought back to the weeks of practices at the pension. Rotund, balding Monsieur Priad was coaching Alice.

He spoke no English: "*Elas, non*," was his quick response when asked. But they got along rather well. He did not laugh at her slow French, and wished her *bon courage* at the end of every session.

Alice was brought back to the present as Madame's maid announced luncheon. Carl, Madame de Sales young son, chatted away in flawless English as he escorted them up to Madame's personal apartment. The dining room table was set with elegant silver and china. Crystal water goblets sat at each place. All five dined and chatted, relaxed and cheerful at the simple meal before them. A roast beef was served with steamed green beans and flaky biscuits with butter on the side. Dessert was American apple pie—a high pastry dome glittered with sugar crystals that concealed the mound of sweet fruit slices.

"Hot biscuits and apple pie, Madame," said Alice. "Oh, you must have known how long I have pined for good old American food."

"We must have you properly fed, as well as practiced, for tomorrow, my dear."

"I feel quite nervous, but I know I will honor all your hard work," said Alice.

"I have no doubts at all, Alice," said Madame. "If you are still here at Thanksgiving, we will have a proper turkey with all the trimmings."

Alice smiled brightly and thanked her hostess, but her stomach knotted. A month ago she was sure the she and Jerry would have been married and back in Chicago for the opera season, her birthday, Thanksgiving and forever.

Her twenty-fourth birthday was tomorrow. Two significant events marked the day. Her dear Thetas had sent a registered envelope with twenty letters of best wishes and heaps of gossip. The distraction of those good letters last week removed the pain of Jerry's delays until she had succumbed once more into worry. Sleep evaded her. Whirlwind activity, such as the teas and luncheons tucked in between lessons and shopping, left her physically exhausted, and her mind found no quiet place to rest.

"Alice, dear," said Madame de Sales, "are you quite with us? You look a little pale. Still thinking about tomorrow?"

"Yes. I guess I am a little tired."

"Perhaps we should adjourn," said Madame. "Carl, my dear, kindly escort the ladies downstairs. Alice must get her rest."

"*Oui, Maman*," replied Carl.

***

Alice arrived at the de Sale's studio promptly at one p.m. Her friends deposited her in the back of the studio to warm up her voice, accompanied by Monsieur Priad. The cellist who would provide music between Alice's songs tuned up in the adjoining room.

At the appointed time, Alice sent a brief prayer to God, took a breath and stepped out into the salon for her first aria. She stood gracefully in her navy

93

tea dress and new hat waiting for the polite clapping to subside. In the hush, Monsieur Priod caught her eye, nodded and began to play. She felt the song rise up through her soul and out into the room filled with her friends and distinguished visitors. Her Italian and German rolled effortlessly through the music. Three more songs, with intervals of graceful cello music to rest her voice, and her recital was complete. The small audience clapped vigorously. Alice felt the glow of pride she had waited all these months to feel. The hard work and lonely months apart from Jerry had come to this impeccable finish. Truly, now, she could go home.

***

October 29th
Sunday afternoon
My Darling Jerry:
It made me thoroughly homesick this morning when I went to the Gare St. Lazare to see Miss F. away. They will sail from Liverpool on the 2nd. If it weren't for Emo I would feel like a mere speck on this side of the globe. I did so hate to see her go; she has rather looked after me. As the funny little train wended its way out of the station I felt somewhat of the same loneliness that gripped my heart as I left you at Toledo all those months ago. I walked almost home, and then into the Rue de Barri Church and heard some good singing. The sermon helped me to forget my troubles.

But enough of this! I am glad Emo and Mildred are here and you have never seen more excited girls than these as they are overseeing and doing all the gay stunts. We have been to the Opera Comique three times—Massenet's *Werther*, which I am to study the mezzo-soprano leading role of Charlotte all of November, and *Manon*. We heard splendid singers. We also saw the lovely music version of the fairy tale, *Blue Bird*. Later we are to see *Louise*. Alas, we cannot wear our new chapeaux as it is against the law to wear hats in the theaters. But a feather or jewel will do, and I have just the things I need.

We went to some lectures on early Italian and Spanish art at the Louvre, given by Emo's new friend Miss Heywood, and they will continue throughout November, if I am still here. I never before knew how to pick out the good points. I feel like I can judge more intelligently.

Little did I think two years and eight months ago—to be exact—that I should be sending you letters from Paris. Good night, my Jerry dear.
Your loving Alice

Chapter 26

Respite

November 21st, 1911
40 Rue Copernic
My Darling Jerry:

Mail came fast and furious this morning so that by eleven o'clock I had the great good news that I am to see you right after the New Year. Oh my, Jerry, I can't wait! Surely nothing will pop up in that time to change plans again. It does annoy me so to think I can't tell you that everything is all fixed for us to be married in England. Mrs. Fogo is still so formal, and I don't suppose thinks yet what a relief it would be to me to have her suggest my coming to establish a residence with her. But I will just have to ask her. I have been thinking lately we are too determined to carry out our original plan, for if you only have a month, two weeks will be taken by travel during stormy weather. Every Chicago paper says Florida is alluring. In Canada, we have an open invitation. But there I would have to share you, and I couldn't stand it. I must see you and you only, my Jerry dear. I have shared you so much with other people that I am stimulated to sheer selfishness in the request, but I must have you to learn more of the real Jerry, who seems to have been snatched away from me so often by cruel and intruding circumstances.

If you say you are coming—no matter how short a time you can spend—you will find me in England waiting for you, or if you say so, I will leave Paree after witnessing the famous way the French have of installing the New Year, and take passage for New York with a bounding heart. This letter ought to reach you by Dec. 3 and there will be plenty of time for an answer unless you relieve an anxious mind by sending a cable.

I will finish my card of lessons with Madame and then I believe I will take a rest up until the last minute. I must confess I have been in bed for the last three days feeling worse than miserable with a cold. I did go down for dinner and was up this evening with Emo in her room. Several days ago Madame gave a lecture on the timbre of voices, and I sang a German song. Mildred, who was with me, said while I was singing Madame leaned over to an old pupil of hers and whispered that I was the best pupil she had now. That wasn't bad, was it, when I wasn't feeling as spry as I might?

Good night, my Jerry dear,
Alice

November 25th
My Dearest Jerry;

Madame says to stop everything and come back and brush up just before Xmas. I guess she is right, so I am going to do it and get plenty of sleep, and then I know I will get fat and rosy. I want to leave on December 6th after Madame's lecture. Everything is almost entirely settled for me to go to a convent—don't worry I won't join the sisterhood—in the forest at Fontainebleau. Emo will come to spend the last few days with me, and Madame says she will try and spend a Sunday. So all this makes the prospect look brighter. ... Don't worry about me. I will benefit by the little change, I am sure. I can't sleep, and that has been going on for some time, and consequently makes me unexpectedly nervous. But I will survive, don't worry. ...

A Mrs. Ridley-Scott, an old English friend of Madame's, is quite the society lady in London. Madame wants me to sing at her home when I pass through. When I come back from Fontainebleau she wants me to give an afternoon myself, and when I gasped, she said she might have a tenor to help out. A tenor and a mezzo can give a good program together, so I hope she lets me. I think the motive of all this is to let me try my "wings," as it were, before I leave her. Isn't Madame a wonder, the way she continually thinks of me?

Wednesday, December 6th
Fontainebleau—Avon
St. Joseph's Convent
My Darling Jerry:
Here I am at last in this peaceful spot, and altho' I have only been here a matter of hours; my spirit seems renewed with the quietude of the place. Luncheon is served at the early hour of 11:30 and I arrived just long enough before to interview Mother Superior, who is in charge of the place and look about a little. When I was coming along the corridor with la Mère Superior, I bowed to one of the sisters I saw standing near and was greeted with, "Good morning, why how tall you are!" in a perfectly delicious Irish brogue. I felt quite at ease then. ...

There is a little French girl here, and although a "Madame," she is about my age, and since luncheon we have been for a long walk in the forest. She quite saves the day, for the others are ancient ladies and I would be quite by myself without her. We have chatted French entirely, for she only knows about four English words, and she helps me wonderfully for she laughs so good-naturedly at my queer mistakes. The huge forest surrounds Fontainebleau and the sections are all marked off with letters and marks on the trees something the way the Indians used to do. There is a large military station here and soldiers everywhere. A group of over a dozen were practicing band music out in the forest, all standing in line with their bugles, and those who were playing kettle drums were bracing themselves up against trees and were working away for all their might. And almost everywhere a sort of Scottish heather is growing like the little sample I am enclosing. We scampered around like children, plucking this and that, and just exalted in the carefree moment. You would think I had been carrying the world on my shoulders from that speech, but the change from noisy Paris seems good for a week or two.

I am sitting at my table in my room, writing by soft candlelight. Nothing more up to date than that, and anything else would be quite out of keeping with the surroundings, to be sure. The sisters are all so sweet and happy, not sad and pious-looking, and are eager to do your slightest bidding. I ought to return to Paris just boomingly healthy and able to sing as I never have before.

The mails go very irregularly now and are posted spasmodically, but I do hope this reaches you as I want it to, to carry heaps and heaps of love to you and let you know I am happy. Bon courage with the contest, my Jerry. And after that the days ought to simply fly. I will be thinking of you.

Your Alice

December 12th
Fontainebleau
My Darling Jerry,
This has been a wonderful day for mail. A card from Miss F. and three letters from you. So you met the little lady at last. Her card was in glowing terms of the nice time she had had, and I know everything went off with much "éclat" if you had the planning of it. …

This is the most glorious day I have had since I have been over here, I believe. Emo came out from Paris and I had made all the arrangements to go to the chasse. Really, you simply must see it: lovely forest with good roads and shoals of by-paths where the whining dogs just darted as soon as they were released. The horses were polished by the grooms to the highest possible degree of perfection while they waited for masters and mistresses to arrive in automobiles. They were Lords and Ladies "Somebody," as the chasse was private and we really could not have seen it had it not been for the kindness of a gentleman whom I asked regarding the rendezvous. There were many others there in carriages whom I imagine were not invited guests, so we felt at ease. And the coachman was most amiable and we learned all about a chasse from start to finish. From before twelve o'clock until dark, four thirty, we were chasing from one part of the forest to the other.

Emo took the train back to Paris this morning and now I am all alone again.

I think I will go back Tuesday morning in time for Madame's lecture in the afternoon. I am like a warhorse pawing the earth—I can't wait to get back into the fray.

Your letter of December 5th arrived letting me know that you are still eager to keep our original plan, which was just what I wanted to know. I have dispatched a letter to Mrs. Fogo asking her outright if she will take me under her wing, and I hope to hear the end of the week. I am thinking no matter how short a time you can spend over here you will have a glimpse which will refresh your very soul for the rest of your life.

I am eager to know the result of the contest. Chicago is taking everything before it, according to the December bulletin you sent. But all that is over by the time you read this. Good night from Fontainebleau, more from Paree, gay Paree! This is rather a hilarious finale.

Heaps of Love,
Alice

Alice returned to the Villa Copernic and fell headlong into Christmas preparations, parties and rigorous rehearsals.

Evening mail on the twentieth of December brought the long-awaited invitation from Aunt Annie Fogo. Alice, who had just come in from a rehearsal, cried tears of happiness and threw her the hat in the air, to the hilarity of the guests in the pension sitting room. Early the next morning, she sent Jerry a long cable of arrival and departure possibilities.

On the twenty-second, Jerry cabled back that he could leave around the tenth of January.

On the twenty-third Alice wrote him that her "afternoon" recital was Tuesday, January ninth and that the following performance in London would put her in Rothbury by the eighteenth. By February fifth she would be ready to be married, and sent a confirming cable.

On December thirty-first at eleven thirty p.m., Jerry closed the contest and sent a cable to Alice with the news that Chicago had taken a first, winning over New York City.

New Year's Eve, Alice was celebrating with Mildred and Emo, arriving back at one a.m. to a late supper with all the pension guests. A Chinese revolutionary prince in the diplomatic service, whose perfect English and good humor kept them in stitches, an Armenian lady, her son and an Austrian gentleman raised a toast to Alice, wishing her *beaucoup de bonheur*.

Chapter 27

The Recital

Musical Courier, January, 1912

Alice Hicks has a voice of strikingly beautiful tone and sweetness, and she uses it well and with much sympathy and intelligence.

January 10
Rue Copernic
My Darling Jerry:
Here I am at last alone in my room, munching chocolates which Mme. Chalamel just brought in to me, and altogether I feel as though "yesterday never was." Last night I wanted to write you and record the great day's events, but I simply could not hold my head up. It is really no joke giving a long program, and on account of the frightful rain, Mr. Gordon Yates did not arrive until late, which necessitated my singing my two first groups with very little intermission.

The wonderful finishing touch was when Madame told me the whole recital had gone off better than any she had ever helped a pupil give—my eyes fairly popped. I thoroughly enjoyed the newspaper reporters and indulged in giving them all the information they wanted, even to the make of my gown, which occasioned a little comment.

Madame was a perfect wonder. I met everybody. There were many of her old friends there and some from London. M. Yates sang awfully well. He has a full rich baritone, and is from the Queens Theatre in London. Mrs. McArthur I had met before, and she played. She is president of the Thursday Musical Club in New York, and a charming woman. Mr. McArthur said he could understand my Italian so I just felt that happy, Jerry.

And now the wonderful thing to look forward to is your coming. Everything seems overwhelmingly lovely these days. Today I got my ticket to Rothbury, going to London by Dieppe and New Haven. That is the longest channel crossing but the train leaves at the best time for me, 10:15 a.m. And I will be in London in time for dinner at seven. I am writing ahead to the Hotel Balmoral where Emo and her aunt were all summer, and she assures me it is a place I can go alone and with perfect comfort.

It seems as if one long dream with many "vicissitudes" is to come true at last. I will imagine you on your voyage and send letters to the Savoy for your arrival. My dear Jerry, au revoir and bon voyage.

Your loving Alice

Chapter 28

Marry Me

Mrs. Ridley-Scott had been a most gracious hostess. The At-Home concert in London had gone smoothly, and the hotel turned out to be as comfortable as Emo promised. A leap of faith, these critical three weeks of establishing residency. Would Jerry's crossing meet with heaving seas and untimely delays? Would Aunt Fogo be kind or cool? Her letters *seemed* friendly enough. Would the rules of foreign marriage suddenly change without notice and foil their plans?

Alice boarded the *Edinburgh Express* to Newcastle from Kings Cross Station at ten a.m. For three restless hours she tried to relax, flipping through her newly purchased posh magazines, pacing the corridor outside her first-class compartment. When the dining car opened, she was the first to appear.

A young couple joined her. They were on their honeymoon, they said. The distraction and animated discussion of their shared newlywed plans got Alice through the next hour. Reluctantly, she parted from the glowing couple to return to her seat, suffering through the next several hours. The air was suffused with scents of damp wool and unwashed bodies overlaid with perfume. Coal smoke from the engine worked its smell through the closed windows, mixing with oven fumes from the dining car, carrying the odor of baked onions. By three thirty, when the train pulled in, Alice was frantic to get off.

Cold, wet weather greeted her as the conductor handed her down to the station platform. Alice gasped, "Thank you," as the northern English winter caught at her feet and legs, seeping through the layers of wool stockings, petticoat, skirt and coat. She pulled her collar up tightly, hugging her furs to neck and chin, and dashed to the waiting room.

Alice approached a blue-uniformed ticket master behind his cage and inquired, "Can you tell me if there is a tea room nearby, and—oh, yes, the Anglican Church. Is it within walking distance?"

"Aye, lass," he replied. Alice saw him look her up and down as if to take the measure of her height as well as her station in life. "Nice tea 'n biscuits just there." He lifted his whiskered chin toward the signed door across the room. "Tha chorch is a different matter altogether."

"Yes, I see," said Alice, noting and rejecting the rather seedy establishment. "I rather need to stretch after the long ride. I thought a walk would do me good, before I catch the next train."

"Aye, mevvies ya hev yornin for a swank place," the ticket master replied, "just roond the reet three block, forst door. Ye go nee but one maire street doon fur ya chorch, canna miss it, verra large, the chorch. Mind tha step in case o' ice."

Alice kept the grin off her face until she was out the door. The "Geordies" had such a delightful brogue. She might just work it into a Northumberland ballad later.

In spite of the cold, it was refreshing to walk. And who could resist this opportunity to window shop? What Rothbury might hold was still a mystery, nothing likely at all between here and the Scottish border. Frilly curtains barely visible through steamed-up bow windows announced that she had found the tearoom. She was escorted to a table far from the door. The taste of good black tea warmed her inside and out. It was laced with cream and sugar, and served with tiny cucumber and butter sandwiches on brown bread, as well as sugary cakes spread with raspberry preserves.

Braving the winter weather again, Alice walked the few blocks to the Anglican Church. She knelt in a pew near the front and sent up a prayer that all would come beautifully these next three weeks. Sacred music from the practicing organist reverberated with treble arpeggios rolling toward her from the huge organ pipes. With a heart full of joyful thanks, she sent a prayer to her mother. This tenuous connection to Aunt Fogo was possible because of her. Alice asked that her mother would forgive her for this far away marriage. And then she walked back to the station, ready to face this one last train trip without her beloved Jerry.

It was as she boarded the Rothbury train that she hatched a plot to surprise Jerry by meeting him at this station in Newcastle at this very time, three weeks from now. How delicious, she thought, to see him alight after this long, long time. She would fly into his arms and feel his heartbeat and his kisses. Just the thought of him warmed her in places never reached by the tea and cakes.

***

Aunt Annie Fogo, dressed in black and wrapped against the falling snow, was standing under a light on the platform. Alice had spotted the elderly woman moving out from the waiting room to the huffing train.

"You look like your mother, dear Alice," were Aunt Fogo's first words.

Alice took her aunt's proffered hand, surprised by the strong grip. They must be made of sturdy stuff, she thought, to survive in this northerly climate.

"How happy I am to finally meet you, Aunt Fogo. My dear mother asked to be remembered."

With that, Aunt Fogo took Alice's arm and walked to her closed carriage. The porter brought one small trunk and strapped it in place. The remaining pile of trunks and boxes had been stored in London for her return.

Aunt Fogo and Alice chatted pleasantly during the ride beyond town to the farmhouse she called Summerville. Aunt Fogo chuckled as she mentioned the name of her little house, especially in this season. But she assured Alice that in the summer the place was a blaze of heat and color. Alice could only take the statement on faith. The home welcomed them with warmth and light. The guests, Aunt Fogo's friend Mrs. Lamb and her niece Viola, both from Oxford, were waiting for Alice to arrive so they could all have their supper together.

During the three weeks of establishing residence, Alice and Viola became friends, accompanying Mrs. Fogo and Mrs. Lamb on neighborly visits. Sometimes they met at the tearoom on Bridge Street, walking afterwards across the medieval bridge just to hear the rushing of the River Coquet under the ice. High Street's dark stone buildings boasted a well-stocked bookseller, greengrocer and stationer, where Alice and Viola occasionally did the shopping.

And, of course, there were several appointments to keep with the rector of All Saints Church. She arranged the simple morning marriage service and some sacred music for the choir. An ancient Saxon stone cross stood sentinel at the door. Alice could not resist touching it as she passed in and out. Except for that artifact of early Christianity, it was all so familiar, just like the parish church in Mitchell, where she'd grown up. And nothing at all like the elaborate social event in Los Angeles that might have been, were it not for Norah.

***

Jerry left Chicago for New York on January twentieth. On the twenty-fourth, he sailed for Southampton, England on the White Star Line's *R. M. S. Olympic*. A large pile of mail from Alice waited in his stateroom. As soon as the ship left port, he went directly to his room, lit a cigar and saturated himself in her news. God, he did miss her.

During the voyage Jerry played the role of chaste bachelor, escorting the ladies on their constitutionals, sitting at dinner each night to entertain the other guests with the romantic wedding adventure that awaited him. "Miss Hicks," he said, rolling out the prepared tale, "told me in no uncertain terms that if she was worth having, she was worth coming after. So, here I am." That it was patently untrue was irrelevant. The statement painted a romantically humorous story—which was entirely the point. The other men, some single, some not, teased him unmercifully about his impeccable behavior, apparently considering the entire voyage one long bachelor party. With no little admiration, the group awarded him a humorous "Certificate of Exemplary Conduct" as assurance to his bride.

Jerry had his picture taken on deck with two of the ladies in question. They stood unsmiling, bundled against the cold wind, their backs to the lifeboats, Jerry with a scarf tied comically over his hat. The shot provided the intended deadpan humor for his onboard audience, and, he hoped, a certain broad smile from his beloved Alice later. He had the photo developed on board and tucked it away with the award for a future interlude.

103

The *Olympic* docked at Southampton on the thirty-first. Impatiently, Jerry milled about with the other passengers while luggage was disgorged from the hold and sorted out on dry land. After a further delay for the customs inspection, he was on the train for London.

He stayed the night at the Savoy. The next morning, he visited Regent Street to purchase a single stone diamond ring, and then he returned to the hotel to bide his time with sightseeing.

Alice had written strict instructions in her letter to him mailed from Rothbury just three days ago. He followed them precisely, catching the ten a.m. train from King's Cross Station.

Be sure and get a first-class ticket. Altho' only "Dukes" and Americans ride first over here, you will see the justice of it later on. ...During your wait in Newcastle I am going to ask you to do something for me. While I was there I wandered around to a cathedral just at the right of the station—St. Nicholas, I think it was called—and gleaned a great deal of information from the verger about the wonderful organ and organist. There is no one here who can play the organ well, and I cannot imagine our quiet ceremony in the little church without some music. Will you go and ask and find out if the organist would come to Rothbury?

Jerry arrived in Newcastle at three thirty. He climbed down to the platform, intent on the letter clutched in his gloved hand. Someone tapped on his shoulder. Puzzled, Jerry turned to see who in the blazes it might be. Alice stood before him, tall and graceful, just as he had seen her almost a year ago—well, minus furs.

"I've changed my mind," she said. "The music in Rothbury will do very well."

Her gray eyes brimmed with tears and a smile blossomed across her face. She drew her hands from her muff and grasped him around his neck. In that instant she was in his enveloping arms.

Alice, stunned into silence by her longing, sensed Jerry's own struggle for words. She simply clung onto his arm to keep him close. Jerry managed a few instructions to the porter about his small suitcase's transfer to the Rothbury train. Then, arm-in-arm, they walked through the waiting room and into town to the tearoom Alice had visited three weeks before.

"You look divine." Jerry gazed into her eyes, drinking in all her features.

"You are handsome as ever, my Jerry." She smiled. "After all the years of letters, here we are."

Conversation over tea was about nothing. The sound of their voices, the physical closeness of their bodies, were miracles to be savored. Smiling, being, touching was all.

Alice and Jerry boarded the five forty-five for Rothbury, sitting tight against each other, which was as much as etiquette would allow. He checked into the elegant County Hotel which sat with its back to the Coquet River and its front in town. Aunt Annie Fogo joined them for supper. Jerry was only required to be in residence for twenty-four hours, and he had timed it to the minute.

On February 5, 1912, Alice Cuthbertson Hicks, age twenty-four and Irwin Johnston Muma, age thirty-five, were married without fuss at the Parish Church of England. The Reverend Charles Edward Blackett Ord performed the brief service. Aunt Annie Fogo and Violet Lamb witnessed the ceremony. After a small but gracious wedding breakfast at the County Hotel, as much celebrating as Mrs. Fogo's Scotch Presbyterian upbringing permitted, the newlyweds boarded a southbound train to Morpeth. There, they changed to the London Express and hung an "occupied" sign on their first-class compartment.

During the long ride south, Jerry wooed Alice gently, calming her nerves and banking the fires of their desire. They arrived in London and checked into the Savoy.

Jerry tipped the bellboy, closed the door himself and turned the lock. Electricity shot through them both, released at last from its firm tamping down. The trolley of flowers, champagne and delicacies Jerry had arranged for was ignored.

No awkward moment followed the removal of their hats and coats. He pulled her close for a kiss. Alice reached up and took the pins from her hair. And they walked into the bedroom that finally was theirs to share.

Alice and Jerry remained at the Savoy until February eighteenth. They planned nothing except what each day might bring. They did not travel to Paris, for Alice would share him with no one. Instead they traveled to Nice and wandered the Riviera until the twenty-eighth. Foregoing the usual formal wedding portrait, they had each other's studio photograph taken wearing the haute couture Americans were crazy for in France. Jerry sported a bowler hat and dark English walking suit, hands propped on a black lacquered walking stick. A black wool overcoat was draped elegantly over one arm. Alice was fitted into a green and blue shot silk suit, with buttons decorating her sleeve from cuff to elbow, a white lace jabot falling gracefully from her neck. A puffy tam o'shanter sat at a jaunty angle on her head, accented with a Scottish thistle. Alice mailed the photos as postcards to her brother George in California, and on the back recorded the colorful details.

***

"Chicagoan Coming with Bride:
Irvin J. Muma Weds in Scotland After Romantic Courtship"
Special to the *Chicago Daily News*
New York, March 13—Irwin J. Muma, Chicago representative of an eastern accident insurance company, with offices in the American Trust building, Chicago, is en route to his home today with his bride, following their arrival last evening on the Rotterdam on the Holland America line, which

steamship had a tragedy in mid-Atlantic March 4, when a great sea smashed over her stern, causing the death of two of her crew and the injury of several other persons.

The homecoming of Mr. Muma closes a romantic courtship and marriage. After his graduation from the University of California he met Miss Alice Hicks, a coed at the same university, at a local function in Berkeley, Cal. Young Muma had been the manager of the Berkeley football team. Miss Hicks, after their meeting, went to Scotland to visit relatives and Muma to Chicago. He proposed to Miss Hicks by mail, asking her to come to Chicago for the marriage ceremony. The young woman replied that if she was worth having she was worth coming after, so Mr. Muma took train and boat last January for Scotland. The couple was married in a Scottish hamlet Feb. 5 and went to Monte Carlo and the Riviera for their honeymoon. They will live in Chicago.

The myriad of other clippings had similar stories, all of them incorrect in some detail. But it did not matter. The outcome was the same. Married to Jerry, finally and forever.

Part Two: Bride into Society Matron

1912–1917

October 18, 1912

To read on your birthday morning

Fear not, O trembling soul, thou canst not see the way of life, and what thy path shall be, but courage, God hath said, to you and and me, "I will be with thee." When all the world is kind and life is bright be glad, O soul, laughter and mirth are right Christ said, "Rejoice with all thy might, I will be with thee."

With fond love.

From Mother

Chapter 29

A Bride Ensconced

A Monologue for Gran'mere

Gran'mere, I have been imagining how you fared during the few months the two of you were snuggled into the posh Blackstone Hotel. It must have been a grand place to entertain the friends Jerry had made. There was the Beaux Arts façade to remind you of Paris and the Art Hall in the foyer to delight your eye with credible classical paintings that you understood from your visits to the Louvre.

Did you meet the wives for tea in the restaurant, and did they welcome you with the Midwestern warmth that belied winter's frigid hold? Those women who surely befriended you had been waiting months to meet Jerry Muma's fearless adventuring fiancée. Those women from the Christian Science Church, salesmen's wives, Rotarian wives—their hearts must have been captivated by you as easily as had your Theta sisters.

I can see you, Gran'mere, fighting off morning sickness sometime late in February as you swept off to the Majestic Theatre, a vaudeville venue across from the Travelers Insurance Building. Jerry would pick you up on Friday nights at the Blackstone, where you would be sitting on one of the gold Chesterfield couches in the lobby, purposefully posing under the rich brass lamplight to catch his eye. You would have taken the Monroe Street trolley and greeted your friends, chattering away as you crossed the theatre's spacious mosaic floor. It was not the opera, after all, but it would do until the fall season began. Except that you forgot to count the months, and you would miss the opera season again, but for a different reason.

Jerry moved you out to an apartment on Chestnut Street when spring came. (I know that because you saved calling cards with May dates from Millie Chessman and Emma Lovejoy, and of course Elinor Flood, who would be your close friend for a long time.) With the new apartment came a maid who would cook and clean. Jerry did promise.

That first night, baked halibut with creamed potatoes and new peas waited in the warming oven for Jerry's return. A jelly-filled sponge roll with sweetened whipped cream sat in the icebox for dessert. Candles wavered atop a damask tablecloth, and the soft breeze of evening was redolent with new earth and spring flowers. In the soft light of your first night, Gran'mere, I can feel your joy of home.

Shortly after you moved, you received a treasured letter from your father in the morning mail. This was only the second letter you had ever received from him, the first being in Rothbury just before your marriage. You tucked both carefully away in one envelope, which was where I found it.

May 12th, 1912
Rancho
My Dear Daughter Alice, Mrs. I. J. Muma,
...We are so thankful that you and yours were not on the ill-fated *Titanic*. Hoping that you and your Jerry are nicely settled in your new home, which must be a great change for you after so much sojourning.

Mother will join with me in kind love to you and Jerry, whom I hope to get better acquainted with in the future.

Your loving father
***

Gran'mere, I had a thought to share with you before I go. You were a feminist, so we were told, and you and Jerry were much impressed by Teddy Roosevelt. Events in Chicago must have inspired you, though you never said. In August, Jerry went to the National Progressive Party Convention. You could not go, of course, being very pregnant and not meant to be seen. The Presidential campaign that year was centered in your city. The Republican primary had nominated your favorite statesman for President, Theodore Roosevelt, in an effort to remove Taft. However, Taft supporters of the Republican National Committee manipulated delegate votes to award President Taft the winning 235 seats at the convention held in the city in June. Outraged Roosevelt supporters, Jerry among them, broke away and immediately formed the Progressive Party, holding their first convention in August—in Chicago.

Jerry went as a delegate, and you must have read every line in the papers and learned the gritty details from Jerry each night on his return. The headlines screamed the news that a woman, Jane Addams, whose settlement work in Chicago had made her famous, actually seconded TR's nomination. Never before had such a thing happened. There were plenty of other women delegates too, doctors, lawyers, and professors. It must have been because women's suffrage was on the ballot. A political movement was being born before your very eyes. Chicago was ahead of most of the country on this contentious argument, but I would imagine that you would have given it all up to be home in California.
***

In September Brother George sent you a poem about being a mother; the baby was churning and bumping. For your birthday on October 18, Jerry brought you flowers, and your mother sent you one of her spiritual gems. Were you beginning to be frightened at the prospect of having your first child so far away from family?

Perhaps sitting huge and uncomfortable for breakfast on November 16, you tried to share the fruit and scrambled eggs with Jerry, but managed only toast with a little marmalade. And dinner never came.

> *Mr. and Mrs. Irwin Johnston Muma*
> *Announce*
> *The birth of a son*
> *On Sunday, November the seventeenth*
> *One thousand nine hundred and twelve*
> *One hundred and seventy-nine East Chestnut Street*
> *Chicago*
> *John Rothbury Muma*

Aunt Annie Fogo sent the dearest white baby dress from Rothbury—a gossamer thing of no practical value and incredible beauty.

When you opened this letter from your dear friend Mildred, were you thinking fondly of your free old days and forgetting the anguish? Or perhaps you were thinking of the distance you have come. You never said.

December 9, 1912 4 Rue de Chevreuse, Paris
American Art Studio and Club
My Dear Alice,
How very glad I was to have your letter. I so miss you. Even now, when I go straying about, it seems as if you are really here and we are still struggling to climb the stairs to M. Priad's little home, or struggle into the hot, crowded Metro. But all this time you have really been living in America. I think of you in your nice apartment, and the wonderful thing that has happened—I can hardly realize it. ...

So glad that you have not let your singing go—and I think you are a perfect wonder to sing when you have so many other things to think about. What an education it must be to start housekeeping! How could you manage a maid where you weren't an expert yourself?—It must be fun, only one would have to have a very strong sense of humor. ...

Much love and a very Merry Christmas to both of you,
Mildred

***

Gran'mere, when I concentrate, I see you sitting with John Rothbury looking out at the snow piling up. You are barely recovered from the birth and have a maid and baby nurse to do your bidding. In two weeks you will stuff yourself as best as you can into your clothes and celebrate Christmas. Perhaps you might even sing during an evening at the club. But, you would still be here

110

in Chicago—not back in LA with dear Mother and Father, George, the babies, and sharp-tongued sister Kate.

Merry Christmas, Gran'mere.

Chapter 30

It Wasn't the Weather, so Much as Jerry Gone-1913

"I had just opened my mail, Alice, first thing, you know. And there's the letter from Travelers Headquarters. Thought it was the news we were waiting for, but no. They turned down my request for transfer back to Los Angeles. Damned sons of—"

"Jerry, shush!"

"The whole lot, Alice, the whole, stupid, thickheaded lot! I just walked out and headed for the Athletic Club."

"I could have guessed," said Alice. "Whew, this jacket simply reeks of cigar smoke. I can just see you seething, smoking, and seething some more."

"Well, I spent the rest of the day closeted in that small conference room, the one with the private phone line."

"You, *and* your cigars," Alice surmised, reaching out her long fingers to caress the dark shadow of his whiskers, shaved clean over twelve hours ago. "Did you call Arthur in San Francisco?"

Jerry pushed his heavy black hair back off his face, then put his elbows back down on the damask dining cloth. "I did not. Old friend he may be, but I didn't want anyone in Travelers to know what I was cooking up until the deed was done. I spent the time on the phone, long-distance. That's going to be quite a February bill from the club, so don't fret—just pay it. Well worth the expense." He stood and paced from the kitchen back to Alice. "Argued first with Travelers Headquarters in Hartford, then called Hartford again, but this time to Aetna." He loosened the top button of his shirt and removed the collar, looking instantly more relaxed.

"You are maddening, Jerry. Tell me. What happened? Are we going back?"

Jerry grabbed her hand and kissed the palm. "Yes, dearest. I have been given the go-ahead to find an office while they work up the contract. Not a word to a soul, understand? This gets out and Travelers will make it a hard go."

***

"No more moving when we get home," Alice insisted later that week, sitting on the bed in her kimono and handing over Jerry's underwear for him to pack. "It's exhausting, an upheaval with all the baby paraphernalia. Please, dear, find us a real house with a long lease."

They had had this conversation before—mostly Alice talking and Jerry nodding—when their lease had expired soon after John Rothbury's first Christmas. They moved to another apartment further north outside Chicago and closer to the Evanston Golf Club, which Jerry planned to be using this spring. It was to no avail, as they would not be here.

***

Jerry traveled east first to the Aetna home office in Hartford, Connecticut to sign the contract for his new job and then straight west to Los Angeles to organize the new office and find a house.

March 14th, 1913
The *California Limited Santé Fe*, enroute
My Darling Alice,
Everything going right. I know you and that dear boy are happy. He is a joy and a blessing.
My very best love to you both.

Ensuing weeks brought news that Jerry had negotiated his 35 percent commissions on most health insurance policies, an annual $18,000 travel expense allotment, and a March 15 starting date. He wrote her anxious letters at two in the morning, almost overwhelmed by his frantic days. Alice struggled to stay positive for him, lonely as she was for his presence.

Sudden lettergrams would fly from Alice to the Hotel Alexandra where Jerry was holed up, sending bursts of perturbation at his inability to find just the right house, and then following hours later with apologies at her lack of sympathy for his plight. It felt like the old days of their long-distance courtship, the dark ones of delay and indecision.

Anxiety crowded under Alice's ribs like some demon being. Snow the previous week turned to a drenching cold rain, and then last night, a tornado swept down the street. She huddled away from the windows with John Rothbury, trembling in fear of being blown out of bed and into the weather, hearing the crashing of trees, ripping roof tiles, and fire engines screaming down Sheridan Road. All that time, the baby slept.

Alice now sat watching the gray dawn appear through rivulets of rainwater running down the window, her eyes streaming tears. Her father's other letter lay in her lap. She pulled it from the ribbon-tied piles, those masses of correspondence saved, starting from the day she had said yes to Jerry.

January, 1912
My Dear Daughter Alice,

No doubt you are surprised to get a few lines from one who hates to write letters, but I thought it my duty to do so as your time is short as a "Miss." Mother and I are so delighted to know that you are going to be married at Mrs. Fogo's, where we enjoyed ourselves so much. I am sorry we could not be present at the ceremony, but will be with you in spirit. … Good-bye dear daughter for the present, with love and kisses over again.

Your loving father

So much had transpired since that unconventional marriage last year: the magical honeymoon—surely it was a near thing not to have conceived this little handsome mite of hers in the train down to London—the return to Chicago, and the mad race to envelop all of the friends Jerry had made for them.

Alice was not prepared for the swift, blinding pain that incapacitated her on Saturday morning. She managed only to call her C. S. practitioner before the headache took over her ability to function. Within the hour, a C. S. nurse, followed by Elinor, had Alice tucked into bed and the baby safe. She slept away Sunday in her darkly curtained room, cradled within the love of Science. The Practitioner prayed with Elinor, and then with Alice when she woke. Monday morning, the headache was gone and the anxiety pushed far back into her unconscious.

Alice busied herself with the occasional concert, church and parties with John Rothbury in tow or safely tucked in at home with the maid. Jerry wrote encouraging details as his new job took shape. His correspondence now came proudly on new letterhead: *Aetna Life Insurance Company, Irwin J. Muma, Manager Life and Accident Department, 534-537 Security Bldg., Los Angeles.* But Alice knew, when her hair started to fall out, that she was not going to hold on much longer. She thought perhaps it was too trivial a matter to bring to her C. S. practitioner. But when every hair on her head looked to be in jeopardy, she reached out to Science, and sure enough, her deep brown mane returned. Just in case, she started a special raw egg wrap that was thought to be good for the scalp, and determined to depart for California whether Jerry was ready or not.

***

The doorbell rang and the maid ran to answer.

"Mrs. Muma," whispered the maid, making her way from kitchen to sitting room in an effort not to wake John Rothbury. "That was Western Union; you have a telegram. I asked him to wait in case of reply."

Alice's head was wrapped in the egg yolk treatment. She looked up from writing a letter to Jerry, having decided to leave for Berkeley next week and then spend a few days with the Thetas while waiting for him to rent them their new house. She had wondered to Jerry how much to pay their maid, who knew they were departing eventually, but not when.

114

"Thank you, Florence," she replied, noticing her maid's anxious smile. The woman seemed to guess that her services were about to be terminated.

Alice sliced the envelope with her letter opener and yanked the paper out.

LEASE SIGNED APRIL 14 FURNISHED HOUSE 976 ELDEN AVE 6 MO STOP COME HOME LOVE JERRY

"Oh, Florence, we have a house!" Alice flew up, knocking her head wrap askew. "Please tell him there will be a reply. Here is a tip to encourage his waiting." Alice saw the worried look on Florence's face and reached over to hug her. "I'm sorry this is so sudden."

PACKING UP IMMEDIATELY STOP WILL SPEND 3 DAYS IN BERKELEY SHOWING OFF JOHN ROTHBURY THEN DOWN TO YOU STOP WILL PHONE TONIGHT LOVE ALICE

Alice ran to the bathroom to wash out her hair, flinging her kimono off on her way. She showered but her hair was too wet for a trip to town, so she had Florence prepare a quick luncheon for the three of them. The day was glorious, as mid-April had brought spring in with a blinding light and a fresh scent of green. The maid would take John Rothbury to the park while she began to pack. She called the nearest photographer to arrange for a formal shot of herself with John. She would surely need to leave many a picture behind in Berkeley to remind them of her visit.

With Elinor and Jim Flood, Florence saw Alice and John off on the *Overland* at Union Station on the morning of April 20. Alice had sent several trunks ahead to the Los Angeles address and one to San Francisco. A single suitcase with necessities had already been stowed in their overnight compartment. She had six-month-old John firmly in her arms and waved goodbye as the train gently tugged them out of the station, blowing steam and black smoke.

She gazed through her window at the endless plains of Iowa and Nebraska, which were ready for early spring planting. Flat eastern Colorado raced by, and soon she felt the uphill drag into the snowy passes of the Rockies. When the conductor announced they had crossed the Continental Divide, Alice felt California pulling her home.

For three nights, unable to sleep for the growing anticipation, she curled up in her pajamas, long hair braided down her back, to watch for the fugitive moon popping out between black mountain silhouettes. Each day she sat in the club car soaking in the passengers' praise for John Rothbury. They could not resist touching his already-darkening blond hair. In Sacramento she changed trains for the southbound journey to Oakland, and thought of the gay summer times with Peggy in Marysville. Sadly, Peggy would not be at Berkeley to share her joy at being back. Nor would Mildred Ahlf have returned from Paris. Nonetheless, there would still be friends enough to greet.

***

Arthur Holman, Jerry's Travelers counterpart in San Francisco and fellow Rotarian, picked Alice and John up at the station and insisted on their coming to stay with him and his wife for the week. After suitable comments on how much John Rothbury looked like his daddy, he broached the subject of Jerry's defection to Aetna.

"Well, you surely surprised us all out here, Alice, when the news of Jerry's resignation came over the mountains."

"No one more than myself, Arthur," Alice lied.

"I thought Chicago was a position of great prestige and opportunity."

"Certainly it was, Arthur, but you know Jerry has a love of California and a taste of what great Western cities are so hungry for."

"Right you are. I have known Jerry since the turn of the century, and he is content only with the whir of our metropolis. Did you know that he started out with Aetna right out of college?"

"Why, no, Arthur. Tell me." Alice deftly turned the conversation away from Jerry's defection. It would accomplish nothing to discuss the phone battles in the smoke-filled rooms.

Alice was scooped up for luncheons and endless teas by her Thetas, most of whom had been following her journey through Europe, romantic marriage, and sojourn in Chicago. As her departure to Los Angeles loomed, she was commanded to give a toast during one such gathering. She felt all eyes on her, and she glowed in the knowledge that she looked perfect. The new blue suit molded her upper body, and the jacket's wide lapels showed off the white shirtwaist and the pearl drops in her ears. The jaunty, small-brimmed hat was accented with a navy bow at the back and set off her rich, brown hair. There was her beautiful son John at the front table, his eyes riveted on her, secure in the arms of Ruth Englis, a Theta from her school days.

She stood and faced the room of young women, her eyes bright and lips parted in a smile.

"I am an ex class of 1913 and purposely avoid meeting the gaze of any of you, for I know your shocked expressions. So this, you say, is a specimen of the loyal Theta we long for to uphold the honor of Thetadom. But let my fate be summed thusly. That the matrimonial snare was so well plotted and laid for me that I fell victim, and forsook my comrades and the path of learning. So with the coming of May 1913, I am graduating with honors other than academic."

She went on to give the history of the Thetas, pointing out how fortunate those young women were who could shelter in the chapter house designed and executed by one of their own, architect Julia Morgan.

116

"I hope many of us will meet at the June twentieth Biennial Grand Convention."

Thunderous applause celebrated the end of her toast and her visit.

***

Jerry could not spare the time to come and get Alice, nor did she expect it, though Arthur grumbled at the lost opportunity to grill his friend. She left from the Oakland station on the southbound train for Los Angeles. John, used to being sorted out here and there, was lulled again by the soft clacking of the train during much of the overnight ride. Alice hopped out during the long stop in Santa Barbara to show her little son the Mission-style beauty she had longed to see.

She tasted the ocean on the wind as they moved past San Luis Obispo, then smelled the forest heat of the San Gabriel Mountains and earthy San Fernando Valley. The stench of raw fuel in the air preceded a preposterous view of oil derricks situated helter-skelter among Los Angeles homes.

There on the platform to greet her was darling Jerry and her dear parents, George, his wife Annie, and little Helen and Aileen. Her breath stuck in her throat and her eyes were rimmed with tears.

She was home.

Chapter 31

The Promise of Home Begins, 1914

It was 7:30 on a dry July evening as Jerry left his office in the Security Building. Adjusting his hat to block the sun's westerly glare, he threaded through the multitude of black automobiles parked at the curb, grabbed the rail of a pausing electric trolley and vaulted up. The heat of the day was softening, the breeze welcome. He watched the mass of drivers teeming toward the suburbs, to homes on large, landscaped lots with deeds restricted to white American families, who waited for supper prepared by Negro servants. Jerry was comfortable with the segregation and lifestyle, seeing it only in terms of the increase in insurance policies one might secure with each additional automobile and house lot. If he was bothered about anything, it was that he himself was not yet driving one of those cars. Not yet, but soon.

He was late coming home but hadn't meant to be. Alice would forgive it; he had called to let her know. She would be sitting up reading, her feet propped on a poof to keep her ankles from swelling, a pillow behind her lower back to relieve the ache of the coming baby. Little Johnny would be tucked into bed after his nightly fairytale, exhausted from a day of running everywhere and charming everyone.

He let himself in, plunking his briefcase down in the den on his way to the living room. Alice looked up and smiled a welcome, shifting forward to greet him.

"Sorry to be late, my dear," he said. "I don't mean to be so, especially now." He leaned down and planted a kiss on her lips, and felt it returned.

"How are you feeling tonight? A little weary?" Jerry took her face in his hands, and saw tiredness written there. He moved his hand gently to her large belly, and the baby kicked.

Alice winced. "That's what I get for changing positions. I'm fine, really. The nursery is almost set up. Are you ready to be thrown out of the den?"

"I will not be king in my own castle much longer, I see. But, I do need a corner of the table in there. I have some work to do after you go to bed." He watched Alice pull a face. "Just a bit, Alice dear—don't look so forlorn."

"It's all right. I was just missing you all day, reminiscing about our move here. John Rothbury was so little. Now we are bursting at the seams."

It had taken just a week for Alice to appreciate the lovely home. Bless Jerry for finding a house with room enough for a piano. To the left of the living room stood a small den with a stone fireplace, the grate stacked and ready to receive fire. This den would now become the new nursery.

***

"The maid has left some cold lamb in the icebox, and a little salad on the kitchen counter," said Alice as she hefted herself from her chair. "Looks less than appetizing. Have the coconut cake instead," she teased. "I'll keep you company."

Alice opened the icebox to retrieve the lamb. Jerry carved a few slices deftly off the bone and laid them on the dinner plate. He scooped some mint jelly onto one side, grabbed the plate of salad and carried it into the dining room.

"God, I'm hungry," said Jerry between bites. "Where'd this mint jelly come from?"

"Anne brought it from Sue when she visited us in April. You wouldn't remember. There was so much going on with the sale of Buckeye. When you're finished, let me take your plate. I'll bring us each a slice of cake. Been waiting all day for it."

Jerry laughed quietly. "All right, I'll be quick about it. You're wasting away to nothing these days!"

"Oh, pooh!" Alice lumbered off. "Two pieces of cake and a glass of milk for me."

While she was gone, Jerry mused about the sale of Buckeye Ranch, his family home.

He was happy to let this burden of his family home go. His father had settled the land, chosen for its proximity to his mother's kin, way back in the 1860s. They had all worked hard in times past, with the dairying and the orchards. Jerry had spent his younger years there, but had left for Oakland to go to high school and had never really been back. His sisters Anne and Sue had stayed. He visited from time to time, bringing Alice more recently. They all had ridden the rolling hills, following the acres of pasture that ended abruptly at the ocean. They'd bring the old buckboard loaded up with Anne and Sue and a picnic lunch, hobbling the mule under the cottonwoods.

Then his father had died, and more recently, his mother. Sue had married and moved away to Milwaukee last November, leaving Anne with the burden of Buckeye and then with illness from the hard work of it all. He had sent Anne to visit Sue to recuperate, with demands only that she rest and come back well, while he put the ranch up for sale.

In April, Anne was in good health and great spirits. He had sent her $150 for the fare on a sleeper and for the new taffeta dress she had seen. She stopped first in Los Angeles for a few days to visit before heading back north to San Simeon and the Buckeye Ranch, ready to clean the house up for the buyers.

Jerry voiced his musings when Alice returned. "Anne seems quite content to stay on the old place and sort out the flurry of would-be buyers, now that the neighbors know we are serious about the Hearst contract. The Evans relatives came tumbling to the door for visits. First Will made an offer higher than Hearst, then Uncle John said he wanted the place, but we all knew he didn't have the money. Some Swiss company approached her, thinking to bring in a dairy herd. They backed off when she shared the ups and down of dairy farming on the place. One year of drought will kill the herd, as we learned often enough growing up."

Alice smiled in agreement and downed the last of her milk. "She's quite smart, your sister. Lucky to have her sorting things out. Wasn't it nice that the old hired hand Rob made a fine garden for her to come home to?"

"And I am grateful to Mrs. Leggett, too, for agreeing to come back to help with the housework." Jerry paused and changed direction. "Phoebe Hearst has been after the Evans cousins to sell to her, you know. In the end she'll get it all."

"Mrs. Hearst's a canny one. George has been dead for over twenty years, and she manipulates the fortune with great skill. Remember all the buildings she endowed at UC Berkeley? But, my goodness, how many acres do they need? Her son inherited 30,000 acres, the whole Piedras Blancas Ranch."

Jerry nodded in agreement while forking the last of the cake into his mouth. "Rumor has it that her son wants to build himself a California castle on the hilltop to hold his warehouse of European furnishings. Right now all he can do is camp at the bottom."

"And, how about this?" added Alice with a tidbit gleaned from a sorority sister. "Rumor has it from the Thetas that our own Julia Morgan will be the architect."

Jerry nodded, pleased that she had this collegial connection to all that was happening in their life together, though he had no particular thoughts on Julia Morgan one way or the other.

"Well, I'm selling to old Phoebe. The agreement is $22,500 in five installments, paid up in thirty months at six percent. Wouldn't surprise me if they were paid in full in just a few months, though." Jerry pulled a letter from his briefcase. "Anne sent a letter down to the office. It just came. I thought you would enjoy reading it."

July 27, 1914
Buckeye Ranch
My Dear Brother,
I am sorry to be so long in sending back this reply on the deeds.

It is a delicate matter indeed to bring up, Jerry, but you know the instructions say that all the money shall be paid to you for us. Your creditors or estate could rightfully claim all, and we would have to go the trouble of proving otherwise. You must fix the paper so that 1/3 of each payment is set apart upon payment into the bank for me, and I suppose Sue would want the same arrangement.

I hope you see things as I do and that I will hear from you soon.

Barney wants Hearst to pay $100 for his 32 dairy cows. They have only offered $50. He's anxious to be gone so he can set himself up someplace else. He's no farmer but not a bad dairyman. A little shiftless perhaps, but deserves that much.

Old Bob is anxious to be off, having done a nice job on the garden and orchard for me. Have you any cast off overcoat that would fit him? He is still wearing the little coat you gave him from college days. He is quite feeble now, tho' we cannot say so to him. I despair of his plan to buy a little chicken farm in Santa Cruz, for how will he manage?"

Love and best wishes,

Your sister Anne

Alice looked up after finishing the letter. "She's watching out. Good for her!"

Jerry said, "Let me have an hour on the corner of your table in the den. I promise to come to bed directly after that."

"All right, Jerry. I am so tired." Alice smiled and hugged him. "Mind the baby doesn't kick you out of bed."

Jerry watched her slow progress down the hall, tented in the light linen smock. He remembered her words, spoken after a particularly bad bout of morning sickness back in February. "This is it, my Jerry, two babies are enough for the world." She had thrown the Margaret Sanger pamphlet on the table. "I have things to do."

Jerry took his dishes to the sink where the maid would find them tomorrow and returned for his briefcase to work in the den. The round oak table with claw feet, the one promised by Alice's mother to the first girl to marry, was loaded with baby paraphernalia. Alice had draped a vibrant silk patchwork shawl over the top, and Jerry pushed it to one side and piled his papers on the polished wood. Pulling up a chair, he sat to think how he should be reacting to the chaotic world events.

The *LA Examiner* had screamed the latest headlines about war in Europe. A month ago the Austrian Archduke was assassinated. Austria declared war on Serbia; the Germans were throwing their hand in with Austria, which galvanized the French to join with the Russians and likely the British. The Germans were building a navy to rival England. And all of Europe had divided up nations in the Far East and Africa to harvest the raw materials for industrial dominance. That was likely the real reason for any war in Europe. Dominance of world markets.

Some said war was impossible. But today Jerry had received a letter from a friend at Travelers in Chicago enclosing an article from the paper, headlined in bold: *Blood Mad Monarchies Prepare Dread Sacrifice. 15 Million Facing Death!* Except for the thousands of tourists in Europe and equal numbers of Americans living in Paris, he mused, what possible repercussions could there

121

be for us? Alice had worries about her friends in Paris, and so he had kept the paper from her today. Time enough for her concern as soon as the baby was safely arrived.

No, Jerry thought, the real danger to the United States business interests was the possibility of war with Mexico, exacerbated by Germany and that damned revolutionary Pancho Villa. German arms had been smuggled in to support an illegal Mexican President, or at least not the one the United States wanted to acknowledge. President Wilson sent in troops but failed to capture the arms. Mexico saw it as invasion.

Pancho Villa and his gang—a goodly portion of his army was composed of, embarrassingly, American citizens—wandered back and forth at will between borders while supporting and then fighting the various Mexican presidents. Villa was both hero and villain, depending on the fight and the day. It was disruptive to American business down there.

American presidents had always supported the man in power to protect American interests. Now, there was growing resentment by the Mexican government at the United States draining off Mexican oil and copper profits. So, if the Germans were running interference, possibly for the sole purpose of focusing Americans on Mexico and not on Europe, President Wilson would need to pay attention. And, President Wilson was at this very moment watching his beloved wife die and perhaps not keeping his focus where it ought to be.

And then, there was the growing violence of the union movement in the mines and factories, fueled by the vicious anarchists. Would the government allow the unions to control prices of critical resources if war were declared?

***

The clock on the mantle ticked in the otherwise absolute silence of the night as Jerry read the note in front of him, then pondered a course of action with his mining partners in the New La Paz Gold Mining Company.

To: IJ Muma, Merchants National Bank Building, Los Angeles, Cal.
My Dear Irwin,

After our conversation today over the phone I am very much pleased at your interest in our case and have the following proposition.

If you and William Kitner are successful in securing a favorable decision for the New La Paz Gold Mining Company on or before 9/10/15, we will hand you certificates for 15,000 shares of capital stock of New La Paz instead of giving it to parties in Washington, DC, as we would greatly prefer having it among our personal friends here, and we feel sure that if you are successful in getting this through by that time that you will have aggregated $75,000 or more. We are confident that that stock will be worth that and more within a year from the time our plant starts to operate.

Yours very sincerely,

O. L. Grimsley
President and Gen. Mgr.

Yes, there were people in Washington.

Jerry opened the letter from Clint Miller, enclosing his deed to the Hazeltine Oil property in Kern County, grunting approval. Gathering all the papers, including the bulky legal papers for the sale of Buckeye Ranch, he packed them into his worn leather briefcase. He yawned and ambled down the hall to the bathroom, brushed his teeth, climbed into his pajamas, and crawled into bed behind Alice.

***

In early August, Jerry watched the papers report the breakout of war in Europe. Though he could not keep it from Alice, he tried to make light of the occupation of Belgium and the push toward Paris by the Germans. With luck, a breezy letter from friends Chauncy and Willis Booth in France showed that, as yet, Europe was not in turmoil. Recounting their trip to London and Paris for the International Chamber of Commerce Inaugural meeting, Chauncy wrote:

Our trip through the Normandy country was bright with crimson poppies and clean, quaint little villages with abundant crops. It was an historical meeting, with Premier M. Poincare presiding. The minister of finance gave a gay garden party and the American delegation was sent to see the northern battlefields. ...

***

Several weeks later, at 10:30 on a bright morning, their little girl was born and with the same blond curls as her brother. Jerry supposed that her hair would darken as little John's had. He didn't care. He adored her.

Jane Erskine Muma
Monday
August the twenty-fourth
Nineteen hundred and Fourteen
Mr. and Mrs. Irwin Johnston Muma
976 Elden Avenue

Alice chose the names to cement her Scottish past to the present, "Jane" for the grandmother from Edinburgh who had died before Alice was born. "Erskine" was a little more obscure, a lowlands Scottish connection brought in by some ancient Cuthbertson, no doubt, from her mother's side. George, Alice's brother, was delighted with the names and the addition to the family, and sent his regrets that he could not be there when she left her lying-in to

123

present Jane to the family. The house filled to the brim with flowers and letters from well-wishers.

And then the celebration of Jane's birth was over, and life returned to normal.

In mid-September the postman delivered Alice a letter from Bath, England from her old Theta friend, Florence Heywood, who had lived in Paris and given tours of the Louvre. Florence had fled to England to escape the awful fate of becoming trapped in occupied Paris.

My Dear Alice, the letter began, with praise for the birth of Jane and salutations to Jerry and little John. Then it turned abruptly toward the plight of the people at war.

I bid you rise and stir up to help the wretched people here—the starving women and children. We (Americans) who are at peace during these dreadful days must exert ourselves to befriend the helpless, and they are legion. As I have written the girls I want each one of you to gather together your friends and appoint yourselves chairmen, each of you to your own committee, and organize a benefit concert, dance, garden party, fair, tea, or subscription list. Each girl can select their right kind of people, generous, active, philanthropic and enthusiastic—you ought to do wonders. If a dozen Thetas will bestir themselves to help in this sad world there will be 144 people interested. These different groups ought to collect a large fund even if only a little be given here and there. And it will mean so much to the homeless and hungry of Paris. The wage earners are on fields of blood and the women can find no work to do. Really, the mind refuses to grasp it. Bestir yourselves like the clever, competent women you are and write me again.

With love,
Florence Heywood

Alice ordered a gown from Paris, a lustrous crepe satin creation with tulle embroidery and a blue belted waist. It was delivered through customs in October. She wore it for the next several years of the Great War while she, her Theta sisters and the numerous charitable ladies' organizations raised dollar after dollar for the starving people in Europe.

Chapter 32

Just Being a Wife

January 9, 1915
230 Franklin St.
Chicago, Illinois
My Dear Sylvia,

So much has happened in both our lives since those halcyon days of the European tour. How hard it is to be limited to pen and ink when there is so much I want to say, but I will pray that a sympathetic grace be lent to what I fain would say. This holiday season brought with it much more than I anticipated, but with the young lady and Sir John, I find my hands filled without anything additional. Some four or five children in the neighborhood came in for the tree and for John Rothbury and his delight was unbounded. Dear little girl Janey—four months old the day before—sat calmly looking on at the noise and laughter from her carriage.

Lest I be assailed by further interruptions I will on to the main message I would send. Oh, how I wish that you could see and know my viewpoint as an old married lady for but in a moment your difficulties would be solved. I know full well what you are passing through in settling this all-important question of your life. How I wish you could profit by my mistakes and blunders and go on to better things without falling into like pitfalls, but then it is to be remembered that no two of us travel just the same way. Many a wet pillow did I have in Paris and long before I ever thought of Paris, but then you are not the same intense nature that I am. This one thing I well remember deciding before I left for Rothbury. "I am doing right as I now see it, whatever may be in store in the years which are to come." And so that has been a comfort many times since. Right here I am seized with a longing to unburden some of the interesting, romantic and yet strange events of my life. It would fill a book!!

How odd that you should meet an Englishman. I understand the "old critters" and I find myself constantly striving to learn the American man. I am going to answer your queries just in the order you put them to me. Even if it is a question you only can finally settle, it is a comfort to talk it over. I am using utter frankness—anything else would be false modesty, for I yearn to help you see married life in a beautiful, yet sane and practical way.

The keynote of married happiness is comradeship. To have either (of you) feel a superiority of interests or liberties does not make for understanding. Whatever freedom to come and go that may be sacrificed after marriage ought to be compensated for by the joy of having someone vitally interested in what

125

concerns you and a feeling in general of being "two pitted against the world, the flesh and the devil."

After all, this feeling of freedom to come and go seldom gets us anywhere, and this thing of living is a serious business.

You know best about your official position with the A. H. Singer Company and if you would be planning to continue your connection with the same fidelity. I would think that that was your most serious problem, especially when the income of so many near and dear to you depend on the success of the firm. As far as continuing your duties along with a home of your own, it is out of the question and an unfair tax upon your strength. We can only do about one thing at a time and do that well. And as for having your mother-in-law live with you, it is the rare exception where one roof shelters successfully more than one household.

What undermines the health of so many women is ignorance. You must know what your duties are as wife and know what a husband's just and unjust demands are. I should always advise any girl to talk with her fiancé and learn if he wished children. If a topic of this kind seems too difficult to broach, remember that the mere exchanging of the marriage vows is no such miracle worker as to make it easier then. If there is not that sweet and sacred trust and confidence before marriage, there will not likely be the mutual understanding afterwards. Plan your children, talk about them and want them, and then they do not come as such little strangers. Or else set about to not have any, and there is every legitimate means to doing this.

Then one sweeping statement to be made in favor of matrimony is the attitude of society generally toward the lone woman. It is so nice to have someone so near to you to be identified with you in all your undertakings—to act as a protector, and yet how up in arms the modern woman would be to that speech. After all, the estate of matrimony is not to sit languidly and gaze into each other's eyes, but to be up and doing, glad of the opportunity and to let love be the sweetness of understanding.

My dear, dear girl, I have not written as I would. It is well-nigh impossible. Many thanks for the concert programs. Remember me to your mother.

Your loving Alice

Chapter 33

War as They Knew It

While the Great War bloodied Europe, England was still accessible to the Americans. Alice was able to stay in touch with her elderly cousin, Annie Fogo. The Rothbury cousin's handwriting was increasingly illegible due to a slight palsy of her hands. It was with difficulty, therefore, that this most recent rambling note was deciphered.

June 6th, 1915
Somerville
Rothbury, England
My Dear Alice,
I was pleased to have your last letter. John Rothbury is getting to be quite a big boy, and the wee bairn still so tiny. ...
I am afraid it is more than sad, so many men from here and also from all the colonies, giving their lives for one man's ambition. Fourteen hundred soldiers billeted in Rothbury for four months training left in April and seven hundred are here now, living in the hotels, school, etc. ... Germany could be beaten and the war come to a finish. ....
What a price butcher meat is getting. I feel for the people who cannot afford the price. ...
Give my love to your mother and father.
I am your affectionate cousin,
Annie Fogo

***

Alice's friend George Manship was a British citizen who had been called up to fight. She had met him at UC Berkeley back in 1910 when they had sung the romantic leads in her debut of *Erminie*. His gallant uniformed snapshot sat smiling out at her from the corner of her desk. It caught at her heart every time to see the photograph; friends in San Francisco had recently reported him killed.

When a letter with the return address of New York Penn Station, Army P.O. 2B appeared in the stack of her afternoon mail, she had no idea of the surprise that was about to be delivered.

29 February, 1916
My Dear Mrs. Muma,

This is just to assure you that despite rumors to the contrary I am still down below. I have heard from several people in California asking me if I was still living, as the report of my death has been published in the San Francisco papers.

Anyway, here I am. At present I am under a red blanket, tucked up in a little bed in the Red Cross Hospital in Rouen. No, I am not wounded. I just happened to be too near a big shell when it burst. It sort of picked me up and threw me against a buttress of the trench, and since then—a matter of about ten days—I have had some difficulty in breathing and have been unable to sleep.

The wonderful thing is that there is any of me left to need either breathe or sleep. I can't imagine how the flying splinters missed me, or failing that, why I was not blown to little pieces. ... The duration lasted about two seconds and I was then picked up by the concussion and thrown back; one gets up and wonders why it hasn't got me. The next thing is to dig in the hole made by the shell and find the fuse cap. I have got mine and he's quite a good souvenir.

The rest has come at quite an opportune time for we had just done three solid weeks in the front line trenches, and after three weeks of knee-deep mud and water with boots and clothes on the whole time, one is quite ready for a rest. Still, one gets along all right and it soon becomes quite natural to sleep so. As the boots are caked in mud, a sandbag is pulled over each just to spare the blanket a little, and one sleeps quite soundly. We had been under heavy shellfire for nearly the whole of the time. ... The name of our billet is the Shell House. The place is perforated all over with huge holes and leaks like a sieve.

The strangest feeling is to hear the women's voices at the hospital, belonging to the nursing sisters.

Slow tears filmed her eyes as George went on to wish her family well and to ask her to spread the word of his recuperation.

God had saved him, after all.

***

Jerry's war was of a different nature: played on the fields of profit against Native Americans and within the walls of the government. The Las Paz Mines—16,000 Arizona acres—were yielding quantities of gold, stock prices were rising, and stock shares were now being offered on the Las Paz Mine Extension. The plan all along was to separate the Colorado River Indian Tribes from that 16,000 acres, and it came to fruition at the end of 1915 when President Woodrow Wilson took the land for the United States by executive order.

The firm of Consul and Hilton secured the decision on November 19, 2015, adjusting the La Paz claim to lie outside of the reservation. The actual mapping would not begin until 1917, a mere formality, in any case, for it had no bearing on the gold extraction.

128

The property lay nine miles northeast of the old town of Eherbert and four miles east of the Colorado River, and a three-day examination showed "good values evenly distributed." The gold had come from mountain erosion. Plans were made to work the claims year-round using a good dirt road already on the property.

Jerry was made secretary of the New La Paz Gold Mining Company. He purchased his first car using 500 shares of La Paz stock for a Cole 860 touring car with a 39-horsepower engine and wire wheels.

Clearly Jerry's "friends" in Washington DC had pulled off the deal. It happened all the time.

Chapter 34

Teach Me to Drive

"Teach me to drive, Jerry. Today, right now!" The words thrilled Alice. She felt her hands wrapped tight around the steering wheel, though at this very moment she was clutching her morning tea. He had promised and promised, but first golf and then extra hours on Saturday at the office had slipped between his agreement and the fulfillment of it. Oh, she thought, the freedom of the motorcar. Why, most of her friends were already driving, flying down the road at twenty-five miles per hour.

This, however, was one of those rare Saturdays that stretched far into the night with Jerry by her side and their maid minding the children. Alice would tackle driving this morning, then luncheon at the club and tour other neighborhoods for the new, larger house required now for the growing children. And, to top it off, the band concert tonight at Westlake would be magical—a full moon. Delicious.

"Can you handle all that power, my dear?" said Jerry. His eyes teased and his lips curled up in a grin.

"Don't be silly, darling. How hard can it be? I've watched you do it a hundred times. My turn!"

Jerry looked Alice over from head to toe as she stood to carry her cup to the sink. "Smart hat, no feathers to fly in the wind. Sensible shoes. You look like a man in that tie, even with all that bosom." He reached for her and nuzzled her neck.

She replied with a slap across his backside and a coy twinkle. Grabbing her coat and bag she towed him amiably out through the kitchen porch to the garage behind the house.

Jerry stopped Alice by the rear of the car. He reached out and turned a switch near the gas cap. "First thing, make sure the gas tank lever is on. I turn it off when I park for the day. Now, hop in."

"I remember what you do next," remarked Alice after plunking herself in the driver's seat. "Leave the choke lever on the steering wheel just as it is. Now, turn on the air pressure and prime it to 1.5 psi—see, I know what that gauge is for."

"So, what does psi mean, Alice?"

"I haven't the slightest, but I do know you need air pressure in the gas tank or something." Alice turned back to concentrate on the task, talking out loud to herself. "Now, turn the key in the ignition one full turn, put my left foot on the clutch, check I am in neutral with the handbrake on, and push the starter, that round button above the brake pedal, with my right foot."

The eight-cylinder engine turned over with a rumble and settled into a purr.

Backing out of the garage was a different thing altogether.

"Remember that reverse is over to your left and down," prompted Jerry. He placed his hand over hers and guided the lever that rose from the floorboards between the front seats. "Good, you kept the clutch down. Now gently let the clutch out and give it just a little gas."

The Cole lurched and stalled more than once, but Alice did manage to back out without denting the fender on the garage door. Jerry could not help but smile. Alice scowled in response, but finally laughed out loud in embarrassed relief.

The motorcar bucked and stalled along its trip forward, but with only one grinding of gears, Alice found her way out of the drive. She turned the Cole right onto Elden Avenue's tree-lined street, passing green front lawns uninterrupted by fences and graced by tasteful front gardens. Within the hour Alice gained some smoothness in her accelerations. Corners were turned at reasonable speed. Alice gleamed with pride over luncheon. House hunting was put off in lieu of another hour's lesson.

Her determination was not tempered by patience. Alice's demand for the Cole vied with Jerry's for the two weeks it took her to be comfortable behind the wheel. She begged him to take the electric trolley to work, and he gracefully agreed; she knew it made him proud to see her in command of the Cole. And, there was more, of course. Freedom to come and go as she pleased was palpable. Would Jerry have understood this? Probably not. After all, he was always free—to play golf on weekends, remain at the office, or even take off for Mexico with the chamber of commerce to explore trade.

Part Three: Socialite and Singer

1917–1925

"And what do you want to do with your voice, my dear?" asked Madame de Sales.

Chapter 35

The Seven Arts Workshop

Alice stood with eyes cast down, posing next to an elaborately carved writing desk. Her dark hair was pulled back in a bun with two ringlets, one by each ear, falling forward by her shoulders. She held a bouquet of flowers and feathers in her hands, obscuring the bodice of her dress. Her cream silk skirt, embroidered with chartreuse and grass-green beads in a lacy leaf pattern, cascaded below the bouquet to puddle gently on the floor. A light silk drape hung behind her as a backdrop.

"That's perfect," said the photographer. "You can relax while we get Mrs. Burton in place."

Alice looked up, and dropped the bouquet on the carved wooden chair behind her. Then she arranged her sheet music discreetly on the desk, away from the eye of the camera. She and Elizabeth had just finished a dress rehearsal for their upcoming performance at the Wilshire Country Club, readings from the play *Monsieur Beaucaire*, interspersed with the singing of old French ballads. The photographer was now taking the illustration for the press release.

Elizabeth walked onto the set, dressed in a dark blue satin evening coat with wide, embroidered sleeves. Her pointed slippers were just visible under the flounced dress. A small book in her hand identified her as the program's reader.

"Look out over my right shoulder," said the photographer.

Elizabeth turned her head, shifting its abundant blonde mane, and gazed at some point above the would-be audience. Behind her was a dark brocade drape.

The photographer came out from under the hood of the camera and lit the two standing candles in their wrought-iron stands, framing the shot.

"Mrs. Muma, back in your pose, please, and we'll get our pictures."

The two partners, Alice and Elizabeth, stood on either side of the desk, the light and the dark, each ready to do their part. The photographer spent ten more minutes taking the formal shots.

Alice hopped down off the set, unpinned the ringlets and grabbed her music off the table.

"We'll make arrangements with the trucking company to pick up the scenery next Wednesday, shall we?"

"The Woman's Club is expecting everything the day before our performance," responded Elizabeth. "That should work. The photographer will take the program to the printer this afternoon. He said to be at his studio by four p.m. to see the proof."

Elizabeth and Alice disappeared behind their own privacy screens to remove their costumes, and soon gowns and slippers had been replaced by light wool suits and sensible, chic pumps. The finery was hung along a pipe rack on rollers holding an array of gowns for their various performances.

***

George Manship's triumph over death had given impetus to Alice's performances during the years preceding this Woman's Club performance. Charged to civic duty by Florence's stirring cry, her soprano voice had carried the songs meant to stir hearts and open purses, singing in all her languages but German. She sang for programs at schools and the Women's University Club, and performed solos at the Christian Science Church in Santa Monica and alumnae functions in Oakland.

Something wonderful happened. By the end of the Great War she had created a unique style: a harmony of poetry, song and pantomime.

Madame de Sales, Alice's Parisian voice teacher, had fled that war-beleaguered city to relocate in New York. Alice wrote to her for advice and approbation on an initial program entitled *The Desert*, involving poems, songs and prayers of American Indians as interpreted by writers and poets.

Altho' not originally sought, this program is almost entirely a California contribution, which of course pleases me no end. This work is the only one of its kind, so far as I have been able to learn, in America. By that I mean, where one common topic is employed throughout and where costumes and scenery are used. It includes the speaking as well as the singing voice, and gesture is used only for dramatic emphasis. No attempt has been made to imitate the Indian, but merely to give an impression of the desert at large, hence the plain costumes which give splendid color effects.

Madame's returning letter of approval turned Alice's sketches and fabric swatches into completed costume design and stage set. Four performances in San Francisco at the end of January elicited this critique by *The Musical Courier*.

February 13, 1919

This is a new art form and very attractive. It might almost be called a bit of poetic fancy, like a scene from an opera. Without actually having a plot, it has all the elements of drama and depicts vividly the life of the American Desert, its atmosphere, its smells, its delightful freshness, the tragedy of its arid wastes—yet the fascination of it, the elusive charm which, it is said, always draws back to the desert anyone who has every dwelt in it. ... The interest grows from start to finish and there is a feeling of expectancy which holds the attention at all times. Mrs. Muma is to be congratulated upon the invention of a new art form, the success of which may be confidently predicted. Further

134

plans for her artistic presentation in other California cities, and possibly in the Middle West, are now under consideration.

Alice had chosen her words carefully during the interview, so the mention of the Middle West was purposeful. It gave a kind of grandeur to the piece, she thought, to think of horizons further than her backyard.. Alice, though, had no intentions of expanding beyond her borders at the moment. She had won, instead, a seasonal spot as a singer shortly after *The Desert* performances in the newly established Entertainment Course sponsored by University of California Extension Department. Ten concerts were held October through April of the following year, traveling by train and taxi, playing to crowds from Monrovia, Riverside, Santa Barbara, Ventura, Van Nuys, San Pedro and more in high schools, courthouses, women's clubs and the Sherman Indian School. She sang "The Twickenham Ferry," "I'm Wearin' Awa' Jean," and the familiar "Blue Bells of Scotland," accompanied by a woman on a richly gilded floor harp. Alice recited Shakespearean readings, then sang English folksongs with a piano accompanist. The stage props and settings, costumes and lighting all came together to packed houses and thunderous applause.

They paid her an honorarium of ten dollars per performance. The money didn't matter, for it was a glorious accomplishment. Besides, Jerry was paying the bills, and he was gone on business much of the time.

***

The Seven Arts Workshop, for which this most recent photo sitting was a fundraiser, had evolved from this last year of effort. She had formed a partnership with Elizabeth Burton. Her partner, a lecturer, artist and member of the Drama League of Los Angeles, would deliver the eloquent spoken words designed to further the "dignity of good English with clear diction," their brochure read, while Alice would provide her "charming mezzo-soprano voice, designed to please both the eye and the ear."

***

By 1921, she and Elizabeth, accompanied by other invited artists to complement the program, performed in private homes and at fundraisers for the Drama League's Committee for Foreign Relief. And so it was that for the early years of the 1920s, the coffers offered in relief of Poles or Belgians or Serbians were filled to overflowing by well-connected matrons of the arts in Los Angeles.

Chapter 36

The House on Windsor Boulevard Has an Opening Night

Alice, in the midst of her blossoming singing career, built a home. Spectacularly. The expensively purchased plot in Windsor Square would house a show piece, a statement about Alice's love for the new California architecture: the architecture of the two-story stucco, with its red tile roof and hidden gardens, captured the richness of the Mediterranean by way of Santa Barbara, with hints of the grand mansions of the California Land Grant aristocracy. By June of 1919, months before she started her UC singing tour, Alice was traveling the short distance from her old-style bungalow to watch the new house come to life on the palm-tree-lined street. Grand, open rooms on the ground floor led out to an arched covered porch. Wings on either side would provide privacy for the garden. And on the left wall, there would be a graceful wrought-iron staircase leading up to the apartment over the garage: something she envisioned with trailing pots of geraniums and vines, just as she had seen in Italy, transforming a simple stucco wall into a stage for family photos and a theatrical backdrop for the garden.

On an evening in June of 1920, the house, full of Persian carpets and well-placed Spanish carved oak pieces, was to be formally introduced to a hundred of their closest friends.

"Your tie isn't right, Jerry. Here, let me straighten it," said Alice with controlled anxiety.

"Don't fuss, I've got it." Jerry turned back to the full-length mirror in their dressing room.

They were both handsomely reflected back from the gilded wood frame. The silk of her sleeveless red-flowered gown flowed seamlessly down over her tall figure; his white tie and tails sat immaculately on his. Jerry gave the tie a twitch and it settled in place.

Alice took a long breath, held it, and let it go. It was an exercise she used to loosen her throat before a performance. This evening was indeed another performance, and she might well sing, too. Tonight was the culmination of a year of planning, this home on Windsor Boulevard into which so many guests would flow. Her ears were alert for the Zoellner Quartet tuning up in the garden and the faint rattle and chatter from the kitchen as caterers prepared to set out the sumptuous hors-d'œuvres. Artichoke canapés, tiny chili relenos, and savory cheese balls crowded the platters. A buffet table held crystal bowls of shiny gray caviar with small horn spoons for the scooping, surrounded by sieved hard-boiled egg yolks and toast points, all nestled atop shallow trays of crushed ice. A white-coated waiter would stand and serve.

"Alice," Jerry said, turning her face to his. "Remember when we finally moved the wine cellar in March?"

The corners of Alice's mouth twitched up. "Oh, yes." She knew he had spotted her nervousness and was reaching for a distraction.

"There I was on top of the wagon loaded with wine and spirits. People were packed three-deep to watch the trip north from Elden to here, over Wilshire. I finally felt compelled to wave the permit in their faces and shout, 'It's legal, all bought before Prohibition!' I tell you, Alice, I feared for my life."

Alice hugged him, her tension abated. "We'll be using much of that champagne and spirits tonight, my Jerry."

Jerry nodded in agreement. He grabbed her hand. "Let's say good night to John and Jane."

They swept down the hall to kiss the children, now camping out in Jane's front room to spy on the entering guests. The maid was with them, her room being next to Jane's. She would spend the night.

They entered to find the maid laying out the pajamas, and the children were plopped on the bed, swinging their feet and laughing uproariously as John's much-longer ones clunked on the floor while Jane's feet swung clear.

"John, don't do that!" admonished Jerry with twinkling eyes and the twitch of a smile. "The guests will think you are on a rampage up here."

"Mummy, you smell good," said Jane. "I know what it is—Chanel No. 5. You always wear that." She slid off the bed and gave her parents a hug.

"Don't tarry too long in John's room tonight, you rascals," said Jerry. He knew they would escape the clutches of the maid to gawk at the guests in the garden over which John's bedroom loomed. "But now, if you are quiet, you can stand on the balcony of the maid's room to watch the guests arrive."

"No hunkering down on the sleeping porch, either," reminded their mother. "You will never get to sleep with all the chattering in the garden. If you are good, we shall swim in the pool tomorrow."

***

Guests entered through the carved squared frame of the front entry. Some were aware of two small heads peering down from the awning-covered balcony.

"How nice of you to come." Alice repeated this to each friend and business connection who arrived. She meant it every time, escorting couples and the occasional lone male to a cluster of friendly faces particular to their interests. Light and air played through deep-set windows, creating a delicious breeze as guests meandered over wood and tile floors and through oak-beamed rooms. Many paused at the sight of the painting of the Black Madonna over the carved limestone fireplace mantel. But the overriding focus, which propelled every

137

guest into small talk this evening, was curiosity to see the Muma home—it meant being seen by the press and therefore appearing in the social column the next day, as well as being able to say to their neighbors what a charming and elegant home had been added to the houses of Windsor Square.

By ten o'clock the quartet was in full swing. Beethoven had been replaced for the moment by Alice's favorite, the Zollner's rendition in strings of two Old English songs. Guests' voices and bursts of laughter mingled with the tinkle of crystal. Waiters passed through the throng with never ending trays of tidbits and glasses of champagne. The bar under the triple arches of the garden porch did a brisk business in martinis and scotch. Above, the dark little heads of John and Jane appeared from time to time in the screened windows of the sleeping porch. Really, thought Alice as she caught a peek and wagged her finger to send them off, it was impossible to expect the children to settle down with all the racket.

Alice never stopped moving; each guest was made to feel important by a comment or gesture of affection. The same questions flowed around her as she worked her way through the crowd. "Weren't you lucky to nab the Zoellners?" "I heard their last performance at the Ebell Club in July." "Wasn't their Hayden, Dvorak and Handel exquisite?" "Isn't Joseph Zoellner's daughter so accomplished, playing violin next to her father!"

There were endlessly rewarding exclamations on the garden's rustic stone paths. Its brilliant red cannas, tall palms, and little trees all created candlelit hideaways. Those accolades provided Alice the proof she needed that the landscaper's bill had been worth the expense.

The guests left in dribbles after midnight's supper was served buffet-style in the living room. The centerpieces were several enormous whole pink salmon, donated by Jerry's fishing club, poached in wine, then jellied and garnished with colorful vegetables. At two a.m. Alice and Jerry were able to make their way upstairs and found the children tucked into their respective beds. The maid had fallen asleep at her post on the sleeping porch. They gently awakened her and pointed her to her room.

"A fine little affair, Alice," said a weary Jerry as he popped his collar off. "The children enjoyed it immensely, did you notice?"

Alice's face hurt from smiling so much. Turning so that Jerry could unzip her dress, she said, "I thought I caught a glimpse of their little heads in the sleeping porch. Don't worry, we will tease them, but still allow them to cavort in the pool during luncheon tomorrow."

Early the next morning the gardener set to work repairing the casual damage to the cannas and cleaning the fallen garden bits from the pool. Jane and John heard him whistling and shot down the back stairs to the kitchen where Hattie was cooking breakfast.

"Ah," said Hattie as she put the butter on the table, "is it the thought of a swim or could you two imps smell my scrambled eggs and toast? Pull your socks up, young John—you look a mess."

"Okay, Hattie," said John. "Please pull Jane's up. She's a mess, too."

"They won't stay up," said Jane. "Can I have more toast, please, Hattie?"

"Me, too. Please, Hattie—and could you button Jane's shoes? You should have been here last night. My, grown-ups make a lot of noise."

"Did they keep you both up? Why, I just can't imagine." Hattie leaned forward to button Jane's shoes while setting a plate of buttered toast on the table. "You two going swimming later?"

"Well," said Jane, "Mother caught us looking down last night, but father will get around her if she's mad," said Jane.

"Sure, we'll go," said John.

"Finish your breakfast and run to the front of the house and get the papers and save me some steps. Food needs organizing before my afternoon off."

"Don't go, Hattie," pleaded Jane. "Can't you stay and play with us?"

"No, pet, I can't. I have my own family to tend. But, I'll be back tomorrow."

***

It was almost noon before Alice and Jerry made their appearance. Shade had come to the back garden, and a table was laid for a light luncheon. Jerry brought out the coffee and tea, and Alice carried a pitcher of lemonade. While the children splashed in the pool, Alice thumbed through the papers for the report of the party. She was not disappointed.

A delightful affair, the *Examiner* reported. *Beautiful and artistic and altogether lovely.* Alice sipped her tea, her heart full of the grand evening and satisfactory report. Her reverie was only briefly interrupted when Jerry interjected, "I have a two o'clock tee time, Alice. Got to run."

"Goodbye, dear. Have a good time. We'll see you at the club for dinner with the children."

Chapter 37

Legs of a Journey, 1923

"I just can't go now, Alice." Jerry was pacing. The headlines of the paper screamed in bold-faced belligerence, *MUMA FACING $312,000 SUIT IN COURT.*

"Miles, the son of a b—"

"Jerry!" Alice, her face tight and heart plummeting with this news, abruptly sat down on the leather chair near Jerry's desk.

Jerry reached over and whacked the study door shut. "He told the press I gave him a tax list of rich men in LA who might need our new tax protection insurance. Preposterous. That's illegal. But of course the courts obliged him with this civil suit. I *gave* him leads; he used that list for two years. Two years, Alice! Made a pile of money for himself and the company. Great commissions. You know I reward my team for their hard work. It wasn't *his* list. It was mine, and there were still names on that list *I* wanted to pitch." He paced back and forth; face getting redder with each step across the Persian carpet. "What's in it for him, this lawsuit? That's the question."

"You have friends at the county courthouse who could ferret this out, I'm sure."

"I sure as hell *will* find out. But can't do it in time for this trip, and I can't leave without clearing up this mess."

"Well," said Alice, hoping to find something to save of this long-planned vacation, "you might get it cleared up in time to join us in Europe." She could see this was probably going nowhere. He hated being bested. She loved his ambition, and the price she paid was loneliness. He wouldn't go anywhere now if it didn't involve business. Alice sighed and stood up to walk off her own anxiety. She was realizing that her honeymoon was the last time he had traveled unless it was connected somehow with making money.

Jerry turned to look at her and continued as if she hadn't spoken. "But this other thing, this reciprocity crap. That's what this is really about. Someone wants me off the school board. Just when contracts will be handed out for that $17 million school bond. What an opportunity! I've been endorsed for reelection to the board by the United Church Brotherhood and the Citizens Committee, for God's sake. I've got a proven track record of good for the schools. People are complaining to the papers that the Citizens Committee is reactionary. What the hell is that all about? I'm a registered Democrat, for Christ's sake!"

Alice was shocked at his language, and bit her lip to stop herself from a remark that would turn his anger on her. They already had battles enough with Jerry's complete disregard for spiritual guidance. Golf on Sunday. Dismissive words in front of the children about Christian Science. What had happened over the years to cause him to reject the very thing he had introduced her to and practiced himself during their courtship?

When he got this way, she was more worried about his red face. "Just loosen your tie, dear, and tell me exactly what is happening. You're going to have a stroke." She sat back down pretending calm in an effort to calm him.

"Reciprocity, that's what this is about. Bristol, this agent I hired last year to sell insurance—he's also a school board member, and he approached this architect contact of mine and tried to sell him insurance, claiming that as manager of Aetna, I would then put the architect's name up to the school board for some of the new buildings. There is no bidding involved in this project; the school board gets to choose the architects they want.

"Now I'm being accused of reciprocity, and it looks bad. Bad for me, bad for the school board, and bad for business. No choice but to pull out of the election." Jerry lit a cigar, puffing thick spirals of smoke toward the ceiling.

Alice coughed and waved her hand in front of her face. To complain that her hair would reek of it would not help.

"Really, Jerry, such a mess. You've been good for the school board. I just hate to see you leave."

"Yeah, well, it's cutthroat, this business." He waved his cigar at Alice. "But let me tell you, this architect will never build a building in this city! Rotary will close its doors to him, and Bristol, he, and Miles will never get a recommendation from Aetna!"

Jerry slowed his pacing and finally plopped into his swivel chair behind the desk. He looked across at Alice and patted her hand, which had come to rest near the *Los Angeles Times* clippings of all the articles raging against him. "Can't go. Just get a refund for the train. Take the children yourself. It will do you good to get away. Better yet, take George's eldest girl Aileen with my ticket. Poor girl, she spends too much time on that ranch with her father." Jerry turned to the address roll on his desk and flipped to the D's. Dropping his now-dead cigar on the heavy glass ashtray, he picked up the phone.

"Bad idea," he mumbled and put the receiver back down in its cradle. "Can't let that busybody operator in on this."

"Visit Eddie tomorrow, Jerry," said Alice, who knew he was calling not city hall but the newspaper editor who was on the University Siting Committee with him. Very influential. "He'll tell you who is behind this. And, well," she added, trying to put a bright face on the mess, "perhaps you will have more time to work with him on the new LA campus." She was already resigned to taking this trip east to Mitchell to visit her aunt without him. As for sailing to England and the Continent, perhaps he would come for that, after all.

141

***

"Line up quickly," Alice commanded. "I hear the train. Father, you in the back. Now, push together. Heavens, Johnny, you are almost as tall as Aunt Sue, but still, get in the front next to Jane. Janey, dear, pull down your sleeves and your socks up, for goodness sake."

Jerry's sister, Sue, grinned beside her husband Griff, whose watch fob glittered across his dark vest. Aileen, George's half-grown girl, stood next, then Father. Anne, Jerry's other sister, came next. Then, dear Jerry, his newspaper tucked under his arm and that ratty old sweater showing beneath his jacket. Glory, would she ever get him to get rid of those awful pale-striped trousers? Her sweet Johnny, named after her father, stood with his mouth agape, and Jane was barely contained in her double-breasted sailor jacket.

What a chubby child she is, thought Alice with dismay. Not at all pretty, that round face framed by the Buster Brown haircut. While Johnny—so handsome and tall at age ten. The train rolled to a stop, a backdrop for the shot, and Alice snapped the picture. She would have it developed in Mitchell and then show it to her family there.

"All right, say your farewells and let's get our seats." Alice slipped on her gloves and put the camera in her satchel.

Their little group dissolved as the passengers flowed into the train. Jerry hugged and kissed Alice and the children and shook his father-in-law's hand. Anne and Sue followed suit. Alice saw with some amusement Johnny's panicky face at his aunts' approach and his deft maneuver of an outstretched hand—a handshake to avoid their embraces.

"He must be growing up," she said laughingly to the startled aunts. "One of these days he won't let me hug him, either." She hustled the travelers aboard, Jane and Johnny at the windows, then Aileen, Alice and her father. Departure was pandemonium: good-bye shouts, the conductor's *all aboard*, the scream of the train whistle, kisses thrown through the hissing steam. The great weight of the locomotive strained forward through the huge, man-high wheels.

Alice sat back in her seat, relaxing into the firm upholstery. She looked around at her collected family, thoughts scrambling around in her head. Was she truly happy to be heading back? It was time that John and Jane learned about *her* world in the best possible light, and then be introduced to that other larger world, England and the Continent, so much more sophisticated even than the metropolis of Los Angeles. Nothing about her poverty as a child would pass her lips, nothing mean and small. Only the best parts of her childhood in Mitchell would be woven into her own children's memories. She would stay positive, study her little Christian Science prayer book each day to find the good truth of her life, and pass it on. She was a different person from that poor country bumpkin who left Mitchell all those years ago.

The three children were chatting a mile a minute, so excited, she knew, to be on their first great adventure. Her father sat calmly, eyes half-closed toward the nap she saw overtaking him. Her mother never did get to go back to the home place, Alice mused. Gone now to Heaven, and her father diminished as a result of that death. It would likely be the last visit for him. She sighed; she missed Jerry already. Jerry. For a shocking second that awful, empty feeling in the pit of her stomach rose up from her memory, bringing with it a similar day twelve years ago, when it had been she on the platform waving just such a goodbye to Jerry in just such a milling crowd of happy excited people—he'd left her alone and moved to Chicago.

***

The family traveled north to Vancouver where George had married his beloved wife Annie, pausing there for a few days to glory in the gardens of Victoria while giving Aileen a proper visit with her grandparents. Alice reveled in the stunning gardens and remembered her feeling of abandonment when George left home to come here. It was 1903: she sixteen and he twenty-four. Nonetheless, he had been the only one of her siblings around for her. He scolded and hugged with love and no doubt some irritation; no one had understood her better. Alice had forgiven him slowly for his abandonment by taking delight in his barrage of letters, and finally, his insistence that she come with their mother to Los Angeles where he had settled into building a real estate fortune. There her life had changed forever. She was full of gratitude.

George was the reason all the Hicks family left Mitchell. Brother Will came in 1904 and went back and forth as their father needed help with the business in Canada. Alice's older sisters, both nurses, came separately just a little later: Kate, now widowed and responsible for her retarded daughter, and poor Jo, now dead. And finally, in 1909, her father came for Christmas and stayed.

***

The family departed by train from Vancouver for the three-day trip east, heading down to Seattle, then following in the path of Lewis and Clark along the border with Canada. The Cascades were swept with blue and yellow wildflowers grown lush from the snowmelt. The Rockies held them spellbound with dizzying crags, snowy caps, and huge evergreen forests. The train rode across the vast North Dakota plains and over high wooden trestles that trembled with their weight. Turning south near Mankato, Minnesota, Alice retold the story the children had heard repeatedly of Jerry's then-ten-year-old Aunt Mary's escape from the Indian Massacre in 1862. "Just your age, Johnny dear. Imagine this landscape bare of civilization back in those pioneer days." Johnny, Jane and even Aileen squinted at the land passing by their window, as if that would erase all signs of habitation.

Breaking their trip in Chicago for another several days, they took up rooms at the richly appointed Blackstone Hotel, where Alice had finished her honeymoon as she waited for a furnished flat. She propelled the children to

143

Marshall Fields and museums. Her father, Mr. Hicks, sought refuge in the riverside park during those times, but was always available to take tea with the family and Alice's numerous friends, if for nothing else than to keep his grandson company. Alice was grateful, for Johnny found it difficult to sit quietly through the nattering of adult women.

After an overnight on the train, the Plaza greeted them in New York with spacious rooms and deep bathtubs. Alice organized the luggage in all their connecting rooms and encouraged naps all around. She herself turned the tub taps on full and sank into the steaming water. One more leg on the journey to Mitchell's bittersweet memories and dear, dear faces.

Nearby Central Park provided a haven for Mr. Hicks the next day while Alice towed the children past the gardens and lawns amid rocky outcroppings to the Metropolitan Museum, and then on a healthy hike across to the Natural History Museum. Before leaving for the train, she taxied to De Pinna's for the flowered silk summer dress and jacket she had ordered weeks ago. The dress was the epitome of good taste and reeked of money, just the thing to show that, while she had left Mitchell after eighteen years of poverty, she would return an accomplished and wealthy married woman.

***

Chatting on their way toward Canada, Alice embellished her father's stories to the children, stories of his adventures as a horse dealer, with the romance of her rare trips around the county with him in their horse trap. She dug through her memories to delight them—sledding in the heavy winter snow, bonfires for warmth and light, pulling taffy, long bright summer days full of fishing in the Thames, and raspberry picking. Raspberry picking? Yes, the raspberries would be ripe before they left for England. Yes, they could go and mind the scratches, and yes, they could help make the jam.

All these things and more she had done with cousins near her own age: Muriel and Jean, Uncle Will's girls. Her cousins had often sent notes in tiny envelopes—rectangles no longer or wider than her thumb, made on heavy cream paper stock, embossed with "Dunelg," the Hicks family manse, begging her to come over and play, or saying sorry when she was sick. Ah, those notes, tucked away with the rest of her correspondence from days and decades past. Treasures, those. Alice had to acknowledge that Mur and Jean never called her poor or made snide remarks, or really, treated her any differently than if she had been a sister.

***

The Hicks family had been a large clan in the small town of Mitchell. Alice's grandfather Hicks, to her enormous pride, had founded the town around 1840, having been uprooted from Devonshire at the age of six. The colonel, as he was called, had been appointed an officer in the militia during the settlement of the Huron Tract, which lay outside Toronto and down the dirt highway upon which Mitchell was founded. He built a hotel and became the

144

postmaster. Colonel John Hicks died at fifty-nine, hugely popular and reasonably wealthy. He left his wife Elizabeth with six children, the youngest of whom was only one year old. Alice's father, who was older than Uncle Will by almost two years, was out working by that time to support their mother and siblings.

Alice had often wondered how Uncle Will had come to own the handsome late Victorian stone manse while her father, the eldest, wound up with a small house. That house, Glenview, was hardly as stately as the name implied. Seven children had been born in crowded quarters, and of them, only Bill and she had been left with their aging parents. Bill was the son to stay and help his father. It was implied that she, Alice, would be a source of comfort and help to her mother, as George had reminded her often in his letters from Canada. Well, Alice thought, it had turned out that she had indeed taken on that role, but not as a lonely spinster stuck in a small town.

***

When they all filed out of the train at Mitchell, they were greeted with enthusiastic hugs and "halloos" by grown-up cousins Jean and Mur. The elderly Mr. Hicks was helped into the carriage by Johnny and Jean, and the driver stowed the immense pile of luggage safely with the ticket agent, to be collected later that afternoon. On the short ride to the Folk Victorian mansion called Dunelg, the children chatted with excitement, asking Jean and Mur a hundred questions all at once about the various adventures planned for their month-long stay. Alice looked up the drive as they turned in from Blanchard Street to see a Dunelg smaller than she remembered. The pine trees, on the other hand, almost obliterated the view of the house from the road.

The carriage pulled halfway around the semicircular drive and stopped at the ornate entry. Alice made herself the last to enter, shepherding the children and her father ahead so that she could take her time walking up the four steps and under the porch roof; its dainty double columns supported the second floor covered balcony. The hammock strung between the columns on the right side of the porch ruined the balance of the architecture, Alice thought at once, but still, it beckoned her. The memories now jumped into her mind of Mur and Jean shouting down from the balcony, "Be down in a minute, I can't find my prayer book!" or, "Race up to our room, why don't you!" Alice fingered one of the columns, noticing that the white paint was peeling, and headed in.

Jean's room, to which she had been assigned because Jean was to move in with Mur for the duration, could have used new wallpaper. Alice couldn't resist flopping on the bed, and she smiled to realize that it was the same after all—that same soft feeling, that slight indentation where Jean had slept in the middle of the mattress all these years. Here, the three of them had told stories under the covers late at night, hiding from older brothers.

Jane interrupted Alice's reverie by flying into the room, clearly excited to explore.

145

"Mother, you ready? Let's go down."

Alice gathered Jane and Johnny in a quick hug, then all three descended to the parlor. Frail and white-haired both, Aunt Marie and Uncle Will were already deep in conversation with Alice's father. After formal introductions of the children, they were encouraged to go out and explore the grounds.

"The poor young ones have been cooped up far too long," said Aunt Marie. "Supper won't be for a few hours yet. Go work up a good appetite."

***

Alice's cousins couldn't get enough of the children, and it was no time at all before there was a gang running free on the lawns, into town, into the shallow Thames River to capture crawfish as bait, and fish. Alice's father put his thin bones down in one of the porch chairs, and except for his nightly sleep, could be found at all hours of the glorious clear daylight, deep in conversation with his brother. They had not seen each other for two years, not since Will had traveled to LA.

Alice watched Jane, Johnny and Aileen submit themselves to the moments of suspended time that early summer. In the evenings, their energy clearly abated after days on the river, picking berries, slipping into Hicks House Hotel to slide up to the long bar for a root beer, they would gather around her while she sang and played the piano or shared stories of growing up in the town founded by their great-grandfather.

"Do you remember," Jean would start, "tennis on the lawn?" and Alice would see herself in hand-me-down dresses and a borrowed racket. And so it went until Alice was begged for stories of the children and Jerry in the great city of Los Angeles.

Jean and Mur hung on every word about the Muma life. Alice had brought stacks of photos to tell the stories: her singing career and the exquisite costumes, golf outings with Jerry in Carmel, the newest movie series, the "Our Gang" bunch living down the street with whom Jane and John played. The family was stunned by the shots of the elegant house on Windsor Boulevard and the descriptions of the parties and fundraisers held in its garden. Clearly, Alice thought, her childhood poverty had been eclipsed.

***

"Oh my goodness, we need a passport!" said Alice, just off the phone with the steamship company. "I guess I just assumed… Because I was born here…" she sputtered. It was a scramble to the Trinity Rectory for a baptism record and to Toronto's Hall of Records for the birth certificate. She cabled Jerry for his own birth certificate and their marriage license.

The *S. S. Montrose* could accommodate just one larger cabin booking. She grabbed it— out of Montreal for Liverpool on July 6—without the required visa, but with a handsomely penned note to whomever, saying she had simply run out of time to procure her visa. The letter of explanation would certainly do.

146

Aileen was packed back to Los Angeles on a sleeper with a large sum of money for expenses. Her father stayed put for another month with his brother.

Chapter 38

Annie Fogo Meets the Children

Wednesday, July 18th, 1923
Central Station Hotel
Newcastle-on-Tyne, England
My Dear Jerry:
The children are asleep and I must tell you what a thrill we have had in arriving at Newcastle-on-Tyne, at the very station platform where I met you these dozen years go.

We have twin beds and an extra cot for Janey. Tomorrow we leave for Rothbury and Aunt Annie Fogo, but in order to arrive at the proper hour and make all the changes, we have had to make this stopover.

We were very late in docking at Liverpool on Saturday. In fact we should have been in on Friday, but we lost time in the icebergs, as they had to stop the engines. It was 6 p.m. when we were through with the customs, and too late to get to Harrogate to Pauline's. So, we went to Chester. The children were agog with delight and had their introduction to the wonders of the Old World—old Roman walls and the splendid cathedral. We rode on double-decker streetcars and had a general survey of the little place, and at noon were back in Liverpool to leave for Harrogate, arriving in as pretty country as surely there is in England! Pauline is beautifully situated, and the gay season is on, and it all quite made me think of Monte Carlo and our honeymoon.

Pauline's children gave Jane and John a splendid time, so much so that they did not want to leave last night. We came on to York in the twilight, and it is not possible to describe the beauty of Princess Mary's country.

York Minster is the king of cathedrals in England, and the verger is taking us around with fifteen others, and making a fuss over the children, so I know it made a great impression on them. If you could only be here to enjoy it with us, you would realize what a foundation is being laid for tolerance and appreciation of what another nation can do. They will have much to tell you, and many times exclaim, "I wish Daddy could see that!" So you see we are thinking of you, and the same strong desire to carry through to success is with me as when I left Rothbury with you and passed this way!

My love to you,
Alice

The Mumas arrived at the Queens Head Hotel in time for late afternoon tea with Annie Fogo. "*The* Aunt Annie Fogo," reminded Alice, "who arranged for me to marry your daddy in England. She's had to give up her farm to live in town, now." The old woman, wearing an extraordinarily large black hat, arrived soon after on the arm of her maid, who made sure of her comfort before heading to the kitchen for her own tea with the help. Tea in the dining room transpired under a beamed ceiling and in streams of light admitted by leaded clear glass windows. All of it was lost on the children, who sat patient and bored. The hat, having its own chair to rest upon during the meal, sat like an enormous black cat. Alice noticed Johnny and Jane gawking at the thing and wondered if there would be giggles forthcoming.

Conversation was mainly between an animated Alice and old Annie consisting mostly of stories of the trip to Mitchell, a hello from Mr. Hicks, and wasn't it sad that Alice's mother, who had visited Aunt Annie so long ago with her then bridegroom, was gone. The children were exhausted from the journey but the teacakes would perk them up. As long as they did not fidget in their seats and spoke politely she would allow them to stay. Alice ignored occasional faces they made to one another over the fish paste and cucumber sandwiches.

Jane began to nod off. Alice saw her daughter struggling to stay upright and took pity on her, bringing the meal to a close as soon as politely possible. Johnny rose to help Mrs. Fogo from her chair. As if by some magic, the maid reappeared. They all kissed goodbye and promised to come for dinner at Mrs. Fogo's home.

Though it was still early evening, the three Mumas walked upstairs to a spacious en suite with two beds and a cot. A maid had already unpacked the trunks Alice had marked, laying out nightclothes. Alice drew a warm bath for the children and afterward tucked them in.

"Why is it still light out, Mother? It feels like afternoon, not evening," Johnny said. "It's so hard to go to bed with the sun up so high."

"Don't you remember our discussion with your daddy about how the sun stays out longer in the summer the further north you go? I'll close the drapes; you'll see you won't mind, at least for tonight. Good night, Johnny dear." She leaned over to plant a kiss on his forehead. Sometimes, as now, her son was not ten, but still little, wanting her hugs and kisses.

"Good night, Mother." He closed his eyes and was asleep instantly.

As for Jane, she was already gently snoring.

Alice kissed her check and then tiptoed toward her own bed. They would have an interesting day of it on the way to Kelso, just over the border into Scotland. Jerry's cousin, at least three times removed, lived in a house called Pringle Bank.

***

"Race you to the top!" yelled Johnny to Jane. Abandoning remnants of a picnic to scavenging rooks and squirrels, they scrambled up to the ruins of

Roxburgh Castle. Alice huffed behind them to the great stone pile sitting on the hill above the Teviot River.

Alice read from the guidebook, "The Scots took this castle in 1313 with heavy losses to the British."

"Are we related, Mummy?" asked Jane, who had been the recipient of a kilt of the Erskine plaid, accompanied by her mother's story of their Scottish connection through the Edinburgh grandmother after whom she was named.

"Weel, noo, I dinna think so," said her mother with a smile and a reasonable attempt at the accent. "We come from lowland Scots, more likely. But dinna fash, there are no ghosties biding here the non."

Jane snorted a laugh.

"Yeah, well I remember you reading in the guidebook," said Johnny, "that later, King James's face was blown off when the British tried to take back the castle."

"Ugh!" replied Jane. "Did he die?"

"What do you think, silly? Of course!"

"Enough! Now sit. Just look at this view of Scotland. This whole area, from Rothbury north to Kelso, saw battles for hundreds of years. Imagine being a British soldier on a lookout tower above us, watching the howling Scottish horde advance. Why, I can almost see the flags flying and hear the beat of the drums over the din of war."

The three then sat comfortably on the grassy tufts at the base of the ancient castle walls, the only remaining stone ruins from the tower that once guarded the English defenses from the marauding Scots just over the river. Through the trees on the Scottish side, they could see the town of Kelso nestled beyond the outward curve of the Teviot.

"We'll be going there shortly for a visit to Cousin Blanche and her mother, Nellie. They are Daddy's cousins, of course, through his mother's side."

"Are they going to fight us do you think, Mother?" asked Jane.

"You *are* a goose," replied Alice. "Of course not. That happened ages ago. The Scots and English live in reasonable harmony these days."

Alice, John and Jane found their way back to the car and chauffeur, crossed the Teviot and arrived at the house called Pringle Bank in time for tea. The children, as always, were well behaved, answering all the questions Cousin Blanche and her elderly mother could think of about their visit to Roxburgh Castle.

"Why don't you go and play in the back garden, then," suggested Blanche after the teacakes had been demolished.

With a pleading look at their mother and her nod, they said, "Excuse us, please," in unison. They made their way quietly to the back door, and exploded onto the grass with whoops and laughs. They played at being the Scots and then the English, taking and retaking Roxburgh Castle.

***

Windswept rains occasionally coursed across the broad hills surrounding Rothbury, drenching pastured sheep huddled against lichened walls. Water flooded the narrow winding streets into town and roared under the ancient stone bridge, making life generally miserable for the village on a day predicted for abundant sunshine. Such was the case as Sunday service closed at the parish church. Alice and the children were hovering in the vestibule, chatting with a trim, black-clad octogenarian by the name of Mr. David Dippee Dixon.

"We'll see you for luncheon in about an hour?" said Alice. "The children are so looking forward to your stories."

"I'm delighted to come, and pleased that Mrs. Fogo will be there as well. It has been awhile since I have seen her." Looking toward Jane, Mr. Dixon said, "Have you seen her big black hat?" and smiled conspiratorially.

Alice looked at her daughter. "I told him, you see, about the tea with Mrs. Fogo. It turns out she is famous throughout town for her black hats."

Jane grinned but said nothing.

They all left, popping black umbrellas open against the downpour and hurrying toward waiting carriages. Parishioners were headed back to Sunday lunch of overcooked green beans, boiled potatoes and mutton, all smothered in viscous brown gravy. Not so for Alice, who would not countenance such a disgusting meal. They would dine at the Queen's Head, eat proper roast beef and Yorkshire pudding, green salad, and have a lemon cake for dessert. The confection was Jane's favorite and a surprise for her birthday.

A grumble of thunder and scant flash of lightening signaled the end of the storm. By the time they arrived back at the inn, puddles sparkled with the returning sun, and the air turned warm. A good omen, Alice thought. Mr. Dixon was a lovely man and somewhat famous all the way to London for his knowledge of local history, archaeology and music. Mrs. Fogo said the town thought the world of him, and the children took to his stories and relaxed manner of speaking. Alice was eager to speak to him concerning his collection of old songs, which he had promised to share. There would be a lot to talk about this afternoon.

***

"What do you think about a trip to Lord Armstrong's castle, Craigside, tomorrow?" Mr. Dixon said over his beef. "I happen to know that he has quite an interesting hydraulic system, John, installed by Lord Armstrong's famous father more than thirty years ago. His Lordship's home is not open to the public, you know, so you would be quite lucky."

Johnny looked inquiringly up at his mother. "It sounds *interesting*. Exactly what is 'hydraulics?'"

"Using water to move things or create things: in this case, elevators and electric lights," responded Mr. Dixon. "But I will say no more, hoping to leave you all intrigued for tomorrow. That is, *if* you are interested."

151

"I think it is a splendid idea," interjected Mrs. Fogo. "Mr. Dixon is librarian to Lord Armstrong's collection, so he knows a great deal about the large estate."

"Then it is decided," said Alice. "We are looking forward to our visit. Now, Janey, please eat those peas. I understand there is something special for pudding today, in your honor."

"Pudding?" said Jane. "Chocolate would be very nice."

"No, actually not pudding. The English call all desserts 'puddings.' It's cake—your favorite kind, lemon.

"With candles?" she said, mumbling between bites of the disappearing peas.

"Yes, with nine of them."

Plates were cleared and the air was full of expectation. The maître d' emerged from the kitchen, winding through the other tables. He held a large lemon cake decorated in icing with piped swags of butter cream around the sides. On top, and brightly lit, stood nine pink candles in a circle. Strains of "Happy Birthday" rang out at the table. Diners from other tables joined in and clapped loudly.

Jane blushed furiously and smiled from ear to ear.

"Make a wish," said Alice, "and blow your candles out."

* * *

The Mumas met up with Mr. Dixon at eleven o'clock the next morning. They all piled into the chauffeured car for the two-mile drive out of the village.

"Beautiful morning for exploring," said Mr. Dixon.

They pulled under the covered entry and unloaded.

"This magnificent home was built by Baron Armstrong, then?" asked Alice. "It appears to be a blend of Tudor, Gothic and Renaissance. I see the half-timbered architecture on the fourth story and the magnificent tall chimneys poking up from the roof. And yet the construction looks peacefully coexistent."

Mr. Dixon chuckled. "Mrs. Muma, I believe he not only replaced the poor thatched cottage with all these bricks and chimneys, he renovated much of the village—all fine examples of late-nineteenth-century town planning. The baron was what they call a 'gentleman engineer.'

"You know, John, the very first electric light in the country, and perhaps in the world, was lit by hydroelectricity right here in Lord Armstrong's house."

The party arrived at the bottom of the hill to see a large pond and imposing single-story stone building out of which humming and chugging sounds could be heard. At Mr. Dixon's "hallo," a large, aproned man appeared from the open door and strode toward them.

"Mrs. Muma and company, this is Engineer Snivley. He is called the Caretaker of the Electric Light. Mr. Snivley has kindly agreed to explain his job."

152

The caretaker spent a few minutes explaining that the pumps in the building pushed water from the pond into a holding tank 200 feet above the house, where water was then fed by gravity through pipes into the house. The water was used in the bathrooms and kitchen. In addition, there was a turbine here in the stone building that drove a dynamo which generated electricity, used for lights and to drive the dumbwaiter in the kitchen.

Alice was watching Johnny's attentive face as the eleven year old took in the story of hydraulics. He was a boy who had as yet shown no interest in things beyond sports and deviling his sister. But now, watching her son take in the power of water, she thought she saw some glimmer of his future work.

"Thank you, Mr. Snivley," said Mr. Dixon. "It was good of you to take the time." The party turned back up the path and walked toward the house. He continued, "Your American inventor Mr. Edison sued our inventor Mr. Swann over the patent for the electric light. The two gentlemen finally agreed that the electric light had been discovered simultaneously in our two countries, and formed a company together in the spirit of cooperation. That would be in, let's see, about 1882, if memory serves."

The group chatted their way back up to the house where Mr. Dixon regretfully refused luncheon, claiming his presence was required in the library for the afternoon.

***

August 27 was sheep market day and the morning of their departure. A bleating, dirty mass of animals greeted them as their chauffeured automobile inched passed on their way to the station. Jane and John thought it was grand to have such an escort. Alice thought it quaint and held her nose at the smell of unwashed fleece. Though it was not the first time they had heard the bleating flocks moving down the streets, it was unique to be caught in the middle. Mr. Dixon had explained that the ancient market cross in Rothbury was the symbol of royal decree required in those early times to hold the sale of goods. Kings and sheriffs would have need of the taxes. Alice found it quite exotic to imagine requiring the king's permission to sell sheep. The whole idea of a decree for commerce of any kind would have been unfathomable to the merchants of Los Angeles. Jerry would have found it hilarious.

Mrs. Fogo struggled out of the car, insisting on waving them off from the station platform. There were hugs and handshakes and promises to return, then the passengers pulled away for the trip south to London.

The long day on the train and the gathering heat made for cranky children as they neared London's Strand Palace Hotel. It was a bath and early to bed for the young ones.

Alice spent the evening planning her trip to the Continent with the Cook's travel brochure. The next morning, they all walked to the agency and booked a tour for the following day: second-class tickets for berths on the long ferry steamer ride from Harwich to the Hook of Holland, and then the train to

Amsterdam. Johnny begged to see a battlefield of the Great War. Antwerp was not to be missed; there was Paris to experience, and a few days extra with Madame de Sales—she had recently moved back.

This last leg of the trip went effortlessly. Jane and John had gotten used to hotels, trains and museums. French was now added to the various English accents already commonplace to their ears. Within a week her children were speaking to porters and waiters in broken French and to each other in the accented Northumberland English. Johnny and Jane kept it up while sailing from Southampton to New York on the *R. M. S. Olympic*, charming the adults at dinner and on deck. Alice could think of no finer thing than to see her children truly transformed. And wasn't it fitting to be passengers on the very ship that had brought her Jerry to her in Rothbury in 1912.

***

Within a week of their return, Johnny and Jane were sent off to the Glendora Foothill School to board. Alice and Jerry drove to Carmel for a golf weekend.

October 23rd
Dear Mother,
I want you to please send me a pair of high shoes and a bathing suit and please send me some good dresses because I need them very badling.
Love from Jane Muma

Dear Daddy and Mother,
Did you get home all right? I wish you would come out here and see me. I am having a nice time putting in stamps.
Love from John Muma

November 8th
Windsor Blvd., Los Angeles
My Dear Johnny,
One of the most surprising things to tell you is that you have been chosen to be the Mascot of the UC team at the big game this year! Our wee Johnny Muma—he used to be so wee—growing up enough to be part of the biggest event that the year will bring to California. I am quite excited about it.

All our adult friends will be there, Johnny boy, and they'll be as proud of you as your delighted Daddy—who has done so much for football in the West.

I am sitting here on our big porch with your aunts, regaling them with our summer adventures. They both agreed that you children gave their mother a marvelous time on that trip. And then to come and go into a real school and live with new boys! It's pretty exciting. ...
With love,
Mother

Chapter 39

Summer of Separation, 1924

How is your father? Aunt Marie had asked in her letter posted late in January. *The people here were all delighted to see him again.* Aunt Marie was still referring to last summer's visit. Aunt Marie, stuck in time, Alice thought, whose own life was swept up in concerts, teas, dinners, theatre classes for the children, and endless demand to entertain Jerry's business friends. *How is your father?* Dead before the letter arrived, was how.

Alice's gray eyes teared at the thought of his passing. Sitting at her desk now in the slanting light of afternoon almost six months later, she could still visualize Aunt Marie's letter jumbled together with all the waiting-to-be-paid bills of winter, the Philharmonic annual subscription, the invoice from the Windsor Square Police, that private service to keep order in her community. She had buried her father next to her mother and Sister Jo in the Hollywood cemetery—the one where in good time she and Jerry would be.

Alice forced her thoughts more toward the present. A new photo sat within her view: Johnny and Jane, he in dark knickers and Jane in white lace, standing by Hattie the cook. My, they loved Hattie. They hated to leave her company and her cooking and were always comparing Hattie favorably wherever they went for dinner. Jerry had taken the picture just before he left for the Democratic Convention in New York.

The morning of that breakfast snapshot, Jerry's delegate certificate had lain between them like some great barrier.

State of California, Certificate of Election Issued to Delegate Irwin J. Muma, Certified Democratic Delegate at the Presidential primary election of June 25th.

And as a delegate, he was going to New York City to elect the Honorable William Gibbs McAdoo from California to run for the presidency.

She and the children would be gone before he returned.

"I know this is important, Jerry, but really! We have planned this summer with you in mind. Johnny is counting on you to teach him to fly fish. You know I can't do it!"

Jerry had shifted the cold cigar out of his mouth, dumping it on the ashtray. "Alice, my dear, you knew of my commitment to the convention way back in March. If you want to travel, I won't say no to being a bachelor for the summer. Simply can't be out of the office that long."

Jerry had been quick to beg off the trip once the whole summer had been planned out. Alice sighed, stuffing down resentment. She shared this feeling

155

with very few of her Christian Science friends. The resentment sprang from Jerry's arrogant criticism of her absolute dependence on C. S. for daily "truth" to guide their lives. The more troubled she was, the more time she spent with the C. S. practitioner who was especially trained by the mother church in Boston to help her pray for guidance. Alice prayed the bedtime prayer with Jane and John. She attended readings and discussions every Wednesday evening. She looked for ways to counter Jerry's growing scorn of the C. S. quest for truth when he was troubled with difficult business decisions. Perhaps the summer away from him would give her some ease, though for sure the children would miss him terribly.

***

So began the long summer separation. Jerry's letters to Alice and the children were full of the excitement of the Democratic convention.

New York papers boasted headlines in favor of McAdoo; the California contingent waved flyers, threw streamers and screamed slogans as the madness escalated. There was pandemonium in the smoke-filled caucus rooms reeking of cigars and Scotch whisky and roast beef sandwiches.

A clipping of the paper showed a photo of a California delegate speaking eloquently to the mad crowd.

McAdoo protected the Treasury—the citadel of government—from attack by the powerful. He organized and put into operation the Federal Reserve Bank system with zeal that knows neither fear nor failure! McAdoo knows the farmers problems and served agriculture conspicuously in 1914 when he organized the War Risk Insurance Bureau that saved the cotton crop. He gave us the eight-hour day with overtime to railroad workers, opened ports and successfully moved our troops and supply trains. ... He is opposed to religious discrimination, leading Congress to act to secure rights of American and Jews in Russia during the persecution there.

There was a fifty-minute demonstration after the nomination, Jerry reported, and he was in the middle of it. Cigar smoke hung like a thick fog in the hall, mixing with the reek of men in sweat-stained white shirts, and cheers echoed off the walls of the convention hall. Apricot colored streamers were passed from hand to hand, and somewhere in the mêlée an unnamed California delegate stole the Illinois pendant.

Jerry penned across the margin of the newspaper clipping,

Why, Alice, the last time we had so much fun was the time we organized the theft of the Axe during the UC–Stanford game in 1900!

An Oakland delegate was carried on the shoulders of the two tallest Californians present. The volume of shouts and screams of the competing candidates raised the cacophony another decibel. In the end, it was Underwood, not McAdoo, who was nominated. But by God, it was fun.

***

156

Alice had to admit that Jerry was a terrific correspondent with the children during their stay at the Idaho fishing camp.

August 11, 1924

My Dear Jane,

You have been a very vigorous correspondent and I have enjoyed your letters very much. I am sorry about your costume. It can't be found so of course I can't send it to you. Besides, you will be home before you could get it, almost.

I am anxious to know where you are going to school this fall. The thought of school comes to mind because the UC boys are all going back to college today.

Hattie calls upon the "fone" quite often. I believe she is as anxious as I am to have you back. How can you stay away from the beach so long? Besides, you are missing a watermelon party that I have every Sunday afternoon. Tell John I sent his malted milk and mother a new lantern.

Best love,

Dad

Late August, 1924

North Fork Fishing Camp, Idaho

My Dear Jerry,

The children are asleep and the day has been a wonderful one. I will let Jane tell you the details, but your package brought squeals of delight. The costume—you found it after all—has been greatly admired and fits very well except the waist, which is much too much of a fit now to allow for growth. She has acquired pounds since we arrived. I ordered a birthday cake in Salt Lake which came Saturday a.m.

Your package came Friday in good season, also the candy. We had the cake Sat. p.m. so the Salt Lake people could celebrate. Two of them treated the whole camp to ice cream, the first we have had since we left civilization. It proved quite an affair. The chef outdid himself and all the children sat at one long table—ten of them. Jane played the hostess to them all very creditably and we had music on The Victor—lovely records. Johnny crowned her with a little wildflower wreath.

The cash arrived safely early this morning and I am very grateful. Now we can wind our stay up on Friday evening, leaving at 8 p.m. with several of the other guests. We have plenty of snapshots so hope we can give you a very good idea of the surroundings.

I realize I have hardly told you how the days go. Some guest fishermen brought in three to four pounders, but some other men just lie around and call that a vacation. Each to his task! The women seem to keep pretty close to bridge for amusement, I regret to say, so I have been glad of the children for an excuse and go out on the river at sunset after dinner and read to them, anchored in the stream. There are walks, and several guests have their motors, and we have been included a few times.

Do not land on John for not proving a better fisherman. All the other boys have their fathers here who go out with them, and of course John had to stay home or go alone. Everyone has an expert's outfit of flies, etc., and John has just what I could get him locally, which is very poor. Someone today at the Flat Rock Club gave him two flies and he went right out and caught a fish. He found another good fly and has it stowed safely in his hip pocket in a folder. He has learned many things and poles a boat like a gondolier and is almost the official boatman. Jane makes friends everywhere and bobs up serenely no matter what. But I do wish you could have introduced them to this kind of outdoor life. I acknowledge I do not know it. For this is my first experience. I have watched out for the best for them under the circumstances.

I am wondering which way you are inclined to route the tickets for Virginia. I realize it is an insurance meeting and not a pleasure trip, as you will undoubtedly remind me, but I like to see as much as possible en route. We can go by New Orleans and return via St. Louis, or must it be otherwise?

I have written to everyone from here so that the house (in Windsor Place) will be going as usual by September 1st with Hattie back again. I am making lists so as to accomplish everything I should attend to before leaving, for I am assuming to get there by September 9th. We should be starting back on Friday, the 5th.

I hope no one has persuaded you into purchasing an automobile. I have thought it over carefully and think I would rather do without one than to in any way have a repetition of the Cadillac difficulties. I do not want to drive another car unless we can pay for its operation. If that cannot be, we will wait until we have a driver who will have sole responsibility. This year the children can go to their lessons via bus. While we are away I plan that Olga shall go with them, except to the school on 3rd St.

This is the last note I can write to you, so look for us Sunday p.m. And I hope you will be as glad to see us as we are looking forward to seeing you.

Our love to you,
Alice

The homecoming was riotous. Jerry met them at the station, hiring two taxis, one just for the family who swarmed into his arms. The din was too much, and Jerry rolled down the windows to let the sounds of the children's voices dissipate into the avenue. The second taxi held the trunks and boxes filled with dirty clothes and presents for Jerry, Hattie and the gardener, and mementos of that long summer away. Johnny and Jane captured their father's attention throughout dinner, and talked and talked until Jerry covered his ears and laughed and said it was time to wind down and go to bed.

"Hattie, Hattie, tuck us in!" said Jane. "Please, just this once."

"Just this once," said Hattie to the pleadings. "I haven't *seen* you all summer!" She marshaled the children out of the dining room and upstairs.

Alice looked at Jerry with such hunger in her eyes that he moved quickly to her side. She poked a finger into a hole in that awful sweater he always wore and he pulled it out to kiss her palm, and then drew her roughly against him. She kissed him hard. He put his hand firmly on her back and propelled her into the study and shut the door.

***

Two days after Alice and the children returned to Los Angeles, she and Jerry boarded the train for West Virginia and the insurance meeting. During the ride it felt like a honeymoon to them both, the emptiness of the past summer still fresh. Nevertheless they remembered to send postcards to the children that mapped their journey through Albuquerque, Kansas City, Chicago, Richmond and finally Hot Springs.

Alice reigned supreme by Jerry's side in the evenings and had him to herself in the dark of night. The daytime was taken by his male only rounds of golf, during which she rode out on groomed trails with a few of the wives, sitting beautifully in English riding habit on a chestnut mare. It was infinitely better than interminable games of bridge.

Chapter 40

Tragedy of Immense Proportion

1925

A Conversation with Gran'mere

Gran'mere, you never wrote a word of that late January day. The sudden death of my Grandfather Jerry was recorded only in public documents. Allen's Clipping Service did a noble job of cutting dozens of newspaper notices, all of which were stuffed, along with an equal number of letters of condolence, into a manila envelope labeled, "What Jerry Muma's Friends Thought of Him—30 January, 1925." Did you put those clippings in your files for me to find, those maddening hints onto which I would hang your private grief?

You left me no choice but to wait for inspiration and a full moon, which always made you vulnerable. So it was that I found you at my elbow one late night.

"Looking back," Gran'mere murmured, "I wonder if my father's death portended some end-of-days for my path in the world. It was one year from his passing that my dear Jerry died. On a sunny Saturday morning in January, he left the house to make a business call. Over breakfast we had finalized our anniversary celebration plans for the following weekend and begun a discussion of a Mediterranean tour for the summer. It was just an ordinary day of extraordinary plans, he said, and laughed uproariously and kissed me and walked out. And he was dead. Collapsed, they said, in the street, taken to the Hollywood Hospital unconscious and died. Cerebral hemorrhage like my sister Jo."

The answer troubled me. "But Uncle Johnny said Grandfather died at the club; after recovering briefly and refusing medical assistance, he died in the elevator." I knew this issue would never be resolved. It is a small fact, considering, but typical of Gran'mere's mysteries.

She went on without acknowledging me. "I remember the phone ringing. I picked up and heard the voice of a man speaking words I could not grasp and then there was a hissing in my brain, and then there was nothing. I heard no birds, no voices on the street, could see nothing, could not breathe… Later, I must have called Annie and Sue, and his cousin L. B.

"We had a service at home. The casket sat in the living room surrounded by banks of flowers. Family and friends overflowed the rooms, drifting quietly, speaking in soft tones. For once there was no music." Gran'mere shuddered. "To this day the smell of lilies fills me with dread. Johnny and Janey were so lost. I found them sitting on the stairs leaning on each other with their heads down, as shocked and full of sorrow and disbelief as I. And the street, well, it was lined for blocks with the limousines that took us to the public service at the Hollywood Cemetery where he was cremated."

Gran'mere went on to describe the dozens of pallbearers at the cemetery as the casket was carried to the crematorium. I remembered, as she named them, that most had been on her list of contacts during the last five years of her life—people from whom she begged money to finance her next improbable scheme.

"We carried his ashes in a beautifully inscribed brass casket to the mausoleum. I asked especially to pass the area where my dear mother and father were interred, and my sister Jo.

"For so many weeks after, I hid my emotions behind a dam. I received so many letters of condolence from family during that time, but it was Cousin L.B.'s that finally broke through."

There was something so direct and masterful about Jerry that his loss cuts deep. I should not be so emotional but I cannot escape those startling and overpowering impulses when I am by myself or with others that simply makes you feel faint. …

"Reading it, I *did* feel faint, as he put it, and became hysterical—sobbed until hiccups stopped my tears and exhaustion swept me into the darkness. And I slept.

"My Jerry left me for good that awful January day. Not a business trip, not a late night at the office, nor the club, not Rotary or the Masons. He was gone. We had not been on the best of terms that last year. Christian Science was creating a great divide. I prayed for him to see the value of it, but he would not. In fact, the ridicule was becoming quite unbearable.

"My good friend Elizabeth Burton remarked quite candidly in a letter to me only a month after he passed that Jerry, while not approving of Science, was now on his way to find God, leaving me free to live the truth and guide the children without opposition. 'I cannot help but feel it is a great liberation for you,' she wrote."

"Oh, my, Gran'mere," I blurted. "That is so harsh!"

"She was right," Alice went on, "though she might have waited another month or so out of consideration."

161

Chapter 41

Three Plans Made, 1925

"Life must go on," murmured Alice to no one in particular. She was standing in the bedroom looking out at March's sweet spring garden. Condolence letters had stopped. In place there was Elizabeth Burton's excited letter from Paris. It hinted at one project, at least, to keep her mind occupied during these "dark days," or "great trouble." Everyone's use of these euphemisms grated on her nerves. Nothing could describe that vast emptiness where Jerry used to be.

After the first of January Alice had contracted with Elizabeth Burton, her partner in the now-defunct Seven Arts Workshop, in a new venture, an antiques import business. Alice was providing financial backing. Elizabeth had already ensconced herself in Paris for the purpose of ferreting out French and Spanish antiques when Jerry's death had sent life reeling out of control. Elizabeth's four-page, closely penned letter announced the imminent arrival of the first crate at customs in the Port of Los Angeles. It fairly vibrated with the thrill of the chase.

I visited more than thirty places until I found as much for your money as I could, then repaired and packed the following: a Louis XVI chest with marquetry, framed mirror with its original green paint still evident, a rare old bed and a Pondreuse, which is a Marie Antoinette dressing table, a bedside reading table bordering on the "Directoire" period. ...

There were more Louis XVI fabrics, mirrors, beds and chairs than could be crammed into Alice's home, and so the garage would become the warehouse.

***.

A second grand scheme had come to Alice one night after prayers—the notion that Jerry's memory should be preserved forever with a scholarship in his name for a deserving male student at UC Berkeley. Jerry's friends would love the idea, she thought, and she dashed off a note to several, naming a committee and asking for their approval.

Their concerted reply was simple: They were absolutely delighted. Who better to chat with than Senator McAdoo, Jerry's very good friend with influential connections? When she left the senator's office she boarded the train for Washington, DC with letters of introduction to members of the Finance Committee and Department of Interior, and would ferret out the potential of her plentiful oil and gas leases to pay for this scholarship.

The last advice Alice received from her committee as she boarded the train for the ride home was this: Send check for the first $400 directly to the

President of UC in Berkeley until we can set up the fund. The first year scholarship was on its way. The financing for the $4,000 endowment looked promising.

There was just enough time to plan the scholarship before she and the children left for their world tour, plan number three.

***

The day after school recessed, the three were on their way to New York to board the *S. S. Oronsay* for the Mediterranean cruise—Madeira, Gibraltar, Monaco, the Riviera, Italy, Yugoslavia, Monaco, Algiers, Egypt, Spain, Greece, Constantinople, and finally, Paris. Paris, where Alice would catch up with Elizabeth Burton and the import business sitting under cover in Alice's garage. Six weeks of adventures. Six weeks to forget the loneliness. Five months since his death.

Alice would skip England altogether, as the elderly Annie Fogo had died this winter. So many deaths, all of them in January—the coldest month of her year.

***

"Wave, you two! There she is—there's Cousin Olive."

"Mummy, we just saw her!" said Jane.

"Johnny, smile and wave your cap. Cousin Olive *will* see it," said Alice. "Listen, my dears. She was kind enough to put us up last night and to see us off and bring such wonderful books and fruit to our stateroom. It is only right to acknowledge her."

The ship's steam whistle let fly a mighty blast as the longshoremen heaved the massive hawsers free of the nautical cleats. Alice and the children jumped at the noise, then whooped and hollered, shouting out to Olive and waving and throwing streamers. The water boiled as the *S. S. Oronsay* pushed away into the harbor. The bow swung around, pointing toward the Atlantic. Red tugboats with their bulky rope bumpers escorted the ship past the Statue of Liberty.

"Time to unpack," said Alice as the tugs turned back to Manhattan. Linen suits and lawn shirts, short pants for Johnny, silk dresses for formal dinners on board, costume bits and pieces for the end-of-cruise balls… All found their way into the wardrobes. Sturdy shoes and dressy evening pumps and sandals were lined up, toiletries organized in the bathroom. At last it was done.

"I have a surprise for you." Alice pulled out three monogrammed black leather logbooks. "Jane, Johnny, make sure to start filling in your travel logs. It will be a lifetime treasure." Johnny pulled a face and tossed his into a drawer. Jane peered quickly into the first couple of pages where the *S. S. Oronsay* itinerary was listed. "Come on, you two, begin today and every day it will get easier. I'll get you started. Now, let's dash up and have luncheon. Who knows what interesting person will be sitting next to us." Alice had a glint in her eye, and the excitement in her voice was catching. She looked at her children and

163

smiled. They grinned back at her. After smoothing her bobbed hair, she gathered them into her arms for a hug.

***

Log Entries for Jane and Alice: Raymond Whitcomb Mediterranean Cruise, *S. S. Oronsay*, Orient Line

Jane—June 27—weather: fare. Got into a fog but got out very soon. Made friends with Mr. Don, had a fire drill and a dance at 9 o'clock.

June 30—weather: fare. Had a talk at 10:30 and ice cream at 12 o'clock. I played 2 or 3 games and we had a talk on the Malay Peninsula and the fishes climb trees winked there eyes at you and then went down and took a shower bath.

July 4th—weather: warm when we got to Madeira but when we left had a big wind. We got off the boat onto a litter and went ashore and got into a bullock cart and went to the railroad station and got on a very funny train and went up the mountain. Then we came down the mountain in a funny old cart on a stone road. We went back to the boat at 3:30 and we sailed at 8 o'clock, 4th of July celebrated at dinner.

Alice—June 27th—after dinner with a new moon above, the children danced on "A" deck.

July 4—Sat. weather: beautifully bright and clear. Sighted land in early a.m. Ran along shore until 10:30 a.m. admiring grape trellises and dwellings on the hillside. Soil red. Early potatoes are sent to England. Went ashore on a tender amid small boats with vendors of Madeira embroidery, crowded stone wharf with steps down into water. Took bullock-cart over pointed cobblestones up to the funicular railway where the ascent begins 3,300 ft. up to the hotel with gorgeous views, where we had luncheon. Descent was made via wicker sleds without crew, only two men with ropes to hold it in check. Heaps of fun to sail around corners. Running water in gutters in which women wash their clothes. Beautiful overhanging gardens bougainvillea, grapes, palm trees. Browsed through some shops where Jane found some peasant shoes and John found a collection of stamps.

***

Donald Rockwell, ship's passenger, upright and congenial, befriended the Muma family for the cruise. They were introduced the first night of formal seating. The balance of the passengers at their table, including the Misses Alton-Brown and Mr. and Mrs. Aikens and their daughter Eugenia, were all delighted with Mr. Don. He was present to sing in a fine tenor voice with Alice at church services and comfortable playing deck sports with the children. He would be found with several of them on the train to Granada and the Alhambra, in Malaga, in Algiers at the Sultan's Palace, then back again to the ship for champagne and a midnight sailing. The Mumas, Mr. Don and one of the Misses Alton rented a car to drive "*Subito!*" through the streets of Rome to gaze at the Villa Borghesi, the Trevi Fountain and the Coliseum. A train took them all to Pisa and back, automobiles took them to St. Peters where pilgrims from all corners of the world crowded through the Vatican treasurers. Naples found them with other ships passengers shopping at the Galleria Umberto, then back on board at the rail to watch Stromboli come into view while sailing toward Messina and the Adriatic.

***

Then, as the sun filtered through a gauzy haze, there was Venice.

"I will show you the beautiful city I explored years ago before your daddy and I were married," Alice said as they stepped into the tender to ferry to the dock.

"When I was here with Miss Freuler, we came by train. Our faces were black from the soot of the smokestack! It was about this time of the year—no, perhaps a little earlier—but it was so hot we had the windows open." Alice fought off the sudden memories of Jerry. She had been a slip of a girl then, and so full of innocent hope, and she wanted him to come here to marry her on a gondola as they rode through the Grand Canal. But then, she smiled to herself, she had wanted to marry him in every city in every country she toured.

"Mummy, it's not *so* hot here. The waves are splashing a bit," said Jane, who inadvertently brought her mother back to the present.

Alice was grateful for the reprieve from her maudlin thoughts. "Janey dear, and Johnny, too, look toward that huge piazza. That's where we are headed— St. Mark's. See that man with the open umbrella? He's likely our tour guide. Try and stay in front of the group so you can hear what he says."

Johnny looked bored as they traipsed through St. Mark's and followed dark narrow streets from one ancient molding building to the next, the guide pointing out endless glowing details about the mosaic floors and columns of yet another church. The only saving grace was the opportunity to feed the pigeons after lunch. But when their breadcrumbs ran out, he and Jane, in a fit of wild abandon and halfhearted scolding from their mother, sent the birds wheeling into the sky.

They spent the afternoon wandering through shops before exploring the last little church. With others of the tour, they all found themselves back at St. Mark's and sank with relief into the rigid metal chairs placed around small, shaded tables at a pasticciera. Fresh-squeezed lemonade and some ricotta-filled pastries worked wonders to restore their energy but did nothing for their blistered feet.

"You have done well, dears. Your reward is a gondola ride through the Grand Canal before dinner." Alice was not above a little bribery to encourage the absorption of some culture. Truth be known, though, she was aching to hear the gondoliers' operatic songs and feel the breezes as they plied the waters, all of it reviving the memories of her stay long ago.

They dashed back to the *Oronsay* for a late supper and an overnight to Ragusa, and the next day took in more mosaic-tiled churches and palace doors

165

of inlaid marble, then moved on to Cattaro, where Jane and Johnny's reward for touring the medieval town was a swim alongside the ship, diving off some small boats carried aboard just for that purpose. Wet and exhausted, the children flopped into bed and dreamed their way to Athens.

That city was a blur of temples seen in bright white light. But it was the rose of sunset, evening star and moon that caught at Alice's heart as they were rowed back to the ship.

Log Book—Constantinople and Beyrouth (Beirut)

Jane—weather—hot and hotter! We got on the tender at 9 o'clock and rode into the city and to the Oya Sophia Mosque and they made us ware funny slippers, then to the Sultan Ahmed Mosque, they made us ware the same slippers there.

We went to the Military Museum we saw the helmets of the Crusaders and then we went to luncheon. We saw the Seraglio Palace and the big kitchen of the Palace. Next we saw the tomb of the Suleiman and Roxalana, the mosque of Suleiman the Magnificant and last of all the Grand Bazaars.

Beyrouth: very hot! We started for Baalbek early in the morning and reached it at 11 o'clock and saw the big temple of Baal. Then we started for Damascus passing over the plains and roving mountains which were bear. Small villages, black goats with Arab Shepards, black tents, drivers sang, past through cool stretches of green trees besides the Abana River. Into Damascus, muezzin (mother spelled it for me) call. Moonlight. After dinner went out with Don and a guide in a carriage with two black horses.

Alice—On Friday, July 31st we took carriages for the mosque and en route encountered a most unique sight in beholding a cavalcade of Arabs mounted on camels from Palmyra. They rode through the streets in colorful regalia en route to fight the Drugges—a tribe which has a secret religion—which is in rebellion against the mandate of the French. ... It being Friday, we were hurried through the mosque, walked to Saladin's tomb and the bazaar before luncheon. After siesta, at 3 o'clock, we went in motors to see where Paul was let down in a basket. A brass factory and chapel founded where Paul had his vision en route to Damascus. As I write muezzins calling in trembling voices.

The next day was beautifully bright and we spent the morning bargaining for costumes and daggers in the bazaar, while Don looked for camel saddlebags and a hubble-bubble. ...

After luncheon we sped away in a hire car over dusty hills toward the Jordan Valley, our driver dressed in a long duster and bright red fez. We crossed a bridge which the Germans had blown up in the Great War. We were much amused by a caravan of resting camels while a Scotchman border guard scanned our passports, formally passing out from under French protection to British Authority. On over bare hills we sped passing the shepherds with their flocks, until as twilight fell, we beheld the Sea of Galilee, on among the ruins of Capernaum.

On August 2nd we were in Tiberium, motoring over the hills where the 5,000 were fed, into Nazareth and Mary's Well. Saw Joseph's carpenter shop, the Church of Annunciation with its lovely oleander, and the synagogue where Jesus preached. Marvelously cool, with moonlight and cypress sentinels and streams of camel trains.

Jerusalem came into view on the 3rd and we spent two days exploring Church of the Holy Sepulcher, the Wailing Wall, and passed by Rachael's Tomb. In the evening there was a lovely moon visible from the Allenby Hotel where we were staying. The sky went from purple to amethyst while a camel train, the beasts hung with Turkish bells, tinkled in tune to their plodding steps.

On the 4th we took the train to Cairo. Sand and oases passed by as we traveled bordering the blue Mediterranean. Across the Suez Canal and through customs aboard ship. We boarded an express train where we had dinner and finished the late afternoon in the Valley of the Nile. Directly to bed at the Continental Savoy, in the Cleopatra's Suite.

The next day we toured by carriage bright and early, along modern streets to the museum, viewing King Tut's charms—canopic jars, jewelry, sarcophagus—our dragoman of dusky hue flicking his fly broom over the poor horse. Then to bazaars and siesta and a treat for the children—overnight in tents in the desert, before which we saw the Sphinx and the Pyramids. There was dinner and dancing and moonrise with camels before we all fell asleep.

Jane—Cairo—In the morning we went to the museum and saw King Tutes things and all sorts of things after that we went to bazaars and stayed there all morning. In the afternoon we went to the lookout and then we started for the desert and slept in tents. In the morning we went shopping. In the afternoon we left for the train to go to Naples.

Chapter 42

Jane's Adventures in Paris

The three of them were all sitting around in the hotel, at tea after their Science lesson.

Alice asked, "Janey dear, how would you like to stay with Mrs. Burton for the fall term at school?"

Jane just knew something was up, but said with a bright smile, "What fun. Will Johnny stay, too? Will we be going to a French school?"

Their mother hesitated. "No, dear, Johnny will be coming back with me. I think that is for the best. You are by far the more confident student, and such an independent spirit. My goodness, it will be no time at all before you are speaking French like a native. Why, Mrs. Burton will be taking you all over France on our quest for antiques. You will have French lessons and of course Science ones, as well. There will be theater and tea dances and all sorts of adventures."

Jane could tell her mother had already made up her mind to stick her with "Tante" Elizabeth Burton, and she glanced over to Johnny, who just shrugged his shoulders. He didn't look happy. Jane liked the "adventure" part, but they would be so far away. You can't just come home to California from Paris whenever you want.

"There is just the dearest fur coat I would like to get you before we go," continued Alice. "If you promise not to grow too much, it should fit you beautifully when you need it later in the fall. I remember such grand adventures in Paris when I was here before your daddy came over to marry me."

"Well, but you were a grownup," Jane said, but liking the idea of the fur coat.

"Oh, but you will have Tante Elizabeth always with you. She likes you so much, and misses her own daughter Helen terribly. Won't you think it a grand gesture on your part to keep each other from loneliness?"

"Will I be home for Christmas, Mother? Wait, I would like to be home for Johnny's birthday in November, actually."

"I will arrange to have you home as soon as Tante Elizabeth can get away, certainly, Janey."

Jane could spot an evasive answer a mile away. It sounded fun except for the part about her brother not being here. This was the first time the two of them would be so far apart.

The next day Jane heard mother talking with Tante Elizabeth as they sat around the tea table in the hotel room. She had been invited in for a cookie and then shooed out. Of course she stayed close to the door where they couldn't see her. Her mother was paying $100 a month "for Jane's keep" she called it, plus a little extra just in case, and $500 to buy more antiques.

**

Early on September 3, Tante Elizabeth and Jane saw Alice and Johnny off. The train was huffing steam as though impatient to get going. Jane decided that really, she didn't want them to go without her and was starting to get a stomachache from all the anxiety.

"Be a good little girl and make Tante Elizabeth and me proud," said Alice, hugging her tight.

Jane hugged her so hard that her mother grunted. "Okay, I'll write you in French every week, as promised. I wish it was cold enough to wear my fur coat! It is so beautiful, Mother. Thank you again."

"Golly, Janey, I am going to miss you," said Johnny. "I'll try and write, but you know me." He grinned and wrapped his arms around her shoulders. "Don't cry. The time will go by faster for you. Just think, ole *Mater* will be nagging me the whole time without you to run interference. Bring me stamps for my birthday. See you before you know it."

"I never cry," Jane said. Of course she wanted to. She was already missing his stupid self and that black hair always coming out from his cap.

**

20 September, 1925

Quimper, Place Saint-Corentin, FranceMy Dearest Alicia,

Well, Janey and I have been enjoying our trip within Brittany, all except the weather. We stopped overnight here and did a lot of shopping, and then spent five days by the sea but were not near a bathing beach. I sketched some and Jane tried her hand, too—then we hunted up furniture and antiques and I bought a bed for you. I can write more about what I saw when I get back to Paris. Jane got herself a jabot and a bit of lace for you.

Our greatest treat was a trip by auto car on a beautiful clear day, where I took Janey to a dear little Breton play, in old costumes, with dances and bagpipes, and she enjoyed it! Our hotel here is in decline but the meals, a la carte, are deliciously cooked.

Janey speaks of her coat many times a day. I can hardly wait to see it. She is as happy as a lark and no trouble at all. I enjoy her company. When she chatters too much, I subdue her for a bit. She is really making progress with her French. I got her some books, as we are having a lesson every day. I venture to say that in three months she will know quite a lot. ...

You are nearly home by now and will see my dear child and give her news of me.

Much love and good cheer.

Affectionately,
Elizabeth

October 15th
Ma Chère Mère,
I am having a lovely time in Paris. I went to the opera to hear *Corneille* and I had a lovely time. It was the prettiest thing you ever saw, but they certainly take a long time to put up the scenery.

I have my eye on a little trunk that is only 90 francs, about $4, and if you send me the money for it now, I will have someplace to put all the new doll clothes I am making. I am getting along pretty well in my French. It is much easier for me and it does not sound so much like Greek.

October 21st
Ma Chère Mère,
I just received my dress and hat and I am wearing them now. I hope you got that little piece of lace and the stamps I sent for Johnny. I went to see a picture show the other day and it was all about Siegfried and it was wonderful—the cast was too. I am going to the opera and to a Sunday matinee and to another play by Molière. I am having such a lovely time in Paris and wish you were here.

I will receive my package from LA tomorrow.
Much love from Jane M.

Oct 26th
Ma Chère Mère,
I think that is a very smart dress Tante is ordering for you in Rome. I like the orange velvet color very much.

Tante's daughter Helen is coming over for a visit to buy her trousseau, and Tante is very excited about seeing her. I will be going back on the ship with her when she returns to get married.

November 2nd
Ma Chère Mère,
I am having a lovely time in Paris and wish you were here too. I went to *Salomé* yesterday but it was not very good. There was too much killing in it, because it was 250 years before Christ. We went to the Louvre the day before yesterday and went through one whole side of it. It was the picture part. I can tell one painter from another by now. Thank you for your long letter. I think I am going to receive your package today sometime. I will celebrate Johnny's birthday when I get home.

November 10th

Ma Chère Mère,

Talk about fun I am having in Paris. I went to see the play of *Jeanne d'Arc* and it was beautiful. I can understand lots of French. I have just covered my trunk with stickers from all the tours we took last summer. Tell Hattie if she would mind me bringing home some lovely recipes from my hotel if I can because they cook just as well as you do, Hattie. Tante Elizabeth asked me to include my French essay on Notre Dame.

November 27th

Ma Chère Mère,

I am having a lovely time in Paris. Yesterday was Thanksgiving Day and we had more fun than you can think because we dressed up in costumes and scared everybody. We had a large cake with American flags on it and I have one on my coat. I have a nice friend to play with and can speak quite a bit now.

P.S. Dear John, I hope you received your stamps for your birthday and hope you had a nice birthday. I did a short essay in French on the revolution. Try and read it.

December 15th

Dear John,

I am having a lovely time in Paris and wish you and mother were here with me. We have had lots of snow in Paris so much that the little birds had nothing to eat so we fed them and got our picture in the papers for it. I hope this little letter reches you before Xmas and I hope you got the great big dog made out of cloth from me. Have a good time with mother visiting Aunt Marie in Mitchell. I bet you will have more snow than in Paris!

Merry Xmas and Happy New Year.

Much love from Jane M.

Chapter 43

Switching Paths

The quiet was suffocating, belying the blue-sky weather outside. Alice had been wandering through the house—home just a week, and the emptiness was driving her crazy. She lingered in Jane's room, feeling a sudden ache for her plain and cheerful daughter.

"You'll wear well," she remembered saying to Jane a while ago to Jane's question, "Am I pretty?" Alice had regretted those words the second they were out of her mouth. Too late! For the look on Jane's face reflected shock, then indifference, a mask surely pulled down to block the pain. Alice knew she had been shut out. Everyone else found her daughter appealing and energetic. Well, Alice sighed, it was an old tension between mothers and daughters. But—Alice knew her favorite was Johnny, and knew Jane knew it, too. The sparkle in her son's eye, his winning ways, his handsome looks... This boy of hers was so like Jerry, and there was no help for it.

The gardeners were leaving, chattering amongst themselves in Portuguese. Their tools clanged into the back of the truck. She wandered out of Jane's room and to the sleeping porches in the rear of the house which framed immaculate gardens. The scent of loamy soil and cut grass relieved her moody thoughts.

This morning Johnny had grinned and waved and was out the door. Gone to catch up with friends and maybe play a little football at the park. Jane—if Alice were being truthful—was dumped on Elizabeth for months.

The life she had been dreading was here: facing the hours without Jerry. She had put it off as long as possible, had tried to stay positive on the three-day train ride home with John. In Chicago they changed trains to the *Overland* without visiting the ghost of her married life and Johnny's birth. Neither the dome car views nor the miles and days through plains and mountains moved her as they had in the past. Instead, she and Johnny had relived the spectacular cruise and replayed the swims and rounds of tennis from their brief stay on Long Island. (In truth, that Long Island visit had more an air of delaying the dreaded ride home.)

Alice had planned so much to do when she returned that she could not, even for an hour, think beyond her projects. All she had to do was start. Piled on her desk were volumes of letters from Elizabeth Burton. The idea of their joint business venture had been a lark. Now it seemed ordinary and, well, distasteful. Elizabeth, who had given up her routine of lectures on art history for this chance to make a fortune from the wealthy LA matrons, was using her own irrefutable good taste and Alice's money. Elizabeth was picking up on

Alice's reticence, and reflecting it back with such maddening composure that Alice was forced to keep going with this project. Elizabeth wrote:

About our venture, I think you are right about beginning quietly and if you want to put it all on to me—the whole "raison d'etre"—I do not mind, altho' I think that after all and if you are honestly going into any business, it is well to have no fear. Otherwise, I may have to come home to organize my lectures for the New Year to meet my financial obligations.

Alice ground her teeth at Elizabeth's ability to maneuver so well around Alice's carefully worded doubts and come through as if nothing had been said.

I think our mutual percentage ought to be decided soon. It seems that 60–40 basis would be about right.

"Agh!" said Alice out loud to the empty house. "Maddening!"

What was the truth of this project? Certainly Alice had prayed every day for guidance on this unending heap of finery stacked in her garage, leaking into the house. Was she being sidetracked by Elizabeth's own path?

***

As fall came, and then the early winter with its attendant parties and opera season, Alice felt the pressure of this business venture tamp down what should have been the heady gaiety of her social life. There was Janey to contend with at the heart of it all. Pulling out on this agreement now might jeopardize that whole plan. Elizabeth was doing a fine job of taking care of her daughter; from all reports there had been only one incident where Elizabeth "had to be severe" with Jane; the actual incident was never explained. But Alice knew Jane could be stubborn to get her own way, so it must have been that kind of incident. Janey for sure had never mentioned it. *She wouldn't have, would she, with her letters likely scrutinized before being sent.* Now Elizabeth's own daughter Helen was due any day in Paris to shop for her trousseau, an unaffordable event without Alice's funds. Well, Alice was good and stuck until Janey was safely back in California. But then, Alice knew she would eventually receive the gorgeous drop earrings designed especially for her—replicating a fine eighteenth-century museum piece—set with precious stones and pearls. There was also to be an orange velvet gown. Both would be ready in the spring. What a glorious statement they would make for her professional opera debut next October: an ensemble of arias of which she would be a part. It was a daring adventure, a first step toward a new life cloaked in secrecy should it fail to ignite decent press coverage.

Early in December Alice made arrangements to wire Christmas presents to Paris. With plans completed for the Jerry Muma Scholarship and the pseudonym chosen for her opera debut, she was restless to flee before the holiday weighed her down. A few weeks later she and Johnny boarded the train and headed east to Mitchell, Canada for Christmas. It was just unthinkable to be in Los Angeles, in her beautiful home, without Jerry.

***

A letter awaited her from Elizabeth when they returned. Alice was pleased at Elizabeth addressing her as Alicia. It hinted foreignness, therefore mystery, while keeping her identity. She had quietly inserted the idea into her letters as the plans for singing took shape. If her singing career took flight, her name would only heighten the romance.

December 29th, 1925
Dearest Alicia,

Two fine long letters of yours are before me to be answered. Dear Helen is gone home and I feel Janey is a comfort at this time. We had a very happy Christmas together, a wee tree and some trimmings for Janey, stockings with little jokes and some goodies. She trimmed the tree entirely herself and also filled the stockings.... Right in the midst of it came your lovely big pink azalea and the box of candied sweets, to make us even happier with the loving card and its message from across land and sea! Gifts galore from her little friends, a fitted workbox from Helen and two parties on Xmas day with little girls from the building. Janey looked quite smart with her new skunk cuffs on her coat and her new brown shoes.

Now about curtain material and also upholstery. Striped silk—18 meters of it double wide for $2 a yard. I settled on the yellow silk for furniture coverings with small stripes of a purplish cast, also some pure Directoire design fabric in rich yellow to be used with the bed coverings. You could put them right in stock for a good profit, and you will have them by January 15.

I am following this with a diagram of decorating bedrooms and sewing instructions for the fabric.

There is a balance of 3,000 frcs left but your earrings need payment as do the Breton beds and Janey's ticket home on the *Minnetonka*. I just sent a cable saying Janey will be traveling with a fellow Scientist from Sunday school, a Mrs. Flanagan, on January 30. Jane is to have her own stateroom just next door to Mrs. Flanagan and will sit at the captain's table. I will provide her with enough American money to pay her tips. I will need to cancel Janey's dentist to allow her to say goodbye to just about everyone in Paris!

Janey is homesick, seeing Helen and all, but the days should pass quickly and she will be on her way! She has kept well except for signs of a cold and sore throat, but I had Mrs. McCallum do some Science work and it was nipped in the bud. She has grown and her dresses have had to be lengthened, and she chats away with French people, but it is hard to get her to speak it to me.

I hope your bairn reaches you safely.

***

Mr. Don from the Caribbean cruise was agreeably imposed upon to meet Jane off the boat in New York. Dear Don lived with his parents in a palatial apartment in Philadelphia. Head of his own company, he had family money and lots of it—and a penchant for remaining a bachelor. Alice had no compunctions about asking this favor, so enamored with the Mumas as he swore he was.

Jane had been safely home a week before Alice received Don's delightful letter.

February 16, 1926
Dear Alicia,

What a pleasure to see Janey's smiling face at the dock in New York and to have a nice visit with her while she was getting her baggage inspected. I did not have a pass to get by the guard at the end of the wharf. However, using a little of the Algerian methods, I worked my way around a cargo of wicker furniture, and after a quarter of an hour managed to make my way past the freight gangway and to Janey and her friend.

She certainly is a sweet little girl and I know that you were glad to have her home again. Her freckles are gone and she is so tall and so completely in charge of herself. You will be so pleased with the changes in her, I am sure.

We had tea while she waited for her train, and she regaled me with tales of her departure, tossing in French words completely unconscious of putting on airs. Apparently her French friends all came to see her off and loaded her down with candy and small gifts and lots of flowers.

I have provided her with the $125 you said she needed for overland expenses. You will know this, as well by my telegram, that Helen is meeting her in Chicago.

Give my regards to Johnny with some for yourself.
Faithfully yours,
Donald

Jane had arrived on the train, stepping down to the platform to wild adulation from a small crowd of family, and good old Hattie. When she was home and thoroughly hugged and fussed over, Alice, Johnny and Jane clattered up the stairs and into her room to help her unpack.

"And this is my fur coat," said Jane with some pride. "Look, it sheds a bit, but isn't it fine!"

Johnny tried to put it on and nearly ripped out the sleeves, and they all chuckled a bit, though Alice pretended to scold.

When Jane pulled out her woolen bloomers, though, they all burst into fits of falling-over laughter. "What *will* I do with these in Los Angeles, I wonder?" said Jane.

"Ah," said her mother, "they served you well in the snows of Paris. Perhaps the poor box will do for them."

So it went until the trunks were empty and the closets full again, and all the clothes stored for her return had been sorted and rejected as unfit for the changed Jane who returned to charm them all.

Alice noted Jane's little autograph book lying on the bed and picked it up to browse through fondly written poems and messages left by nine months of friends. Yes, Alice thought, everyone loved Jane. Which was why she was jolted out of the pleasant reverie at the trite and mean verse left by Tante Elizabeth.

There was a little girl, who had a little curl,
Right in the middle of her forehead.
When she was good, she was very, very good,
But when she was bad she was horrid!

Even the purser on board the *Minnetonka* had more imaginative and complimentary things to say about the half-grown and always-cheerful girl who loved to dance. It was definitely time to separate herself from Elizabeth Burton.

Chapter 44

Local Matron Sings in Opera

March 1st, 1926

My Dear Alicia,

…Now, this thing is on such a large footing, that I think if you frankly come out with the fact that you have gone into business, as well as I, you will then be in a position to put things before your friends and the public much better than if you say you are merely selling them for me. You know that nowadays there is no longer any opprobrium attached to a woman going into business. We are too earnest Scientists to harbor any false pride, aren't we, dear Alicia.

Affectionately, Elizabeth

Nasty pressure between Alice's eyes had grown more annoying as she scanned the balance of Elizabeth's letter. False pride, indeed! The nerve of the woman! It was time to end this farce. Nothing short of a drastic move would get rid of the import business and the frightful emptiness in the house that Jerry would never fill again. After a night of prayers, the idea came.

After lunch a couple of weeks later, she sat Johnny and Jane down in the garden room.

"My dears, I have made some decisions which I hope you will honor enthusiastically."

Alice could see her children look up with wary expressions, and then shift toward each other, their black leather chairs almost touching. After the initial euphoria of having Jane back in the fold, there were days when the very air vibrated with tension.

"I miss Daddy," Jane had wailed one night. "I see his fishing hat in the back hall, and it makes me so sad."

Johnny walked around as if he had no cares, pretending that hugging his sister was all he needed to do. But Alice had caught him at odd times with his eyes downcast in disappointment when there was no father to cheer him on at the football games. Occasionally he snapped at her and left the house. It wounded her, his reticence about his feelings, but she tried to understand. They were both a handful these days, half-grown with hormones clouding their reason.

"What we need is a complete change," Alice continued. "I have decided to close the import business with Tante Elizabeth. To that end I have arranged for all the items to be placed in storage. We also need a fresh start in a new place." Here she paused, as the children's faces registered true alarm.

"I like it here, Mother," said Jane in a steely voice.

"All our friends are here," said Johnny, his tennis shoes hitting the floor with a thump as he bounded up to pace the floor. "Father's guns are in the rack, his hunting jacket is still in the back hall. I miss him, too, you know. Don't pull us away from his memory just like that. Who cares, anyway, about Tante Elizabeth and her stuff? Why did you start with her when all you want to do is sing? I won't go, I tell you. Uncle L. B. and Aunt Sue will agree with us, I am sure!"

"Johnny, don't be impudent," Alice blurted. "Calm down and hear me out!" His father had *never* disciplined him, had left it up to her, and it was difficult; Jerry was never around, just like now.

"He was never around," Jane said as if listening to her mother's inner turmoil, "but I loved him so!" It was Jane's turn to stand, and she angled across the room, bare feet marching over the jute rug. She moved to the credenza and picked off the small, framed photo of her father, his profiled face topped by a battered fishing hat.

"This is mine. If all we will have of Daddy is memories, I am claiming this." She held the photo to her chest, walked back to the chair and sat, tucking one leg under. "And don't yell at me for putting my feet on the furniture!"

Alice waited a few beats to calm her temper.

"I have heard of a new development in the Santa Monica hills called Castellamare. I think it would be a good investment to build a house there, and I have my eye on a lot with views of both the Pacific Ocean and the hills. I would like you to come with me and take a look at it next week. I promise to move all of your favorite things into that house so you can call it your own. In addition, I am having Tante Elizabeth purchase some antique Spanish furniture just for us."

"Will we go to the same schools?" asked Jane.

"I would like to remind you that you both will be changing schools in the fall in any case," said Alice.

"When will we be moving, then?" challenged Johnny.

"I have made arrangements for us to move almost immediately into an apartment at the Women's Athletic Association, downtown. But you will finish this year at your old school."

"But what about Hattie?" asked Jane.

"Hattie will be let go, Jane," replied Alice. "I have already spoken to her. Perhaps when the Castellamare house is finished next year, she will join us." She tried some levity, "You know I can't cook." And she blew out her breath to release the tension in her voice. "Johnny, dear, change into your whites and put on clean tennis shoes. You have a court date at the club."

Jane padded out to the kitchen. "Going to see Hattie," she fired over her shoulder.

Jane landed on a gray-painted chair and drew a shaky breath. "I'm going to miss you, Hattie."

"Same for me, Miss Janey," said Hattie, moving away from the hot range to give Jane a hug. "Now, how 'bout some of that fresh coffee I just perked, with lots of cream?" Hattie made her way back to the gas range and pulled off the percolator, grabbed a cup, opened the fridge for the bottle of cream, and had the fragrant brew in front of her Jane before she could answer.

Jane jumped up, tears flowing. "Nothing is the same since Daddy died, is it? I miss him, then I had to miss you all that time in Paris. Now I come back and you are leaving and we are leaving. It's not fair!"

Hattie opened her arms and gathered Jane close. Cushioned by Hattie's ample bosom, Jane let the tears flow over the pristine white uniform while Hattie gently rocked her.

"Come on then, Miss Jane. Let's have a celebration." Hattie released Jane and disappeared into the laundry room, coming back with the ice cream maker. "Let's you and me make some vanilla. Maybe there will be a little left for that brother of yours when he gets back from tennis. Now get the rock salt, and a hankie while you're at it."

***

The home on Windsor Boulevard was inventoried and rented partially furnished. Johnny and Jane fretted. Alice exhausted herself with the enormous task. Elizabeth Burton, at first shocked to hear of the upheaval and then resigned, came back to help dispose of the goods. It wasn't a month before they moved into the downtown apartment within the Women's Athletic Association. Alice didn't have to manage staff, think about menus or feel the ghost of Jerry's presence in her bed. She could focus on her career and the new house.

Rehearsals for her October concert began just as schools let out for summer vacation. The children were excited to go to their first sleep-away camp, a cowboy camp in New Mexico for Johnny and a sailing camp for Jane on Catalina Island.

John's arrival at the Los Alamos Ranch School was a tangle that ended well, thanks to the good graces of Mr. Connell, the director. Alice had applied way back in January but had become stalled by what she felt was impertinence by their refusal to treat John with C. S. methods were he to become ill. The camp became filled in March. Undeterred, Alice sent him there anyway, with a letter:

June 29th

Dear Mr. McConnell,

It is presuming, I know, to send John to you, but I assure you I do not do it in a spirit of rudeness, only knowing that you are liable at the opening of camp to have a vacancy. I felt a personal interview might result in your being attracted toward the boy and allowing him to stay. He has in his pocket the papers you require, together with the necessary check. If you have no place for John, he is to withdraw quietly and return to the city. ...

Yours very sincerely,
Alice Muma

July 3, 1926
Los Alamos Ranch School
Otowi, New Mexico
Dear Mrs. Muma:

I am going to be frank and tell you that I do not like your methods. I told John that I had no place for him and that my camp was filled. He asked if he couldn't come up and see the ranch. I could hardly refuse such a request. As he seemed to be so heartbroken at the thought of leaving, I decided to make room for him and keep him for the summer. This has put me to considerable inconvenience.

I will never understand your sending the boy on that way, subjecting him to the humiliation of being placed in the position of an unwelcome intruder. He seems to me too fine a boy to treat that way. However, now that I have decided to keep him, we will try to give him the most wonderful summer he has ever had. ...

Very sincerely yours,
A. J. McConnell, Director

***

She would miss them. Better that than having them in her hair. While they were gone, she gave a performance of Scottish, French and Italian songs at the Women's Athletic Club, testing the professional waters, as it were. By the time Johnny and Jane returned for school in the fall, Alice was rehearsing four days a week for her secret October debut and visiting with the architect for a new house in Castellamare.

It seemed to Alice that when you follow the truth of Science, all is possible.

***

LA Times, October 18, 1926
"Local Matron Sings in Opera"

The diamond horseshoe of Los Angeles grand opera was mildly excited the other evening when friends of Mrs. I. J. Muma, prominent matron, observed her on the stage in an ensemble. Mrs. Muma's musical talent has occasionally led her outside her family circle, but heretofore, she has appeared only in civic or philanthropic endeavors and never professionally. ...

That evening performance—on her thirty-ninth birthday, no less—had required unremitting commitment over the year. An expensive year, too, what with the move, the second successful Jerry Muma Scholarship award, summer camp, and on and on. Worth it, every penny, down to the dangling gemstone earrings from Europe. Alice could envision them as her signature jewelry for future performances.

Had she been silly with her secret performance? After all, on the night and before the performance began, her face was visible to all. The shame of failure might have motivated the secrecy, for so much was riding on this initial success, this extraordinary move toward a different life.

Chapter 45

Casa Chiquita at Castellamare

"Shirred eggs with mushrooms and that lovely lemon tart for me," said Alice to the waiter in the Women's Athletic Club dining room. "Jane will have the chicken with sweet potatoes, and John the lamb chops and peas. Ice cream for both of them afterwards."

"Casa Chiquita? Really mother, who named it?" asked Johnny. "I think it's silly."

"Well, I like it," said Jane.

"Dudley—Mr. Corbett—made the suggestion once he could see the house taking shape," Alice responded with a smile. "It suits the place, I think. Oh, you'll like it well enough! And now that the windows are in, and the wooden ceilings installed…"

"What does he know?" scoffed Johnny.

"Well, aren't you Mr. High and Mighty about this, Johnny dear."

"Mr. Corbett is *very* artsy," said Jane. "He writes books and articles and puts on plays."

"He is a good friend and fellow Christian Scientist," said Alice. "Why, Johnny, don't you like him? He thinks *you* are pretty fine."

"Well," grumbled Johnny, "he's always hanging around."

Luckily, luncheon arrived to stave off further disconcerting remarks about Dudley Corbett, whom Alice knew was developing a huge crush on her. She *was* flattered, and he was good company, and that was that.

Within the hour the family climbed into their car for the drive north along the coast to Santa Monica. A right turn off the highway put them on Tramonto Drive, where hairpin turns on new pavement climbed steeply and ended all at once on top of the hill with a stunning vista. Construction progressed here and there, but only a few homes were inhabited. All had the look of the California dream house: stucco walls with red tiled roofs and little gated entrances hiding luxurious interiors and millionaire views.

At Casa Chiquita, a truck piled with flagstone commanded the front entrance. Voices carried across the lot along with the thunking of shovels and a mallet. The third and final patio was in process.

The Mumas parked on the curve just beyond the house. Johnny and Jane piled out of the car, slammed their doors, and ran pell-mell through the front gate to a grand flagstone garden.

Jane hooked a left and made for the recessed, arched doorway into the living area, which was still bare but for the huge fireplace and the red tile floor.

She passed the little door of the dumbwaiter set in the wall at a convenient height. Johnny, right behind her, peered out the deep-set casement windows of steel-framed glass. They all were greeted with a fresh breeze redolent with scents of eucalyptus and pine and saltwater.

"Mother," said Jane to Alice, who took up the rear of the mad dash. "Never sell this! I want you to will it to me." Jane flew out into the garden again, past the master bedroom with its own entrance, down a flight of uneven stone steps and onto another patio near the kitchen, only stopping as she reached the low wall guarding the end of the property. There in front of her, Topanga Canyon lay almost invisible, folded into the mountain range that headed unbroken to the sea.

Johnny and Jane spent another hour inspecting their bedrooms, guest quarters and kitchen, gabbling away about the move. Alice took little notice, engrossed as she was in discussion with the contractor concerning installation of the bathroom and kitchen fixtures. As the sun dipped toward the Pacific, Alice found her children speaking Spanish to the masons as the crew thumped the last flagstones in front of the guest quarters off the garage. The family gathered back into the car and headed to the Athletic Club.

"Now, after dinner—homework," said Alice. "Next week you're to start rehearsing for that O'Neill play at the Majestic, Johnny."

"What about me, Mother?" said Jane.

"You're one of the children, Janey. Be patient. John is playing the role of young Jim Harris, and has a few more lines to learn than you." Alice smiled at the thought of her youngsters in their first grownup production, *All God's Chillin Got Wings*. "Won't it be exciting, both of you on stage. You're going to have to study for school *and* rehearse at the same time. Opening night is just after school closes. Now, off to your books."

Voice lessons had not shown either of them to have inherited her musical ability. Jane, though, should be quite accomplished at the piano if she stuck to it. Johnny—well, he would be as handsome as any man in the movies, and he did have some acting ability.

Alice planned an early night, hoping their schoolwork would be quickly finished. She had to be up with the dawn, as she had many times before, to drive downtown to pick up several daily laborers to work on the new house. "You are such an unconventional adventuress!" Dudley had said to her months ago. She had to admit she *was*, rather, always enjoying the feeling of stepping a little out of the ordinary to meet her goals.

While the children plied away at their spelling and math, she pulled up at her own desk to review the prodigious file of papers finally signaling the settling of Jerry's estate. It would be May next week. Two years. He had left no will, lots of debt and very little cash. Eleven months of hard work it took with her attorney just to appraise the estate at a little over $341,000. After the evaluation, many stocks and bonds were sold off to pay the debts.

She had decided from the beginning that the wisest course would be to give up her executrix claims and hand them over to Jerry's longtime friend and attorney, Gurney Newlin. Gurney had promised not to collect fees for settling the estate, but he was also in charge of the guardianship trust for the children, which was in effect until Johnny and Jane's respective twenty-first birthdays. The court set the annual fees. Alice would have to justify all the children's expenses on separate forms and keep receipts, and pay for the privilege. And she resented, in advance, every penny she would fork over.

It was embarrassing to find out that Jerry had never paid his sisters Sue and Anne their share of their father's estate, sold so many years before. It was with abject apology that Alice wrote the checks to each of them for $1,814.

The court had allowed her living expenses of $1,000 a month, which Alice continued to exceed without fail. Gurney was always sympathetic. He would come up with a little extra cash, generally from the stream of ongoing commissions from Jerry's insurance sales.

The $16,000 for Casa Chiquita was mostly covered by a second mortgage on the Windsor Boulevard house, but there were items of furniture to be purchased, the moving expenses, and voice and coaching lessons for her budding operatic career.

Alice insisted on keeping some land in Yuma, Arizona that Jerry had purchased—with a whopping mortgage. It was a desert parcel with the rich promise of irrigation from the Colorado River. And why not? The California desert had proven a rich resource for fruits and vegetables when irrigation was introduced. If crops were making farmers wealthy in California, the land in Arizona would respond similarly as soon as the Colorado River was diverted into the pipes and canals, just as Jerry envisioned years ago.

Gurney had great sympathy for the scholarship fund, too, being one of Jerry's closest friends. Alice had no trouble insisting on her portfolio of oil and gas leases to fund it. She also kept her 50 percent interest in her brother George's ranch in Riverside. George and his wife always paid on time, so that was a guaranteed income. Jerry's life insurance policy provided, along with some stock dividends, the $18,000 necessary to purchase more of the fabulous Laguna Land and Water Company Stock.

Gurney warned her, "Your stock portfolio is heavily overloaded with that one stock, Alice. I don't recommend it." Never mind, the dividends would provide a handsome allowance for the children as well as herself. The stock had a bright future with all the new building in Los Angeles. The market was making millions more every month.

***

Summer's crescendo was the christening, as Dudley called it, of Casa Chiquita. But not before John and Jane's play *All God's Chillen Got Wings* was a sellout performance and Alice hosted the Women's Athletic Clubs opening musical evening of the season, and auditioned for a part in *Il*

184

Trovatore. The two parts for mezzo-sopranos were exceptional, even for Verdi. If she could capture the role of the younger woman, Inez, it would be an excellent launch to her career. But first, she must present Casa Chiquita to her friends.

***

On the night of July 24, the house was opened for a party. The promised Spanish antique dining table and enormous carved chairs, which Elizabeth Burton had hunted down, had a place of prominence to one side of the fireplace. On the mantle stood two large pencil sketches of the children by an up-and-coming artist, Herman Amlauer. Jute and Persian rugs graced the tiled floors. Two wrought-iron floor lamps sent golden light through their parchment shades. A baby grand piano commanded considerable floor space under a north window, and from it, Alice played and sang to her guests, including bits of Scottish and English folksongs. There were even strains of "Bye, Bye Blackbird" and "My Blue Heaven," both commanded and sung by her guests far into the night.

The tinkling of glass and conversation resonated throughout the house. People meandered over the patios as the music drifted around them; greetings and introductions flowed liked a river from upper to lower patios. Guests poked their heads in to see the guest quarters, which were outfitted with yellow-painted wooden beds from Mexico, and Alice's own bedroom with its carved mahogany bed, Regency Period, and block-printed curtains lined with ivory sateen. An eighteenth-century Dutch marquetry walnut secretary fit nicely into a corner by the window.

It was Dudley who capped the evening for Alice. For as the last guests departed in a flurry of praise, he kissed her cheek and said, "You have breathed a living spirit, part of your own soul of joyous hospitality, into this home. Good night, Alicia. Sweet dreams." And he departed.

Chapter 46

Limelight

Alice sat at the breakfast table, bleary eyed, gloriously tired and still giddy. A pile of newspapers were strewn about in her search for reviews of *Il Trovatore*. Last night many of the flowers strewn on the stage had been for her. Still, she hungered to read whether she had pleased the music critics. It was her birthday today and no praise could be too high.

LA Examiner, October 17, 1927
"Los Angeles Civic Opera Opens with *Il Trovatore*"
The debut of Alice Muma in the role of Inez was cordially received. The singer's ease of manner bespoke no insincerity, and her singing was commendable for clarity of tone and enunciation.

Alice snorted in disgust at the lukewarm pronouncement and moved on to the *LA Express.*

Alice Muma, prominent in social circles, made her debut in the role of Inez. Endowed with a charming soprano voice, she manages it to good effect. Few first appearances show such security of vocalism and diction, both of which carried well into the far corners of the large hall, as the applause showed. To tonal expression this new Inez adds histrionic spontaneity wanting in the "old timers." As a result, Alice Muma could not only share numerous curtain calls, but the footlights were banked with flowers in her honor.

"That's more like it," she gloated aloud, and leaned forward to take her tea, noting with disappointment that neither paper used her new stage name of Alicia.

"What's 'more like it,' Mother?" asked Jane as she pecked her mother's cheek and plopped herself on a chair. "Happy birthday, and here's my card. I made it myself."

"You're awake early for a young lady up late last night," replied Alice as she leaned over to give her daughter a hug. "Thank you for remembering. I wonder when you had time to do this. Is your brother stirring?"

Jane shrugged. "Let me see the paper, Mother," and she grabbed the *Express* to read for herself.

"Yes, I am, and you were splendid, Mother!" said Johnny as he slid into the remaining chair and snatched a piece of cold toast from his mother's plate. "Forgot my card. Tia Lala and Tia Patsy, Aunt Sue, Uncle Grif, Mr. Corbett, Mr. and Mrs. Dickson... Just everybody was there. We cheered and cheered!"

"Tia Lala gasped when you made your entrance," Jane said, "and remarked how beautiful your gown was. She said she didn't know why you thought it didn't fit. It was just perfect. Then Mr. Corbett leaned over and said you looked so Spanish in your part, a credit to the opera, and no one else looked the least bit Spanish."

"How was the party last night?" asked Johnny.

Alice beamed, reveling in her children's excitement, feeling the glow spreading through her heart. The exhilaration of last night had overcome the exhausting weeks of rehearsals, voice and diction lessons, and fittings. "It was fine, Johnny. A supper party for over fifty people. The Dicksons were there, likely because of his managing the newspaper, and guess who else? Xavier Cugat! And movie people too numerous to count. And, of course the cast of the opera and *moi*."

Alice's eyes scanned the dining room for the bouquets of roses and carnations someone had scooped up for her from the stage's apron.

"I thought I would never experience a night like last night. A mezzo-soprano rarely sings an aria or plays next to the leading tenor. This was certainly the most spectacular birthday present I could have imagined."

"Last night you proved you could be a great star," said Johnny. "All the cheering, and clapping…"

"And the curtain calls—don't forget the curtain calls," piped up Jane. "And Tia Lala is getting a copy of the libretto bound in brown leather with gold letters saying *Souvenir of Mother Singing Inez, Love from Jane and John*."

"Jane!" shouted Johnny. "You weren't supposed to tell!"

Alice sat quietly after the children had left the table, reviewing all that had preceded opening night. *Il Trovatore*, one of Verdi's beloved operas, was set in fifteenth-century Spain and came with opulent costumes. Most of all there were some treasures of mezzo soprano roles.

The work of honing her part continued with long weeks of rehearsals and extra coaching. Her costumes were fitted; Alice insisted on controlling their creations. Posing for the press photos, she stood proud and smiling in a square-necked velvet bodice with a lace insert down the front, flowing skirt panels of golden brocade and short train of burgundy. Sleeves, puffed at the shoulder, were caught tight above her elbow and lace flowed gracefully to her wrist. The pearl and gemstone earrings from Paris set off her long neck. Her dark brown hair was carefully waved. Perched on top was a pillbox crown draped with a lace mantilla.

***

Monday morning the mailman delivered heaps of mail. A note from Dudley gushed, *Your appearance was stunning. A great night and the reward of real work, the result of an unfaltering ambition. More roses to you.* Alice's sister-in-law Sue pronounced Alice's gown striking and her performance fine and sweet. Notes in a similar tone poured in from a panoply of friends.

187

However pleased she was with the praise of friends, it was a formal letter from Max Wieczorek, a Western artist whose landscapes were filling galleries and private collections, whose request left her stunned. He wrote that he had seen Alice in the production and asked her to sit for a life-size portrait in pastels. Of course there was no refusing such an invitation.

A week later he had chosen her gown: emerald green cut velvet with a plain round neckline, accented with a large peacock feather fan. By the December 7 opening, the large painting was hung with others in the Sixth Annual Painters of the West Exhibit at the Galleria in the Biltmore Hotel.

Elizabeth Bingham of *Saturday Night* pronounced:

The portrait was outlined with spirit and sureness... deftly done, the light touch and the vitality of the figure blending well with the delicacy of the pastel medium.

The review reprinted a photo of the portrait.

"Gorgeous in color, but that is about all that can be said," remarked Alice to a friend after walking through the exhibit. For all that, she purchased the portrait and hung it to the side of the fireplace at Casa Chiquita.

***

Anxious at the thought of Christmas in Los Angeles without Jerry, Alice arranged a family cruise to Hawaii in mid-December, and a stay at the upscale Hotel Halekulani with its views of Diamond Head. It was not world-class, but it was acceptable.

Dudley's prose followed her to the island hotel. With the children occupied at the tennis courts, Alice picked a chaise on the lawn and stretched out her long legs to read.

A boundless horizon with all sorts of new scenes and adventures... a comfy deck chair, a book and the blue Pacific, Dudley began. Alice smiled in agreement at his romantic prose. She had always adored to ride the waves and remembered with a flash of nostalgia her first trip over the ocean from New York to Italy bundled in a coat and lap robe against the spring wind. He did know her pretty well.

I wonder what you will really get out of your trip. There is a restless, unappeased urge in your spirit that may make it a bit difficult to find all you seek...

Alice put the letter down in annoyance. How dare he demean her spirit! But she allowed the delicious breeze to calm her. Slowly the peace that she came here for enveloped her again. Dudley was wrong—Dudley was certainly wrong. She knew the right of it, this new path of hers. Prayer and hard work were showing the truth.

Dudley was nonetheless a good companion and dear friend. She remembered with fondness the Halloween night just past. They had been talking about this new novel of his and a myriad of other things. Alice had been boosting his confidence, for she felt somehow that without encouragement he was too scattered in his interests to be a serious author.

He had taken her hand and said, "Would it be too plebian of us to go to the Ocean Park Carnival on Halloween? I would love to take the children if they are free. We could take a glorious swim and then a stroll through the fun sideshows to watch humanity and study types."

"Oh my," said Alice. "Would this study be for your novel? I thought I was inspiration enough." And she laughed at her own silliness.

"My dear, grateful as I am for your confidence, and the many charming things you do for my pleasure, I was thinking of being a child again, just for the evening. It would do us both good. Now, I must to the typewriter go, to reduce my scribbled notes to cold letters."

Alice said yes to the idea, whether or not John and Jane could go, and had given him a peck on the cheek and sent him off down the hill to Los Angeles.

Then, two days later, in November, a letter arrived from him containing the usual small talk of mutual acquaintances and progress or lack thereof on his novel. At the end of the note he had written,

The green patterned seahorse handles on your new cupboard that you showed me were astonishingly lifelike and stick in my mind. I can still feel their swelling breasts thrust forward to surmount the tide. A sign and portent perhaps of a door that may be opened for me?

What was she to make of that remark? Alice had always thought Dudley a confirmed bachelor. His father had been grossly overbearing and a cold fish, to hear Dudley talk. Dudley therefore had made it a point to be affectionate, demonstrative—quite good qualities, really. But alarm bells were going off in Alice's head. And now, coupled with his comment of her "unappeased spirit," perhaps she should heed them.

Enjoying the breeze across the Halekulani Hotel's lawn, she wondered if he was implicitly asking her to marry him. Clearly he liked the children. Jane certainly thought he was interesting, but John, that was another matter. Dudley thought well of Christian Science and admired her for her beliefs.

"Drat!" said Alice aloud as she folded Dudley's letter into her purse. Her peace was gone. She would go for a walk and find the children, who should be winding up their tennis game. She would calm down and not think of anything serious for the next few days. Rest and renewal—that was the order of the day. This was just not the time to think of remarrying, whoever the groom might be.

Chapter 47

Winds of Change - 1928

A Conversation with Gran'mere

"It's so far away, Gran'mere," I said, watching her reading a letter from a Miss Lillian Weaver. Suddenly, in her mind, the children were receiving an inadequate education at their schools. Perhaps it was true. What *was* true was that Christian Science had become her guiding light. So much so that, without her knowing—and, of course, how could she have my perspective?—she was in danger of making an irrevocable decision.

February 20, 1928
Andrebrook School
Tarrytown-on-Hudson, New York
My Dear Mrs. Muma,
Thank you for your inquiry about Andrebrook School. Yes indeed we are a Christian Science school. … We don't usually take girls as young as thirteen but I do acknowledge the special opportunities Jane has had. The trip to Munich will be organized for August. It is the capital of musical and artistic charm of Europe. Please keep in touch. …

"Jane will be on that boat," said Alice with assurance. She pressed her manicured fingers to her eyes, probably to relieve the ache of hours at her correspondence, glancing with annoyance at a bit of ink from her fountain pen staining her thumb.

"It's from your letter to Cousin Jean in Mitchell," I said. The sealed envelope with its address and stamp sat atop the pile of correspondence going to the post office. I suspected Gran'mere was feeling Jean out for a possible visit from Jane in the summer, so confident she seemed of the Munich opportunity.

The Hicks family in Mitchell was quite diminished. Uncle Will and Aunt Marie had passed on and the cousins scattered throughout Canada. Only unmarried Jean was rattling around in the tattered mansion called Dunelg. How strange life can be, I thought. Alice, who had once secretly coveted the Dunelg Manse, now owned several homes which quite outshone the stone home of her childhood dreams.

"I think this is a bad idea," I continued. Jane's attendance at this school would alter the course of the Muma family, and not for the better, although Jane herself would receive one of the best educations offered in the Western world. I knew what was to come and was already cringing.

"Boarding school looks to be a solution to a number of problems," Gran'mere replied, ignoring my warning. "If the children are going to be away from my guidance, they must be in the right atmosphere."

"Too far," I cautioned.

"It can't be helped. There is nothing here in Los Angeles."

"What of Johnny? Andrebrook is only for girls."

Alice tugged her tweed skirt back over her knees before reaching further into the desk for the Los Alamos Ranch School brochure.

"While not Christian Science, it is strong in academics during the school year, and hosts disciplined outdoor activities in the summer. Johnny wants to go there again—'cowboy camp,' he calls it, in New Mexico. Uniforms are required. They are run like the Boy Scouts—camping trips on horseback, fishing, hunting, polo, solid education… Sparsely furnished cabins kept ship-shape by the boys… It gives them a taste of the simple lifestyle, and carefully chosen instructors guide them—no nonsense and plenty of good food. His daddy would have approved."

"But what if both Johnny and Jane are thrilled by those schools?" I asked. "What then?"

She smiled, perhaps pleased that I had discovered her plot. "My thought exactly. Should they like it, why not suggest they stay on? I would have some peace of mind that their care is in the hands of competent people while I am struggling with all my might to succeed at my singing."

"I don't think this is a good idea at all," I said, as if pleading would make any difference.

Alice scoffed at my concern. "You know nothing of the difficulties. Johnny will not study and is often unruly. He needs discipline, accountability and a strong hand. There are no men in my life to take him under control."

Never has been, I thought, remembering the comment made years ago before that "her Jerry" had never once disciplined the children.

"The LA schools are no challenge for either of them. Johnny refuses to work at his lessons, and Jane is stubborn." She sighed. "Both are so bright. Janey needs a private school, but it must be Christian Science that guides her. Johnny, well, he will focus on Science if I nag him, but he is always losing his books and finding a way to avoid Sunday school. Jane is more malleable on that score."

By April Alice had decided on summer camps, and several thousand dollars were allocated from her dwindling supply of cash. Both Jane and Johnny sat in turn for new passport photos with serious faces—strong eyebrows over dark eyes. Both had thick brown hair carefully combed; Johnny's slicked back,

191

Jane's parted in the middle and held behind in a soft bun. They had their father's heavy jaw, a feature that looked rather better on Johnny.

***

The words from Gran'mere's correspondence gushed forth with clarity as the spring sped into early summer. Rehearsals, voice training and diction coaching culminated in a brief three minutes of Handel's orchestral song, "Ah, Let Me Weep, Lord," with the Los Angeles Symphony and later in the summer, a solo program of songs produced by Dudley. Alice wore a black satin gown to both performances, stunning audiences with her soaring bell tones. Between performances, she squeezed in concerts and dinners with friends and, always, church on Sunday and a C. S. meeting every Wednesday evening.

Become a landlord, Alice, wrote Elinor Flood, Alice's best friend from the Chicago days. Alice took her advice. One Miss Klumb was hired to manage both the Windsor and Castellamare homes and their annoyingly expensive repairs. A third rental property was almost ready to purchase. Alice dubbed it Kings X for its being located on Kings Road, and it was a collection of tiny apartments with a spectacular view of the Hollywood hills.

The very same John Rankin who escorted her during her college days at UC Berkeley was now an attorney, and she hired him to do her legal work—the most immediate crisis being the threatened lien on Castellamare for late mortgage payments. Ah, Gran'mere, I thought, your fanatical timeliness with personal correspondence did not extend to your finances.

John Rankin became her champion. His glib tongue, meticulous work, and affection for her (though he loved his wife dearly) would keep him in her employ until her death.

"What I would have done without his correspondence throughout the remainder of your life, Gran'mere, I do not know." His letters were long and detailed, factual and funny.

Gran'mere also hired a secretary, a Miss Moore, to deal with all manner of correspondence, keep the bank accounts, send out checks, coordinate the efforts of all her businesses and work with both Miss Klumb and John Rankin.

Of course, there was her clipping service.

***

July arrived, and with it the complicated plans for camp. Gran'mere insisted that each child have a friend in tow on the train through Chicago: Jane and Marjorie in one compartment and John and Hal in another. She mapped the route, bought tickets and packed trunks. She organized friends to meet Jane along the route from Chicago through Canada to New York. Jane wrote about that trip:

192

The four of us had a marvelous time going to Chicago, but Marjorie was awful, she was so crazy about John and Hal. She has still got John's class pin. P.S. I'm afraid I am going to have to ask you for more money. I only have two more checks and about eleven dollars in my purse. Johnny borrowed forty dollars. …

The two men across from me are discussing Al Smith and Hoover and I think that you and everybody else in C. S. should do their work! One of the men is for Al Smith and is trying to make the other believe Al Smith is THE MAN. BUT HE IS NOT.

"She is a worldly young woman for her age," remarked Gran'mere.

I couldn't have agreed more. "Gran'mere," I said, "Johnny and Hal left Chicago for New Mexico and the Los Alamos Ranch School. But Jane continued on alone to Canada—Mitchell to Jean, then North Hatley to your old Theta friend Peggy and her brood. She crossed into New Hampshire for a week with old friends before being driven to Tarrytown-on-Hudson, then boarded a boat to Europe. That seems an extraordinary thing, sending a thirteen-year-old girl unescorted across the country for a late summer adventure in Europe with people you never met."

"Janey was well protected," said Alice. She glowered at me in indignation at the very thought of impropriety. "But, yes, it was brave on all sides. Janey carried on splendidly; everyone remarked how like me she was! My goodness, she positively glowed in her letters with each adventure. Really, though, there was no other way. Sending both my children off to be with people I never met was a risk. I simply could not afford to travel to their camps.

"It was her last correspondence in New York which convinced me that my plan for boarding school was working."

July 31st, 1928

Dear Mother,

This is the last letter I can send you until I get to Paris where I will wire you. I just met Miss Weaver, and Mother, she is so nice. She has a beautiful garden and a Boxer dog and there are about seven horses here. I certainly would like to come here for high school.

"Of Johnny, I was not so sure. Letters from him from the Los Alamos Ranch School were full of the joys of riding through the desert and cliff climbing, some of it quite reckless, no doubt, as boys are wont to do. And, of course, he had been there the year before. I felt the need to remind him, *don't forget to say your daily prayer for protection.* He was wildly happy, even when composing the required letter home every Sunday. Oh, that pleased me. I hungered to know every minute of his day. However, it did bother me that Sundays did not include church."

193

"You had adventures of your own that summer, I believe." I said. "Your little Whippet sedan was stolen right from the front of the Women's Athletic club."

Gran'mere grimaced. "I had to rent a car from Hertz Drive-Ur-Self at the Biltmore for a day! My car was used in a holdup, of all things. The police found it the next morning. The Whippet was not damaged, but my beautiful yellow voile dress and big black straw hat were crushed in the trunk box."

God, I thought, there was drama in Gran'mere's life even when she was not in control!

"Both children were wild to have me purchase a new car, a bigger one, and offered to give fifteen dollars a month out of their allowance to help pay for it. It is really sweet of them to think of me."

"Tell me about the opera season," I asked. She had been oddly reticent on the subject this year.

Gran'mere wavered a bit and finally began. "Dapper, slim and thinly mustached Gaetano Merola: It was on him that I hung my star. He had launched the San Francisco Opera Company in 1923 and partnered the formation of the Los Angeles Grand Opera Company. California's operatic future was rich with promise on his arrival. I had already performed with him at the Shrine Auditorium the year before, although it was not, of course, a full-blown opera. He was augmenting his San Francisco performances there in Los Angeles, a gorgeous auditorium, as you know.

"While the children regaled me with letters of their adventures, I rehearsed the role of the Countess in *Andrea Chénier* until my coach pronounced me ready for tryouts. Merola was due back early in August to prepare for casting. I spent the remainder of the week beforehand—that would be late July—in Santa Barbara celebrating the Old Spanish Heritage Days. So many Pasadena and Los Angeles friends. Very gay, it was."

Gran'mere's countenance now reflected utter happiness at being immersed in the social high life. Her gray eyes sparkled and smile lines appeared on her cheeks, for she was no longer young. She stood and walked the room, suede pumps making soft sounds on the carpet. And yes, I saw her pose here and there, as if remembering a stance during conversation with a significant conductor, perhaps, or a university vice president.

"First the parade with Senator McAdoo. He was resplendent in purple velvet on horseback. The silver buckles and ornate bridles tinkled as he and everyone else rode their magnificent steeds. Men and women marched on foot in Mexican costume, pirates and forty-niners. At a tea afterward, old ladies who were born from the original Land Grant families sat in Spanish dress and received their court. Dinner followed, and then off I went in my own black Spanish dress, all done up with a mantilla and silver hair combs, to the stadium to view a dramatization of the early days. We met friends later for waffles at midnight.

194

"The next two days were filled with teas and a *dansant*, and theater parties late into the evenings before we motored the long way back. I rested on Sunday, needing the peace of church and Science to prepare for the opera tryouts ahead of me."

I watched her gather herself in, and saw her frown as she prepared to tell me bad news.

"Johnny and Jane were wild with plans to come home to hear me sing, but it was not to be. The tryouts lasted two weeks." Her voice turned to a whisper. "All that work and expense—for nothing.

"Merola told me that he was giving the part to someone else conditional on her improving. If she did not, he would give me the part."

"What did you say to that?" I asked.

"I said I would be grateful for the chance and would not give up the part but perfect my Italian diction and coach for dramatic action, as the part demanded. Merola dismissed me saying, 'Right you are.' And that was that. Now there was no real reason for the children to stay away, but the die was cast."

***

Jane swept through Paris, had her fourteenth birthday in Munich and wrote to Johnny.

August 27, 1928
Care/Frau Prof. Jank
Karl Theodore Str. 25
Munich
Dear John,

I am in Germany at last. It is a very clean country. It would be so much fun if you and mother were here. I am learning a lot of German words at Frau Jank's villa. It is three floors and we have the top floor to ourselves. It's hard to believe that I am fourteen whole years old and can have a driver's license. Miss Weaver is taking us to Cortina. ...

Jane returned with Miss Weaver late in September to enter Andrebrook as a freshman. Jane, who had not the least idea how to study, learned quickly enough under the strong and loving care of Miss Weaver. Alice felt redeemed by her choice of school for her blooming daughter.

***

Gran'mere, who would never live full time at Casa Chiquita, but try and rent it out, wrote from her downtown apartment:

August 15th, 1928
Women's Athletic Club, Los Angeles
Dear Johnny,

195

We shall have 10 days to play on your return before you go back to school. How do you feel about Los Alamos for the full school year? I am hoping you can catch the train on the morning of the 31st to make it back in time for the last concert of the summer. A cable came from Jane in Munich letting me know she had arrived. It was welcome, for I cannot describe my feelings as I realized she was off and away with someone I never met. Rec'd the usual mid-camp letter from your director, Mr. Connell, who is very content with your entering into all the camp activities. I am very pleased. Can you make inquiries for me on recent oil development in South East New Mexico? The agent who sold me Castellamare is trying to interest me in acreage down there in Lee County in exchange for my Wilshire Country Club Membership. Make your inquiries like a businessman.

I feel badly that you should be all summer without your C. S. books. It is not right and you know it, when we are relying on C. S. for our help and protection.

Johnny continued to evade Science. And Mr. Connell did not allow his boys free rein to wander about the large state of New Mexico on a mother's errands.

He returned to Los Angeles, accompanied his mother to concerts, packed his trunk, which included a new set of C. S. books, and returned to Los Alamos for his sophomore year in high school. The students, all boys, were held to high academic standards in preparation for Ivy League college. In this, Alice was pleased. However, A. J. Connell would brook no interference from "coddling mothers." Had Gran'mere understood this, no doubt Johnny's education would have been quite different. As it was, disaster was inevitable.

***

Gran'mere needed another career opportunity, now that the children were expensively away in school, and the opera was no longer an option to pay for it. A chance exchange of a few sentences with George's daughter Eileen during her younger sister Helen's wedding suddenly opened a way.

"The fire's out!" George shouted down the phone. "The wedding cake you ordered has just been delivered, so the wedding's on."

Had the fire been fiercer, as fires can be in the Sequoias, the wedding might have been held with the justice of the peace, and Gran'mere would have missed the conversation.

"Aunt Alice," Eileen had said, "I see the State Department is hiring diplomatic staff. I wish I could afford to take the course and stand for the exams. I just can't afford it with my college debt at Stanford, but it's just the thing for you, don't you think?"

Gran'mere visualized the romance and intrigue of working in the Foreign Service. Why not? Anything was possible if you followed the path. Surely it would be a way to parlay her love of travel and languages.

***

196

Surely not, Gran'mere, if I were you. But, I could understand your need as I understood the consequences.

Chapter 48

Dear Mother, How Does It Feel to Have Both Your Little Bums Away at School?

"'God is ever present. His love will meet my need,'" Alice recited as a mantra against her anguished thoughts. Over all that was to come this year loomed the nagging fear that failure to win a part in Merola's opera company truly meant the end of her singing career.

"'Shepherd, show me how to go / o'er the hillside steep. / ... I will listen for thy voice, / lest my footsteps stray / I will follow and rejoice, / all the rugged way,'" she would whisper from a favorite poem of Mary Baker Eddy. Vigilance with these Science prayers of protection was her refuge.

Determined to stay with her music as best she could, Alice performed again with the LA Symphony's mid-January production for ten whole minutes on stage, offering two songs this season. Johnny was part of the enthusiastic audience for her new rendition of *La Mort de Jeanne d'Arc*, and a repeat from last year, *Lascia Ch'io Pianga (Ah, Let Me Weep, Lord)*. And then there was the more intimate musical program for the Women's Athletic Club later in the month.

"So, that's something." she said to her son after the performances. But she didn't feel it. The expensive alternative lay before her, waiting for her to decide.

***

With a $3,000 bank loan application applied for in late January waiting approval, she enrolled in the Foreign Service course, put her son on the train back to Los Alamos, and traveled the lonely miles to Washington, DC. The world would lay open to her after the course, she was sure; China, Burma, Germany might beckon her to a majestic and romantic calling.

She agonized over the loan until it was approved—March 3 had been a long time to wait, especially as she was already in residence, daring to start her classes. She shipped an enormous box of furniture and knickknacks to her DC flat from LA as a familiar touchstone.

March 9, 1929
1803 Biltmore St., Apt. 211
Washington DC
Johnny Dear:

This has been a very full week for me, up at five o'clock and working until midnight. If it weren't for C. S., I could not push on.

At the close of Friday I look back upon one of the most interesting weeks I have ever had. I am very gratified with the course, the textbooks and above all Dr. Crawford. Little by little he drops a bit of his personal background, and I find he is a Virginian from English parentage. ...

I cannot tell you how much I wish I might talk with you tonight. You did not enclose Mr. Hitchcock's plan of studies for you for the next two years, and I must insist on this matter being cleared up before I give my consent about the Grand Canyon trip. I have only your few remarks regarding your schoolwork, and it looks very much to me as follows. Spring vacation is almost here, and with three subjects only, we are anything but getting our money's worth. I am not imagining this. They are putting it over on you and me. Mr. Connell's letter said that he had turned over to Mr. Hitchcock all matters pertaining to your course, so I am writing him tonight. In short, I am demanding an explanation, and it is up to you to see that I get it. The only thing that will cause me to consent is a satisfactory assurance from Mr. Hitchcock that you are working to the maximum of your ability.

You may be amused to know that I am going to the Chinese Legation and ask if they have someone to help me learn the rudiments of the Chinese alphabet.

Good night, Johnny dear, and please know that I am anything but happy to be forced to ever speak harshly or unpleasantly about the old schoolwork.

Love,
Mother

Sunday
Los Alamos
Dear Mother,
I suppose by the time this letter reaches you, you will have already sent your decision. Mr. Hitchcock has sent you all your required data. I do hope your answer is to the affirmative.

I passed all my subjects this week.
Much love,
Johnny

He did go on his trip. However, the tension between Alice, Johnny and Mr. Connell escalated to the breaking point when, just days before the end of exams, Alice demanded that he leave school.

Oddly, in early June, before her own exams, Alice abruptly left the Foreign Service School, put her crate of furniture and decorations in storage and drove to New York in time to meet Johnny's train and witness Jane's year-end activities. "Les Mumas," as she was now fond of calling the little family, had a grand time traveling, chatting their way west, sharing only the happy adventures of their recent semesters at school. The three had been apart for six months. Their brief joy at being together masked their individual failures and loneliness.

Jane's successful debut as an actress in *Prunella* got a guffaw from Johnny: "What a name for a play!" Johnny's adventures riding a mule down and back up the rubble-strewn path in the Grand Canyon brought appreciative gasps from Jane.

Alice regaled them with a tale of President Hoover's inaugural ball: "It was a charity ball, and evidently, the day for such glamorous affairs is over in Washington. The world and his wife was at that one. Not an ounce of dignity in it, but likely the community chest gained a substantial amount of money."

The children roared with laughter. It was so "Mother!"

The three arrived in Los Angeles and took up their residence at the Women's Athletic Club. John worked his part-time job running errands at a brokerage house. As a homeowner, Alice was still entitled to beach club rights at Castellamare and the two children made their way by bus from downtown Los Angeles to the Santa Monica coast almost every afternoon. Alice was rarely available to join them.

Jane would be going back to Andrebrook, announced their mother. Johnny would be going somewhere, but no one was up for discussing it. Behind the closed doors of Miss Weaver's office during Jane's end-of-school activities, however, Hackley School, only a few miles away from Andrebrook, had been suggested. The Hackley School application had come, and Alice filled it out, deciding on a whim to call him "Juan". Quite quickly, the application was accepted. Miss Weaver surely had influenced that decision..

During those times without Alice hovering, Johnny and Jane caught up on those missed months.

"Golly, Janey, this is swell," said Johnny, sinking his weary body onto the warm sand, luxuriating in laziness. "Mother's little bribe of a tennis club membership for the summer didn't work today. No courts available at five in the afternoon. Just as well; I'm pooped." His sturdy legs stretched out from under the beach umbrella, his muscled body in the swimsuit turning the heads of all the young girls parading on the beach.

Jane, sitting cross-legged on her own beach towel, leaned over and nudged him with her shoulder. "That's what you get for staying out so late last night. Mother got you into Hackley."

Johnny tensed up. "Don't bring that old mess up now, will you? I told mother in June that I only wanted to go back to Los Alamos or else here for high school. And she said no *most* emphatically."

"Yes, well Hackley's in Tarrytown. We could be together. I miss you, you know. Besides, you never write. How else am I going to keep track of you?"

"It's not a C. S. school like Andrebrook, is it?"

"No, but they do tolerate us C. S. folk," said Jane with a grin, trying to lighten the tone.

"They don't have any horseback riding. What am I to do with the polo equipment Mother let me buy?"

"You can ride with me at Andrebrook on the weekends," Jane replied. "Maybe I can use some of your polo stuff next year on the senior team."

"They don't have such swell guys. Be a bunch of stuck-up rich kids," grumbled Johnny. "I won't go and she can't make me."

"She can, and you know it. Look what she did to you at the end of school."

Johnny felt his heart race with anger and helplessness. If only he could forget the humiliation. His grades were not the best, he had to agree. Two problems—failing geometry and that damnable fourth subject he could not manage to take.

"I want to hear how you mean to make up the fourth subject without being a year late in entering college, which would be a disgrace," his mother had railed in a long-distance call one Sunday night.

"But, Mother!" Johnny had tried to reason. "Mr. Connell says they are not available."

"Nonsense, my dear boy," she had fired back. "That cretin headmaster, Mr. Connell, is putting it over on you and me. And, why are they not tutoring you if the courses are not available? I want a direct answer to this question: Are you getting your money's worth? I sent you to him to be thrashed into shape, if need be, but to make your grades. I could do it, but I paid Los Alamos to do it… I thought that private schools functioned to meet whatever need presented itself through paid tutoring."

For Johnny this grade thing was a bitter pill. Jane was carrying six subjects, riding, jumping, performing plays, doing piano lessons and going to the opera. To her credit, she never lorded it over him.

That March letter from Mr. Connell really capped it. Mother sputtered with indignation when Mr. Connell suggested that she never made him work, nor appreciated the necessity. Why, all Mother did was nag. The letter had ended with a parting shot: *In another month the faculty will vote as to whether John should be invited back.*

Jane tapped him on the shoulder, and Johnny blinked and took a deep breath.

"Sorry, Janey, I was just remembering all the rotten stuff that happened. You know I was so mad at Mother that I deliberately forgot to send her a Mother's Day greeting."

"Boy, she was upset about that all right!" Jane said. "Wrote me that she was the only mother without flowers or at least a cable of good wishes from her son. That's okay. She was really furious that I spent all that money on new clothes before I went to see her in DC for Easter. You know she always forgives us in the end, right?"

201

"Yeah," said Johnny. "I got my trip to the canyon."

"And your polo equipment, as well," said Jane. "Mother and I did have a splendid time for a week, riding and going to teas and such."

"But Janey…" he said with a catch in his breath. Suddenly, the dam behind his emotions burst. He dug out a handful of sand and flung it with all his might in the direction of the water. "It was Mother who rigged it so that I would not finish the school year. I guess she felt that if she pulled me out before my geometry final, the failing grade wouldn't count. And, she couldn't stand the humiliation of my not being asked back, and at the same time she hated Mr. Connell. Well, the feeling was mutual. I went in to have a talk that he asked for. He said it wasn't my grades but Mother's attitude! Bossing him around, demanding this and that. He told me she had asked them to vote not to bring me back just to teach me a lesson but not to tell me she said so."

Jane sat very still while her brother poured out the misery of his last months at the Los Alamos School. During the ride west in early June, the talk had been so full of happiness. At home, there was no time for the two of them to be alone. At last she was to learn just how badly things had gone for him.

"Then I started passing geometry, and wrote her that I might pass the final, and I insisted that she let me take it. But, no, she would have her own way. You know what she wrote to Mr. Connell? 'You had your chance, now it's too late!' I call that pretty vindictive, don't you? I was trying so hard to please her.

"And then, 'Be on the train and don't let them trick you into missing it.' Why would Mr. Connell have any earthly reason for me to miss a train?"

"But you did miss it!"

"Only because Mother's telegram came too late!"

"Ah, but you didn't miss my play and the horse show." And Jane gave him a big hug.

***

Early in September the children boarded the train for New York for the four-day ride. The two spent many hours discussing their mother's foray into the Foreign Service.

"Why do you suppose she made all that effort and spent all that money, then did not even stay to take the exams?" said Jane.

"Don't ask me," said Johnny with a shrug. "She kept writing me that the work was getting harder. Perhaps that French test she was supposed to take was too much for her."

"She would never admit it, though," said Jane. "My goodness, but she was enamored of the instructor, Mr. What's-His-Name. Positively agog about his English forbearers."

"I thought she had fallen in love with some German fellow?"

Jane laughed. "Could be. I saw some correspondence from some woman lawyer who was answering Mother's questions about property rights and dual German citizenship and things.

"I mean, really, Johnny, there she was living in her furnished apartment, and she sent for a huge crate of her own things from Los Angeles. 'I just feel I could not do without my own things surrounding me one more moment longer,' she wrote. What about us, far from home in strange surroundings and nothing but the clothes on our backs!"

Johnny said, "You know, she wrote me that she was taking a speedwriting course in March, in case she was too old to be in the Foreign Service she would have 'something to show for all that effort and be prepared to reenter the secretarial world.' What was this 'too old' business? You'd think she'd checked that out beforehand."

"But here's what I really think," said Jane. "She got wind that she could try again for the opera, and just gave up the whole Foreign Service idea. You know she's been very occupied with voice lessons this summer, and spent a huge amount of time at tea with all different musical people. I heard something about the cast being pressured to buy in to the opera company. I'll bet she's going to try again."

A sly smile broke out across Johnny's face. "So, Janey, sister dear, tell me what really happened at that speakeasy you went to in New York last Christmas?"

"Okay," said Jane, as she pulled out a cigarette. "Got a light? I hate to disappoint, dear brother, but I only had one gin and tonic. I know it would have been a quite different party had you been there."

***

Jane saw Johnny off at Hackley and continued north to Waccabuc to stay with friends until school started for her in early October.

August 30, 1929
Dear Mother,
We had a pretty good trip east. Every night we got together in the compartment and played games. We had a pretty good time. Thank you for the nice stay at the Biltmore and all the rest. I think John is settled nicely at Hackley so you won't have any more trouble there.
Love Peter (Jane)

Dear Mother,
Last Sunday I went down to Miss Weaver's and Jane came down from Waccabuc and went to chapel with me. The week went along fairly well until I heard that you are allowed to hang up in your room only one framed picture. You know, Mother, I wasn't built for a school life like this. But I'll try to hold on. I worked hard and got on the football team to surprise you. We went to the Statue of Liberty and the aquarium but nothing has happened to me since then. Please, I need money for another suit. I'd tell you more about school life but I have to go to physics.

203

All my love,
Johnny

October 4
Hackley School
Dear Mrs. Muma:
You will be interested to know that Juan seems to be getting along. He has been at my table and I am indebted to a rather close and pleasant acquaintance with him.
Walter B. Gage, Headmaster, Hackley School

Dear Mother,
About the suit, I can get one for about $45 and it is really very smart. Jane came to take me to Sunday school. It was very nice.
Please send my Laguna stock check. I got $20 stollen from me during a football game. I don't know what you told Mr. Gage, but if you wire many more times like that, I'll get kicked out of here just the same as Los Alamos.
Say, when are you going to write me something about yourself? I know your busy and must be likely opera but still I'd like to hear something about it.
Love, Johnny

Oct. 7th
Andrebrook School
Tarrytown-on-Hudson
Dear Mother,
I got to school on last Tuesday and helped Miss Weaver fix the rooms for the girls. I have been asked to the Halloween dance at Hackley. It is going to be such fun. I saw John's room and I'm going to do my best to fix it up, because it is such an awful place. Dilly, my drama teacher as you might remember, is quite interested in me and my ambitions for the stage.
All my love,
Peter (Jane)

Oct. 14, 1929
Hackley School
My Dear Mrs. Muma:
No doubt Juan has written you of his adventure last week. On a recent evening, five boys including Juan made their way out of the dorm and went to New York, returning to the school about four o'clock in the morning. While their presence in the city was harmless in itself, the offence is, as I am sure you will agree, serious. The penalty imposed consists of detention at school during the first three days of vacation.
Walter B. Gage, Headmaster, Hackley School

Dear Mother,

I told you I was getting my privileges back because I've been so good for the last three weeks. I call that using my head. And another thing, I carried the ball in the football game for five yards (I am in the backfield). Jane invited me over to supper tonight and I had a pretty good time.

Jane and I are going into New York for Thanksgiving and I wondered if it would be asking too much if we had a little wider margin to travel on.

By the way, you didn't have any stock on the New York Stock Exchange, did you? Because I suppose you heard about the tremendous break which ruined hundreds of people.

I hope your a big success with all your parts. I know you will be.

Good-bye Mama dear, lots of love,

Johnny

My Dear Mrs. Muma:

Except for the telegram received this summer I have had no word about bills either for last year's balance or this year's tuition. I am sure this is a mistake and that you will let me hear from you. I need to know quite definitely so that I may keep Jane's expenses within the budget you have decided upon.

Cordially yours,

Lillian C. Weaver

Nov. 2, 1929

Dear Mother,

I hope you are getting along with your singing and that everything is all right.

I got my evening dress for the opera season just now, so thank you very much.

Miss Weaver wants to know if John and I could go to Europe with her this Christmas—to the Tyrol and to Munich, each for three weeks. We would ski over the Alps with a guide, and Miss Weaver thinks this would open John's eyes. I told her that it might just fit in with your plans to be taken care of at Xmas. I got my evening dress just now so thank you very much.

Love,

Peter (Jane)

Hackley School

Dear Mother,

Here's just a hasty letter to tell you I made a touchdown! And after that Jane took me into New York to a show on account of my birthday. That was pretty good fun. ... After that, the Gages invited her over for dinner. It was awfully nice of them.

Love,
Johnny

My Dearest J and J,

Pipes have burst at Castellamare under the patio. I rented a car to go and see repairs in progress, and to the C. S. meeting that evening, stopping by the newly acquired Kings X studio apartments to drop off some things.

At rehearsal a week ago with the Columbia Grand Opera Company, I learned I am singing the roles of the Countess de Coigny in *Andrea Chénier*, the Countess Ceprano in *Rigoletto*, and Inez in *Il Trovatore*. During the months of December through April, our itinerary will take us all over the western coast, with trips into Montana, Colorado, Oklahoma, Texas, New Mexico and Arizona.

I am enjoying your letters much more of late; they have more news in them, which makes me so happy.

Much love,
Mother

Dear Mother,

I am so happy—I just heard that you intend to let us go. That's awfully sweet of you. I know we are going to have a wonderful time. It is going to be a heavy drag on the funds, but I think it's worth it.

Lots of love,
Johnny

Chapter 49

At Some Distance

"Dearest Aunt Alice!" said George's recently married daughter Joy, who was hovering in the doorway. Alice could see her spritely form.

"Come right in, Joy. How lovely of you to sneak backstage."

Alice, wrapped in a kimono, was sitting at her dressing room table after her performance as the Countess in the opera, *Andrea Chénier*. The garish lights of her makeup mirror illuminated a face reasonably bare of the heavy greasepaint. Her hair was plastered close to her head, and the disembodied wig, a tall, powdered affair, loomed bizarrely on a stand nearby.

"You *did* invite me," said Joy, who sidled up to the wig and stroked it with her forefinger. "Father declined to come in, thinking perhaps you were in a state of, well, you might put it, deshabille."

Alice laughed in agreement and opened her arms to give her a hug. "Rightly so, too. Lovely to see you, truly. Did you enjoy it?

"You cannot *know* how much. The very way you made those deep curtsies without even a thought to that wig!" Joy paused to catch her breath. "May I see your dress?" Joy twirled around to where Alice pointed behind the changing screen and made her way around it. "Oh my, it is every bit as lovely as it seemed from my seat. I just adore those delicate lace sleeves." After a brief touch of the voluminous taffeta skirt, Joy walked back to Alice at the makeup mirror.

"Could you hear me?" asked Alice, knowing full well that the acoustics in the college theater in Pasadena were just about perfect. Alice craved all the praise she could garner, anxious because of the poor ticket sales following their previous performances.

"Father whispered that your voice was clear and soft at the same time. I couldn't have agreed more. And your acting, Aunt Alice—most realistic!"

"You know, my dear, that the Louis XVI period is just a treasure for me. It must be why I love this opera and the costumes."

"'A tapestry come to life,' Father said during your curtain calls." Joy giggled. "You know Father tends toward flamboyant speech. But in this case I totally agree. And the people around me were whispering, 'Charming and graceful.' They adored you."

Alice glowed with the praise. "Thank you, my dear, for all your fine compliments. Now, I must ask you to let me finish removing this makeup and struggle into my clothes. One of our patrons is giving a supper party for the cast. Please tell your father that I will meet all of you for luncheon tomorrow, my treat."

"I will, I will. Thank you again for the tickets."

Joy gave Alice another hug and was out the door.

Alice could hear Joy exclaiming to her father as their voices faded down the corridor. When the stage door clunked shut behind them the sound felt somehow ominous. She shook it off, dressed and left by the same door.

***

It didn't matter that the society pages wrote glowing columns about the "who's who" in attendance at the after-performance soirées. It didn't matter that the cast was made more glamorous by an Italian tenor and baritone. It didn't matter that Alice and the cast were required to front money for the season. On February 1, the Columbia Opera Company failed.

Alice slunk back to Los Angeles, but the thought of moving back to the Women's Athletic Club and answering the inevitable questions was unbearable. She went into seclusion in one of the three tiny apartments at Kings X. She had only one tenant—"that Russian," as he was known to her agent, Miss Klumb—a struggling actor always late with the rent. The remaining space was jammed with furniture stored from Casa Chiquita and Castellamare.

For more than two weeks there was not a single communication to her children or her friends. Even Giuseppe Barsoti, the lead tenor of the opera company who had pursued her passionately for the month of January, was not privy to her whereabouts. Alice had tucked his love letters away beneath her clothes in the trunk. His notes, all of which ended *with all my soul, I love and adore you, amore and baci*, would come to nothing now, had there even been a chance at courting throughout the opera tour.

Alice brooded for days before hiring a C. S. practitioner for help with her desperation over this failure. Headaches, insomnia and heart palpations all worked to break her spirit. But not quite into sickness. The practitioner provided the solace for sleep and repaired her wounded soul but did not resolve her dwindling income.

What was she to do? Both children had begged to continue with their schooling. Jane's school tuition was overdue for this semester, and just how was she to pay for next year? Well, one thing was definite; she set pen to paper and wrote Jane that she could not go back to Andrebrook the following fall. Johnny, however, was a different matter. She must reward his fledgling efforts to study. He was so close to applying for college that she could not pull the plug. She telegrammed thanks to Miss Weaver for taking Johnny under her wing in Munich and gave permission to keep him studying throughout the

208

remaining winter. She sold some Laguna Land and Water Company stock—by pure dumb luck, just before the company lowered its dividend—to pay for Johnny's tuition, private tutoring and the C. S. practitioner who would keep him on track with his studies.

On a lovely spring morning Alice emerged from the tiny apartment. She had hatched a plan for a series of costumed recitals to be given in Australia. She closeted herself with her musical friend, Olga, to develop several music programs. Over the next weeks, she collected her props. The tenant at Casa Chiquita was delighted to allow Alice to pose in the garden while a photographer captured charming shots of her looking smart and smiling in tweeds and an elegant cloche hat. That would do, Alice thought, for some of the newspapers. For the recitals she collected all her costumes. With the help of her clipping services, she collected and filed every single article ever written about her performances over the decades, sketches on scrap paper, and precious large black and white photos of her posed in costumes for the various operas. She would be writing all the publicity once she reached Australia.

She cut a record of her singing "Hayfields and Butterflies," a delicate ballad piece that she and Olga chose from one of the few women composers around, Teresa Del Riego. One copy went in her luggage for the cruise; there was a likely chance for a radio interview and the music would suit. The other copy was sent to her Foreign Service classmate Byrne in New York. She was fishing for compliments and knew he would deliver.

My Dear Alicia, replied Byrne, not another day must pass without my thanking you for that wonderful record. What a voice! Stop bossing those Mexican workers, take off your work overalls immediately, and come to New York to the Metropolitan. You could make a fortune recording professionally. You are singing as I write. Emily is entranced. ...

Alice smiled, her soul warming at the praise so richly supplied, and tucked his idea away for another year or two.

A few days later Alice drafted a press release for her departure. She and Olga had accomplished a masterful blending of operatic arias from her recent performances, with those staged dramatic productions she had invented in the 1910s.

Los Angeles Times, March 16, 1930
"Opera Singer Embarks"
Alice Muma, soprano, sailed on the *City of Honolulu* to Honolulu, Australia, and New Zealand after the debacle of the Columbia Opera Company. She plans to return from her costume concert tour a little in advance of the homecoming of her children, John and Jane, now away at school. The

Muma house at Castellamare will be the setting for many gay affairs during the summer season.

Mme. Muma has won success both in the concert and operatic field in that of the costume recital, in which she has specialized to a considerable extent, with felicitous results, for her programs are far from the usual stereotyped costume recitals, revealing a striking originality and creative imagination both in concept and in production. A unique and fascinating program which was instantly popular was entitled *The Lute of Jade*, presenting Oriental songs by several composers. Mme. Muma supplements her musical program with a perfection of details in costuming, stage-setting and lighting effects which add immeasurably to their effectiveness, presenting also songs from Monsieur Beaucaire, and an old colonial ballad called "Washington," by Percy MacKaye.

Alice stood with the other passengers crowded by the rail, all flinging gaily-colored streamers toward the wharf and shouting to friends and family who were seeing them off. The band played "Aloha Oe," the traditional number for all Hawaii-bound steamships of the LASSCO fleet. Alice remembered her first trip, a healing time from the desperate years after Jerry's death. This trip would be the same—a slightly smaller ship with the same elegant layout. Well, it wasn't the same at all, really. For this voyage was one of discovery and hope. Would the name she made for herself internationally give her a leg up on others, come California's next opera season? She would only know after it was over.

It was exhilarating, this leave-taking of solid ground. She could not help but be uplifted by the joy all around. And the single screaming toot of the *S. S. Honolulu* seemed to salute her hope. Black smoke billowed from the two stacks and the engines pounded as the ship inched away. Guided by the harbor tugs, the steamer, with mail and cargo stowed and excited passengers above, turned west into the Pacific.

Alice clamped her hand on her hat as the stiff breeze from the open ocean threatened to steal it. Now was the moment to walk down to her cabin to read the letters from her children. Was it just this morning that her postman had put them into her hands on her way out the door?

March 4
Munich,
Dear Mother,
If you go to Australia, this letter will just make it. Please add on to the allowance of $168 for cleaning and new clothes. I only came to Munich planning for a month.

You know, you have to write letters, too. I am very lonely. But I am making the best of it. Thank you for letting me stay. Miss Weaver has said that she has "cobbled" together all my various credits from the schools so that if I study hard this spring, I will have a normal senior year at home in the fall without worrying about enough credits to graduate.

The thing is this, the professor only speaks German, and it takes so long for me to work through the lessons that I am far behind. Mutti Cranston is helpful, and I like her very much. She takes me on little trips on some weekends. ... Say, she wants to take me to London for a week in the early summer, just before I take my college boards.

Love,
Johnny

Always more money, while I am trying to save every penny, thought Alice. But—he is correct, he does need clothes. She ignored the gnawing feeling in her stomach.

Gratitude toward the Munich school director Mrs. Cranston came with a niggling doubt triggered by Johnny's affectionate use of the name Mutti. It meant "mommy" in German. Was some of the closeness she hungered for with her son being transferred because she was not there? She didn't like the jealousy that word set off in her heart. There was nothing to be done but continue moving forward. She would trust in God and C. S.

March 7, Andrebrook
Dear Mother,
I hope your costumed concert will be all right. Please write and say where you are going on this trip and what's it all about.

My arm is much better after the car accident Miss Weaver had with me sitting in the front. Miss Weaver says it is healing perfectly because of C. S. The doctor says the cast can come off in a few weeks.

It is going to be terribly hard to tell Miss Weaver that I won't be coming back next year because I have grown to love this place so much that I really began to think that I belonged here.

Of course I realize how much has been paid for us, and I will keep within the hundred dollars' allowance for the spring. I have already made one dress this year to save money, which came out well. I don't know if you remember or not, but you said that perhaps you would let me have one of your black and silver foxes because wearing both was overpowering.

Lots of love,
Peter

Alice rankled at Jane's signing herself "Peter." She refused ever to acknowledge the reference, never mind instigating a conversation that might bring to light just why Jane would want that name. Perhaps all girls these days were taking on pet boys names. It was just a phase.

She did indeed remember Jane's asking for the fox.

But, no, you cannot have it yet, my dear. It will make a splendid finish to my outfit during the interviews I am planning in Sydney. Perhaps next year.

***

Alice arrived in Honolulu after four glorious days on the sunny sea. Before even the last rope was tied up, the freight gangplank came out and long jumbled lines of luggage began to form on the dock. She would change ships to the smaller but no-less-elegant *S. S. Tahiti* for the long haul to Australia. She could only have faith that her own trunks and boxes would make the switch. One could not do these costumed recitals without costumes.

And there was Olga and her husband, Clifton, having arrived several days ago for their own vacation here in Hawaii, "hallooing" her from the dock, then encircling her neck with a fragrant lei and speeding her off for a luncheon at the gorgeous Halekulani Hotel. They sat on cushioned rattan chairs around a glass-topped table. The dining room shutters folded open to the brilliant ocean. The waiter suggested the catch of the day, and brought them snapper sautéed with butter and redolent with chunks of ginger-spiced pineapple.

Lazing on chaises under the trees after the meal, Alice and Olga nattered away about the upcoming cruise and tour. Clifton wandered away, amiably grumping about women and their "noise," to walk the beach.

"We had begun to finalize my publicity for Sydney," said Alice. "Have you had any further thoughts? I don't want to leave it to the locals."

"I have come prepared!" said Olga, reaching into her handbag. She whipped out a scrap of yellow-lined paper. "I am thinking you might say, With an enviable reputation throughout America and Europe as an interpretative singer of art and folksongs, blah, blah, blah. You'll see it there. You must also tout your training with Hageman and make sure you tell your audience that he is famous with the Metropolitan Opera."

Back and forth Olga and Alice went, revising and reorganizing the one-page flyer to include no fewer than eight little delicious blurbs of praise from various news clippings and a small headshot of Alice in costume.

"Worthy of a world class prima donna," said Alice. "Now, let's call out to Clifton. I must make my little boat."

On the return, Alice collected mail from the steamship office, a single letter from Miss Weaver, before climbing on board the new ship.

Alice settled in to the ship's library for tea and opened the letter.

March 13
Andrebrook
Dear Mrs. Muma:

Jane brought me your letter today. We mingled our tears together. Of course you are writing me and I will know why you feel it necessary to remove Jane from Andrebrook. I can't tell you how much I regret this and how sincerely I hope you have not yet made a final decision. It would be a pity to make a change. She is growing in every way. You spoke in the telegram of the enormous expense of the children. You are perfectly right. They have seemed to me so large that I have used the greatest care to make the money go as far as possible toward the things that you have wanted for their experience.

You said to me in a letter early in the year that it was a great relief to you to have me looking out for your children while you were occupied, and therefore I have been trying to take your place and spare you in the matter of Jane's everyday material needs.

Our Munich director, Mrs. Cranston, will be writing to you about John. She thinks he is doing well overall. He bought a motion picture camera but then refused to take pictures, said he wanted to remain in school there, but then initially refused to attend classes. It seems to be working out well in the end and he is reported to be studying hard. Though he resents your insistence on Science Church, Mrs. Cranston has won him over to church on Sundays. C. S. is very big in Munich.

I ask you if you would not be able to spend the summer, all three, in Munich so that he could continue. It would be a most happy experience for you during the Wagner and Strauss Festival, and residence in Munich can scarcely be more expensive than in California. ...

Very cordially yours,
Lillian C. Weaver

Alice bristled at Miss Weaver's suggestion of a summer in Munich, overcome with a tidal wave of jealousy at the thought of both of her children being guided by strangers. Miss Weaver was being impertinent at the very least. Mutti Cranston... No! The children would come home to California. They belonged there. She belonged there. It was all getting out of hand. She jumped up in disgust, in her anger knocking the cookies off the tray on the table. Ignoring the tea, she huffed her way to her cabin. *Jane, at least, I will have back under my roof*, was her last thought as she slipped off her clothes and bathed. Alice slipped under her covers and consoled herself with some readings by Mary Baker Eddy.

Miss Weaver's query about the children's summer remained unanswered throughout the cruise.

***

When Alice arrived in Sydney, she worked with the publicist for the Town Hall Symphony to produce posters and flyers. It cost her a great deal of money, which she hoped to recoup and then some, with the three concerts. Very little in fact came back to her. The orchestra was a credible volunteer group of out-of-work musicians. The ticket charges barely covered rental of the hall. The audiences were enthusiastic, and for that, at least, Alice was pleased. And then there was the fascination of being in Australia, the supper parties and meeting all the dignitaries.

For the radio show, Alice billed herself as a Canadian mezzo-soprano, creating a kinship from the Commonwealth. The script she had prepared was delivered to the airwaves almost wholly.

I am a colonial, too, for I was born under the British flag in Toronto, Canada. I call the world home now, and I have always meant to see my fellow countrymen in the Pacific, so here I am. My great regret is that I cannot stay with you longer, but I must return to America until September, when I will set forth again on a concert tour of the Hawaiian Islands, Japan, and China and the Malay Straits. ...

She sang a group of three songs, Chinese in flavor, and played her record.

Alice had caused enough of a pleasant stir to pique the interest of the society tabloid, *Daily Pictorial.*

They are to do a spot on my human side, she reported to her friend Olga, to whom she had sent the article. You can see that this was the perfect opportunity to drag out the Castellamare-in-tweeds photos! Nary a mention was made of my singing, but I suppose publicity of any sort will do to get my opera career up a notch.

They asked me how old my children were, and I wouldn't tell them for fear they would discover my age. "Never a question to ask a lady," I fired back to the reporter.

I am coming home soon, with brief stops in Samoa and Tahiti. You should see me in town by mid-July. I am looking forward to having Les Mumas under one roof. I have missed them so.

I have missed you dearly, as well, for you as accompanist would have been the perfect thing. We would have sailed well together. But I am grateful at least for your kind company in Hawaii. My warmest regards to Clifton.

Love,
Alicia

Daily Pictorial, May 16, 1930
Sydney, Australia
"Top Rung Not Too High for Woman: Prima Donna Tells of Feminist Work in America"

Alicia Muma, a feminist prima donna from California visiting Sydney, looked smart in a black and white floral two-piece ensemble banded with black fox fur. An off-the-face hat of black velour was touched with white. The finishing touch to the outfit was a two-skin silver fox stole.

Mme. Muma is a life member of the Los Angeles University Women's Club and a founding member of the club publication, Women's Vocational Guide to Services, whose mission is to find work for university-trained

214

women. The University Club has also established an innovation in publishing a little monthly book reviewing the content of children's movies for appropriateness.

Madame is a keen feminist and sure that her sex can attain anything.

Indeed the top rung of the ladder is not too high, she is sure.

Alice was in a fury coming home to an empty house. Time to take a firm stand, she thought, against the manipulation of Miss Weaver—for it had to be that canny businesswoman's grasp on her children that was forging their love for the East Coast and Munich. Alice would consider sending both Johnny and Jane to the C. S. boarding school in Kansas City. They had wanted to be together, so together they would go. Cheaper and closer to home, as well.

Alice placed a very expensive long-distance phone call to Miss Weaver, now back in Tarrytown-on-Hudson at Andrebrook, demanding her children be returned to her. Miss Weaver went to great lengths to explain the necessity of Johnny's remaining expenses and hinted that a partial scholarship would be available for Jane. Alice felt nothing but shame at Miss Weaver's attempts to downplay the financial mess Alice had gotten herself into, and the long silence on her part that had led Miss Weaver to make decisions, or not, based on what the children would have her do.

"I do feel," Miss Weaver said at the end, "that the development of the children has been what you desired and your desire has been our guide and aim in planning for them."

"They will come home to me," said Alice. "That is my decision, and you will abide with it."

"Have a pleasant summer," said Miss Weaver.

Chapter 50

Johnny and Jane go to California—and Back

Jane was sweltering in the 99-degree heat at the Brooklyn pier the afternoon of July twenty-second when a long nautical hoot reverberated over the water. The German liner had arrived. Mother had written that Byrne would meet them. Jane hadn't bothered to look. She was oblivious to anything other than her long-away brother's arrival.

She had put on her best dress, a blue ruffled affair with polka dots, deciding also on a little black straw hat and black string gloves. The train ride down from Tarrytown-on-Hudson to Manhattan and the ensuing subway trip to the pier left her wilted. She was dripping perspiration from under her hat. Her hanky was soaked. Nevertheless Jane joined the throng of other happy people waving madly.

Suddenly there he was, striding smartly from the second-class exit and clearly looking for her through the crowd. Jane rushed into his arms for a giant hug. Johnny's gray suit was crushed in the ensuing welcome.

"My God, it's hot, Janey," he said, standing back from her and grinning. With a swift tug, he took off his green tie, stuck it in the pocket of his jacket, and before Jane could say a word, peeled off his jacket as well.

"Hello to you, too," said Jane, grinning broadly through tears.

"Come on, then, you weepy female, let's go find the baggage. I only have two suitcases. Left the rest in Munich." He hung his jacket over his shoulder, putting his other arm around her shoulders. They meandered through the throng, looking for all the world like two tall and elegant young people at peace with the world. Which was mainly true, now that they had each other in view.

Byrne found them in the baggage area, greeting them both with hugs and words of welcome and eventually loading all into a taxi. Johnny held them in thrall with a torrent of commentary on his delightful life in Munich. He would go back for the fall term, his grades were good and the professor was the best, the mountains the highest, girls the prettiest… Jane and Byrne just listened and smiled and nodded from time to time until the taxi pulled up at Byrne's apartment in Manhattan.

"Janey must come with me this time," said Johnny. "Man, I was so lonely for my only sister!"

Jane nodded in agreement. It looked like she was having a hard time speaking. Then she managed to overcome her emotions long enough to squeak

216

out, "Wouldn't that be wonderful? Andrebrook in Munich, and I would be near you."

They hauled Johnny's two bags and themselves into an ancient elevator and up eight floors to the elegant high ceilings and spacious rooms of the Maconnier's post–Great War abode. After a brief but necessary wash and brush up, all three waited for Byrne's wife, Emily, to return from work then hurried off to a tiny French bistro for dinner.

"I thought you might like a change from schnitzel, Johnny," said Bryne. Which brought a laugh from everybody.

Johnny ordered steak, rare, and pomme frites, *s'il vous plaît*. Jane followed suit. The fried potatoes were delicious, and just salty enough.

"I don't suppose we could have a tad of wine with our dinner," suggested Johnny. "I've just about drunk all the German beer there is and their wine is too sweet for me."

"Why not? I am all for a little wine myself," said Emily. She signaled the waiter and ordered a bottle of Cabernet.

The four turned down dessert in favor of an early night and walked the short, hot blocks back to the apartment. They were finally all talked out, sated from the rich food and sapped of energy from the muggy air. By unanimous agreement, they all wished each other a good-night and slowly made their way to their bedrooms.

When bathroom visits had finished, and bedroom doors were left ajar for the miniscule breeze, Byrne, in bed by that time, looked over to his wife and said, "Don't they seem great pals?"

"Yes. It sounds to me as if they don't ever want to be separated again."

"I'm just a little worried," Byrne said. "Alice is too strict with them, overall. She abhors drinking and smoking; the children do both. You remember, Emily, Alice admitted berating them constantly in a letter to me months ago. She is making a horror of their bad habits and it will only drive them further into misbehaving."

"But they seem sensible, Byrne. In charge of themselves, for the most part. Heavens, look how much time they spend miles away from their mother. I find it a little sad."

"Yes, and if Alice keeps on nagging, they will spend even more time apart. They are high-strung, like Alice, and quite charming, also like their mother. I can see why they might send sparks flying between them. Perhaps Alice should say something like, 'This drinking and smoking is ugly, just like lying or animal passion. If you do it you will be unhappy.'"

Emily sighed and pulled the light sheet off. It was a hot night even with the fan blowing and the windows open to a fugitive breeze. Cars were still motoring down the avenue, but the disembodied voices from the street had quieted.

"Do you think Alice will send them both to the C. S. School in Kansas City as she suggested to you? At least they would be together."

"They would run away within the week!" said Byrne. "Kansas City indeed! What is there to do, for Heaven's sake? No. New York or Europe for that bright duo." He plumped his pillow and sighed with pleasure. "That was a wonderful dinner. Now, we must get some sleep if we can bear up under the swelter. Johnny and Jane need to be on the train early in the morning. And we still have to rescue Jane's luggage from the locker in Penn Station."

***

Les Mumas had all of six weeks together at Casa Chiquita. Rancorous debate occasionally bounced off the plastered walls: arguments over schools and money, for the most part. Alice finally agreed to send Jane back to Andrebrook, embarrassed as she was with the scholarship that was probably charity in disguise. Adding to the mix was Alice's unvoiced guilt at having spent so much of their dwindling funds on the wild goose chase that was Australia. It didn't help that Jane berated her for it during a scolding by Alice on Jane's requested allowance increase.

Johnny had begged to be sent back to Munich for his last year, agreeing, in exchange, to apply to Cal Tech, not some Eastern university, when his college boards were completed sometime the following spring. Alice was bribing him back to California and searching frantically for an enticement for Jane, as well. For how could it be that the pull to the East Coast and beyond would rip them asunder from her beloved California? It was unthinkable, and yet the signs were there.

By tacit agreement anger was suspended for their last night together, the Belair Beach Club picnic. For a few hours as the late afternoon blended into evening, the sound of ukuleles, snapping bonfire and rushing waves acted as a balm to their edginess.

September came around again, and with it the children's departure for the East. Johnny left Jane ensconced at the Barbizon in Manhattan, where friends would pick her up for a two-week stay in the country prior to her own school start. Twelve days later, Johnny was in Munich under the loving and watchful eye of Mutti Cranston.

Perhaps that loving and watchful eye of Mutti Cranston became too much for Alice. Perhaps an embarrassing lawsuit from her car company for non-payment of her loan had made her flee. Whatever the reason, in late November, she dropped a press release to the *LA Times* as she boarded her train for the East that she would spend the winter studying music and the Christmas holidays with her son, who was attending school in Munich.

Miss Moore, her secretary, would hold the fort in California.

Arriving in New York, Alice applied for a visa for France from the consulate in Manhattan, preferring to apply for German and British visas abroad. While she was waiting for her application to be approved, she spent some days with Jane at Andrebrook, discovering a yet-more-grown-up daughter fully adjusting to the rigors of academics, piano lessons, horseback riding and drama class. Alice took a great deal of pride in Jane's accomplishments, but did not approve of her daughter on the stage. There was something less—*acceptable*, about actors. Overall, the profession lacked the class of opera. But she said nothing, for decisions were not imminent. Jane's drama coach, Dilly, was firm about an additional year of training. And, most of all, perhaps Jane would not be there, but back in California.

The two Mumas shared the Andrebrook School box at the Met for the last opera of the season before Alice sailed away. Jane was left alone, briefly loved, and dismissed yet again in favor of her brother.

During the Atlantic crossing, Alice read her lawyer's typed letter outlining the process for being deposed in France for her trial in Los Angeles over the car mess.

December 12th, 1930
My Dear Mrs. Muma,

In regards to the Chrysler automobile lawsuit: *Commercial Credit vs. Muma*, your trial is set for May 31, 1931. Being prejudiced in your favor since 1909, I of course think you would make a good impression on anyone. You must realize, of course, that anger at the system will get you nowhere.

I recollect that you claim that the Commercial Credit Co. demanded the car when they took it, or the man said he demanded, or words to that effect. Think that point over. I will want a good answer, conforming to the truth, of course, in your deposition to be taken in France at a time set by you possibly in March. Papers will come through the American Consul and back here by April 20th, so I can prepare the trial. You will have to cooperate a lot to win this case.

I hope you are having more leisure over there and can spend a part of all the hours I put in on this case, too. I suggest that you not be too ambitious.

Best regards from Enge and me.
John Rankin.
P.S. Miss Moore just phoned me that the appraisal company (for the inventory at Castellamare) approved $5 for the missing knife and is begging to be paid their $75. She is hoping for money for me by the 10th of the month.

Well, Alice thought as she put the letter down, Miss Moore is certainly earning her keep. But that's an exorbitant expense for inventory for a five-dollar knife. Alice sighed in exasperation, then gave up the worry. Miss Moore was just the organized person to handle the minutiae.

The specter of the dreadful collection agency man, however, was not so easily dismissed. She couldn't help reliving that awful afternoon when that other man made such a fuss and took her car. Were the neighbors watching? Surely someone would have wanted it for what was left to pay if they had just waited. Such a mess! And the man was rude, and probably in a fit of pique she had been rude back, without a thought to consequences. John Rankin was right, of course. She might win the case, though it was improbable, but at least she could not be hounded by the press while she was in Europe.

Alice buried her lawyer's letter among her other correspondence, to be brought to light when she had to face being deposed in France months and months from now. She allowed the ship to carry her toward Cherbourg. For a time, for this coming winter and spring, there would be singing and Johnny, life in hotels and tea and luncheons and new people. Perhaps she would meet a baron or two. Thick on the ground they were in Europe, all breeding and marvelous taste and no money.

Alice landed on the coast of France and took the train to Paris. There she lived with Elizabeth Burton and celebrated Christmas with her old friend. She whittled away the weeks with visits to the Louvre, and planning her concerts with Madame de Sales; and waited with some impatience to meet Johnny in Cortina at the end of his school vacation.

Chapter 51

A Vagabond Existence

It wasn't all just waiting. There was the magic of reacquainting herself with Paris, gay even in the rain and cold. Madame de Sales saw her frequently to conduct voice lessons in preparation for Alice's recitals in Europe. Elizabeth was a gracious host and was busy herself still buying bits and pieces of French and Spanish antiques, and had forgiven Alice months ago for Alice's refusal of a loan for the purchases. Harmony reigned within Alice's sphere. Expectation replaced anxiety.

On Johnny's last day of skiing down the Italian slopes, Alice boarded a fast train to collect him. She piled him, his skies and his friend, Ted, onto an overnight train to Venice. (It would be economically adventuresome, she felt with no little pride, to let the train be their hotel and just zip into towns for a peek.) The three dashed through the brilliant sunshine of the next morning into the Doge's Palace, then by powerboat to the Lido, and then over to the Island of Murano to gaze at the glass production, then finally luncheon and another overnight train for Milan.

After resting until noon in a dayroom at a hotel, they stretched their legs with a hike to the cathedral and poked into some shops. The reward was a long luncheon, Alice watching the boys with pleasure as the trio consumed a risotto creamy with Parmesan, followed by salad of bright young lettuce delivered only yesterday from Sicily's warmth. Veal scaloppini in a rich wine sauce followed.

"Which is as close to wine as you two are getting with me," scolded Alice but in a soft voice and with a smile. Recalling the lecture Byrne had given her late last year on being too strict, it was the best she could do to thwart an outright refusal for wine with their meal. She herself was drinking *aqua minerali* (sparkling water), encouraging them to do the same. They ended their meal with the tart-sweet taste of blood oranges, also from Sicily, which stained their fingers with the purple juice as they peeled the fruit.

At seven p.m. they boarded the train for the overnight trip to Munich. Alice said good-night to the boys, stepping into the cabin next door, and if she could have locked them in, she would have; there were a few pretty young women on the train. Curled up and wide-eyed from the excitement of being with such young companions, she watched the snowcapped mountains slip by, lit only by the cold moonlight. Thoughts buzzed about in her brain of what was to come from this visit to Johnny's world in Munich.

Miss Weaver had arrived weeks earlier with a new gaggle of girls for their month of vacation, just as Jane had done the previous year. Would she and Miss Weaver be able to develop a respectable relationship in spite of Miss Weaver's meddling? Alice, awake for most of the night pondering the issues, fell asleep just before the porter knocked on her door announcing breakfast.

Once in Munich, Alice began to ingratiate herself with the community that was nourishing her son. She explored his room and memorized every detail, saving them so she could picture him in his daily routine. She met often with his professor, Herr Dr. Pfeiffer, for tea. Discovering that the Humplemeyer Restaurant was everyone's favorite for dinner, she would go there several times a week with some combination of Johnny and Ted, the young women Miss Weaver had brought with her, and Miss Weaver herself.

Occasionally they all met at the Rathskeller and she didn't raise an eyebrow when Johnny and Ted ordered beer.

Mutti Cranston became a friend during that short stay in Munich. No one was more surprised than Alice herself, whose fear of being eclipsed turned out to be unfounded. Miss Weaver became an ally in turn, but the relationship held a measure of reserve. Alice had to respect a professional distance, on the other side of which was a school director facing both the challenges of a shrinking economy and the responsibility for developing the students in her charge. The torrent of wealthy daughters applying to the school had become a trickle. Alas, Jane would become another victim of that deplorable economy at the end of the school year. Alice had begun to formulate a plan to get Jane into college by skipping her senior year—and back to beloved California.

Too soon, Alice was returning to Paris and rehearsals with Madame de Sales; Alice's first concert was two weeks away at the end of January. Her program repeated many of the songs from the Australian recitals, though the performance was somewhat constrained by fewer costumes—a trunk had been mistakenly left behind in New York. The rigorous schedule of practice, rehearsals, and French conversation lessons left little time for walks in the Tuileries. The small concert at Madame de Sales was well attended. Disappointingly, it earned no interest from opera companies. *The state of the opera in the Western world*, wrote her friend Olga from California, *is in desperate trouble. From Germany to Chicago, the companies are hanging by a thread.* And Paris as well, grumped Alice.

In March, Alice scheduled travel to London to hire a manager for her concert there in May. Her Kirkby cousins lived just outside town, having fled from China months ago to avoid the bloodshed. Miriam was begging for a visit. It had been a long while—Miriam's daughters were almost grown now. It would be a treat to go for tea. Truth be known, Alice was lonely for family. Miriam was her small attachment back to Canada. The two had played together as children, before Alice immigrated to America and Miriam married a diplomat.

On a lark, Alice booked a flight from Paris with Imperial Airways. A normally full day of travel would be reduced to a few hours.The airline, in business in England since the mid-1920s, was as heavily subsidized by the British government as its competitors were in Germany and France. All were vying for the lucrative passenger, freight and mail routes. Air travel, albeit still combined in places with rail travel, offered such speed now that one could travel to Cairo from London in less than a week instead of a month. Alice squelched her longing to revisit Egypt.

As happened, however, with some regularity, fog in the Channel canceled the air crossing. She and the five other passengers disembarked from the wooden-framed twin-engine biplane in Boulogne to ride in first class on the train to the coast, crossed the water by steamer, and boarded another train in Dover for London. She saw Miriam Kirkby and her daughters for tea, spent the night at the Savoy, interviewed and hired a manager for her London concert, and the next morning flew back to Paris. The magic of air travel was born in her from that day.

Chapter 52

East Coast Forever

Winter and spring of 1931 Alice was a blur on the landscape between Paris and Beaulieu, then Paris and The Hague, then Paris and London, and Paris and Munich.

Gown fittings, rehearsals, printing and placing advertisements kept her in Beaulieu for the last two weeks of March. On the thirtieth, after the concert concluded at the Beaulieu Casino Theatre, she boarded a sleeper train for Paris.

At breakfast in the dining car, driven by desperate measures to get Jane educated, and in California before the money ran out, she drafted a letter to her lawyer in Los Angeles asking him to contact UCLA about enrolling Jane as a freshman before she had finished high school.

She also wrote a letter to Miss Weaver at Andrebrook instructing her to enroll Jane in summer school.

In April, Alice dashed for a long weekend in Munich and environs with Johnny and Mutti Cranston, motoring madly at 4:30 a.m. toward the mountains for a sleigh ride on the late spring snow, then a nap in the sunshine on the hotel terrace, then back to Paris for voice lessons with Madame de Sales.

Early May Alice traveled to London for her concert at Wigmore Hall. Dinner beforehand was at the Savoy, of course, her treat, with Cousin Miriam and her daughters.

"*Au revoir*, Alicia, good-bye," they shouted as Alice and her trunks left on the boat train to Harwich, where an overnight ferry would take her to the Hook of Holland. *Apple trees and lilacs glowing in the twilight, cows and hedgerows speeding past*, she noted in her diary, as she sat by a window in her leather cloche hat and stylish tweeds, looking like landed gentry and conversing with interesting people.

In Paris, Jane's letter awaited.

Dear Mother,
Please understand that on June 20th I am without a home or money. At the present moment I have less than a dollar and debts. ...

Only Alice's bedside C. S. readings and her bible anchored her to hope. Debt was looming, having borrowed an enormous amount from the bank and from an old friend: $2,500 for Johnny and $1,900 for Jane.

***

Mutti Cranston met Alice in The Hague a few weeks later and kept her company through final rehearsals and hair appointment for the concert on the eighteenth. One more recital, one more monumental push for recognition and money. Then, the mad schedule was suddenly over. The concert, rather than being a joyful event, signaled the end of months of travel and expense.

On May 19, Alice swept into Cook's Travel for last-minute mail, then boarded the train for Paris.

My Dear Mrs. Muma,

We have been trying to get together a single statement from the many involved and detailed pages of college requirements. The documents show that Jane must have fifteen units to try for college, which she will have in June of 1932. It would be impossible to take so many credits during the summer. She has taken her practice College Entrance Exams. We will proceed to get ready and wait until the last minute to pay fees and get tutors in case your plans call Jane over to you. I realize John's school does not close till July tenth and that other opportunities over there were anticipated for him. I know you will all want to be together in Europe as the shared experience will bind you all so much more closely. Jane can stay here in Tarrytown until your way is clear.

Yours very truly,
Lillian C. Weaver

Alice wanted to beat her head against the train window. NO! Janey could just go to summer school at Andrebrook, and they all would come back to California, and Jane would enter UCLA, and Johnny would enter Cal Tech. After all, Johnny was due to take his college boards, and oh-so-much was riding on his passing. This whole expensive school year was preparation for college, and if he did not pass, no one would want him.

She arrived in Paris at 7:30 in the evening and made her way to the Hotel Beausejour, where she had moved after her initial visit with Johnny in late January. There was always a moment of lightness when she entered this hotel. It was home for a while, the black iron grillwork reminding her of California, a place she always came back to in this vagabond existence. She headed inside, commandeered a porter for her considerable luggage and headed upstairs for a hot bath, a cup of strong tea, and a soft bed. She would wait a day or two to collect her mail. Surely there was no good news.

Over toast and marmalade late the next morning, Alice scribbled a new list of to-dos on the back of an envelope. Clothes needed mending after the hard wear of the winter; a corset stay threatened to impale her from so much work bolstering her in her costumes. She could do, as well, with a spring frock that would carry her into the summer and back to Los Angeles. Chase Bank was a must, if only to check on the paltry remaining sum in her account.

225

She turned, then, to file some papers away in the Luis Vuitton traveling secretary trunk. Alice had purchased it in a fit of pique at not having a portable desk on which to write and type during her travels. It had suited her hotel room and would do for the boat trip home with Johnny in the summer. It had space, even, to store a portable typewriter, as well as a proper file bin with dividers, and storage drawers for writing supplies. A small writing surface was cleverly stowed away and could be assembled in a minute.

***

Jane's scathing letter arrived on the twenty-fifth, leaving Alice as bereft as if someone had died.

Dear Mother,

I will get a job as a junior counselor at my camp in Maine, so it will not be necessary for you to give me any money, and then you will only have to take care of John this summer. All I ask you to send me from next month's Laguna Stock check is $125. You must realize that ever since last February I have had only about $35 and most of that was spent for vacation. I have had to skimp even to be able to have enough toothpaste. It's been perfect HELL! I really think, Mother, that during all these months, when you have been getting $400 or sometimes more than that and then borrowing, you can at least give me that much. You said you were trying to economize. Why, when you come to think of it, I have spent much less than you have. ...

If I don't come back here next year, there is no place to go; college is absolutely out of the question. Besides, it's a lot cheaper here because Miss Weaver is asking no tuition. All I would need is $25 a month. But if I do this there must be a written agreement that a certain amount would arrive every month at a certain time. And I imagine if Miss Moore had charge of it, it would be even better. I beg that the next amount of money you borrow go to paying bills here. If you can't do that, you can give me my third of the money left in Daddy's estate and I'll take care of myself. ... Within a year or so John and I should sally forth for ourselves. But I feel that John should have his chance in Munich. Surely it is the only recompense for his interrupted study.

Mother, I don't think I could ever forgive you if you insist upon dragging us home to Los Angeles this summer because it just means the finish. If you don't mind my saying so, I think the attempt to economize this winter has been a pretty good fiasco. I'd like to have my share of the estate and see what I can do myself. You have always said you wanted us to take charge of ourselves in every way. But you never, never, never have gone through with it. You always step in at the end and change the way you want it to go. I'm not trying to be ungrateful or anything, I'm just trying to help you at a time when, from your letters, you were at the end of your string. I've worked hard and tried to make you proud of me and I hope I've succeeded.

Loads of love,

Peter

Following shortly on the heels of Jane's letter was one from Miss Weaver.
Dear Mrs. Muma,

I don't see any unwillingness on Jane's part to meet life and its responsibilities. I understand perfectly well your desire to plan for the children and of course do not want to interfere. Standing outside I look at the three of you with great interest and sympathy. However, of course, you recognize that I understand Jane's needs, having watched over her almost constantly for over three years. ...

You are mistaken in thinking that Jane, with her scholarship, holds any different position here from any of the girls. No one will know she has any special concessions. Please do rest, my dear lady, in what good opportunity comes to meet the present need.

Please do not feel that the child is putting up opposition to you. You have asked her to do something she knows is beyond her, to be one year older than she really is.

I will gladly offer her a fourth year, giving her a home and academic instruction. She has earned this by her beautiful useful life here. I'll be glad to have the money you are sending for Jane's last school year, but from this time on she will have only personal expenses to consider.

Yours faithfully,
Lillian Weaver

Alice could no longer pretend to be in charge of Jane. Clearly the influence of Miss Weaver was absolute.

For the remaining month of Johnny's school, it was luncheon at Rumpelmeyers, tea with Johnny and Mutti Cranston almost every day, and walks in the Englischer Garten. A tutor schooled Johnny in chemistry after he completed the college boards, and so he finished his fourth year of high school. Now it was time to return to America and face the future.

Alice and Johnny checked into the Hotel Washington in New York, making a point of having tea with Cousin Olive, sharing the latest news about the London cousins. They all went to see *The Barretts of Wimpole Street*, after which Johnny took the train to Boston while Alice made a quick trip to Washington DC.

They met up a few days later in Boston, booked into a C. S. retreat and hired a practitioner for Johnny. After registering for summer school, they dashed to Cape Cod for a quick visit with Ted, Johnny's friend from Munich.

Alighting briefly back in Boston, they drove overnight to Maine for a half day visit with Jane at camp, barely getting in luncheon and tea before the grueling ride home in the fog and the first day of summer school for Johnny.

Alice hunted up an apartment one block from MIT. Johnny left her alone in it the very next weekend to enjoy her view of the Charles River, while he again drove back to the Cape to visit Ted.

Part Four: Fait Accompli, Unfortunately

1931–1938

New England does not seem the place for the free Californian spirit to develop.

Chapter 53

Finally, Repose

A Conversation with Gran'mere

It was then, Gran'mere that I found you in repose, gazing from your living room window, moonlight twinkling over the river. Did that bring us together, this shared, magical view of water in moonlight?

"I've seen it so many times in my life, Gran'mere. It never gets old." I decided to jump right in with my question. "What possessed you to go to Washington DC all of a sudden?"

"I went south by train to Washington DC on business, meeting my good friend Anne, whose husband is connected to the Smithsonian. They were the ones, you may remember, who were on their way to China when I took the State Department course for the Foreign Service. At dinner she came up with the idea that I might make a concert tour of the British West Indies this coming winter. I came back by aeroplane."

"Was this trip just an excuse to take the plane back the very next day?" I asked. She had not written one word about the purpose of the trip.

Alice almost grinned in delight. "I took Ludington Airways, landing first in Baltimore, then Wilmington, and Philadelphia. You can't imagine the beautiful views of Manhattan, landing in Newark." (But of course I could.) "I took a taxi and train to Penn Station, stayed overnight at the Biltmore and a midnight train to Boston. Now here I am."

"Boston seems, perhaps—*less* than you are used to, culturally," I ventured. "What will you do all the months you're to stay here?"

Gran'mere moved around the room, touching the rented furniture with distaste. She sighed as she pulled her hand away from the dark upholstered chair by the radio.

"I miss my things," she whispered. "These are just awful."

"Boston is a wasteland," she continued in a louder voice. "The only two friends I know well are in Europe for the year. No culture to speak of, but, there are movies. Johnny and I could relate to them, having met so many movie people. Let's see—Dressler in *Politics*, Bennett did *The Millionaire* and also *The Smiling Lieutenant*. I also saw that character Will Rogers in *As Young as You Feel*. I'm sure there are more to come.

"The Mother Church is here and gives me solace. The seat of all knowledge for Christian Scientists: Mary Baker Eddy's works are there for us to read. All the church practitioners are trained here. The place is fairly humming with devotion and love. Without that, I feel I would disintegrate."

It was obvious to me that Gran'mere was also here to monitor Johnny. The apartment was close to MIT and C. S. practitioner guidance, and she would guarantee his attending the Mother Church in Boston by her mere presence.

To put a lighter touch on things, I asked, "Was this where you learned to cook?"

She laughed. "I urge you to try and picture me cooking breakfast, luncheon and dinner for a hungry schoolboy."

"I have a hard time with that, Gran'mere." I laughed in turn.

"Well, it is a measure of my devotion to that young man that I learned. I bought the *Fanny Farmer Cookbook*, and dredged up my notebooks on cooking and nutrition from my college days."

"Surely you don't carry those notes around with you."

She snorted. "No, they managed to get into my costume trunk last year. Olga's idea of a joke, I think, for which I must thank her."

"Jane did drop in for a quick visit after camp was over in mid-September. Did you mind, after all the bitter words?"

"It was lovely to see her. Really, she is a treasure, and growing prettier every time I see her."

I noticed that she did not answer my question. "Gran'mere, were you able to resolve any of this turbulence between the two of you?"

Alice pursed her lips and would not hold my gaze. "Les Mumas were together for only a few hours. I put her on the midnight train and have not seen her since. I have not had a minute to be sad since Johnny officially entered as an MIT freshman, because then began the clamor of fraternity rush. I was so afraid that it would consume him. Don't forget, I know firsthand what freshman rush was like back in my day.

"I managed to buy a Ford in October, having loved the rental in the summer, and broke it in driving to New York and back to view the foliage. I popped in to see Jane, but she was gone on some school camping adventure

"I knew when John failed to get into Cal Tech, and Jane could not enter college with only three years of high school, it meant that Les Mumas had switched coasts. Though Olga makes a case that the opera company in LA is still in existence, I can't go back.

"I can't go back," she said again, the agony of the decision written on her face. "Can't leave Johnny to the distraction of rush week, so I take little vacations to ease the boredom of Boston. The steamer to Provincetown with its quaint shops and scurrying sailboats is a sight to behold. There *are* symphonies, so Boston is not entirely without culture. A horse show, occasionally... Breakfast in Harvard Square when I am absolutely off cooking. I am muddling through. But my heart isn't in it the way it would be in Los Angeles. I am just dazed by this ruthless severing of plans."

Alice drifted away from me, her fears expressed. Where better to find peace than in the healing love of the Mother Church?

The living room window was open to the breeze, and a scrap of paper drifted along the floor. I caught just a few words written in her own hand before it slid under the dark upholstered chair.

Thou shalt not be afraid for the terror by night, nor for the arrow that flieth by day.

I believe it was part of Psalm 91.

***

Thankfully, the year drew to a close on a more positive note. In a single-spaced, four page typed letter, John Rankin listed the status of the numerous tasks Alice had assigned him. With the expected dry humor, he related that she had escaped jail: the Chrysler lawsuit against her was dropped by the judge as the company did receive her car in good working order, Castellamare would soon be rented, and she owed the carpenter $200 in repairs to set the kitchen right.

Jane came to Boston and was beyond excited to be Johnny's date for the Yale–Harvard game and fraternity dance. Gran'mere was overjoyed to see her daughter in a new gown that evening, being whisked away by her handsome son dressed in his tuxedo, driving the new Ford.

Gran'mere announced at Christmastime, as Les Mumas gathered in Cousin Olive's apartment at the George Washington Hotel in New York City, that she was going to tour the West Indies. Olga would be sending another trunk of costumes.

Chapter 54

Alice Conquers the Caribbean

Sailing January 9, noon, 1932
C/o *S. S. Zacapa*, Pier 9, North River
United Fruit Co., NY City
Dear Alicia,
Margery and I would have been there to see you off except for a prior engagement. We wish you success in your ventures. I enclose letters of introduction for Mexico City.

I will arrange the details of your publicity in the *Broadway Magazine*, the *Radio Dial*, and the *Radio Guide* while you are gone, so that everything will be in readiness when you have the pictures taken.

Between the typed lines in invisible ink I have written all the little things which I would say to you if I could sit on deck in the moonlight and exchange confluences.

Here is a toast to my motto for your new coat of arms—"High, Wide and Handsome." This in red letters on a silver background engraved on a scroll beneath the crest, an airplane, the Pacific Ocean and you in a stunning negligee.

Smooth seas, balmy days, brilliant nights. Hurry home to tell us about the whole wonderful experience.

Affectionate regards,
Don

Don Rockwell. Alice grinned at his outrageous note and felt the tension of the last few weeks unwind. *Margery will keep Don in line. Nevertheless, a little safe flirting would surely improve the spirit.* Alice, used to his ways, knew he never stepped out of line, at least not with her. As her business contact and publicist for the hoped-for radio programs in New York, he was the best there was, and she had cultivated both Margery and him as friends of the family.

Sitting in her tiny stateroom, Alice looked into her hand mirror, seeing a face that was forty-five. It was full, as full as the body that went with it—filled out by marriage and two children. Brows arched over gray eyes; only a hint of crow's feet. *Not bad, given the stresses of the last several years.* She touched her hair, now short and gently waved, but still the rich brown of her youth. *Little else left of the life with Jerry.* Thoughts raced through her mind, the increasingly fugitive commission checks, the money just scrounged for the hotel management course scheduled in Washington DC after she returned from the cruise. The course must not fail to find her a job. Singing careers these days were scarce, and yet, this last attempt to sing abroad, coupled with a radio debut in New York... She pushed back the fear of failure, covering it with hope, managing it with Christian Science. Alice placed her little C. S. reader on her pillow.

It wrenched her heart to think of never living in Los Angeles again. That thin thread of Cal Tech had dangled before her, promising to draw them all back. But then had he gotten in, her friends would know the depth of poverty facing the Mumas. The nightmare of accessibility to her creditors made her shudder. Perhaps it was better this way, but it was agony to be away from the homes she loved. Windsor Boulevard was sold at last after years of being rented, Castellamare's Casa Chiquita was still vacant, still waiting for a buyer. The last, King's X studio apartments in the Hollywood hills, was rented to an actor who could not pay the bills. Out of work like the rest of us, she thought. *My beautiful furniture, hidden away in those homes. I dream of it.*

John had failed his midterm exams in German and was summarily kicked out of MIT. The money Alice spent had been all for nothing. In a few months he would go to Munich to study German, determined to reenter MIT in September. But with Hitler on the ballot in Germany, it was not safe to send Johnny until the election was over. What to do?

Jane had found a home at Andrebrook and would finish in the spring. The upside to that was that her financial dependence on Alice would end with her graduation. Jane, stubborn beyond all, would not entertain a university but perhaps might opt for teachers' training instead. What a waste. She should go to college. There had been enough disaster to upset Alice for a lifetime, and she vowed not to think of it for a week. The basic tenant of her C. S. studies was that events might try to make one upset, and through study one could overcome all negative thoughts.

She tucked Don's letter into her traveling secretary trunk, which held her life on bits of paper. Should its dark file drawers be exposed—like Pandora's Box, the truth of her poverty would fly out to the world. Utterly unbearable.

Dear John Rankin... She paused remembering her frantic telegram to her lawyer and confidant, begging for news of her tax refund review, because $1,150 hung in the balance. He telegraphed back just before Alice boarded,

COLLECTORS OFFICE SWAMPED TREASURY DEPT LOW ON FUNDS NO POSSIBILITY EXPEDITING

There were stacks of other letters trying to make her desolate. Her diligent California secretary, Miss Moore, sorted bills and forwarded mail with a dribble of commission and dividend checks. Miss Klumb, the house agent, lived in her precious Castellamare villa while searching for buyers in a depleted market. Prospective buyers for her gem of a house slipped away as they saw their stocks fail.

John Rankin and Miss Moore guarded Alice's whereabouts, providing only her permanent Women's Athletic Club address when pressed by creditors. John was especially good at keeping the vultures off. Here she was, spending her last nickel, while she could hardly afford to pay him, in fact had fired him just because she couldn't. But he continued to shore her up. The dear man could not afford to take his wife, Enge, on vacation.

So, when Alice dropped this delicious bit of delight from Don into her traveling trunk, a little bit of light shone in the darkness.

Alice slipped into a wine-hued linen skirt that fell just below her knees. Silk stockings shimmered underneath. She pushed her feet into low, vamped pumps. The matching boxy linen over-blouse hung beautifully from shoulder pads to disguise a thickening waist. Clipping pearls to her ears and a strand of the same around her neck, she bent over the roses, sent by her son, to inhale the scent. With the powerful memory of Don's love note to buoy her, she went out to meet the forty-nine other passengers.

They were all lined up at the starboard rail to watch the confusion of ships departing with them. Less an armada than a rout, she counted twenty-five sea vessels in all, scampering out of port and in danger of ramming their neighbor. As the *S. S. Zacapa* passed the Statue of Liberty, the chill wind drove them all inside, Alice to tea, and many more to the bar.

Rough weather kept some away from the dining room, but Alice was brave enough to dine with the purser as his only guest. He was a handsomely uniformed man and probably over two hundred pounds, which he carried elegantly on his tall frame. He said his name was Boschen, and they chatted pleasantly about his brother, a U.S. Army colonel, and a nephew who had graduated from MIT. Alice, lying in spite of herself, said she had a son just starting the engineering program there, and she was traveling to Jamaica and then on to Mexico City to singing engagements yet to be booked. Mr. Boschen said he had the perfect contact, a Mr. Ernest Rouse, who would certainly be of service with her plans for a concert in Kingston. Alice said she would be delighted to meet the gentlemen, and rose after coffee, feigning fatigue, to return to her cubbyhole.

The first night out was rough. Alice was not bothered. She read in her little C. S. book before retiring. And slept soundly for the first night in months. She had a contact for her Kingston concert.

The *S. S. Zacapa*, more a shiny white yacht than steamer, plowed the now-calm seas with the coming of dawn. It was owned by United Fruit Company; Alice envisioned bananas stuffing the hold on the return trip. She thought with a shiver of furry tarantulas touring her trunks down there in the dark.

After luncheon the second day out, Alice was waylaid by a flirty bachelor much too young to be taken seriously, a Mr. Walter Chemowsky. After speedy introductions, he invited her to join a table of passengers nearby. They all sat around, clothed in linen suits and dresses, determined to embrace the warmth of the Caribbean, which had yet to arrive.

And the conversation drifted, as it does with new acquaintances, around a myriad of subjects, never straying into politics or religion. It was drawn to a close with the mention of Alice's forthcoming hotel management course in Washington, and the promise by the Cottons for an invitation to dine when Alice arrived in their hometown.

***

Walter Chemowsky attached himself to her throughout the cruise, regaling her with silly stories and threatening to make her stay in Kingston fun. Though Alice spent much of her free time in her cabin reading, she was not immune to his charms, and felt herself relaxing into the comic romanticism of the voyage. Remembering the shocking behavior of some of her fellow singers on her cruise to Australia last year, she kept Mr. Chemowsky at a certain distance, but never once let him abandon her.

He appears to have a full purse, Alice wrote to Jane later, *and is a scream of fun. I have asked him to call on you on his return in March or April. He is from Augusta, Maine and knows all about your camp in Harrison. That should be a good talking point. Though he says he is traveling for his health, he appears to be in the peak of it. ...*

The little ship docked in Kingston harbor on the fourteenth. The Myrtle Hotel porters met Alice and the Muma entourage of costume trunks, and by two o'clock, the luggage and Alice were comfortably arranged in her small room on the second floor overlooking the street. Mr. Rouse, of Rouse Transportation, had agreed to call at two thirty. He showed up in an open car; Alice watched him unfolding himself to over six feet of linen suit and pith helmet. She moved forward to greet him, and her red-feathered dress especially purchased for this Caribbean adventure shivered a little in the breeze. Mr. Rouse's carefully arranged expression as he took Alice's hand could not conceal his delighted amazement with this charming new bird.

Within an hour, they were off to investigate the Bournemouth Swim Club, having a sunset tea with Mr. Rouse's sister. They sat outside under the canopy of a flamboyant tree. Its glowing red flower clusters sat atop feathered leaves, dropping occasional flowers on the table. From their view of the sea, they could see a boat docking. Mr. Rouse said it was the mail hydroplane from Cienfuegos, Cuba. *Wouldn't that be a jolly trip for Johnny boy?* she thought.

The next day, Mr. Rouse left Alice in the capable hands of the manager of Ormsby Hall, Kingston's biggest auditorium. Before long, arrangements had been made for her concert on January twenty-third, rehearsals scheduled, publicity submitted and tickets printed.

The Gleaner, January 23, 1932, Kingston, Jamaica

"Mme. Alicia Muma Charmed the Audience with her Fine Technique"

Those who were fortunate to be present at the Ormsby Memorial Hall last night enjoyed a treat they will not easily forget. ... A program of 21 items, the first 6 extracted from her costumed song recital in a dramatic setting. The second part was three groups of songs, "Youth," by Catherine Barry, "Love is in the Wind," by Alexander McFaych, and "Hills," by Frank la Forge. All were skillfully handled. The second group was a collection of French songs with which Madame Muma displayed great artistic ability. ...

The last group of 6 songs was Madame at her best. She has a pleasant easy manner and sings with culture and sympathy.

Sunday, January 24, 1932

Aboard *S. S. Empress* of AustraliaMy Dear J and J:

To find myself again on board a splendid 20,000-ton Canadian Pacific liner is almost unbelievable. She has just made a cruise along the north shore of South America to Panama and is now en route Havana, Nassau and New York. The cruise is manned by the nicest Canadians—Mr. Ross, Mr. Willmot and Mrs. Kerr, hostess—but the passengers are rather terrible types of Americans. So very much has transpired in such a short space of time that I am almost dizzy.

I hope you received my first letter (sent airmail) telling of the trip down to Kingston, and now just a word about my stay there. My hotel room was rather hot, so to offset that disadvantage I held "court" in pajamas every day from just before luncheon until as far into the afternoon as possible with engagements in a small summer house in the hotel garden looking toward the sea and the bathers. Here I studied and received callers and it worked beautifully. ...

Wednesday I added a Christian Science meeting. There I met some charming Jamaicans—which means that they have some colored blood. They mingle freely with the whites, and color means less in Jamaica, probably, than any other place on the globe.

Thursday I rehearsed at Ormsby Memorial Hall, testing lights, etc., and then Mr. Rouse took me to a cello recital.

Friday was my big day and I could not have had a more cordial reception. They seemed to feast on my songs, so many of which they have never heard. Many came backstage and I was deeply touched by my lovely flowers. Mr. Rouse topped it all off with a cool, refreshing drive and I had the satisfaction of feeling a tremendous amount had been accomplished. Saturday, with all business concluded, I claimed as my day and hired a car to take Mr. Rouse—in an effort to show some appreciation of his kindness—with me to tea at the home of a friend about 50 miles away.

I have no adjectives to describe the country through which we passed. Majestic silk-cotton trees; I picked and crushed leaves from which allspice is

237

made; red seeds were drying in the sun like California raisins, to be sold all over the world for coloring: Jamaica ginger was drying on large flat trays. There were markets all along the line with gay, picturesque natives singing, etc. We had a charming tea with Mr. and Mrs. Lewis and drove back to Kingston in time for a dinner engagement. (Remember the dinner hour in the tropics is anywhere between eight and nine.)

I have had so much attention and have been so happy, I feel twenty years younger. It was with many feelings that I watched the lovely harbor and the new friends on the dock fade into the twilight—but on to new fields we go! Have just met a Professor Hanbury from Oxford, who has especial charge of Rhodes scholars in law while at Oxford. He is charming. Have listened to the Sunday evening concert with Mrs. Kerr, the hostess. Am rehearsing with the English accompanist tomorrow.

More from Mexico, my blessed pair,
Mother

The *Empress of Australia* docked first in Havana, where Alice repacked, sending most of her trunks on to New York with the ship. She waited three days to catch the steamer to Mexico and she missed it, all the fault of American Express, for which they paid dearly in hotel bills and city tours. Alice fumed some of each day in the Christian Science reading room, practicing to get over it. This had cost her missed opportunities in Mexico City which would never be repaid.

***

She wrote to Jane and John.

My sentence expired on February 5th and I got aboard the *S. S. Orizaba* (named after one of Mexico's most beautiful snow-capped mountains resembling Japan's Fujiyama), and dear kiddies, do you recognize the date— February 5? Twenty years to the day since I married your dear daddy and went with him to London Town. I found myself sailing west into a sun that was setting over the Maya ruins of Yucatán now overgrown with jungle, telling a story of a civilization that was in its first empire when Jesus the Christ was born. ... On the *Orizaba* I found myself very happily seated in the dining room at the first officer's table. He was a jovial Estonian, speaking excellent English. The other guests at his table were a German by the name of Mr. Balz, who had lived through Mexican revolutions; a young Spanish pianist, who has been studying in New York for five years, a young New York girl and her father. On deck my steamer chair was in an alcove with a very nice Mrs. Emerson from New York and a Mrs. Spong, an American who had married an Englishman and lived most of her life in Egypt—and had Louis Vuitton baggage!

We entered the historic port of Vera Cruz at sunset on Sunday. ... The swarthy skinned descendants of Montezuma attended to our baggage. Such absurd duty on my record collection forced me to ship them back to New York rather than bring them in to Mexico.

Picture a fairly lighted station early in the morning with scurrying Americans, disgruntled foreigners, and endless Mexican mothers and babies—all piling aboard for this long-heralded climb to Mexico City over a railroad construction which is one of the greatest engineering feats in the world. The cars were Pullman-made. ... I was joined by several families I had met on the voyage, including a German couple with their children, all of whom spoke English and Spanish. There is no yardstick in the world to measure my insignificance at such a time. I am determined to study Spanish. We rose through the air, and the villages through which we passed were enchanting, pausing now and then where eager natives tried to vend their queer wares. Think, though, of being able to buy a section of hollow sugar cane soaked in water and filled with about two dozen gardenias for twelve American cents! Tropical scenery like a South Sea Isle, we rose over five thousand feet in about fifty miles. Once over the divide, the country was flatter and dustier, with cactus everywhere. Towards dusk we saw the two great snowclad mountains which stand guard over Mexico City, affectionately known as "Popo" and the "White Woman." Here I was at last at this great city which had fascinated Daddy. I felt him very near as I entered it and came to this most unique hotel. Indeed, during these last few days so much of what he told me has come back to me as I gazed upon its wonders.

After touring the city, the handsome old cathedral, the Aztec calendar stone, markets with every kind of fruit and vegetable, I sought the Christian Science Society. Such a happy, eager group. And so, with them and the nucleus of *Orizaba* steamer friends I am faring very well.

I have sung over the radio but have abandoned the idea of giving any other program due to my shortness of time imposed by my Havana delay.

February 17, 1932
New Orleans
My Dear J and J:

Two things I have always wanted to see in the United States—a Kentucky Derby and a Mardi Gras in New Orleans. I would have seen the latter except for the delay in Havana. The old city looks rather shabby after the gala event, but I find fascination in the Cabildo, St. Louis Cathedral, Jackson Square and Pirates Alley. I had luncheon at Gelatois and I would say unhesitatingly that all that has ever been said of the French cuisine in New Orleans is unquestionable true. It was as perfect as anything I ever had in Paris.

I had the thrill of my life flying in the cool of dawn ere the sun get too hot, from Mexico City last Monday morning. We flew right over the Pyramids of the Sun, over orderly haciendas, with every changing types of scenery from wooded mountains and gorges, into fog banks as we neared the coast at

Tampico. The plane was absolutely full and the type of service given by the Pan-American Airways is excellent. ...

Not many days now until I will again be in New York to see what I can do about radio programs. I hope good letters from you both will await my return.

Good-night,

Mother

Chapter 55

Johnny's Difficult Journey

"Why don't I send you on a quick trip, following my itinerary through the West Indies?"

Johnny knew that it was not a question. Once Mother had decided…

"Following my steps through Jamaica and Mexico will open your eyes to the beauty of another world. And, a business opportunity may present itself. Don is working on it secretly, a film distribution company. You shall fly my route in just a week. Then go to Munchen to study as planned."

Johnny retorted. "You are just trying to keep me occupied."

"Only until the middle of March, when the world might be a little saner. The Nazi unrest during the primaries has spilled over into Geneva. No, dear boy, this will do you good. All you think of these last years is how glorious Germany is. There are other places of value, Johnny, which you must consider."

"But, Mother, the expense…" There was no arguing with the truth of their finances. His father's life insurance had been paying for schooling. Mother had spent a lot on her tour of Australia last year and the Caribbean adventure last month, booking singing engagements en route. Both Johnny and Jane suspected that she paid dearly for her recent adventure, not only the stateroom but the entertainment of business connections in Jamaica and Mexico, booking the hall and public relations.

"Janey will likely be in Munich over the summer. You could study in the spring, perhaps, and certainly work with the professor of hydraulic engineering during July and August. The Alps will be wonderful then. You could come back with her at the end of the summer."

What she meant was—and he and Jane had talked about this—that he was too attached to Munchen and to Mutti. But whose fault was that?

"I thought we agreed that I must go and study German for the summer, come back and take the exams to get back into to MIT?"

"We did. I am thinking, though, first, of a business opportunity for you. Don is a great friend to the three of us. He admires your winning ways, dear boy, and feels it would be worth it to train you in sales. He has a Spanish business contact making inquiries right now. Don could expand Columbia Phonograph's reach into another continent. You could make a fortune.

"So," said Alice, "while I settle in to Washington for my hotel management course, you can carry on by yourself for a week."

"It's no fun by myself."

"Nonsense, dear. You've had plenty of traveling practice."

Johnny filled a suitcase and flew down to Miami.

1932 FEB 26 PM 11 59 MIAMI
MRS IJ MUMA CARE AMERICAN EXPRESS CO = WASHINGTON DC

LEAVING FOR HAVANA TOMORROW SAT STOP ON TO KINGSTON MORE WORD FROM KINGSTON STOP AM FLYING TO CUBA IN ONE OF THESE BIG CLIPPER SHIPS CARRIES 40 PASSENGERS LOVE = JOHNNY

1932 MAR 01 AM 11 01
MIAMI FLO
MRS ALICIA MUMA
AMERICAN EXPRESS CO 1414 F ST NORTHWEST WASHINGTON DC

ITINERARY JOHN MUMA AS FOLLOWS MIAMI HAVANA ON CLIPPER HAVANA CIENFUEGOS SATURDAY NIGHT TRIAN STOP CINEFUEGOS KINGSTON SUNDAY STOP KINGSTON CIRSTOBAL FROM THERE TO VERACRUZ VIA SALVADOR STOP VERACRUZ MEXICOCITY AND RETURN BY TRAIN STOP VERACRUZ MIAMI VIA MERIDA YUCATAN ON PLANE STOP HIS TICKETS ISSUES WITH UNLIMITED STOPOVER PRIVILEGES HENCE DATES OF ITINERARY UNKNOWN STOP HE IS EXPECTED RETURN MIAMI BY MARCH TENTH

The ensuing days were filled with missed connections, rerouting instructions from Alice and broken appointments from Don's secret business deals. Johnny was feeling both led by the nose and arbitrarily allowed to flounder by his mother. Finally, physical and mentally exhausted, and several days late, he arrived in Miami, wired Alice, and fell into an exhausted sleep. Johnny took the train to Washington DC, then moved on to New York with Alice to stay with his cousin Olive Kirby. Alice focused on publicity for the promised radio show promotion. She did not understand that her son's lack of concentration was anything more than exhaustion from the rushed and ruined trip. She left for Washington DC before Johnny boarded the boat for Germany.

March 16th, 1932
Columbia Phonograph Company
55 Fifth Avenue, Sound-on-Disc Division
D. S. Rockwell, Manager
New York

Dear Alicia,

Sorry to hear that Johnny had to rest in Miami to recuperate from the effects of such strenuous journey and that you will not be up until next week.

Star-Dust has agreed to a quarter page photo and write up for $50. Kesslere Photography tells me he has some lovely portraits of you, as well as of Johnny. Enclosed is a printer's proof of the article.

Hastily and with affection,

Don

March 28, 1932

*S. S. Ile de France*Dear Mother,

Well, we made it. When I sauntered on deck this morning there were white chalky cliffs of Merry England. Never looked so good before.

Oh yes, thanks for the Science work. You must have received my wire about four hours after I sent it, for at that time I was greatly helped. Now I am more sure than ever that Christian Science is the only real thing. And I'm going to get it, on an average of about every ten minutes. Last night there was a gala and concert. The later half of the voyage has been fairly rough but the sun came out this morning. The waves went down and all the other passengers and little Johnny Muma felt much better.

Adios,

Love, Johnny

04 APRIL 1932

POSTAL TELEGRAPH MUENCHENMADE IT AND AM ALL RIGHT STOP SEND ADDRESS OF YOUR PRACTITIONER LOVE JOHNNY

WESTERN UNION 05 APRIL 1932 WASHINGTON DC

READ CONSTANTLY YOURSELF CLAIMING AMPLE HEALING IMMEDIATELY STOP WRITE WEEKLY LOVE MOTHER

April 8

Columbia Phonograph CompanyDear Alicia,

Star-Dust article on you entitled "American Song-Bird" out today. You are opposite "Is Garbo Dead?" I managed a half page for you and hope you are pleased.

I guess Johnny is safe in Germany by now and I hope everything is going the way you want. I believe I can arrange your radio broadcast.

Affectionately,

Don

WESTERN UNION EASTER GREETING TO
VALLEY VISTA APARTMENTS WASHINGTON DC

HAPPY EASTER PLEASE WORK AM ALL RIGHT

WESTERN UNION
PLEASE ASCERTAIN IF SON J MUMA HOTEL SAVOY LONDON IS
ILL STOP
ALICIA MUMA

POSTAL TELEGRAH
MUENCHEN
ALL SCHOOLS CLOSED EVERYBODY AWAY WHEN CONSUL
RECEIVED JOHNS CABLE NOTHING COULD BE DONE TILL THIS
WEEK THOUGH SERIOUSLY ILL HIMSELF WILL HAVE MATTERS
ARRANGED SOON AS POSSIBLE
MUTTI

April 19, 1932
1414 F Street, N.W.
Washington, DC
My Dear Mutti:
You will never know the comfort which your weekend letter brought to me yesterday. The dear boy's constant repetition that he was all right made me realize that he was indeed so only by the grace of God. I have told him he is forgiven this time, but I have cautioned him that it is kinder to state the facts even though they are distressing.

I know that in asking the wonderful lecturer and teacher John Doorly to call upon John in London was exactly what I would have done. What a strange experience has been mine in watching both John and also the daddy in their struggles, knowing that Christian Science is their only help, but having to keep hands off until they rouse to that fact themselves. While I know the Caribbean air trip was really unnecessary and hard on him (but very much an eye-opener) I realize that he has been rushing along without pausing to take stock, as it were. Now he can, and I am sure he will work to completely overcome the situation. I do not have to assure you that this thing must be absolutely routed and calls for good, consecrated work. John has his part, however, to do, but unless he is studying and reading the literature in obedient desire to replace in his thinking what has brought this about, he will not receive his healing.

While it tried to upset me very much when he flunked out in February, I can see that this pause will put him on his feet for life. He shows not a shadow of doubt in his desire to return to MIT in September. I feel he will take hold.
…

My letters to John are not going to be as long as heretofore, for I recognize there is nothing short of an issue over this matter of correspondence. I wish to make reasonable allowances for the physical, but it cannot go on the way it has other years in constantly urging him to write. He is never going to be a success in business or the world at large unless he expresses himself more practically. I recognize it is practically his chief stumbling block in his college problem. I will make a concession that his letters be dictated, hence my reference in a wire about insisting upon a stenographer to dictate letters to me. ... While I am waiting so earnestly for your letter telling me more about the situation, I am hoping that his improvement is sufficient to permit him to take some trips.

I am hoping for a chance any minute to sing on New York radio, in which case I will feel I have rounded out the season. If a job is forthcoming as a result of this hotel course you may hear of me accepting it.

Matrimonially speaking, the light seems to have gone out.
Affectionately,
Alicia

Mutti Cranston took control, keeping John with her because of his initial weakness and trembling. She allowed no visitors, no excitement, no upsetting letters from Alice, no studying. In a couple of weeks his heart felt normal. Mutti let him out for walks, and a few times down for tea with several of the girls. John was still nervous thinking about studying German in a classroom, so she let him work alone in his room.

Mr. Husgen, his C.S. practitioner let Johnny read his letter to Alice beforehand so there would be no secrets between them.

My Dear Mrs. Muma:
...John suffered immensely during the passage... overreaction of the heart bringing extreme unrest and fear. I have asked John to stay quiet and stop studies until he has regained his normal strength. I am pleased to report that last Saturday he walked a long distance and was perfectly happy, sound and strong. ... As Mrs. Eddy says, "willing the sick to recover is not the metaphysical practice of C. S." John will take up his studies very soon. He is quite eager to get on in his profession and also pass the German examination.
...

May 20, 1932
Munich
My Dear Mutti,
I am taking that hotel training course here in Washington, and I find it far exceeding my expectation. If a job is offered me when I am through the end of June, I would like to accept it, but if not, I am definitely investigating the possibility of getting land and opening a small but enlargeable hotel on the wonderful new Pan-American Highway lying between Monterrey and Mexico City, Mexico. It is a wonderful new field and the idea thrills me. I feel equipped to do it after this course. Also I am mindful of the fact that if John is unable to

continue at MIT for whatsoever reason, it will be someplace for him to come where he can work and accomplish something. (Although wide of the mark for what I would hope for him.) With these tentative plans to drive into the wilds of Mexico, leaving July 1, you will better understand my anxiety to get John provided for ere I go. Then I may have to go to California to ship furniture and settle up, but I cannot speak yet of that. Jane's attitude of not wishing to go to college is trying to disturb me tremendously…

Affectionately,

Alicia

June 7

Dear Mother,

My next project is to pass intermediate German September 16 and reenter MIT. I came over here to get technical German, which was not fulfilled. There are so many expenses, especially the trip from Plymouth to London and Paris and then that trip to Italy which cost $100 for 10 days. This brings the total of extra expenses to $350.00. I have only $325 left, and bills of $265. Please don't give me your little Johnny too much worry over money matter at present. It literally sends a cold chill through my heart, which won't help it. When everything is all right then I'll take it on the nose, but not right now, please.

David Anderson is going to New York July 1st. When I am with somebody I know very well my fear is greatly diminished. The shortest time on the ocean is best and only attainable with the larger ship. I must be high up and have a lot to do, which is only accomplished in first class. The *Bremen* leaves on July 1st. Wire me and I'll let you know the exact particulars. My capital will get me through the month and up to the *Bremen*. From there you'll have to carry me.

Love,

Johnny

Dear Jane,

David, a guy from school over here, booked a third-class ticket, but I know he can spend time with me so I am trying not to worry. He could not leave with me, so I took the train to Paris myself, after saying good-bye to Mutti and Mr. Husgen.

What happened is that I don't remember much, but I did send a telegram to Mutti after a week in Paris. I got scared again and couldn't go on by myself, so I came back to Munchen. Then all heck broke loose and cables flew from Mother and Mutti and Mr. Husgen. Well. I guess we all thought I had seen the light but it sure disappeared in Paris. Mother decided to come and get me and Mutti had to leave for New York to figure out how she was going to make money as the school closed. I stayed with Mr. Husgen and was quite able to study, as he was good company.

246

Mother seemed to take this all in stride, arriving on the 25th, packing me up and coming back on the Bremen to New York. She seemed relieved to see that I was not at death's door. And her suspicions that I was faking it were gone quickly. We made it back to New York safely, and went with haste to Boston to the C. S. sanatorium called Chestnut Hill, and found a new practitioner for me.

Love,

Johnny

Don, literary agent and publicist, could not sort out a date for Alice to sing on the radio, nor could he justify the expense of $10,000 startup costs for the Mexico film distribution business. And so for different reasons, both plans were dropped.

Chapter 56

The Quest for El Caravanera

"Acapulco," Alice's newly christened Ford station wagon, sat in the drive with its tailgate yawning open.

Johnny ran his hands gingerly over the hood; it was blistering hot in the late August sun.

"Mother, it sure beats out our old Ford, 'Kaiser Wilhelm,' sitting in New York all tired and worn. Man, just look at those red wire wheels. Did you check out the V-8?"

"Yes, Johnny dear," replied his mother. Alice, like Johnny, was sweating. Open collars and rolled up sleeves both stained and grimy. She smiled at his enthusiasm, grateful for his advice when picking out this automobile which was to cover so much ground in the next months. They had gone together to the showroom to bargain for this new Ford. The car company was in a desperate battle with the popular Chevrolet in a dwindling market. This new five-door model, with its V-8 engine, was working its charm on a lot of folks, Les Mumas included.

Yes, she thought, Johnny was ready to be here in Boston on his own, in the care of Science at the Chestnut Hill Sanatorium. He would study hard to pass his German exam, and, Lord willing, reenter MIT. He had cost her a month's delay and too much anxiety, but it was worth it to see him so well. Her chest squeezed tight at the thought of the long drive to Mexico by herself. She would *not* permit her need of him to show, or he would have an excuse to accompany her, and she might weaken and let him.

"Let's get the luggage rack on the roof, so I can pack her up," Alice said, with false confidence.

Upright wooden posts, two on a side, had been attached to the roof in order to accommodate the rack. Johnny lifted the rack and the two of them strapped it securely to the posts. Then her luggage in turn was fitted inside and strapped down.

Into the back went some bed linens and pots and pans, then a hammock and sleeping bag, a couple of army blankets and cot, rolls of packing (for who knew how much furniture would have to be shipped across the border), ropes, a bag of tools, and lastly, her traveling secretary trunk. A tarp was stretched over it, and the rear window curtains drawn against curious eyes.

"Good-bye, Johnny dear. Let me hear from you at the Hermitage in Nashville."

"I know, I know, Mother," Johnny responded, his arm around her shoulder. "Have the schedule. Don't live too rough in between. God speed."

A hug, a wave and she was gone into the late morning haze.

By the time she passed Tarrytown, Alice's nerves had quieted. By the evening, she had pulled in to Mutti's little house outside Philadelphia, eager to curl up for a chat. Over a late dinner and endless cups of tea into the wee hours, they talked through all that had passed since Johnny's episode in Munich.

By the end of her second day on the road, Alice was shed of the fears and fatigue that had dragged her down in the months after her Hotel Management course.

Sunday, Sept. 4th, 1932
Nashville, Tennessee
This city seems to fall naturally at the end of the first lap of my journey. If I could only have had your company along the way. I have sung, whistled, gone over my opera parts and repeated psalms from the bible to keep awake, and press on. The new car is behaving wonderfully, in spite of being very heavily loaded. One old Virginian at a gas station pronounced it "a right smart outfit." I declare one needs an interpreter to understand the speech in these parts. Actually, I have heard with my own ears "taint fur," "baccy," and "taters fur Mammy." Little inspiration has been received from the names of hotels. "Eatwell Inn" was on "Purgatory Creek," and I felt no urge to enter when I read the sign "Petunia Hotel." El Caravanera grows in favor, n'est pas? Should I add "International Cuisine" for this trip? Even this fare proves beyond a doubt the need of better cooking.

I have been going slowly on account of breaking in the car, but with more than 1,000 miles accomplished, I can soon speed up. The sunsets have been magnificent. One night such a cold blue; another night like an Australian fire-opal... I have driven until midnight each night, and rested from noon until four p.m., seeking a riverbank with trees or swimming pool to pass the time.

I feel better already with this pause at the Waldorf-Astoria of Nashville. If I reach San Antonio next Friday for the weekend I shall be content. I am getting more and more thrilled as I approach Mexico again. Surely this is an idea productive of interesting results.

Adios,
Mother

WESTERN UNION HERMITAGE NASHVILLE SEPT3 1932 12 3 5 25AM
EVERYTHING OK READY FOR EXAMS ON YOUR HORSE LOVE = JOHNNY

Sunday, Sept. 11th, 1932

San Antonio, Texas

Dear J and J:

You see I made it on schedule. Monday was Labor Day and I came along through Tennessee from Nashville, and all the colored families were in their best bib and tucker and riding to town. I reached Memphis by noon, having luncheon at "Houston's"—Mrs. Houston being the entire firm. She was immensely interesting with her bright red hair, and unconsciously dropped many trade secrets. ... I spent the hot hours of the day at the Hotel Peabody where the lobby was air cooled. Towards sundown, I set out again and crossed the mighty Mississippi, entering the State of Arkansas, the last state of the great Union for me to see. Cotton fields with miserable little shanties were on every side. The country was beautifully green, having had much more rain. At Little Rock I slept most of the day from exhaustion from the severe heat. The highways and bridges increased in magnificence, but I was told the State Treasury was a little empty therefore. The earth is terra-cotta color, and one little town of simple charm seems to melt into the next at not a great distance. ... After Texarkana I began to see Longhorns, horses with easy riders, ten-gallon hats, and hear the real Southern drawl. The earth is just as black as it was red in the former state. One likes the feeling of freedom in the wide-open spaces. I found more loose gravel roads than elsewhere and could not make such good time. ... I reached Dallas and the Baker Hotel by 6:30, and found the Christian Science Church. ...

I reached San Antonio Friday afternoon at four, parked the car and took a taxi survey of the various hotels. I came to one called Hotel Plaza, with a river on two sides—really the San Antonio River diverted in a unique flood control—and from my room can hear a charming waterfall. I spent dinner with the brother of a nice woman I met in Washington this spring, and saw the movie, *A Successful Calamity*. This afternoon I spent an hour or two in the Science Reading Room. There are a few outstanding historical landmarks, chiefly the Alamo and Brackenridge Park. As seems to be my good fortune on all trips, I have had the glamour of gorgeous moonlight all the way along.

Hope you like the postals. I found lots of mail from East and West waiting for me here at the Railway Express Agency. And, have arranged with a professional shopper to buy for me should I remain in Mexico. With a thriving Sears-Roebuck just across the street, I feel no matter how I find things in the interior that a good source of supply is near at hand. I secured from the Mexican Consulate a visitor's card good for all Mexico for six months.

Now that I have accomplished [so much] thus far, I can scarcely realize that it will soon be over. ... I think I shall leave Wednesday morning, making the 150-mile run by afternoon, remaining overnight and pushing through to Monterrey, Thursday the 15th. More from that famous old city.

Much love,

Mother

Alice found Laredo by dinner. Parking her dusty station wagon at the hotel, she took a taxi to the stark white Christian Science Church. Late afternoon service had just begun as she entered. A few heads turned, acknowledging Alice with a smile. Outside, afterwards, a middle aged woman greeted her.

"I saw you come in. Welcome to our small community. My name is Miss Rizer. I run a little tearoom in town."

"Mrs. Muma," replied Alice. "I feel refreshed in spirit from the service after my long drive."

"Where have you come from, then?" asked Miss Rizer.

"All the way from Boston," Alice said, enjoying Miss Rizer's eyes widening in disbelief. "But only from San Antonio today." Alice smiled trying to make light of her long pull across the country.

Miss Rizer went on. "You look tired, my dear. Perhaps I may offer you a ride back to your hotel?"

"I accept with pleasure, Miss Rizer. Most kind."

Miss Rizer's tearoom, it turned out, sat between her hotel and Netzler's Storage, where Alice would store what she did not need for her trip into Mexico. Alice promised to come for breakfast the next morning, as she was too tired even for supper. With just enough energy left, Alice washed out a few garments, draping them on the short laundry line over the tub, and fell into bed.

Early the next morning, avoiding the heat and dust that was sure to come, Alice repacked the car, storing hotel supplies at Netzler's Storage. Then she walked next door to the tearoom. Miss Rizer had sliced mangoes, rich cinnamon buns and a pot of tea waiting. They sat for an hour sharing breakfast while Alice told her of her adventures crossing the country and of her plans to locate land in Mexico for a hotel. Bowled over, Miss Rizer promised to send Science prayers every day for the success of the hotel.

The following morning, Alice climbed back behind Acapulco's wheel and drove over the International Bridge into Nuevo Laredo. Customs charged her a bond for the car and a deposit, just for what was deliberately vague and irritating, yet unavoidable. Her luggage, except for an overnight bag, was sealed with paper strips, and she was told not to tamper with them until after the inspection again at Monterrey.

The road lay flat and straight for more than forty-five miles. Nothing grew but the occasional cactus and dracaena palms. Then, butterflies by the thousands appeared, *and, alas*, she wrote to Johnny and Jane, *they did not discriminate. I could see them decorating the front of every car radiator that passed.*

Close into Monterrey, Alice was forced to stop in the middle of the road to avoid hitting a herd of goats and a rag-tag goat herder, not ten years old. Alice offered him some fruit, and the boy, hesitating at first, suddenly pin wheeled his sandaled feet in her direction, grabbed the bag, uttered, "Adios," bowed, and fled. Alice followed him with her eyes as he disappeared west into a magnificent sunset.

***

Monterrey was in full parade for a saint's day as Alice entered the bustling commercial downtown. The music wrenched her back with sudden bittersweet memory to the music being played on the streets of London as she and Jerry were checked into the hotel for their honeymoon. *Now gone these eight years, here I am, dear Jerry, embarking on the most daring plan and I wish...* Shaking herself back into the moment, Alice eased to a stop in front of the Hotel Ancira: *every bit as ostentatious as the brochure in the travel office suggested.* How bizarre it all was—opening the year she and Jerry were married, 1912. *Looks a little French as well.*

A white-colonnaded entrance stretched along the sidewalk and up five stories to the mansard roof. Wrought-iron balconies stood out from the upper floors. Unfortunately scaffolding ran amok with the architectural splendor. The new Spanish owner was making extensive renovations.

The doorman ogled her station wagon as she swept by to the desk. The clerk, who could see her car, asked her in crisp English, "Madam, are you part of the Smithsonian team?"

Alice, startled but flattered at the unexpected question, replied regretfully, "No. I have reservations, Mrs. I. J. Muma."

Two bellmen scooped up her luggage. The three walked to the elevator over huge black and white checkerboard tiles. They passed by a wide, white, curving stair leading to the mezzanine. It was newly painted—she could smell it. Alice thought it likely, seeing the extensive renovations, that the humorous rumors of Pancho Villa stabling his horses in the lobby were true. With a practiced flourish the bellboys stacked her bags, opened the windows and then handed her the key with an open palm.

"Gracias," said Alice. She placed the required pesos in his hand, a false smile on her face. *It would not do to offend, but I am so annoyed at the constant tipping. It will drain me dry. The American Express office had better be holding my monthly check or I will be doing dishes for a month.*

Alice walked to the window to survey her kingdom for the next couple of weeks. The view settled her after the exhausting drive. She was looking east toward the whitewashed cathedral and its three-story bell tower. Bells chimed the hour of eight, though it was not much more than seven fifteen. Still, it was grand. Worth exploring in the days while she waited impatiently for the chance to bolt for Mexico City.

Refreshed with a bath and change of clothes, Alice came down to the desk to collect her complimentary card for dinner at the Deutcher Club next door. The kitchen and dining room of the Ancira were also under renovation.

Another good sign, she thought—the Spaniard must know that the Pan-American Highway would indeed bring him business.

The familiar sounds of the tourists' German conversation brought sweet memories of her travels. Used to her own company, Alice managed her veal and potatoes comfortably alone, then left for her hotel and a good long sleep.

The next morning her alarm was the melancholy cry of a street vendor under her window intermixed with the silver sounds of cathedral bells. She took breakfast in a little hotel close by and was delighted to find another American.

Alice asked, "May I join you?"

"Please. It is nice to hear another American voice here. Place is crawling with Germans, never mind the Mexicans. My name is Mrs. Mathews."

"Mrs. Muma." Alice extended her hand and received a firm handshake. "What an extraordinary ring, Mrs. Mathews. I could not help noticing."

"Thank you. An unusual lapis lazuli stone my husband found in his travels."

"Do I detect a hint of the Old South in your speech, Mrs. Mathews?"

"Yes, I'm originally from San Antonio. Married an engineer and here we are in Mexico."

"I recently passed through your lovely city. I am on my way to Mexico City and waiting for the rains to stop."

"A wise decision," said Mrs. Mathews. "The Pan-American Highway is still under construction to the south. Going through the mountains is impossible with all that rain."

They became traveling companions for the several days Mr. Mathews was away on business. During these times, Alice related her plans for a hotel in Mexico and her quest in Mexico City to find out government rules concerning owning and building on land in the country.

"Allow my husband to introduce you to another American engineer who lives in Monterrey, Mrs. Muma. His name is Colonel Woodyard. He has a construction business in the north here, with an office and apartment atop the Banco de Leon. Come for dinner the day after tomorrow. I expect he has a great deal of accumulated experience in dealing with the government, and he certainly knows how to work the Mexicans."

***

Colonel Woodyard turned out to be a wealth of information. He was also attentive, tall, and bald except for a ring of white hair.

"May I say, Mrs. Muma, your plan for El Cavanera is ambitious."

"You may, Colonel. One must take the calculated risk. I'm not afraid of work. Americans will be flooding into the country." She paused, feeling perhaps too bold in her statements surrounded by such company. "Just where my hotel may be remains a mystery I am hoping you will help me solve." Turning the spotlight on her hostess she said, "Mrs. Mathews, your cook is to be commended. So far on my journey, food has been forgettable. This chicken is delicious."

"Cook makes the best Chicken Mole in Mexico."

The colonel took up the challenge, knowing that Mrs. Mathews had thrown down the gauntlet. "I beg to differ, not on the excellent Chicken Mole, but on your cook. Mine was trained by the best. Were she a man she could boast a top chef position anywhere in California *or* Mexico."

"I surrender," said Mrs. Mathews, laughing at this banter. Turning to Alice she said, "We have this conversation every time we dine together. How the colonel manages to keep her, though, is a wonder. With all his traveling, he is never there to eat her food."

"Speaking of traveling," said the colonel, "I am driving to Saltillo in a few days. You were both there, I know, but you missed a treasure—the tile factory. I am placing an order for a client. Would you like a tour?"

So began Alice's friendship with Colonel Woodyard.

***

September crept along toward the promised dry season of October. Every day in the rain Alice dashed to the American Express Co. for her mail. Days were consumed reading and responding to her letters. Telegrams followed pages of typed comments. Carbon copies sent by airmail were followed by originals sent by land. John Rankin sent back pages of reports on the lack of progress on the sales of her Castellamare and Kings X homes. He created lists of her debts, balance sheets on dwindling stock dividends, and forwarded mail from her permanent address at the Women's Athletic Club in Los Angeles. As long as he moved heaven and earth to send her monthly income check from Jerry's life insurance, she would be able to pay her Monterrey bills.

There was a letter from Jane, grumping that her mother had not told her where she was or what she was doing. Alice felt a prick of conscience, vowing to write the children a good long letter as soon as she was settled in Mexico City. There was the long-awaited, joyous telegram from Johnny boy, who had just passed his German exam and required $270 to reregister at MIT.

The hardest part of this awful waiting was the lack of a Christian Science Church in Monterrey. Every night she poured through her C. S. reader, looking for inspiration and calm from Mary Baker Eddy's words. Every morning she was awakened by the cries of the street vendor or the cathedral bells in concert with the increasingly bright sunlight flooding over the mountains and into her room. She gathered her courage to face another day, at the end of which the colonel might be there with his sweet attention, and his advice on realizing her fantastic plan for El Caravanera.

***

The rain refused to quit in early October. Alice, desperate to get to Mexico City, booked a train and stored her beloved station wagon. Panicked at the extra expense, she telegraphed her lawyer,

254

IMMEDIATE SELL WINDSOR BLVD HOUSE FURNITURE GETTING FIVE HUNDRED STOP SEND TWO SEVENTY JOHNNY BOSTON STOP ONE HUNDRED MEXICO CITY STOP ARRIVE OCT TEN STOP THANKS ALICE

She put in a plea to the Lord to find her a cheap casita at the elegant San Angel Inn, and she boarded the train.

A few hours into the trip, Alice walked to the dining car, and was joined by a Mr. and Mrs. Bensel. All three drank their tea and pushed food around their plates. The conversation, which began by agreeing that the fare was truly awful, moved to the reasons for their travel.

"Mr. Bensel and I are looking for land to purchase next to our ranch. It is a lonesome place off the Pan-American Highway, halfway between Monterrey and Mexico City. Just outside the village called 'He-Cow-Ten-Cattle,' but it is written thus." Mrs. Bensel pulled out a pad and wrote, *Xicotencatl*. "I had thought to put in a restaurant or perhaps a small hotel. We have been twenty years in Mexico, and love it."

"I hear a British accent in your speech," remarked Alice.

"Oh, yes. Mr. Bensel is German, of course. And you, Mrs. Muma?"

"I am originally Canadian, with good Scottish blood, but now a true American. I have come to explore the possibility of buying land and opening a hotel. How extraordinary that we should meet."

By the time the train pulled into Mexico City, the Bensels had agreed to look into buying land for Alice, and Alice had agreed to visit them to flesh out plans for the hotel when the dry season permitted her to return to Monterrey and drive her car back.

Chapter 57

The Mexican Saga Takes Form

"Happy birthday to me," said Alice to the purple bougainvillea on the morning of October 18. The cascading vine had an electric presence on her tiny patio. She had a room at the glorious stucco inn, which reeked of centuries-old colonial architecture.

Alice slit open Johnny's letter, hungry for his words.

Mi Madre,

Sirvase V. ourme? Me hable V. a mi! Hot Dog, me speaka good Spanish, he? Just a little incoherent note to wish you many happy returns of the day. A week ago I went down with Ted and some of his friends. Had a swell time sailing in a nice big boat all afternoon.

Worked a little harder last week. Am getting back into the regimen. And what do you think? I got the third lead in a tech drama shop production. I am an oily Frenchman.

I want to go to the Dartmouth football game and so will try to get the $4.00 together.

Love and love,

Johnny

Would he make it without her, Alice thought? Organizing her finances to provide him $125 a month was almost impossible. Johnny would have to learn to budget. Time for her strong arms to let go. Didn't Jane say so on every occasion?

Looking at her watch, Alice gasped in dismay. Too much reverie would cost her this appointment. Dressing gown flying behind her, she raced into the bath and then into the bedroom to slip on a linen suit and her pearls. She chose open-toed flats—one just did not want to be taller than the man, if it could be helped.

Mr. Albert Blair was waiting for her in the glamorous lobby. He looked the same, lines of character just forming on his clean-shaven face. Indeed he was perhaps only three inches taller than her. It was a pleasure to see him again after their brief introduction on her previous trip to Mexico City.

As the manager of the Vacuum Oil Corporation in Mexico, Mr. Blair was in the thick of business as it was done in the capital. He could help her ferret out the complexities of the Mexican government requirements for foreign investment. Alice had corresponded with him briefly before her long drive to

Mexico, asking for his advice when she should arrive in the capital. It had culminated in this appointment.

They made their way to the dining room and were seated at a small, table by the window. Stemware glinted in the sunlight. Brightly painted Talavera pottery plates ornamented each setting.

Alice smiled and ran a finger over the decoration. "I have not seen this majolica on a table since it graced my home in the Santa Monica hills. And though my house is just sold I cannot bear to part with the plates." And, she thought, it sits in storage gathering debt with so many of my other treasures.

Mr. Blair said, "They say sixteenth-century monks brought it over from Talavera, Spain. I claim no understanding of it, really."

Alice replied, "It bears a striking resemblance to all that type of pottery in Spain, Holland and Italy. Likely the Moors introduced the process."

"It seems the Caribbean isn't your only sphere of travel, then, Mrs. Muma." Mr. Blair smiled in encouragement, and then broke off a small piece of roll and popped it into his mouth.

"In my day I did quite a bit of touring. But we seem to circle back to Mexico. My late husband, Jerry, had quite a liking for business opportunities here, especially in Mexico City. He worked with the Chamber of Commerce in Los Angeles on several exploratory trips in the early decades of this century."

"Ah, yes. Diaz was responsible for much of the early foreign investments here. Half of Mexico was owned by foreigners. Wary of Americans, though."

"Mexico seems poised for invasion with this new highway cutting a swath through the mountains. I noticed a few hotels run by Spaniards and Germans. British and Americans have invested in oil. Your own company, Mr. Blair, seems successful. Do you not think the time is coming, with the Pan-American Highway almost complete, that Americans will spill over the border on holiday?"

"I believe so. It appears that civil war is a thing of the past. The bloodshed under Pancho Villa, Zapata and the rest is long gone. Generals are no longer assassinated, Catholic clergy no longer executed." Changing his remarks to less gruesome subjects, he continued, "That famous Californian, William Randolph Hearst, you know, has poured a fortune into this country."

"Has he, then? I didn't realize. Do you know his interests down here, Mr. Blair?"

"Real estate mostly, Mrs. Muma. But I would imagine he has fingers in many pies."

The waiter appeared with tortilla soup, and conversation stilled as the man placed bowls and filled water goblets.

"Wine, Mrs. Muma?"

"Thank you, no," she replied, "but please—for yourself."

"So tell me, Mrs. Muma, what news of your prospects for a hotel?"

Alice related the opportunity she had been offered by the Bensels on the train ride down from Monterrey.

"That is why I felt I must meet you at once."

"I'm flattered by your confidence in my advice. I can put you in touch with some government officials to discuss your issues. This I do know, however, that you may not start negotiations for land purchase or building until you have been here for six months, and have received a permanent visa. Then you must leave the country and reenter. If you are caught even speaking to a builder, believe me, there are people who would report you and out you would go. You must also prove you have 10,000 pesos to invest in a project. So, there you are. While you wait, you can find investors in the States who might back such a venture."

By the time the flan had been demolished, Mr. Blair had outlined a plan of official visits that Alice should make over the next weeks along with his letters of introduction. He promised to set up several appointments and escort her to them.

"Let's walk in the garden, shall we, Mr. Blair? My mind is in a whirlwind now that I have sensed my plan unfolding."

They strolled through the garden, talking about the importance of Mary Baker Eddy's formulation of Christian Science, the quest for truth through God's guidance. Alice knew at once that she had found a worthy companion. Mr. Blair, a recent widower with half-grown children, was schooled in simple graces and a devoted Christian Scientist. She counted him too young to be a serious romantic involvement. Perhaps, though, Jane would find him interesting.

Before he departed, he had asked her to the Wednesday evening readings.

"We often discuss current events from the Monitor. It keeps us up on the world from our little provincial outpost here."

"I will thoroughly enjoy those evenings. I have not been blessed by C. S. since Laredo. It is such a comfort to be around caring people again."

***

By suppertime Alice was deep in thought about just who might respond to an investment opportunity. She dashed off a letter to Mrs. Bensel sketching a more complete version of her hotel dream and suggesting a meeting late in November, when Alice would return to Monterrey for her car. Her typewriter clacked into the night, churning out pages of demands to John Rankin to forage for money. She pulled names from her memory of well-heeled men in Los Angeles she and Jerry had known, including even Mr. W. H. Hearst, to whom she would draft a letter explaining the benefits of investing in her project. Her missive was, as always, one original and two carbons. The first mailed by land, one carbon by air, and one for her file.

November 1st, 1932

My Dear John:

Holidays in Mexico are something with which to reckon. All Saints and All Souls Days came upon me unawares and it is well-nigh impossible to do anything. Every day the shops are closed from one until sometimes three thirty, and I assure you it is disorganizing. While I am so happy to be here, there are plenty of things to be noted ere I plunge in business. However, I go back to this: I would rather be here on a shoestring than in Los Angeles where I could not maintain the old standards. I want to work, and the widow of Jeremiah Muma should not have to do that. I have spent as I have for I never had wealth, and I despise the small fry who pretend. My concern now is not necessarily to let Los Angeles know how really low I am. Befriend me in this, please, for I am working earnestly in C. S. and the testimonies teem with acknowledgements of help received in such circumstances. If God can't help us, who can? ...

Frankly if the new owners default on installment payments for my Castellamare home, I am still glad I am here, for I will go instantly into the wilds, where I know I can live for about $25.00 per month, letting my $144.25 monthly Aetna check go to Johnny until something can be sold. ...

Locate Hearst's right-hand man and pitch my hotel idea to him. Something after this fashion. After introducing yourself say it is the widow of I. J. M from whom W. R. H. bought the two Muma ranches at San Simeon in 1914. That is my hope of establishing a tie, for I know W. R. H. must be hard to interest. Say I am down in Mexico to buy land on which to build a hotel on the Pan-Amer. Highway before next summer's inrush of tourists. ... I wanted to know if Mr. H. would be disposed to lend money on a project of this kind. ... Superb pinnacle for unique hotel overlooking canyons 5,000 ft. high... First unit a modest fifteen or twenty rooms... architect drawing up plans... I would need from $20,000 to $40,000 to start.

I am very hopeful. You may laugh, John, but it occurs to me that he might be just struck by the outlandishness of the things, and oh boy what a spot it would make. Don't waste a minute in going after it, I beg of you. I will be going to the property after Thanksgiving, returning to Mexico City for Xmas or not, according to finances. ... (I dread spending the holiday with Germans deep in the country.) If you get the interest of W. R. H. wire me here in couched terms. ...

This month's Aetna income check of $144.25 must be in my hands before I leave here. Indeed you must know that I am in the habit of making my situation more acute by owing a hotel bill which the check I ask for must cover before I can make my escape. Little does anyone know how the elegant Mrs. M. would be utterly undone if you failed her in these present urgent requests. Go to bat with Hearst, bringing it to a point of refusal rather than to be ignored. The amount available on insurance loan is so paltry that I would rather leave it alone unless I just cannot help myself. In any case it would likely not cover the entire investment required.

Best wishes to you and Enge,
Alice

Several days before Thanksgiving, Alice boarded the train for Monterrey with a stop at the Bensel ranch. Going as far as Cuidad Valles, she hired a car and driver to cover the distance over the dangerously rutted mountain road to the Bensels. Once arrived, Mr. Bensel, on a brown gelding, and she, on a bay, wandered over the ranch and onto some of the seventy-five neighboring acres that Alice was interested in purchasing. With polite reserve, he pointed out the slope of the ground, the natural spot for a hotel and the river, which would draw tourists for boating and swimming. Alice sensed his enthusiasm for her project was perhaps more to support his wife than belief in her vision. Was he reluctant to enter into partnership? She could not purchase this land herself. Even she knew there were certain skills better left to qualified individuals. And a woman, especially in Mexico, did not do this sort of thing with any frequency, even in these modern times.

Heavenly smells wafted toward them as they returned from their ride in the late afternoon. Mrs. Bensel was standing in the courtyard, her boldly striped apron announcing her recent departure from the kitchen.

"My dear Mrs. Bensel," said Alice. "Something smells delicious."

"We will dine shortly, Mrs. Muma," replied Mrs. Bensel. "Gallina Rellena, a little recipe I picked up ten years ago. Spanish, really. I hope you will like it. Mr. Bensel will see to your horse."

"How kind. I'm afraid if I don't change, I will bring the horse to dinner! Do I have a minute?"

Mrs. Bensel chuckled. "Plenty of time to freshen up."

An hour later, all three sat down to enjoy the excellent dinner. Though the conversation wove around the day's ride, very little of substance was mentioned about the possible purchase of the land. Alice received the impression that business was never discussed at table, and so did not press.

After dinner, Mr. Bensel retired to his study. Mrs. Bensel leaned over to Alice.

"Don't you worry, my dear, it will all work out. I am thrilled at the idea of a hotel. Perhaps we will have some good news when you return in a few days."

The next day Mr. Bensel escorted Alice back into town in time to see her off on the local bus. She rode north with Mexicans whose faces reflected their Indian heritage rather than their Spanish conquerors'; their language was incomprehensible. Produce for northern markets was stuffed in every conceivable place on the ancient bus: pigs tied to seat legs blocked the aisle, chickens on laps and in crates on top of the bus roof, cones of sugar stashed underfoot, dried beans and slices of orange pumpkins in sacks under the seats.

The noise and smell was frightful, even with the windows open. At Cuidad Victoria, a frazzled Alice booked a bunk in the one Pullman coach attached to the back of a freight train going to Monterrey. Squeals of pigs punctuated her dreams.

***

"La Princessa, due in about ten minutes?"

Colonel Woodyard glanced down at his wristwatch. "The elegant Alicia Muma will always be fashionably late. Give her twenty, Joe."

"You goin' anywhere with this?" asked Joe.

"Too soon to tell, but she's a fine specimen. Perhaps a bit high strung, a class act, nonetheless," replied the colonel. "I got the martinis. Grab the guacamole, Joe."

The two men walked into the spacious living area of the colonel's second-floor apartment.

Joe's wife, Sadie, and two other American engineers and their wives were scattered around the room. The buffet on the low wall separating the dining area from the living room was crammed with food left over from the Thanksgiving feast the day before. The colonel's cook had made up turkey sandwiches smothered in mayonnaise and cranberry sauce between the halves of puffy white Mexican rolls. Pies and pastries, and a huge bowl of sliced mangoes took up the remaining space. On the bar sat a sparkling pitcher of fruit juice, "for La Muma." The cook approved of Alice's temperance. The colonel's ex-wife was an alcoholic.

Footsteps were heard making their way up to the apartment; a short knock, and in swept Alice.

"Good afternoon, Colonel."

"Wonderful to see you, Alice. What, it has been twenty-four hours since our American feast? Same crowd, same food. You are a brave woman," he joked.

"Nonsense. It's good to see your friends. I enjoy them immensely. I hope you don't mind, but I have routed an expected phone call to your phone. Will that be all right with you?"

"Of course, my dear. Delighted to be of service. Anything I can help you with?"

"No, thank you, Colonel. Just some business from California on the house closing."

Alice walked from the entry directly into the living room. She eyed the colonel's old military buddies from West Point, now living in San Antonio. Alternately during the months, they and the colonel visited back and forth. The men worked and played hard, enjoying the camaraderie on their occasional weekends with dancing and drinking late into the night. Alice loved being able to spend these last few days being "American."

Today, especially, she needed the camouflage of this social occasion. On edge yet again, she was desperate to hear from American Express that her monthly check had arrived so she could drive back to the Bensels and then to Mexico City.

"Hello, everyone. Good to see you all again."

"Are you ready for the Army–Navy game, Alice?"

"Looking forward to it," she replied.

"We have some time yet," said the colonel. "Shall we have some luncheon? Martinis are ready or beer if you prefer."

Luncheon was consumed with the relish only Americans have for Thanksgiving leftovers. There was lighthearted banter over memories of other shared holidays, and bets placed on the final score of the game and who would be ahead by halftime. The noise level rose around the dining table as the amount of alcohol was consumed.

Colonel Woodyard excused himself to warm up the short wave radio and set the dial for the broadcast from Franklin Field in Philadelphia. "Ready to go, all you American vagabonds. The crowd is cheering. We will be sitting on the Army side."

During the game, the visitors were intent on the announcer, yelling "Go Army!" when West Point scored. And score they did. By the third quarter Army was ahead twenty to nothing. The crowds on both sides of the short wave radio were wild. Alice pitched in pretending attention, and growing more panicky as the hour for her expected American Express telegram call grew near, and then passed. In agony that could not be masked one more second, Alice excused herself to the hall phone table and began to pencil a draft telegram to John Rankin.

Get Dickson on the phone immediately asking hundred fifty or two hundred dollar loan wiring money here Monday. Must leave for ranch early Tuesday morning…

She was interrupted by the ringing of the telephone. Her hand shot out to lift the receiver. "Hello, the Woodyard residence, Mrs. Muma speaking." The voice from American Express on the other end calmed her. Her cash had been received. Alice placed the receiver gently on the hook, took a few deep breaths and returned to the party.

The colonel glanced her way, raising an eyebrow in question. She responded with a brilliant smile as if to say all was well.

The game over, and the beer and martinis drained, the crowd filtered out to their hotel. Alice bade the colonel good-bye, turning down his invitation to breakfast. She would be up before dawn.

***

The Pan-American Highway, the newly dedicated but still-incomplete Mexico Route 85, stretched south through mountains and jungle. She drove for two hundred miles, turning off at Xicotencatl. After stopping for something to eat, she filled up the station wagon with gasoline, arranging to store the automobile for several days. Holding her breath that the phone would work (Mexicans seemed not to understand the importance of reliable service), she called the ranch to let them know she had arrived. Mr. Bensel answered, telling her where he had left her a horse. After changing into her riding clothes, she rode down the same winding, narrow, dirt road she had come before. With the jungle close and the bright birds flitting and calling, Alice let her mind wander back to the letter of invitation for this visit.

Now she understood why Mr. Bensel had written of the arrangement with the telephone agent for weekly delivery of mail and paid one Jesus Guillen handsomely, by Mexican standards, for the Sunday mail drop by mule. Alice snorted, "By mule, no less," to the horse. She was anxious that her mail, batched by American Express in Mexico City, had actually arrived here, and was waiting for her.

I am consumed, she thought, to know whether the new owners have made the $300 payment on the Castellamare house, and how it stands with the sale of Kings X studios. Mrs. Klumb says it might bring $10,000. John Rankin disagrees, insisting that the poor quality of the road it sits on will discourage any but the movie crowd I am already renting it to. I will just sell it furnished, if need be. Withal, I must clear my debts and profit by several thousand dollars if I am to see this through. That sum will get me through Christmas. The children need a vacation and I mean for them to enjoy a few plays in New York. ...

Alice rounded the last twist in the drive and came to a halt in front of the ranch house. A "hallo!" from Mrs. Bensel brought her into the present.

Throughout the next several days, the three spent hours around the kitchen table sharing ideas for the hotel. Mr. Bensel promised to pursue purchase of the 75 acres they had ridden through. It was Alice's assumption that Americans by the thousands would be drawn to Mexico, and she would cater to their tastes. They planned for a modest beginning, perhaps near the Sabinas River, using a boat Alice that would bring from storage in Los Angeles for the guests' entertainment. A thatched roof building would suffice at first. Alice could live in it while the builders went on to build guest quarters. The initial building would eventually be turned into an open kitchen and recreation area for the guests. Just before she was to leave, the Bensels agreed to build a room onto their ranch, which Alice would furnish. She could live there while plans were finalized, the builder located, and so forth.

Alice could not wait to get back to Mexico City and write to Jane and John of her success.

Alice was packing her meager wardrobe in preparation for departure when the Bensels' phone rang. Jesus Guillen was calling, informing them that the roads had been torn up due to highway construction south of Xicotencatl. The Bensels insisted that Alice hire a chauffeur for the long trip back to Mexico

263

City. Alice, remembering difficult motor trip north, gave in. The Bensels rode back with her to the town to organize what they could.

He was a Basque having traveled all over the world, she wrote John Rankin later, *and speaking every sort of language and dialect. He was unshaven and terrifying in appearance. I felt I owed my life to him and his careful driving over those treacherous passes. But I hardly knew what sort of stiletto he might draw from his boot, if your money had not been forthcoming.*

***

A visit to the Christian Science church set her mind at ease, and provided an answer to her housing problems. Staying at the San Angel Inn was getting too expensive. She found a notice on a C. S. bulletin board for a house to rent, owned by a Californian. By the week before Christmas, Alice was living in the cottage at 100 pesos a month, roughly $25. Only a telephone remained to be installed, and that was quickly arranged. One of the two bedrooms was to remain available for the owner or her son, who might visit from time to time. Alice had the house to herself—and the pleasure of fine linens, silverware, heating and light. It was exquisitely designed by an interior designer from Los Angeles. Still, the loneliness of Christmas away from home gnawed at her, made worse by the letter awaiting her from Albert Blair that he had departed for a month long business trip to the home office of Vacuum Oil in New York.

Alice spent the holiday with her typewriter, telephone and the owner's dog, hatching a plan to get Jane married off, if not to an opera critic of culture, then to a charming oil man named Albert. Jane, always so self-sufficient, was beginning some serious courting and occasionally asking for advice.

JANUARY 8, 1933
DETAILED AIR LETTER POSSIBLY DELAYED STOP WRITE OR TELEPHONE ALBERT BLAIR CARE VACUUM OIL CO 26 BRDWY ROOM 1343 INVITE HIM OUT TO SEE YOU OR DINNER OR SUNDAY SUPPER OR HORSEBACK RIDE STOP I AIRMAILED HIM CARD OF INTRODUCTION TO OLIVE KIRKBY ASK HIM IF HE RECEIVED IT OTHERWISE YOU ARRANGE THAT THEY MEET STOP HE WANTS TO MEET YOU MUCH LOVE MOTHER

Sunday, January 9th
Broadview, Tarrytown
Dear Mother,
I just received your wire. I asked Mr. Blair out for Sunday dinner but not to ride, as it is too expensive. He sounds nice.

Johnny's and my vacation is a long story. Believe it or not Johnny really danced. We went to two dances at the Sleepy Hollow Manor Club. Once with an old friend of Johnny's, and another at New Year's Eve. We spent Xmas Eve day with my riding instructor and his family at their house. And also a few

264

evenings with Ted's family, having lots of good fun with the boys. We all talked Munich until we were blue in the face. The money you sent was spent on two plays, *When Ladies Meet* and a musical called *Take a Chance*. Thank you so much.

Johnny went back last Tuesday with Ted on the train. The car license is no good.

I continue to go to the opera with Mr. Thompson. It has been very gay. I bought myself a very beautiful black velvet dinner dress with sleeves and made myself a black velvet hat with ears and a net crown which shows my hair through. I had no business to buy the thing but I want to have Mr. Thompson proud of me. At least we had such a good time that we went to a little Mexican café, in honor of you, he said, and there I tasted mangoes for the first time in my life. My, but they are good. All in all it was a most thrilling evening especially to be escorted by a high hat and silver-topped cane. ...

Your plans for the hotel sound interesting. Do let me hear more about it. I enjoy your bulletins very much, but real letters are much nicer to get, and reading those typewritten pages of descriptions always makes me think I am reading Stevenson's *Travels Abroad*. ...

Love,
Jane

Jerry's old friend from the days of setting up the U.C. Los Angeles campus, Eddie Dickson, popped into Alice's mind as a possible investor; efforts with Mr. Hearst had come to nothing.

My Dear Eddie Dickson:

... Mr. Bensel, this very minute, is trying to buy about seventy-five acres of land, on which the taxes have not been paid for six years, and then sell it to me. I expect the cost will not exceed $500.00 (American currency). You may say such a price is incredible, and so it seems, but it is to be remembered that the present owners are ignorant peons who are descendants from Aztec days, when the land was held after the community idea, now called "Agraristas." I await news from Mr. Bensel telling me the exact cost. I have letters in hand which I will present this week—now that the holiday is over, securing permission from the government to bring all my Los Angeles furniture in free of duty. Also I will secure a license to enter the hotel business, which will entail becoming a permanent resident. I will make sure of these fundamentals before purchasing any land. ...

The land has been inaccessible except by horseback until this highway is penetrating its jungle filled with parrots and armadillos. ... I will concentrate on clean, good food—which I can testify will be the first found anywhere after leaving Monterrey—and only have accommodations for about six or eight guests at first. I am working with Mr. Paul Williams of Los Angeles, my architect of Windsor and Castellamare.

Here I am, on the ground floor as it were, ahead of everyone else—although I understand there have been over 6,000 inquiries from those who plan to build camps or hotels of one kind or another—and I feel I can make a go of it. Another most important item is the fact that already a replica of the temple of Uxmal, Yucatán is being built at the Chicago Exposition next year. The Americans are woefully ignorant about Mexico, and touches of its ancient wonder seen at an Exposition should start them a-traveling on their own North American Continent. You see, I am impressed that this is the year of all the years to get going.

The dollars necessary to make the purchase of this land I count on receiving from the sale of the Kings Road Studio property, which apparently has a buyer although at a pathetically low figure. I am glad, however, to get it off my hands now that it is clear that the children will continue their college education in the East. I am forced to see that we will never again live in Los Angeles, and if I can make some money on this highway, I will be as happy as can be. I do ask you if you would consider lending me the $500.00. If that amount is not forthcoming from Kings Road at the moment, I must have it to secure the land. … I will work hard and you know nothing can stop vision coupled with a capacity for hard work. Except perhaps a revolution. But Mexico looks as safe as anywhere else at the moment, and I am game to go down with colors flying rather than sit around bemoaning the state of affairs. Will you please indicate to Mr. Rankin whether you feel you can help me at this point?

I am delighted with Mexico and really am enthusiastic about living here, although it is but a shadow of its pomp under Profirio Diaz. Those must have been great days. You must come and see what it is all about.

That ought to do it, thought Alice. A masterful weaving of the personal, the romance of a new venture, and an appeal to his wallet, a little "maiden in distress" thrown in. *Well, in truth I am!*

***

A cardinal landed on the flowering peach tree just outside her kitchen window. It was a beautiful day. February in Mexico was breathtaking. A little beauty to offset the great disappointment of Johnny's failure at MIT was welcome.

10 FEB 1933
DIDN'T MAKE THE GRADE SORRY HOPE YOU ARE ALL SET
LOVE = JOHNNY

Her response was immediate; her words flying on paper to mask the panic rising up from her heart.

Feb 10, 1933

GODS HARMONIOUS LAW JUST AS OPERATIVE NOW AS EVER STOP THERE IS RIGHT THING NOW DON'T WASTE TIME STOP SUGGESTIONS IN ORDER OF IMPORTANCE STOP BOSTON BUSINESS COURSE INCLUDING TYPEWRITING COMMERCIAL LAW CONTRACT AND FULL SET OF BOOKS COMPLETING COURSE FAST AS POSSIBLE CERTAINLY BY JUNE STOP GIVING YOUR SERVICES GRATIS TO CS PUBLISHING HOUSE STOP RENTING ACRE OR MORE GROUND BOSTON AND PLANTING VEGETABLES STOP SUMMER GO TO GERMANY WASSERWORKS STOP YOUR DECISION NO MONEY FORTHCOMING TO YOU UNTIL YOUR DECISION STOP PERSIST IN DAILY SCIENCE WORK STOP I LEAVE FOR RANCH BEFORE MARCH FIRST STOP LETTER IN AIRMAIL ABUNDANT LOVE = MOTHER

Johnny enrolled in a short commercial course, with hope to then see the road ahead. He had done it without her physical presence, and that counted for something. It was stopgap but better than floundering. Funding at least a few months of his venture was a three-hundred-dollar loan from Jerry's business connection, Mr. Wilson, thanks to a masterful piece of negotiating from her lawyer.

***

Alice took a moment to savor her success. Mr. Blair had called yesterday to ask her to come to his office for a chat at noon. "The Customs Official has some good news to report," was all he would say. At the end of the hour she was given permission to buy land and the status of temporary permanent resident to go along with it. She came away with an English-language copy of the law regarding duties on building materials and furnishings for hotels.

That afternoon Alice went to the American consul to confirm that all was in readiness. He acknowledged it with a firm handshake and well wishes.

She had barely a month to pack, drive up to the Bensels to check on the progress of property negotiations, and get the Ford over the border before her permit ran out.

Her phone rang and Alice moved to the living room to answer it.

"Hello, Alice?"

"Yes, speaking. How are you Albert?" How nice it was to have him back.

"I am well and thinking we should celebrate your victory. I know Mexico City rolls up the sidewalks by nine p.m., but there is a dreadful movie playing which we might sit through. How about dinner afterward and perhaps some dancing?"

Alice laughed. "Typical of these foreign colonies—bad movies, no theater. Let's settle for whatever passes for a movie tonight. I would love dinner and dancing."

"Wonderful. I will take us to a German club. A waltz, a foxtrot, and perhaps a tango?"

Alice put on her red feather dress. It would be a real celebration.

***

The first week in March Alice packed her belongings back into the Ford station wagon for the grueling drive north to Laredo. The portable toilet was the last to go in. Riding shotgun was nineteen-year-old Tom, son of the owner of her rental house.

"How was the flight to Oaxaca last week?" asked Tom as they started off.

Alice launched into the subject. "I asked the aviator to fly over to the coast. I am looking for alternatives to the hotel on the highway if I don't build at the Bensels'. The Pacific Coast would offer opportunities for American tourists. I wanted to see how accessible it would be."

"Food's all grown there. Mother says some gets imported to California," said Tom. "Indians grow pineapples, avocados, beans and stuff. The best coffee around comes from the mountainsides."

"The aviator mentioned, also, there is a flourishing gold and silver jewelry business. Prices are better than in Mexico City. That would be a draw."

"If there was a way, as always, to get across those southern mountains," said Tom.

Alice sighed, nodding her head in agreement. "North or south, it's always the mountains."

***

The paved surface of Highway 85 disappeared just north of Pachuca where the mountains rose up to challenge their driving skills. It was these 122 miles through the rugged passes that remained the engineers' nightmare for the Pan-American Highway completion. Alice and Tom shared the driving as they wrestled her trusty Ford over the steep dirt roads, contending with ruts dried hard from the rainy season last year. They made it after a twelve hour day as far as the mountain town of Tamazunchale, in the dark, with the fog leaking its blinding blanket over the narrow road. Alice was so tired that she begged off supper, sending Tom into the bar for what he could find in the way of sustenance. She collapsed onto her narrow bed in a closet sized room. She dreamed of the bearded Basque driver peering from nightmare trees like some Cheshire Cat. She dreamed that the fog was the mist of her desperation, and through it loomed the three homes she had built and loved. "Don't leave us," they whispered, and then whirled away into oblivion. She awoke and named the fear lodged in her heart—that she might never again have a place to call home.

***

Halfway to Valles, Alice and Tom came to a small river that required ferrying. They loaded the station wagon onto a chalan (one car ferry) and were winched across by an unshaven, rumpled man with a cigarette dangling from

268

his lips. Alice tipped him a few pesos, on top of the fare. He touched his grimy brimmed hat in acknowledgement.

"I'll be more than glad to get out of Mexico. The tipping is driving me mad," grumbled Alice to Tom. The fully-loaded station wagon pulled off the chalan and began to climb the hilly road in front of them. Suddenly over the top came a coupe, which stopped at the crest and blocked the way.

"The idiot must move," Alice said. "Can't he see that I have no place to go?" She was forced to stop the heavily-loaded wagon on the steep grade. And her car began to roll ever-so-slowly backwards. The sound of gravel crunching under the tires was the only noise Alice could hear besides the pounding of her heart. She could do nothing except stamp on the brake and pray. Finally the car came to a stop on the river's edge. The chalan was still docked, but had shifted just a few feet downriver, exposing the gravel lined edge of the water. Had it not moved, Alice would simply have rolled safely onto it. Alice, shaking with rage, got out to survey the damages. The rear wheels were swamped.

She made her way to the ferry operator. "Do you have a shovel?"

The man shifted his cigarette from his hand and without a word, reached back for a shovel and handed it to her. Before Tom could take charge, Alice marched to the rear of the Ford and began to dig the wheels out. Within minutes she became aware of a pair of boots standing by the back of the car. Someone was intruding on her annoyance. Continuing her gaze upward, she saw that the boots were connected to riding breeches and a khaki shirt, and a man with no hat.

"Here, let me have that," the khaki shirt said, his tone brisk, his English heavily accented. "This is no business for a woman."

"Who are you to take charge?" Alice let fly, assuming the man to be the owner of the offending coupe. "First, you block my way when you could have moved, then insult my intelligence by telling me I am not capable of taking care of myself. Get out of my way." She continued to dig.

"Madame, your papers, please," demanded the shirt.

"Please identify yourself." Alice raised up to her full height and looked him full in the face. "When I see your papers, I will be happy to comply."

The man made an irritated snort and ripped the shovel from her hands to finish the job. "I have no time for this."

It took no longer than fifteen minutes for the whole ugly scene to play out. They exchanged papers. Alice was free to go. The offending man drove his coupe on to the chalan, and Alice and Tom continued to the border.

"He was a government official," Tom remarked, his voice low. "There may be consequences."

"The man never identified himself as such. He was rude. After all, one does expect the courtesy of an introduction and some sensibility, even in Mexico."

***

269

It was just as the mountain pass climbed down to a more respectable altitude that the Ford encountered a rut that diverted the wheels into a roadside ditch. Luckily it was on the outskirts of a village and near a farm. A magnificent red tractor growled into view, dirt flying out from the deeply treaded tires. The driver, dressed in the ubiquitous white pants and shirt of the Mexican peasant, stopped. Tom took charge. A lively conversation ensued. After excited gestures and friendly shouting in Spanish, and much walking around the car, the Ford wagon was chained to the tractor and pulled free. After doffing his wide-brimmed hat and receiving many a "gracias" plus a few pesos from Alice, the farmer departed.

"That went well, don't you think, Tom? One more crisis behind us."

"Oh, yes, Mrs. Muma. He was honored to be of assistance to 'the American señora.' He thought me your son, and I did not disabuse him of the fact," he joked with a grin.

"Is he one of those Agraristas we have been reading about in the *Monitor* lately? He looks pretty wealthy for a peasant."

"Probably a PNR party member—against the Callista regime," replied Tom. "This depression hit the farmers pretty bad. All the progress of the cooperative farms, the schools, everything stopped. That's not a new tractor."

"Those PNR fellows sound more like socialists to me," said Alice.

"Yeah, well, it's hard to tell who's who in Mexico."

"Nationalists, socialists, Agraristas, an occasional dictator—the politics of Mexico are unfathomable; Catholics murdering teachers, presidents assassinating rivals. At least now all that violence seems under control."

"But they say General Cardenas is sure to win this election," said Tom. "The Agraristas all over Mexico are supporting him. They love him as governor 'cause he was the only one to continue land distribution and loans to the farmers."

Alice retorted, "Mr. President Cardenas had better put more pesos into this road or even the tractors will find it hard going."

Several more nights put them in proximity to the Bensel ranch outside Xicotencatl. This time, Alice drove her car down the long drive to the Bensel ranch for the short visit. She was greeted by a gracious but low-key Mrs. Bensel. There was no evidence of the promised addition of a room. At lunch, Alice's cheerful announcement of her temporary permanent status was met with Mr. Bensel's vague mumbling about the lack of progress on the purchase of the seventy-five acres for sale next door. Mrs. Bensel's delicious roast pork congealed on Alice's plate. The anxious pall hanging over the dining table did not diminish Tom's appetite, though.

Over coffee, Alice handed Mr. Bensel a card with John Rankin's cable address.

"Please feel free to cable my attorney collect with any progress on the negotiations," said Alice. "I will cable you myself when I reach Laredo."

Shortly after midday dinner, the Ford wagon and its occupants headed back down the drive, hoping to reach Ciudad Victoria before nightfall.

Late in the afternoon of the next day, they entered bustling Monterrey. Alice's happy anticipation at seeing the colonel broke through her depression. He was such a good man, Colonel Pancho Woodyard, she thought, noting that she had chosen not to mention him to Johnny and Jane just yet. Which might mean a contender for the place Jerry had held in her life? Should she offer to have him visit her in New York? What would he be like, deprived of his ex-military friends and out of his sphere of influence? He was openly appalled at Christian Science, and that bothered her. Aghh! Best to let it unfold.

The colonel had been adamant in his last letter that she spend several days of rest here before moving on. But Alice would not be scolded into more than one overnight. She arrived at her hotel and called him at his apartment. He arrived an hour later, dressed in a white linen suit. He doffed his straw hat in a cavalier manner, revealing a suntanned pate.

Alice came to greet him, a picture of elegance in a sleeveless flowered dress with a raw silk jacket draped over her shoulders. They gathered in the lobby while Alice introduced the colonel to Tom. There were handshakes all around. The colonel took Alice's arm to escort her to the automobile, giving her a subtle squeeze of affection with a wink and a grin. She returned a deep smile, keeping the pleasure of this meeting unspoken until they could get rid of Tom.

The three climbed into the colonel's open-topped Buick and drove back to his apartment. Tom went off to supper with two of the colonel's friends, chaperones against the antics that might drive a nineteen-year-old boy to trouble in the city.

Alice spent a precious evening dining with Pancho. She regaled him with her road trip adventures, laughing at the dangers and soaking in his attention. At their favorite casino they danced. She allowed him to pull her close enough to feel the warmth of his chest against hers. But Alice knew she was courting trouble if she accepted his offer to make her the fragrant Mexican cinnamon hot chocolate—in his apartment.

"Hasta la vista, Pancho," said Alice. Her voice danced lightly over the pat phrase. She could afford no drama in this parting. He attracted her more than she should admit...

"Princessa mia, will there be a next time?" Pancho asked. "For us?"

"What do you mean, my colonel? Of course. I'm off to Laredo, then to California to close my affairs, collect the furnishings for the hotel, meet with my architect... There are a thousand things to be accomplished ere I drive this way again." Alice made an effort to acknowledge his deeper question. "I'll be back by August."

"Will you telegram your return to Laredo? I would like to meet you there."

"We'll see. Perhaps I will need to go to San Antonio for additional furnishings. I remember a Sears and Roebuck that is perfect for outfitting the

271

hotel." She leaned over and kissed his cheek, inhaling the lovely Bay Rum scent on his clean-shaven jaw. "I will be back."

***

The whole trek north took a week. At the border she was met by a customs official who insisted on escorting her into the office. She handed Tom the keys, told him to guard the station wagon, and followed the official inside. The office door shut behind her. The official forced papers into her hands.

In English he announced, "La Señora Muma, you are being held under arrest for insulting a government official and refusing to show your papers."

His accusation did not sink in at first, and she stared at him with a blank face. Then in the next instant, Alice remembered the incident at the riverbank and wanted to die for shame. Tom had been right. This ignominious thing was happening to her.

She could only find the breath to say, "But, I did not know he was an official." Next, righteous indignation, fueled by adrenalin, made her furious. Every word was a barely controlled response. "He was wearing no hat, no jacket, no insignia, nothing! And I definitely did show him my papers. I demand to call the American consul."

The customs officials listened in stony silence but agreed to the call. After speaking with the consul and explaining the incident, she handed the phone to the customs official who had issued the charges. When the conversation ended, the men in the room appeared to argue. The rapid-fire Spanish was too confusing to follow. Fear piled up in her throat. How could this be happening to her? What awful sum would the charges be? She had literally a peso in her pocket, not counting the train fare to California for Tom.

In the end, the customs official demanded only a fine of $60, and she would be free to go. That was exactly the amount of her deposit on the station wagon that she had left as security, here at the border, six months ago.

Now fuming, with a new fear piled inside that the incident would cost her any chance to do business in Mexico, she asked Tom to drive across the border to Netzler's Storage in Laredo. They pulled into the yard. It must have been the opening and shutting of car doors that alerted Miss Rizer, whose house and tearoom were next door, for as Alice ducked into Netzler's to retrieve a packet of mail, she came out to greet them.

"Mrs. Muma, and you must be Tom, at last! Come in for a cool drink. It's just wonderful to see you. Shall I take your bag into the guest room?"

The two women hugged each other with genuine affection. Alice thought there wasn't another person within a thousand miles to whom she could speak of the misadventure at the chalan.

"Miss Rizer," said Alice. "I feel I have been away for a year, so much has happened. This is Tom, my trusty driving companion of whom I wrote. It was a grueling ride, but we are here. I will regale you with our adventures as soon

272

as I send this poor boy back to his mother. Do you think you could find something substantial for him to eat before I put him on the train?"

The meal accomplished, Alice drove Tom to the station and saw him off to California.

Alice stayed up with Miss Rizer relating highlights of the trip, but found she was unable to speak without tears of the ferry incident. When Alice could no longer keep her eyes open, she excused herself to bed. Not wanting to know what bad news might lurk within the letters—surely John Rankin had his weekly, long list of problems—she placed the unopened packet of mail on her dresser.

Early the next morning Alice opened the packet and fished out one letter from her attorney.

March 10, 1933
Dear Alice:
I hope you have received my previous letter, listing your total indebtedness. Please acknowledge after you come in from the wilds of Mexico. As to my part, the charge of $1,500 does not include the sale of King's X studios, which is now delayed yet again, or any moving or shipping costs involved in removing your considerable furniture stored in one of the empty studio apartments. Your request to pay the back taxes on your Yuma property remains unfulfilled, due to the present bank situation. How we will muddle through remains to be seen.

The owner of Castellamare, who has reneged on recent installment payments, has had a stroke. His wife blames it on the bank moratorium you may or may not know about, as it happened while you were driving north. ...

I put your remaining $195 in cash not in the bank, but in my safe deposit box. It is all that stands between you and starvation. ...

Chapter 58

California or Bust

"And so, Miss Rizer, I throw myself on your tender mercy. There is no money coming in the next two weeks that I can fathom. Dear Jane has offered to tide me over while she secures my Aetna check from the Hartford office. But everyone is powerless with the bank moratorium."

Miss Rizer patted Alice's hand. "You must not worry your head a moment. Nothing is gained by the gnashing of teeth. The truth will reveal itself. Stay here with me. Rest. Put all your things from Netzler's Storage in my attic. See, there are solutions presenting themselves. One just has to let them come."

Alice did rest—against the day she knew she had to leave for California. But her sleep was tormented by despair. It often lurked at night. The three-year-old memory of her Brother Will's epithets, trying to extract money, still frightened her. Afraid of real violence, she had called her editor friend Eddie Dickson to ask that if anything disagreeable happened that reached the papers, he might stifle its publication.

A friend had just written asking whether Alice would be served papers on account of the San Francisco Opera Company going bankrupt, and was that why she was staying away? Alice almost laughed. The pitiful $100 investment of hers had disappeared with the rest of the investors' money. And the mounting debt waiting in Los Angeles? If she announced herself, they might all pounce, impound her Ford, her trusty "covered wagon," and her beloved furniture.

Still, she had to go. She set up a plan with John Rankin to forward all mail to architect Paul Williams in Riverside, with whom she would meet for her Caravanera Hotel plans. Then she would sneak into Los Angeles to organize the furniture to be bought back to Laredo for the hotel. While there she would meet with investors who might back her project, see Mr. Wilson about the repayment of his $300 loan to Johnny and deal with guardianship issues. The list was painful.

Alice hired two men to consolidate her goods from Netzler's Storage into Miss Rizer's attic. Upstairs went trunks and tables, trays, her "In-A-Floor-Safe," cartons of kitchen equipment, German records, woven reed folding screens, wicker furniture, and a Russian samovar. As a gift, she kept out the copper kitchen utensils for Miss Rizer to use. In payment for Miss Rizer's kindness, Alice painted the windows and doors of the café and treated them both to a movie. *Rasputin and the Empress* was in town, and all three Barrymores appeared in it together. It was exceptional.

On the morning of April second, Alice headed west. The grueling 1,400 miles was broken each day only by the necessities of fuel and sleep. First she followed the Rio Grande, then lost it as the road wound its way through the Big Bend Mountains. Picking up the river again, she paralleled north to El Paso where she collected mail. She sent letters to prospective investors in LA *so that they could have time to think about it and give me an answer when I arrive,* she wrote John Rankin.

New Mexico brought ugly memories of the oil and gas leases, unpaid these last years, and so forfeit. "Don't let discouragement get in," she had said to son Johnny after some disappointment. "It cripples one for action." Who would know better than me, she mused.

The late, sweet spring of a green Sonoran Desert was fired with red cactus flowers along the route. At Yuma, Alice paused at the tax office to locate the 250-acre property Jerry had bought for the day irrigation would be available. Back taxes were owed, but if paid might provide yet another place for her hotel. Office clerks would look it up and report back to her, they said. She ticked off a note to get her attorney on it.

She followed the Colorado River north, then turned west again at Blythe. Joshua trees stood silent on the landscape, bizarre primordial yuccas guarding the ancient round boulders which seemed to have been scattered on the plain by giants of a previous age.

Riverside at last came into view. Alice found the Mission Inn an oasis. There she showered off the dust of the miles and met with her architect, Paul Williams. He sketched plans from her book of inspiration, Fred Richards' *A Persian Journey*, creating her vision of thatched-roof bedrooms called Pangos, adding Mexican tiled floors, an outdoor kitchen, a doghouse and aviary, a boat launch and swimming beach.

Sketches beside her in the front seat of her Ford station wagon, Alice drove the few remaining miles into Los Angeles.

Two weeks in California would be enough to say good-bye to friends and gather her furniture for Laredo. Alice stayed the first week with her C. S. practitioner, feeling the strength flow back within the space of a day from the kind ministrations of prayer.

She booked a room at the Biltmore in San Francisco then placed an ad in the San Francisco paper saying that she would be "at home" to all at the Biltmore in two days' time. If my creditors take note, I will have come and gone before they can act, she surmised. She took the train from Los Angeles and deposited herself regally. Her old Theta friends poured in, and many of her Berkeley C. S. family sat and sipped tea while Alice held them spellbound with her adventures in Mexico and her plans to build a hotel called Caravanera on the Pan-American Highway. She even hinted that there was a new man in her life but refused to give up his name, claiming that his children in Los Angeles had not been informed, nor had her own dear Johnny and Janey in New York.

Alice rented an empty storefront in Hollywood and contracted to have most of her furniture moved into the space. Lyons Storage was cleared out, for by some miracle John Rankin had found the cash to pay for back storage charges. Her paintings and some benches and drapes had been held for her in the attic of the now-sold Windsor Boulevard house, and these were loaded into a van bound for the steep King's Road to collect the mass stored in one of the three studio apartments. The Castellamare house, recently sold, had been abandoned but was not yet foreclosed; the rooms were clear except for some beds.

It was a long two days—sorting, packing, resorting and distributing the pile of belongings. At the end, her two friends took what they wanted to use in their own homes, on loan, they agreed. Alice commissioned one of the two loyal friends helping, her Theta sister Helen Kincade, who was also a C. S. Practitioner, to see the furniture off to an auction house.

The items for the hotel venture went into her fancy new trailer: two ice cream freezers, tables, living room chairs, a kitchen cabinet, chests full of linens, mattresses and box springs, drapes with their rods, fishing poles, and brightly striped cushions: all certified by the State of California for transport to Laredo. Was there anything this station wagon would refuse to do for her, she thought? My constant companion through these last months, without whom I would have failed to accomplish this daring dream. Made for hauling, it could be converted into a camper. Alice would live in it while the first few Pango units were being constructed on the Sabinas Riverfront.

She sneaked out early in the evening to make the Mission Inn at Riverside, but her night at the peaceful hotel was restless. The anticipation of the lonely drive back to Laredo with an overloaded car was not pleasant, nor was the absolute silence from the Bensels. Alice had dashed off a letter the day before to Mrs. Bensel with more bravado than she felt. In an elegant, offhand manner, she described her jaunt to San Francisco, deliberately naming the fancy places she stayed and the innovative gathering of her belongings in the empty store. It was imperative to maintain a certain image, after all. In closing she added, as an afterthought,

I hope to hear from you in Laredo, to let me know what shopping I must do. Wait till you see the results of the architectural drawings for Caravanera. I am very eager to have news from you both.

I am

Yours very truly,

Alice

Alice took eight fiercely hot days to drive the distance back to Laredo. She loaded everything back into Netzler's Storage, along with the goods left behind in Miss Rizer's attic.

In 102-degree heat, Alice left for New York. Behind her in California, John Rankin was working to begin foreclosure on the owners of the Castellamare house. Passing Washington DC, she thought of the apartment furniture still stored there after her hotel management course. Janey could not use it in her small room at school. Nor had Johnny's recent ad in the *Monitor* raised any buyers. A trail of belongings strewn from coast to coast. Markers of her passage.

On arrival in New York, a letter waited for her from the American consul in Mexico City.

Dear Mrs. Muma,

In reply to your letter of May 1, 1933, concerning your desire to obtain an extension of the period allowed by the Mexican Immigration Bureau to prove your investment of ten thousand pesos, that request has been denied.

As to the other matter the officials in the Department of Migration felt justified in imposing a fine of 200 pesos against you, and that issue is now closed, the fine having been paid. ... Should you wish to appeal...

Alice was so exhausted from her journey that she could not find the energy even to be angry. She would file all the consular papers together and revisit the matter when her mind was clear. Perhaps, after a summer of quiet study, she would find a path back to Mexico.

Chapter 59

What to Do?

June 11, 1933
Beacon Hill, Boston
Dear Mutti,
One week ago today I arrived in Boston, the previous Sunday I arrived in New York, the Sunday before that I left Laredo. It has tried to be very exhausting, but I am still alive to tell the tale. ...
Alice

***

"You did well, my boy. You have a head for business."

"Mother," said Johnny, "I have my certificate but no job. I went to see Babson Institute as you suggested, and I should like to go."

"A sound decision, Johnny dear. I need to explore a loan to get you through." What is left to beg or steal? she agonized. John Rankin can check my life insurance policy for a loan. The Wilson loan for the MIT debacle was long gone, and not repaid. She looked at her handsome son. Hollywood might still be the answer. If only he had more confidence. Well, another stab at a movie career for him would be worth the possibility of a studio contract. Either way, she would have to borrow the funds.

"Johnny, I have contacted Mutti on your behalf." She watched his face become guarded. "You know Mutti is scouting for the studios."

"Mother, she lives on the east coast."

"She can get you a screen test. She's moving to Hollywood soon to work for the movies. I can arrange for you to stay with her, or perhaps you would prefer the Bel Air Bay Club. Daily C. S. treatment will be there for you, as it is here at Beacon Hill."

"Mother, you know this is a sore subject. Why can't I stay here for the summer? It would be cheaper. Just how you will find the money for school and this ridiculous trip west is the question." He paused, his voice less strident. "Ted and his family have invited me to visit."

Alice pretended to ignore the last remark, knowing his fear of travel was behind all this. "Nonsense, Johnny. You are quite capable of taking the train to California. You can even meet Mutti in Chicago and travel west together. If there is no contract, come back and go to Babson in October."

"Will you come with me?"

"I've said my good-byes to California. Truly, I must have some rest from the rigors of the last six months. There is a studio on the old Gould Estate, near Janey's school in Tarrytown, for a summer of quiet study. Perhaps I will apply in the fall for practitioner instruction at the C. S. Mother Church."

"Is Mexico out, then?"

Alice shrugged her shoulders. "I just don't know. Perhaps I will try again when the rainy season is over. But we were talking about you, dear boy."

Johnny turned away. Alice could see his agitation in the hunched shoulders.

"I'm going to visit Ted for the weekend," he shot back, and he shut the door of her room.

Mutti was her last hope. While it made Alice uncomfortable to make Mutti so important again, she would play this final card. She dashed off a letter to her friend, begging for support for the Hollywood venture. Mutti, she knew, was dying to see Johnny and make him part of her life again. Alice knew the risk—that her son simply couldn't face it—but she had to try one more time. It would mean a job for him, and his handsome face and bright personality would light their way back to the old life. She was so hungry for it. For that she would be willing to take back all her good-byes.

***

Alice left late in the evening for the Tarrytown studio.

July 8th, 1933
Broadview Studios, The Gould Estate
Tarrytown-on-Hudson, NY
Dear J and J:

A week today since my arrival. I drove south as you suggested and had dinner at the "Lobster." It was so sultry that I could not manage sleeping in a hotel and drove straight through. Flashing lightning all around and the smell of sweet hay was almost intoxicating, and assuredly took me back to my childhood in Canada. I went through Danbury a little before daybreak and reached White Plains by six and Tarrytown shortly thereafter. I took a single room overlooking the garden rather than the studio, which had a kitchen and did not interest me. I have ordered a carpenter to put in shelves and give everything a good coat of paint.

Monday I went to New York to collect mail from American Express and almost needed help carrying it. I sat down to read, and who should I see but Cousin Olive, who stayed with me and brought me back to Tarrytown.

Alice fought for serenity. Throughout the remainder of the summer's hot days and occasional cool nights, the difficulty of selling her houses and the search for money threatened to unhinge her. John Rankin's pile of responses to her queries and demands threatened to topple from her desk. Invitations for tea and an occasional swim were her salvation.

On Sundays, Alice played the piano at church and then submerged herself in Science with the small congregation in another part of Tarrytown. Most days she studied for entry to the practitioner course at the Christian Science Mother Church. Mary Baker Eddy's works lined her bookshelves. Notes on scraps of paper stuck out with abandon in bedside book stacks. Once she qualified to help others as she had been helped, there would be a small and utterly satisfying income.

From Jane, working at camp in Maine, she heard little of consequence. It was such a relief, really, to have at least one child out of the nest. She needs me now, Alice thought, only to sort out her love life and her wardrobe. Of John, ensconced in the Christian Science Beacon Hill Sanitarium, she heard nothing until his letter in early August announcing an impromptu visit to his sister. The letter arrived on a dreadfully hot day. She was gripped with an anxiety that clung like the humidity.

August 7th, midnight
Johnny Boy,
I am disturbed and disappointed over your gallivanting to Maine. Every effort was made to give you an easy and helpful summer for maximum result in the autumn. Why are you not going around with Ted? As to Janey's visit, clean your teeth and have cavities filled before going. Don't disgrace her by taking old clothes, but don't get a horsy odor all over your good ones. You must include in your money something for Jane for her birthday on the 24th. Give her of your love and affection in unstinted degree. It will enrich you both. Mother love and brother and sister love is bound to smack of loveliness in uplifted degree. ...

And so, dear boy, I will try and stay put while you go further and further away from me. Please write. Mutti has been helping me for fainting and pain in my back. It is the beginning of the end. I have carried the worry so long. Please let me feel your strong help and interest.
Much love, Mother

Alice sealed the letter as perspiration dripped from her forehead onto the envelope. She did not notice. *I can't see where he is when he is with Jane.* Panic flooded her chest. *I need to see where he is. When he is in Boston I know every room, the building, and the streets.* Alice collapsed onto her hot, damp bed as pain clamped down on her back, and she moaned into her pillow.
***
August 8, 1933
Babson Park, Massachusetts
Dear Mrs. Muma,
I am sorry my letter of July 1 went astray. It has not been returned so probably it is still following you, hence this copy of that letter.

I am pleased that you have asked John to send me photostat copies of his MIT records. As soon as the enclosed application and the records are received, I shall present them at once to our board of admissions. We have heard from Professor Joseph Pfeiffer in Munich and received a splendid letter from Mr. Hitchcock, headmaster at Los Alamos School. I have every reason to believe that John's application will be approved. The term opens next month. I look forward to welcoming John to Babson Institute.

Sincerely yours,

W. R. Mattson, Assistant to the President

August, 1933

Dear John,

Please ride herd on the best offer for Casa Chiquita at Castellamare. You should consider taking up residence and sleep in Jane's old room where two beds still remain intact. The house key went missing after the owners left, and it was a hard scramble to find one with the realtor, but once it was accomplished, and the property listed and advertised, you could then be on hand to show the place. Still, the most likely candidate for purchase, a Mr. Sokolov, keeps trying to lower the price below the $10,000 listed. ...

After this, please consider yourself discharged. ...

Alice

September 8th

My Dear Alice:

The house is worth at least that. I have included in this letter a note for $1,750, which is my bill. Please sign this note back to me, discounted for $1,600, so that I can make a lien on the sale. You would net $2,500, what with the $4,000 still owed on your second mortgage, the commission to the realtor, etc. I enclose bills from Babson and the guardianship for $100. Your San Diego County Water stock is hard to sell. Remember to pay your Ford automobile insurance.

I am perfectly used to being fired and do not resent it this time or any of the other times you have done so. However, there are still many envelopes of yours in my safe. I went to the Women's Athletic Club today and found that your mail was still waiting there, so I took it, hence the large envelope. Your bank accounts are now all empty. I enclose a list of bills to be paid. If it makes you feel better, the Biltmore has not been able to pay its light bill for months.

Aetna can send you a check for $2,000 as a loan against your monthly $144, which is what you said you wanted for John and Jane's college. John starts on the 29th, I gather. His transcripts have all been received from his various high schools. ...

The last I heard you discovered that the Pan-American Highway would not be finished for another two years and that the Bensels had finally written to

281

say that a tornado whipped though their town and tore up what little had been accomplished of the road. I hope that is the last of it.

I do wonder how I will get on not knowing what you doing, though it will be peaceful.

John Rankin

November 27th
Myles-Standish Apartments
Boston, MassDear Mutti:

I am off to New York at midnight to return with Jane on Wednesday. I prefer Thanksgiving in New York, but Johnny only has one day off. ...

I am glad Johnny finds interest in Babson. He discusses his work with me and has never done that before. I am grateful beyond words that he feels he has something to offer the world. He goes to his practitioner all the time and I see him on Wednesday evenings and Sunday at church. I still want John in the movies but he has asked not to talk about it.

My Christmas plans are not complete. I stand on call if they put on my pet opera, *Andrea Chénier*, and if so I will sing at the Hippodrome in Boston, and remain eager for C. S. instruction any time after the New Year. ...

Love, Alice

Chapter 60

What About Jane?

Jane skimmed a letter from their mother that Johnny had enclosed with a rare one of his own.

January 9, *1934*
Barbizon Hotel
New York
Dear Johnny;
Along came your welcome wire. I have been pretty ill and I feel I have escaped something pretty formidable. My voice is not back yet, but I have been quiet. Please let us get closer and closer for I need you terribly. My spirit seems so crushed I can't seem to rise above it. I know I am a proud, haughtily ambitious old dame!
At least that is the false me. …
Jane is coming down from teaching at Broadview to a recital on Sunday and following reception and tea in the studio. …
I think of you so much,
Love, Mother

Her poor brother was always front and center with their mother. Jane did go down to New York to watch over her mother's bout of pleurisy. The illness was perfectly timed to ruin any chance for performing in the Hippodrome's production of *Andrea Chénier*. Or, Jane wondered, was the sickness *caused* by her being rejected? Or exasperated by Johnny's failure to travel to California at Christmas? The trip had been a present to the both of them. Really, they knew it was one more attempt by Mother to get Johnny to Hollywood for a screen test organized by Mutti. He only traveled as far as Chicago and turned around. Jane continued west. Mutti was an attentive host. The weather was sublime. It just felt like coming home, though Jane tried not to be jealous of the new owners of the Casa Chiquita house at Castellamare that her mother had promised her.

***

February 9
Broadview School
Tarrytown, NY
Dear Johnny,

Got your letter this afternoon and it brought on great shouts of joy, you may well imagine. I was beginning to wonder about our ski weekend. I am free the week of March seventeenth, and I guess that will be just about right, won't it?

It's seven below tonight, so the garage man told me. "Kaiser Wilhelm" is doing well and starts at the first touch of the starter. It's almost too cold to skate comfortably, so we've taken to sliding with the sledges of the lower school. I've been riding a couple of times, too, Of course the horses have been terribly frisky because they don't get near enough exercise. My horse bucked, kicked and pitched like a Wild West show.

But the biggest news of all is that I've heard from Mr. Thompson and have seen three beautiful Russian operas with him. The taxi strike added much zest to our evenings in town. Sherry goes along with me, for his son Hugh who is entranced with her, I believe. She is quite a dear this year—we are getting along very well. Isn't it funny that never in my life before have I had friends that I could really laugh and joke with. I must say, that there is one thing about teaching at Broadview School—that there's goodly friendship and give and take.

Speaking of plans for summer, Miss Weaver would like me to get together a group of girls for Europe, which would make me my passage. I don't know how that will work out but this I know, that I don't want to go back to camp next summer nor come back here next winter. I have to study more before I have the nerve to teach anymore. Perhaps by the time I see you I will have something more definite to say.

Best of love,

Jane

P.S. I'm trying to find the time to read Hitler's autobiography.

June 18, 1934

Boston

Dear Mutti:

With chagrin, I am clearing my desk before I embark upon my next venture—what I know not as yet. I have kept the dollars flowing for John's expensive year at Babson. It has come out wonderfully, and here we are winding out our affairs, and expect by this time next week to be in New York, with my apartment furnishings in Boston stored in Tarrytown awaiting autumn developments.

A really lovely opportunity has come to Jane to attend summer college at Weimar, Germany from July to the middle of August, studying German and literature and living in a household in the quaint little old town. She sails next week. Then when she finishes there, she is to go down to Munich where Miss Weaver has offered her the job of chauffeur to motor the summer girls through the Dolomites and Northern Italy. She does not expect to return until September. I am thrilled that she is at last to be away from the camp in Maine.

I have always felt she should be in more broadening surroundings. She had a very good foundation in German but lacks fluency. This will enable her to carry on a better conversation with John and Ted, and thus help John to maintain his German.

I am in the midst of the class instruction which will enable me to practice C. S. whenever I will earnestly use what I know. You know how long I have wanted it. It has come in a most miraculous way. I finish next Wednesday and will immediately pack up. John will return from visiting Ted and come with me to New York to see what it offers.

And now for a word about the movies, which I am sure you are wondering about. It would seem that he has given up all idea of it. I doubt that he could stand all that is involved. If he only had some of my fighting stuff. Until he rouses in confidence, nothing can be done that I can see. ...

While I think of it, the Mexican Highway situation is turning out and in a very different manner from what I had foreseen. Mrs. Bensel at the ranch is agreeable to a partnership in opening a tearoom in her new ranch home. That will be an excellent way to learn the trade without involving too much expense. Anyway, the low price at which I had to sell Castellamare took the wind out of my sails for the whole venture. My things are still down on the border awaiting the decision. The rainy season will be over and an official party is going down assembling at San Antonio, and I had hoped to be along for that means the Pan-American Highway will be officially opened. The day I have waited to see.

With the best of good wishes,
Alice

Alice tucked the four-page, single-spaced letter into a large envelope, and the carbon copies into her file.

June 23rd, 1934
Broadview School, Tarrytown
Dear Mother—
I am sailing tourist third-class on the *Bremen* Saturday night, June 30th—
Enclosed is a red feather. If you can find a pair of evening sandals with no more of a heel than the black-and-white pajama shoes which you gave me, please have them dyed the color of the feather. But they must have a low heel. My dress is progressing and promises to be very nice.
So glad your class is wonderful. ...
Must get this off. If you can find a little evening bag to dye color of shoes.
Thanks for the money,
Love, Jane

Chapter 61

The Path Back

Alice sat in the Boston apartment gazing with some comfort at the rooms furnished with her own belongings that she had finally shipped out of storage from Washington DC. She was ready to move back to New York. Most of the reason for this apartment had begun with the necessity to be close to John; to know what he was up to and keep him from associating with the drunkards in the business program at Babson. To Johnny's credit, he studied hard and would have nothing to do with the lower elements. Now the school was providing him with job leads in Manhattan, however discouraging the salaries. Perhaps the best hope lay with Mildred Ahlf's husband, Jimmy Strobridge. Jimmy and Mildred now lived in New York, he being the branch manager of Strobridge Lithographing in Cincinnati. What a lot of life had happened since Alice and Mildred's days in Paris.

Anxiety surfaced and forced her to her feet to make tea. There had been some terrible bumps in her road in spite of her son and daughter's success. The Science lesson in February often came to mind now: *With every increasing certainty we can by persistent, daily effort fearlessly affirm that matter and material sense, time and space—limitations of every name and nature—are apart from God and therefore are without actuality.* Another mantra to recite when her mind would not focus on the positive.

After her class was over and Johnny had graduated from Babson, she had motored with him to Chicago for the World's Fair. Johnny refused to go any further, so she continued west alone to Hollywood to visit Sue and Grif and her recently widowed sister-in-law Anne and her son Dan. Her car broke down, necessitating an emergency air trip and ensuing scramble for funds. The debt of the plane ride and car repairs resulted in an embarrassing overdraft.

She was glad to have been there, nonetheless. Jerry's older sisters, Sue and Anne, had been a source of comfort and contact with her beloved California during these years of her widowhood. Though Sue had married Griffith Williams and moved to Wisconsin, they had returned on Griff's retirement.

Anne had married Murray Lee, an engineer who took his family to Mexico to build the railway and then returned to work in the deserts of California, where he had just died of a heart attack. It was chiefly for her and her son Daniel that Alice had made the effort, and endured the lonely ride home.

On her return, Alice had thought to start up an insurance career in New York and had contacted Penn Mutual Life, suggesting she start her training in the summer, hoping, as she said, to write "a risk policy or two during her training." They were happy to train her, they said, and would she please send her California broker's license so they could check on its reciprocity in the State of New York. It was certainly a piece of luck that she had kept it up all these years. But it didn't look promising to make some quick money.

John Rankin's awful flow of bad news continued. Guardianship papers were to be filed and paid. What stocks to sell or transfer in the children's portfolios now that Johnny was coming of age? The tenant at Kings X, who was offering to buy, was very ill; Madame Estelle firmly demanded payment for clothing, as did Altman's Department Store; Mr. Wilson was threating to sue Alice for the $300 loan; and the awful mix-ups of returned checks, cancelled checks and missed payments.

The bad news followed her to the new apartment in Tarrytown: liens discovered on the King's X property during the agonizingly slow closing; the inability to sell any of her furniture at the auction house in Los Angeles, or at least not for the price she needed; the huge inventory in the Kings X studios which must be vacated.

It was therefore a welcome respite from grim reality that Alice sat down in her new apartment to read Jane's letter from Germany. The news had taken a circuitous route from the address at 5th Avenue's American Express general mail drop, forwarded to John Rankin in Los Angeles, and from his office to Tarrytown.

Thursday August 25th
Weimar, Germany
Dear Mother and John—
I got your letter yesterday, Mother, and was a bit cheered because at least I know what you plan to do now even thought I can't know just where you are.

Germany is quite quiet with no outward evidence of turmoil or break. This morning we saw about one hundred soldiers marching through town, the watch all dressed in black and looking like big black devils. ... I heard Hitler speak, but I couldn't understand such a queer Austrian accent.

Last night I went to a gathering in Weimar Halle to hear a chorus, and there was much raising of the right arm and "Heil Hitler," which is now the proper greeting in Germany. It amuses me no end to do it, but seems a bit childish. The grown-ups still speak of Hitler and his politics in hushed tones, but the younger generation calls him the "Savior of Deutschland."

Alice had worried that the trip would be spoiled by the growing political violence. Jane, though, she saw, was weaving it into her life as part of the excitement of her summer. Traveling third-class aboard the *Bremen* had put her in with other students, including a Rhodes Scholar from Yale who had promised to look her up when they would both be in Munich. A young German

287

poet was apparently smitten, as well. Alice could see her cultured, grown-up daughter enjoying the attention of the opposite sex while keeping her head, as well as her priorities. Jane continued:

My Schiller course comes at nine o'clock at his house. We sit among his belongings while the professor lectures in German. Then at ten we go to the library for another lecture on modern literature, including Wagner. At eleven we go to the Goethe Archives. At various points during the lectures we are allowed to finger manuscripts and priceless bits of paper.

We are on our own until four when we have our German grammar lesson, often followed by a reading of *Faust* and *Don Carlo*. With dinner parties most evenings and weekends spent touring, it is a wonder I accomplished nine credits studying only between midnight and three a.m.

Miss Weaver brought champagne and a beau brought me a birthday cake for breakfast at the hostel. I got a nice letter from Johnny and your telegram the day before, which makes everything complete. ...

Please send the eight dollars for your knitted suit and five of my ten in marks if you can do it.

Best of love,
Jane, Sim, Peter

Janey would be home in a couple of weeks. It would be good to have her back.

September 10th
Dear Alice:
I just don't know what I am going to do about my situation with you. I recently told you the depleted condition of my exchequer. The only way I can possibly get any money is to have plenty of time to work on estate and other cases I have. ... I am really down to the point where I really should not, in all fairness to my paying clients and my family, work extensively on matters without a retainer. ...

John Rankin

October 10th
Tarrytown
Dear John:
Your patience has been justly tried. Do not construe my silence as indifference—with receipt of your letter I went right down in illness—I allowed myself to be exasperated and worried. I went out to Jane and John, and there I had to remain until I could walk again. It all came just the last week of my probation with the insurance sales training, so I will have another chance later.

288

Please let Spinnel, Estelles Gowns, Mr. Wilson and the others know my New York address.

Now that the King's X is organized for sale, I am taking a quick motor trip to Mexico to get the new project going. Mrs. Bensel wrote me earlier this year that she is willing to be partners in a tearoom. We are planning to do a formal affair for the group of investors from San Antonio. As you know, Senator McAdoo is a personal friend of mine, and he has promised a letter of introduction to the San Antonio Chamber of Commerce. ... I expect to be there a week, which should put me back in New York on November 15. Let me have a letter from you waiting on my return.

To say I am indebted to you is putting it mildly. Certainly the California chapter is closed. Life begins anew in New York. Jane's school started October 3rd. She is teaching German, etc. John got a job with Chrysler Air Conditioning last week and was dining with Chrysler Junior in his Park Ave apartment before the week was out. So I hope the Muma Red Sea is passed.

My best to Enge and you,
Alice

***

Alice left for Mexico on her birthday, October 18. The Tarrytown ferry carried her across the Hudson. The road south passed through Hagerstown, Knoxville and Memphis on its way to San Antonio by the twenty-third. Colonel Pancho Woodyard met her in Laredo. She stored her trusty Ford station wagon, Acapulco, in Mary Riser's yard and left with him for Monterrey.

Sunday, November 4, 1934
Hotel Monterrey
Dear J and J,
These have been wonderful days since my last line to you from San Antonio. Nothing has been omitted by the colonel for my pleasure and comfort. ... We crossed the International Bridge and sped south on the splendid highway. We suffered with huevos rancheros at a wayside place with plenty of atmosphere. It was midnight Friday when we pulled into Monterrey, and it looked fascinating in moonlight. I was glad to be back. ...

It has been the sweetest courting any woman could receive. Each day I have lunched with him at his apartment. Each evening we have dined together and mostly at his apartment. Herlinda, the cook, and three servants wait on the colonel hand and foot and he only punches a bell or claps his hands and things are accomplished. ... He has a son, Pancho, who is also an engineer and is now in LA with his little family, there being little work for Americans here now. His second son, Edward, is a lieutenant in the Navy and just graduated from Annapolis. His daughter, Helen, recently remarried after her first husband was

289

killed. She lives in Bremerton, near Seattle, with their little son. All have suffered with the alcoholism of their mother, and so draw close to one another.

Wednesday we drove to the Bensels and I found the tearoom idea to be off. Mexico is about to blow up momentarily in religious strife. I find it hard to make that statement. ...

The colonel wants me to step right in—to come into "the firm" and help him in his architecture. Doesn't it sound splendid, and yet behold the fly in the ointment—he ridicules Christian Science. ... And so the whole thing rests. I must see clearly and I will.

Within hours, the colonel is driving me back to Laredo. I have all my plans to dispose of the stored articles and will bring only a few items back with me. I should be with you in New York by next weekend. I will let you hear from me as I get near.

Devotedly,
Mother

December 22, 1934
Los Angeles
Dear Alice,
Merry Christmas to you. Your telegram came this morning and I am grateful for your love and for the appreciation, too, of the unfolding of the Christ in our thinking. A phone call from the auction house says they have a buyer for the piano, but they are crooks, and you should have nothing to do with them. Mrs. Klumb and I went over to see their books for your inventory and they would not show us the records. If you want to take it up with the police commissioner he could force them to show the records.

We haven't good news from the galleries. Enclosed is a money order for $13.70. Things went for such a low price it is heartbreaking.

I am happy the insurance is developing.

My love is with you,
Helen

Chapter 62

The Last Stand at a Swank Address-1935

Alice walked around the apartment with her tea. The living room window of 35 Sutton Place South, Apartment 3W framed the 59th Street Bridge, and the morning sun was magnificent as it danced off the river. She signed the lease without a qualm last October, and it was now almost April. It was this panorama of the East River and Welfare Island and further east to Queens for which she was paying a dear $1,200 a year. Her strategy to sell insurance to pay the hefty rent was yet another failed plan, and the issue of her finances grew more acute as winter released its wet, cold grip.

She looked around, feeling miserable that her furniture barely covered the place. Dear stubborn Johnny insisted on keeping his distance in Tarrytown and commuting to his job in the city. Still staying close to his sister, Alice thought with some jealousy. Inseparable, those two. He would not share expenses by taking up the second bedroom. Nor could he afford to help pay back the $500 loan she signed to get him through that final semester of Babson. Dunning letters from the school sat in the pile on the desk.

Helen Kincade's latest from Los Angeles was just as depressing. *Now, Alice, only good is unfolding and we are in line for it when we recognize we cannot be separated from it.* Helen, both Alice's C. S. practitioner and the designated saleswoman for her goods in storage, felt bound to point Alice to the truth in Science while bemoaning the lack of buyers for her furniture. Alice saw nothing "unfolding," not a glimmer of success in all the years of plans and push and prayer. It could not be borne, this sham of unrelenting hope that things would work out.

And then, Pancho's latest missive burned with his diatribes against C. S. Alice put down her tea and picked up this letter that was so hard to read.

Can't you see and feel that you are wrestling and struggling all the time, and you are lulled by mere mental hypnotic dope? But I suppose that will always be the insurmountable barrier between us—and that frustration is mine as well—and what seems to me the most clear of all things, is in your mind merely blind stubborn obtuseness—a rather-to-die-than-say-yes. And you know we are so attuned in everything else!

It was true, Alice admitted as she wore out the carpet with her pacing. He seemed delighted with her gifts, a silly little eggcup one month, photos of her with her children the next, a poster of Rockefeller Center, which he had framed and mounted in his office. Where is your beautiful, graceful princess? his friends had asked. No, he could not make a visit to New York in June, but come out to Mexico, he begged. He marveled at the letters Jane sent him and seemed as pleased as she was herself over Jane's A in German at Columbia University. But, overall, his snipes at C. S. had turned his loving attention to ashes in her mind.

***

For a month, while daffodils and cherry trees sprang to life in Central Park, Alice paced, and prayed over a way to salvage her life. And she came up with a plan when a ridiculously small check for $100 arrived from Helen for the sale some bits and pieces of her furniture.

She would go to California in June. Pancho wanted her to take the southern route and stop in Monterrey. She would not. Instead she would travel straight to California and load up all the precious furniture that she could use both in her Sutton Place apartment and another, less costly one in midtown. Johnny had agreed to stay in that one if she promised not live there with him. Yes, she would be in the real estate rental business, sublet the Sutton Place, and find roommates for Johnny. If she could not sell her furnishings, then she would darn well make them work for her. A dinner party—no, too expensive—a tea party would be just the thing to send her off.

***

"Janey dear, here is the ham and chicken for the French sandwiches. Roll them tight and cut them on the diagonal." Alice was fussing. Guests were due at four o'clock.

"Mother, remember I taught you how to do this." Jane smiled and patted her mother's shoulder. This was a rare time for them together. Jane was still teaching at Broadview School and dashing to Columbia to study German. Alice's parties had always had an aura of elegance that made her guests feel special; Alice had allowed the caterers, the cook and now Jane to create food to match. The tattered *Fannie Farmer Cookbook*, stuffed with notes on scrap paper and menus from friends' parties, was Jane's source of inspiration.

They sat briefly, looking at the splendid view of the river and swirling the last of the percolated coffee in the bottoms of their cups.

"Remember the strawberries and fondant cakes, and the lady fingers..." Alice went on.

"And I will see to the cream and jam for them, shall I?" Jane laughed. "And, set the kettle on to boil. We have hours yet, Mother."

"Well, you're right to scold for once, Janey. Now then, tell me more about your summer stock."

"I will play Portia at the onset. Don't know what will be next. The thing is, I am enjoying it immensely. I'm getting mighty tired of teaching these little brats."

"The stage is calling you, is that right? And don't call them brats, my dear. It is not becoming."

"Well, they are. And, the theater *is* getting its hooks into me. I am thinking of having my voice tested early next year for the radio shows."

"Should you go back to Pasadena to the acting school there, do you think?" said Alice.

"No, Mother, really, all of that is available here. I have met the nicest young man, name of Gordon. He lives in Connecticut, part of the stock company."

"Is he courting you, Jane?" Alice tried to keep the concern out of her voice. A man of the stage, was... Well, one never knew.

"No, not yet. Mother, don't worry. I am all grown up."

"Well, young lady, you are not of age yet." Alice softened her voice. She desperately didn't want to spoil the moment, or the party. "But soon. I will be writing to release your guardianship bond and get you the portfolio of Laguna Land and Water Stock that has been paying your bills these years."

"Maybe we should sell it to pay your loan from Mr. Booth?" suggested Jane.

"No, that would not do. Perhaps I can convince Willis to wait until your guardianship payments stop. Actually, the Laguna stock has lost quite a bit of value—the market is gone for it right now. But, don't mention this to Mr. Booth today, my dear. We want this to be a gay affair."

"I hope this works, Mother. To bring all your things East is a big undertaking."

Alice understood that Jane meant "expensive."

"I hope so, too, my dear. My future depends on my making a go of this rental business. Besides, won't it be wonderful to have our precious things around us again? I am already imagining your father's steamer trunk in John's apartment. And I haven't even rented it yet! And you, if you do what you plan, next year you will be living here, as well." Alice tried hard not to take offense at Jane's references to her financial constraints. For the sake of a nice afternoon, she would let it go, but it was becoming increasingly difficult to countenance interference in her affairs.

Their conversation meandered comfortably through the guests who would be coming. Chancie and her husband Willis, Jerry's pal from UC and now vice president of a bank in town; her dear college friend Mildred and her husband, who was now Johnny's employer; old friends the Langways, minus their son Ted, who was away in Europe at the moment. Johnny would be disappointed for sure. Lillian Weaver would be here. Yes, it was a well-traveled group, comfortable with their worldview. It suited beautifully.

Alice smiled for the first time in weeks. New plans always gave her hope. And she had given her son the job of renting out her apartment in her absence. That would keep him near.

293

She walked into her bedroom to shower and change for the festivities, and thought suddenly to draft a note for Willis to be delivered the day after the party.

Dear Willis,

May I telephone you on Monday and learn if you are willing to let me extend my note even further? In marrying, my personal income will be released and I can repay you. I will forget all about a trousseau.

Fondly,
Alicia

***

Alice traveled by train to San Francisco, and then visited with friends on her way down to Los Angeles. She spent long, exhausting days with Helen sorting through the mass of belongings stashed with friends and in the auction house. John Rankin had hours of paperwork to discuss.

She invited Pancho's son and his wife for tea at her club. Why not? The life membership was not selling, so she might as well use it. In the small hours of night, exhausted beyond sleep, Alice pondered a life with this American engineer, Pancho Sr., wedded to the Mexican economy. She made lists of things she could do as his wife: start a lending library, study language, sell music, and host trips throughout Mexico and Central America. It was a list of a woman hardly in "repose," as he imagined she would be in his letters.

On July 29, a frazzled Alice sailed east on the *President Pierce*, most of her precious possessions in the hold. She failed to collect a letter from Johnny mailed to the Women's Athletic Club in LA confirming the details of her sublet. It eventually caught up with her in New York.

Dear Mother,

Well, it's rented and for the mighty sum of $135 through to October 1. I have taken $5 to cover your safe deposit box in Tarrytown. The remainder I am paying to the Sutton Place South Corp. This leaves you still quite a sum to be paid to complete your contract with them, and may I suggest that you come back with money in hand as the apartment corp. is not going to grant you much more leniency. It would be very unpleasant to lose our tenant and be forced to refund part of her money. I have given my word to the apartment house attorney that you would pay unconditionally. I had to because they were quite close to dispossessing. ... Your phone bills must be paid as well or both our credit is ruined.

Hope I have made everything clear.

Johnny

***

During the days and nights of the cruise, Alice drew strength from the smell of gardenias and ginger flowers. She read her little C. S. guide and slept late

294

into the mornings. She conversed from her assigned seat at the chief engineer's table with passengers who had traveled as she had, to Honolulu and Paris. She watched all three movies on board, on deck, at night, under the moon and masses of stars, as they passed by Manzanello and through the canal.

Mail from Pancho awaited her in Havana.

July 3
Monterrey
Alicia Dear:
Two very sweet letters from you to date. Yours of Sunday came today. I am glad to know that my son Pancho and his wife Sadie came to see you. ...

I am sorry to know that you are still going—everlasting going—getting your things together—auction—ever going on! Don't you ever let up the tension? Don't you ever run down? What pursues you, Alicia? You are such a lovely person—such a dear—and you owe it to yourself not to have such a complicated program. And maybe it would be a good thing if you would allow yourself a little time for recreation. You go like Hell on fire every minute you are awake and then drop to sleep—of exhaustion...

Alice put down the letter and took a few breaths. There it was, the constant criticizing. At least this was not about C. S. He was right, but it didn't matter. She would do what was necessary, and who was he to tell her differently. Pancho continued:

Damn it all, I wish we could be where we could see a lot of each other for a couple of months and every day of that time and see how we get along. Why don't you come right here and stay in Monterrey and spend some time, and to the devil with what others might say or think. ...

The pull to Mexico, the possibility of matrimony with this man who adored her, could not be ignored much longer. If she could sell that Dutch marquetry desk for $1,000, her debt would be all but wiped out. She might be free to pursue this chance. For now, she would economize by staying with a friend in Tarrytown and pay most of the back rent to Sutton Place South Corporation with the commission checks still dribbling in from Aetna Insurance. All those accounts Jerry had established so many years ago were almost terminated.

In October, Alice moved back into the apartment, renewed her lease, and painted every room. The marquetry desk had not sold, and so was here. The mustard rug with persimmon border went into the dressing room she painted butter yellow. She finished the living room with embroidered hangings from Spain, copper plates, a red lacquered wood box with Chinese characters and a Japanese Tansu chest. Her blue octagonal Nankin dinner plates decorated the glass-fronted highboy near the dining room. She found another tenant, this

295

time at a profit, an older couple who wanted to enjoy the winter season in Manhattan.

Her second apartment, a few blocks west on 56th Street, was in a five-story walkup with a roof garden, heat, hot water and a view of the river. It had two suites; at least one could look at it that way if one didn't count but one kitchen. Perhaps next year she would try to divide it and rent it out to two separate tenants. Johnny had promised to move down from Tarrytown with some friends and help her move in the furniture. Red woolen curtains were hung in the bedrooms; the smaller room held an officer's cot, and the larger two, each a twin bed. The Kenwood plaid blankets, in warm browns and lavender, made a cozy statement. Not quite the Adirondack look, but close enough. Alice placed the brass dinner gong in the kitchen, along with dishes purchased from a cheap purveyor downtown.

Still, there was furniture left over to be stored at the warehouse facility nearby.

***

Alice left for Mexico early in December. Best wishes from her friends sat well in her mind. One imagined a large square diamond engagement ring for Alice; others wished her a life of ease. But she had to laugh at dear Byrne, that flamboyant and devoted fan. His parting letter made her giggle, and she pulled it out to read again as the train pulled out of Penn Station.

Alicia, la Muma,
Too, too bad to give up that nice name on the envelope! Soon to be…Mrs. Stockyards!! Stockyard…dooryard…coalyard … I can't bear it.
Must you!
I'm going to start turning my malicious animal magnetism on him. I'm going to do my best to arrange for one colonel less by the time you reach Miami.
Grimly determined,
Byrne

Chapter 63

Litany of Failure

Alice disappeared into Mexico to decide about her colonel. Abandoning the respectability of chaperones and separate abodes, she slipped into Monterrey to join him in his palatial apartment.

Pancho's recent and recurring malaria was subsiding, but his work had suffered badly during a months-long bout. When fever and trembling overtook him, Alice nursed him and managed his office. On the days when he could travel, she and Pancho drove to construction sites in his blue Buick convertible.

For three months, they talked and scolded, made love and breakfasted together. In the end, he would not countenance Science; she would not live without it. She heard from him once more, a postcard of the San Angel Inn delivered to her in San Antonio on her way home.

Alice returned to New York in March to find the Midtown brownstone apartment in shambles. The young men renting the apartment had been loud and late with the rent. Johnny, working now six days a week, had no time to act as a property manager. It fell to Alice to throw out the offending tenants and move herself in, as the Sutton Place apartment was still sublet. If she thought at all about her vagabond existence, it was sublimated by her need for shelter.

***

The downward spiral toward madness continued for the remainder of the year. Service Please, a company catering to the needs of wealthy clients judged her over qualified for the tasks, and lacking the required humbleness of spirit.

The position of guide and counselor to children on a European camping trip offered nothing more than expenses.

The job promised her after Labor Day in Wanamaker's faded away when the Philadelphia department store didn't open a branch in Manhattan.

A letter of recommendation from the vice president of Chase Bank failed to land her a job in the travel department of American Express.

In despair, Alice wrote to Helen, her C.S. practitioner friend, who reminded her that *if one is working in Science, no exact job in the world was promised even to the most faithful.* Alice found no solace in the message, though she certainly understood the truth of it.

In July, Alice applied for a loan to turn a dressing room of the brownstone into a bathroom, hoping to create separate apartments within the one larger one. The apartment managers accused her of intending to turn the rooms into a boarding house. Despite pleas to the contrary, her request was denied. But they were willing to renew the lease, they said, if she would pay the arrears. Alice found a new tenant, a young woman in business, whose wealthy and respectable father was good for the rent.

In September her friend Willis Booth and wife Chancie steamed back from their annual summer in London. Alice sent them a note of welcome home appending an offer to sell them her rare Bokhara rug for $35 and asking if she could pay her loan on installment. Willis and Chancie said yes, of course.

Alice moved back into her Sutton Place apartment in October with no roommate and a rent increase. She was forced to beg another $100 from Willis, and when he consented, signed over some of the Laguna Land and Water Stock as collateral, now almost valueless due to a Federal lawsuit over the company's back taxes. It bothered her greatly that the stock was actually Johnny and Jane's, but her children had consented.

Out of the blue, the life membership in the LA Women's Athletic Club sold. Alice could not believe she was holding a check for $300. Wanting to pay off her debt of $500 to Willis, she invested the entire check on a tip from a private bank in San Antonio. By December the investment and the promised profit had evaporated. Alice was forced to beg Willis yet again for an extension.

***

On a brilliant day near Christmas, with the treasured view of the 59th Street Bridge back in her view, Alice sat amongst a pile of hectoring mail. The estate of Mr. Wilson of Cleveland, Ohio, wanted its $300 immediately. Babson College would discount their loan if only she would pay it. A third bill from Macy's demanded payment for the blue silk dress Alice had gifted to Jane to attend as a bridesmaid at a friend's wedding. At least Janey enjoyed her weekend, Alice mused, remembering the long excited letter she had received while in Mexico last spring. Jane had thought to ask about the colonel's health in that letter, and when they would meet him. Never, as it turned out.

Weary to her bones, Alice sat down to pen a note to Willis and Chancie Booth.

December 23, 1936
Dear Chancie and Willis,

Not only at this holiday season am I thinking of you all. You must know I have thought of you often, and only because of "deep water" have I kept silence.

There is much to be grateful for; however, we are still intact, so to say.

John is still at his same job—with such a tiny salary, and Jane has given up her connection to Broadview and is without a job as yet.

It is all so different from my expectations and I am a bit weary of the never-ending pull.

I never thought I would write like this and I know you will not betray me.

298

I have had several interesting prospects of jobs fade and one wonders where lies the right thing. Surely this is my period of readjustment on all scores. Somebody or something must need me, even if I cannot find any more "colonels."

I do hope you are wonderfully well and happy.

Affectionately,

Alice

Chapter 64

Devoid of Joy

1936 had died devoid of joy, with nothing to hold despair at bay but sparse memories of brave little teas and desperately cheerful islands of gathered friends. This new year, 1937, promised little, but then, it was early. Alice looked around the tiny place on 45th Street which she had rented in January. It was 300 square feet, one bedroom, galley kitchen, and living room with a cot for Johnny elegantly screened from view. Now, on this dispirited and freezing February day, three of them were crowded around the kitchen table. The printed cloth Jane had whisked on it five minutes ago made a brave attempt to warn away the threatening gloom.

The one teabag that had dragged through each of their cups of boiling water lay exhausted on a saucer. The Depression still full on, they had grown quite used to the weak brew, as likely had the remaining tenants in this apartment building, and for that matter, the balance of all the tenants in every apartment in all five boroughs. Brown bread sandwiches spread with tuna salad provided the centerpiece to their afternoon gathering. A few cookies rounded out the menu. Alice managed, just, to avoid them. She had gained weight lately.

The apartment was taken mostly to keep Jane with Johnny in New York—to save Jane from an imprudent affair with a Russian actor met during summer stock. Jane talked about this dashing foreigner with entirely too much romance in her eyes. Alice feared the consequences of this new involvement, more even than this Gordon fellow from Connecticut. Preparing for the possibility of impromptu wedding, she had contacted a friend to borrow a wedding dress for Jane—in case. And she also had ready all the information on purchasing a diaphragm from the Sanger Clinic in New York, if it wasn't too late.

Twenty-three dollars a month it cost Alice, and with her furniture and decorating in place, she collected forty-five from Jane and Johnny. At last, there was a small profit coming in from her real estate attempts. Her children could both afford it; Johnny had gotten a raise over his base salary of twenty dollars a month. He could also take over the life insurance premiums for himself and his sister, another financial burden lifted from Alice. Jane, unemployed except for occasional radio spots, was paid well when she worked. Jane, ever frugal and self-sufficient, contributed her share to the expenses.

Her children had shown less-than-enthusiastic support for her new project. A haze of disapproval hovered over the tiny kitchen.

"I'm going and that's that." Alice's voice was tight with suppressed indignation. "You are always against my plans. I won't have it."

"Mother, be sensible for once," Johnny retorted. "The Yuma land is lost."

Jane added, "You are finally making some money on your apartment rentals—from us as well as the Midtown apartment—almost $60 a month to add to your $105 monthly life policy from Daddy. With your new roommate at Sutton Place, that more than pays your share of your own rent."

"Your daddy bought 240 acres in the desert against the day when the Boulder Dam water would be available. Last year that dam opened. If there ever was a time to sell this property, it is now." Alice was anxious to make this deal. If she could find a buyer for just $2,000, her indebtedness would be wiped clean.

"You have paid no principal since 1932," said Jane. "Surely it is forfeit."

"No, I went by it last year. There is a moratorium on back taxes. Last month I went to Washington to see some farm people about irrigation possibilities. They were not particularly forthcoming, typical of civil servants." Alice frowned, remembering her useless circular conversations in that stuffy office with two badly dressed young men. "But they didn't discourage me. I must go to California, contact some tax lawyers and advertise this property. Flying, of course, is out of—"

"How will you pay for this trip west on the train, then?" asked Johnny.

Alice lowered her voice and her eyes, dreading the outburst that would surely come. "I have taken a loan against the silver flatware and tea service."

"Not again," yelled Johnny. He started up, and then sat. Alice felt the tension as he lowered his voice to continue. "Will I need to go back to that pawn shop in two weeks to bail you out?"

"We do what we must," was all Alice could mumble. She jammed on her fedora, grabbed her coat off the back of her chair and fled before her anguish could fill the room.

***

Alice was back in New York by the end of February. She had tracked down two landowners of nearby Yuma property whose advice was to wait awhile for the value of the land to increase. Undeterred, she searched out an interested buyer in Los Angeles who might offer $2,000, but not before all the Arizona back taxes of $580 were paid.

She wrote Willis of the project, asking if he would extend her the back taxes in exchange for the Certificate of Purchase. *I will keep trying to sell the property, and at $2,000 that would square my entire indebtedness to you and let me give up any idea of realizing any value out of the venture.*

Willis refused.

***

Alice toyed with a fantasy of a summer trip to Scandinavia, which might allow her to go into business with her young friend Reidar, who sold women's undergarments. (Jane, to Alice's utter disgust, refused the idea of marriage to him.)

And then, the World's Fair in Flushing was hiring, and she thought her Spanish would give her abilities as an interpreter for the South American contingents. She wrote to old friend Senator McAdoo for a letter of introduction, which never materialized. She concluded that the senator was too busy with his new young wife, and all Washington was waiting for the Senator to die of a heart attack from so much lovemaking.

And then, there was the plan to buy up apartments in Queens to rent out to visitors of the World's Fair.

May was a month of strange ups and downs. The coronation of George VI was televised, but of course she had no way to see it in the apartment. The radio would do, and Alice changed back to a Canadian for a while to enjoy it to the fullest. It was right on the heels of the Hindenburg blowing itself up. One could not get away from the dreadful *Times* headlines, day after ghastly day, even while wrapping kitchen scraps in yesterday's edition. Those poor dead Germans; rumors abounded that it was a plot to discredit the Nazi regime. It could certainly be true.

Then, Amelia Earhart provided months of uplifting adventure. Alice was riveted to the *Times* reporting of the aviatrix's journey from Oakland in May. In the evenings she and Jane and Johnny would review the route: Tucson, Miami, San Juan, Brazil and across the Atlantic to West Africa and out to Asia. The absolutely thrilling voyage came to such a tragic end on the flight to Howland Island, and brought Alice into July thoroughly depressed.

There was an anodyne to the downward spiral, the Centennial Celebration of Mitchell, Alice's hometown. Her grandfather was being honored as the founder. Les Mumas tootled up on the train, spending the nights in Dunelg with her cousin Jean, and having their photo snapped in front of the stone commemorative. The weather held warm and sunny. Jean was beside herself with joy with the visit. Most of the Hicks were in the graveyard or in Western Canada, so it was quite a family reunion for all the surviving members.

During the summer, Jane went to the Hudson Valley to do Shakespeare summer stock with Gordon. Sergey the Russian had fallen by the wayside. Johnny fell in love with Edith, whom he met by bumping into her as she emerged from the Empire State Building.

None of this good news could counter Alice's remove from reality.

She wrote a check for $540 to the Phoenix office of the State Land Commission, $40 short of what was required to wipe out the back taxes for the Yuma land. It would have bounced if she had not cancelled it because of the error. By September she owed two months' back rent on the Midtown brownstone, and paid that late with the meager funds she kept for her share of the rent at Sutton Place. She was already being harassed by the paper for the expensive ad she had placed to sell the Yuma land. When the estate of Wilson demanded yet again that she pay them the $300 owed from Johnny's last semester at Babson, she wrote back that as long as she could not sing she could not pay, and that was that.

Johnny found her in the brownstone on her birthday, sifting through papers in storage.

"I can't find my will, Johnny dear," she said.

Chapter 65

Say It Was Heart Trouble

Alice and Jane picked one of the shiny tables at random, grateful to be sheltering at the Horn and Hardart Automat. The late winter gale whipping the Midtown canyons had left them cold to the bone. She and her mother had just blown in from the trek to the Grand Central Annex, where Alice picked up her mail each time the Sutton Place apartment was sublet.

"Coffee?" asked Jane.

"No, dear. Why don't you get yourself a cup and me some tea? "I'll be back with luncheon," Alice said over her shoulder. Alice dropped her gloves and handbag on the table. Damp letters landed in a pile nearby. A letter from Peggy in Toronto just happened to be on top.

Jane put her money in the slot and received the black brew, then on to the hot water for tea. Walking back to the table, she held the thick white china cup up to her face, hot vapor delicious on her cheeks and warming her enclosing hands. She sat with elbows plunked on top of the table and watched her mother clink the nickels into the slot, turn the crank that opened the little glass door, and slide the macaroni and cheese onto her tray.

"Jane, here's a fork. We'll share," said Alice as she slid in. "Thanks for getting my tea." She sat staring at the macaroni, a finger absently tracing the green decoration on the rim of the plate.

"Mother, aren't you going to open your letter from Peggy?"

"In a bit, dear. She is mad to know more about Johnny's engagement. That's all."

Alice ran her hands over her pale face. "Excuse me, Jane. I feel I need to use the ladies' room. Be back shortly."

Alice made her way back to the table. She was a little unsteady. One glance in the restroom mirror had shown her the face of a woman utterly defeated. In addition to the guilt brought forth by what she just knew was in Peggy's letter, there was the issue of the tenant at Sutton Place, whose rent would not cover the monthly obligations.

As if Jane knew the single conversation that would brighten her mother's eyes was Johnny's fiancée, Edie, she drew on the topic as her mother sat back down, and they both picked up forks to stab at the congealed pile of macaroni.

"How long will it be, Mother, before we can see Johnny's new house?"

"We have all been invited out to see the place as soon as the closing— perhaps two weeks."

"That will be exciting. Wonder if the weather will ease up a bit into early spring."

"Edith says spring comes early out there."

Conversation ground to silence, replaced by the scraping of chairs, clinking of china and the hum of strangers' voices.

Alice opened the letter once safely home.

Alice Dear,

I find a letter from the Empire Trust Co. returning your cheque with a protest from the main office of the Bank of America in Los Angeles. Our account has been charged $2.50. How would you like to arrange about it?

We are sure it is his savings department mistake. Would it be too much trouble to see the Empire Trust Manager on Broadway and settle the matter?

The bank insists they can find no trace of your deposit. I am a pretty poor businesswoman, I fear, but I can't bother Sidney with such things at the moment.

Peggy was her intimate friend of so many decades, a Theta sister from way back in 1910.

***

April second, and without the blessing from her children, Alice packed her bags, closed the door on her brownstone and abandoned her just-empty Sutton Place apartment. Inside were all her precious possessions and a plague of bills. She said she would be back by May. She had told Jane to take the keys from the tenant and complete the inventory.

The train sped south to Louisiana then west toward Texas. Alice's sleeper car was her kingdom in motion. Cocooned thus, she began to feel calmer. Edith was in charge now. Johnny was unwell again, and Alice had been rebuffed in her attempt at Science healing. Time to remove herself for one last effort to wrest a life from the desert.

April 4
Tucumcari, New Mexico
My Dear Edie,

You have been a great comfort to me, and are still—in knowing that you spend each day with Johnny. Tell him that the sun is especially bright in his New Mexico. From Tucumcari we are only five hours over two full days from New York—exceptionally good ground covering, I feel. My destination is Bisbee, near Tucson, and here's to my bold venture!

In the leisure of the journey, I find myself hopping back to my last Sunday's trip to the new house. Delighted in every way with your undertaking there. Johnny is obviously happier than he has been since his return from Germany, and has at last communicated to me, in his unexpectedly shy way, that you are the cause of it. I'm all for you, dear, and there has always been a place in my heart for you, I realize now. I used to wonder where you were, and when he would find you. And so at last it has come, bringing, I hope, abundant happiness to you both.

Affectionately,

Alice Muma

Alice reveled briefly within the alpine feel of Bisbee. The town hovered green and hilly over the Sonoran Desert, an oasis within reach of Mexico. The driving force to its economy was the Queen Copper Mine.

She took a train to dusty Yuma and then to Aztec in order to keep an appointment with the Farrins. The couple, long established in Yuma County and proprietors of a guesthouse, had written to her in New York about cautious interest in her property, should it still be viable. They also claimed some knowledge of complicated financial disasters that had befallen some of the landowners hereabouts.

For two weeks, Alice searched courthouse records and talked to the tax department, visited her property by taxi, and drove east with the Farrins to their guesthouse. Would the Farrins buy her land in in trade for some land near their guesthouse for a tearoom? They had barely nodded assent when Alice rushed to hire a well driller. By then, she was almost ready to faint away in the crushing heat.

At the end of it, Alice discovered that her land, though still in her name in Phoenix with all its unpaid back taxes, had been sold off years ago by the town of Yuma. Her "bold venture" to drill for water on her property and start a tearoom had been wrenched away. In retaliation, she hired the Farrin's attorney to begin a lawsuit against the town of Yuma. The trial was set for midsummer.

Fleeing the heat to Los Angeles, Alice bumped into an old friend—Polly, an administrator at the posh Bel-Air Sycamores, who offered her a job. Alice gladly chauffeured Polly, wrote menus, arranged flowers and managed banquets. She was summarily dismissed within the month when a group complained bitterly of the tiny portions of turkey served.

It was obvious, she wrote to her children, that Polly didn't want my help, although very friendly. Same old story—I knew too much. I do things too perfectly, and what appreciation I got from those who did know how things should be done?

***

The promise blithely made to be home in May had evaporated. As a result, a dispossess warrant was issued on the Sutton Place apartment. Jane, Johnny and Edie moved Alice's possessions to the new house. They wrote to Alice of this disgraceful exit of her beloved furnishings, but all her mail reposed with attorney John Rankin in Los Angeles, and she had yet to pick it up.

Alice hid out for a day at her old Bel-Air Beach Club and met someone with a beach house to rent.

Just the thing, Alice thought. Right on the sand, and close to my precious Castellamare house. The bus will let me off right on the block. Polly had paid her for the long days of her work, and there was enough in her wallet for a month's rent and train fare back to Yuma for the trial.

Dear old Mutti, I must visit her, Alice mused as she gathered her belongings for a ride to the beach house. And she formed a note in her head, to be written down and mailed immediately. John Rankin must bring his wife for a visit and kindly take charge in any emergency. She would ask him to do so, and to deliver her mail.

Alice turned the key and let herself into a bright rattan-furnished apartment. She brought her suitcase into the tiny bedroom, opened it and pulled out a filmy caftan, exchanging it for the suit she had worn. The sunny beach beckoned, and she plopped herself on the sand, running her fingers through its softness, enjoying the bit of grit remaining between her fingers and toes. So long, too long, since she had sat on her beloved California beach. Her mind followed the sun. You could pretend it fell into the sea like some fairytale ending of a story told once to John and Jane. They were grown, so no more stories for them. Not here with her, as she had assumed they all would remain, but on the other coast they all fled to, hunkered down after school. That same coast she had just left, through all the hot days, insulated by the air-cooled train. Well, what was left for them? Three houses gone, all for a song. But, well, her songs were gone, too. Life's grand plan, she saw, had taken quite another direction with dear Jerry's departure. It had been a slow slide. She had not seen it, and then not wanted to. Now she sat, hiding from her friends, from the mail sitting with her attorney who never brought good news.

The last bitter pill was the firing—by a longtime friend, no less. Word of her humiliation would spread. Surely now the veil of pretense would be ripped asunder to reveal her utter failure to remain the well-heeled widow of Jerry Muma.

***

Evening brought a stronger breeze. She washed her feet under the outdoor shower, settled into the living room and turned on some lamps. The sun was no more than a rosy glow which never lingered long. Alice picked up her writing materials to begin to type a letter to Jane and Johnny.

What remained? Perhaps swim to China. Pretend to catch the falling sun. Yes.

June 25th
Old Malibu Road,
Dear J and J,

I haven't been so happy in years, in spite of the shadow of the decision I've been making. But it is made. I never thought the temptation would ever come to me. My decision is to swim straight out to China, which will take nerve. Don't comment on my ability as a swimmer. I can't face poverty. I had 18 years of hunger and secondhand clothes. Please destroy my C. S. notes in my secretary trunk. I know C. S. is Truth, and I know this act will darken me spiritually. I always knew when my spirit drooped, the light would go out. An odd result for wanting to excel and not be mediocre.

There will be no disgrace here, for I won't fumble things. Please fly out. You can borrow money on pending settlement of my estate. Bring Edie if you are married. It will clarify with Edie much she likely cannot understand, and prove that our background in California was quite as favorable as hers in New York.

Alice typed on to organize where they should stay, and how to manage the unveiling of their father's memorial bronze at the tenth-year anniversary of the founding of UCLA and please probate her will in New York so that no one out West would know her plight.

When John Rankin forwarded her mail she found a terse letter from Johnny describing the dispossess warrant and the cartage of her belongings to Johnny and Edie's new home.

Furious, she responded.

How dare you. If you meant to add cruelty, you succeeded. It never entered my mind to walk out and leave so much that is disagreeable for you to clear up. I feel that if I could have known the instant they served papers that I could have managed. Does this mean it has been imposed upon Edie?

Alice zipped the letter angrily from the roller, and inserted another set of sheets with a carbon in between. A letter to Edie followed, punched out in kinder terms, apologizing for imposing all the furniture on her. Practical even her extremity, she attached a two-page inventory of the belongings still in Los Angeles, should they ever want them.

A day later, Alice had packed her bag and was watching a school of seals cavort off the beach when the doorbell rang. A friend had arrived, and instead of swimming to China with the seals, Alice accepted a ride into town and an offer to stay the night.

Alice caught a train for Arizona the next morning. She arrived in Yuma to visit the Farrins to discuss the lawsuit, and phoned to find them in Aztec, a hundred miles to the east.

July 4
Aztec, Arizona
J and J,

I exited the beach. Drama has always placed comedy and tragedy nearby. I want to get as much information as I can on the lawsuit and what has been going on hereabouts over a period of years. I have the guesthouse to myself, as the owners also own the airport gas station and stay in one of the air-cooled rooms of the cabins nearby. I am sending this letter to Jane's apartment. Traveler's insurance extended to Sunday, July 10th. I hope you kept the Grand Central PO box. If either of you do not want the traveling secretary trunk, write to Professor Hering. They leave for a cruise to Australia and may need it.

It is high noon of my first day on the Arizona desert. Indoors, a tiny thermometer marks 100. I have hosed the cement floors of the dining and living rooms and had a nap after luncheon, which consisted of two Arizona grapefruits. I can look to the Aztec Hills and down the San Christobel Valley. The sagebrush stretches to the mountains, some red, some purple, and every blend and tint. An outlying vegetable garden is hedged with spines of Ocotillo, and beyond are chickens and turkeys, and the precious water tank which turns the trick hereabouts from arid waste to flowering beauty. I look forward to sundown, for there will be the moon, too, and the stars, which I contemplated coming along on the train last night. And the sight and smell of the night-blooming cereus.

Alice then wrote to her attorney back in Los Angeles.
July 5
Aztec, Arizona
Dear John,
This will undoubtly reach you along with a hasty note mailed yesterday. You might as well know, my old heart—weary of plans deferred with this lawsuit, etc.—is skipping beats in this heat. I rather wish it would stop altogether—a new feeling for me. Please don't worry, but may I ask you to hold yourself in readiness to come for me this coming Friday or Saturday and help me out of here if I don't feel better. Trains are air-cooled. But don't come unless I wire for you.

I will go directly to New York from Yuma after traveling back with some friends to see an attorney. Anybody asking for me, tell them I have fallen by the wayside on my land here on account of heat, en route to New York. Tell them I do not repudiate any of my obligations and that you are coming for me end of week if I am not better.
In haste,
Alice

Johnny, desperate to find his mother, whose abrupt departure from the beach was followed by her sudden movements back and forth from Yuma and Aztec, telegraphed Alice's attorney.

July 5th
COULD YOU LOCATE MOTHER STOP AM MARRYING JULY TWELFTH

And again later the next day.

July 6th
MOTHERS AIRMAIL ARRIVED FROM AZTEC ARIZONA TODAY. MUCH WORRIED ABOUT HER STOP SUGGEST YOU SEND CHEERFUL MESSAGE STOP FEAR SHE IS MUCH DISCOURAGED.

July 7th
Los Angeles
Dear Alice,

I am much distressed to hear of your physical condition. I suppose I can assist, but it is difficult at the end of this week, as I have no partner to help with the practice.

You have much mail and several messages; would send them on if I was sure it would reach you and not be lost, but you move rather suddenly and unexpectedly. I have left several long-distance calls with the gas station at Aztec.

Very affectionately yours,
John Rankin

P.S. A telegram has just arrived from your son John and I replied to him with your Aztec address. His wire said he was marrying on the 12th.

July 6th
Aztec, Arizona
Dear Polly,

In spite of the heat here I am attending to a few things on the land before hastening to New York for John's wedding on the 12th. Got his news by wire suddenly. I sent for my suitcase in your garage and wanted you to know. Expect to be in Arizona again in October.

Much love,
Alicia

Saturday, July 9, 1938
Arizona Hotel, Phoenix
Dear Johnny:

Only last night I learned you had tried again to get me through Yuma and Aztec. Undoubtedly that means operator never told you correctly that there were no booths for privacy in Aztec. It would not have been worth the cost involved to talk in a general store with all the neighborhood listening in.

I came to Phoenix Thursday night to lessen the heat, and on arrival early Friday morning, I sent you a wire which told you my Phoenix telephone was registered with Western Union. Then when I could talk with you, you never called again, and long distance said you had taken the call off. I waited, wondering if you really wanted to give me an invitation to your wedding. I came east to Phoenix to be nearer than Yuma, and in a bigger community. By so doing, I seem to have missed you. The little country operator in Yuma said she was going to tell you I refused to talk. I hope she didn't. Apparently you have moved to the Plaza.

I have no facts. It is all so strange. I find myself wishing I knew where your wedding will be, and at what hour—at your new home, or in church, and where you plan your honeymoon. Daddy would surely like Edie. Tell her so. Is Edie honoring Jane in the wedding party? I have wondered down the years how it would all come to you, and behold, *what irony*.

But here's my best wish and hope for you. May much that is exquisite and idea come to rich fruition. Wooing is a gentle art; women thrive on it, when beauty is rekindled fresh and true. Let not the sun go down upon any misunderstanding, is an excellent idea of keeping happiness at the tip-top.

Good-bye, dear,

Mother

After Alice finished her letter, she delivered it to the front desk to be mailed. She also handed the clerk a note stating that her heart was acting badly, and that if anything happened, to telephone her attorney John Rankin in Los Angeles. She appended a request that no doctor be called, as she had no use for them. She also gave them a short telegram of congratulations to send to her son. She then asked to see the manager, and when he arrived, asked him to call her room the next morning. When he called, she asked him to call again at a certain time and finally again to come to her room that night, just before 6 p.m.

When he knocked, there was no answer. In some alarm from the strange phone calls made to him previously, he pushed open the unlocked door to find Alice stretched out on her bed in her street clothes. Her face was unnaturally flushed and her breathing so faint that he dashed down to the front desk phone to call the doctor and police.

"Dead of cyanide poisoning," said the doctor. "Happens almost immediately, you know. Nothing you could have done. I see the note on the nightstand requesting the police report the death as heart trouble. Can't do that, I'm afraid. Coroner will be notified of the facts."

An hour later a telegram was delivered to the front desk for Alice.

DELIGHTED TO RECEIVE YOUR WIRE PLEASE CALL AND REVERSE CHARGES TWO HOURS AFTER RECEIVING THIS TELEGRAM. JOHNNY AND EDIE.

311

Afterward

On July 11, Gran'mere was cremated as she had requested. Her ashes were mailed to her great friend Mutti in Hollywood. They were interred with those of her husband Jerry in the Hollywood Memorial Park Cemetery. The box, still in its brown paper wrapper from the Phoenix Crematorium, was shoved into the space's dark reaches.

Jerry's little casket, with his name engraved on the front, would eventually rest elegantly near two similar caskets, those of his sister Sue and her husband Griff, who died well after Gran'mere. Alice's humble box was noted in the office records, but the delicate, scroll worked names on the mausoleum's faceplate failed to note her resting place.

On July 12, her son Johnny and Edie were married, and they honeymooned in Germany until the political violence stirred up by Hitler forced them home.

Jane, John Rankin and Mutti dealt with the initial and myriad details of death. The press on both coasts reveled in the juicy suicide, following as it did so quickly before the marriage. Her friends, on the other hand, were gracious in their sympathy.

It has been a matter of concern and sadness to me ever since my friendship began in 1916 that Alice was not able to see how to use her studies in Christian Science so as to bring about a more harmonious relation between herself and her children, or to free her mind from every personal ambition and the will to carry out such desires. Dear Mrs. Muma is beginning again, I believe, a new life unencumbered by this world's limitations. Peace and love ever surround her and guide her toward happiness.

Mrs. Clint Miller

Gratitude

My support community for this endeavor is no small thing. Thank you.

To the HighlandScribes in Denville, New Jersey for their loving critiques as the chapters unfolded over the years.

To Editors Rob Palmer and Sarah Cypher for their insightful corrections, remarks, and cajoling.

To readers Cathy Salge, Pat Fell, Joan Hacker and Bernadette Cicchino for their encouragement, suggestions and stamina.

To Brother Jerry Beardsley, for his research on the Colorado River Indian Tribes return of the stolen La Paz lands in 2005. 90 years, it took, for the US Government to make amends.

To Brother George Beardsley for his constant encouragement and feedback on the initial draft of the novel.

To Nephew Jason Beardsley, for his research on the Muma family homes, and the beginnings of the Rotary movement in the west.

To Shannon Bae for her creation and production of the book trailer.

To my Mother Jane and my Uncle Johnny, for their ability to take only the good things their mother had to offer.

And, lastly, to my Grandmother Alice and Grandfather Jerry, whose files allowed me to know them.

Thoughts and queries for discussion

1. Suicide's effects on family is not really discussed. Rather, the book is a journey of the "why" of a suicide of a particular person. Did knowing right up front of Alice's suicide prompt you to work along with the author to discover some answers?

2. This novel, really a biography of a complicated woman, raises some issues, one of the most interesting is Alice's inability to balance her hunger for social recognition with her feminist career goals. Is this a universal issue for all women? For all women of social/financial privilege?

3. The moral dilemma implicit in Jerry's trying to break his engagement to Nora is made darker by the pregnancy and abortion. Ethical/legal issues of abortion are still very much with us. What visceral reaction did you have to this section of the book? How timeless is this issue of abortion?

4. Why do you suppose, with all of the single women in Alice's great collection of friends succeeding in supporting themselves, did Alice never learn to do the same?

5. In the brief example given of the stealing of the Colorado Indian reservation land proved to have valuable mining deposits, what do you think about the morality of legislative and Presidential theft of lands for the economic benefit of big business at the expense of underserved populations? Does this make you uncomfortably aware

of how your ancestors might have made their money? Or, were your ancestors part of the great poverty-struck population who toiled so that a few white men could become rich and powerful?

6. Why do you think Alice was so emotionally dependent on her son for love and attention?

7. What was Alice's state of mind in the last few years of her life? Did she have psychological issues which had first shown up during college? Or was she just the "drama queen" Jerry thought she was?

Made in the USA
Las Vegas, NV
11 April 2022

47259229R00194